T0208667

BORN IN HELL

VESNA HERMANN

iUniverse, Inc.
Bloomington

Born in Hell

iUniverse books may be ordered through booksellers or by contacting:

iUniverse
1663 Liberty Drive
Bloomington, IN 47403
www.iuniverse.com
1-800-Authors (1-800-288-4677)

ISBN: 978-1-4620-0833-9 (pbk)
ISBN: 978-1-4620-0102-6 (ebk)

Printed in the United States of America

iUniverse rev. date: 3/28/2011

This book was based on true events that my family and I experienced while living in Banja-Luka Bosnia and Vojnic, Croatia. All of the characters names have been changed, along with some places and events being switched around.

Many thanks to my amazing husband
Michael for his great support
My kids Bryan and Helene for letting me write
My great friend and person who helped
me so much Lamphone Schueder
My best friend Amanda Rose Penton
And a very cool guy Marcus James Clay

Thank you all for supporting me, and coaching me through the whole book-writing process. Without friends like you I would of not have made it to where I am today.

CHAPTER ONE

IT WAS STARTING TO GET very white outside. The roads were icy and the roofs were beginning to look whiter. Everything she saw was white and it was very depressing, but she had to look outside anyway because it was one of those nights that was important to her. Jean had freckles all over her face which she hated because she thought she looked ugly. No matter what anyone told her, she stuck with what she believed in. She had gorgeous green eyes like the grass outside right after the rain. Her hair was brown and long past her shoulders. She liked the way she looked tonight, and she couldn't stop looking in the mirror, but she knew she had to go and beg her mother to let her go to this party that everyone had been talking about all day long. She knew her mother very well, she was a very stubborn woman and when she set her mind to something there was no way of changing it. Jean, her sister Marta and their mother Sophie had been living by themselves for about nine years now, and that was how all three liked it. Marta was as beautiful as Jean and they both got their looks from their mother. Their father was killed in a car accident, but to their mother he was never a good man anyway. So it was just them three. Both girls were working at the Inn and making enough money for them to live comfortably. They had something that most people dream about; they had each other. Well, she was going to stop being a wuss and sit in her room; she was going to talk to her mother and see if she can change her mind to go to a party tonight.

"Jean you are not going and that's it," Sophie said. Jean knew this was going to be hard, but if she really wanted to go she had to get through to her mother.

"Mom, it is only for a few hours," Jean began, "we will be back before you know it." Jean saw a change in her mother and knew this was going to be a positive yes. All she had to do now was make her sister say yes, too. If Marta said no, then she would not go for sure. Mom would never let one go if the other could not or would not. She walked in the room where Marta was resting.

"Good, you are here," Jean said. "Have you heard people talk about that party tonight? Mom said we can go if you come with me." Marta looked like she did not want to go, but she also did not want to sit in the house all night either. And if Mom said they could go, why not? It's not every day that their mother would be generous enough to let them go to a party. They got dressed and went to see their mother before the party. Jean was wearing blue jeans and a yellow turtleneck. She never wore makeup, but tonight she added a little black eyeliner and a bit of lipstick. Marta was looking good as always. She was not like Jean, she liked makeup and liked to look good. They went to say good night to their mother before they left for the night.

"Don't stay long," their mother said, "because you know if you stay longer than you promised there will be no next time. No matter how much you beg me."

"Yes mother," Sophie said.

"We know," said Jean. "We won't be long, just to see what all the talk is about." Their friends were waiting for them, they did not have a car and the party was not that far, so they would just walk.

"Aw, Jean, you look very cute tonight," said one of their friends, Carl. "Is there a guy in your life that I do not know about?" Carl had been Jean and Marta's friend since they were little kids, and he was always there for them. To Jean he was more like a big brother than a friend.

"No, there is no guy," Jean said, "but you never know who I might meet. Maybe tonight is the night that I meet the man of my dreams." She did not believe in what she just said she knew she was only going to have fun. Her mother always said men are nothing but trouble and Jean believed her. She never really had a long relationship, she only had guys she would see for a week or two and they would be gone from her life. But tonight she wanted to think that maybe life could be different and everything could change. After all, it was time for a change in her life, she was just hoping it would be a good one.

While Jean, her sister and their friends were on the way to a party, twenty miles away was a person that was not even thinking about one.

Mitch was thinking about going to bed early for once and making it to work on time. His boss had been on his butt for weeks for not coming to work on time, and always being late. But, he could not help that the alarm did not want to work right. He made a note to himself to fix that, too. Mitch was twenty years old, and a good looking guy. He had long curly hair and smoky brown eyes. The girls liked that about him-well that was what he was told, anyway. He was sick of parties. He had had his share. Just three months ago he got out of jail for robbing a store and stealing cigarettes. He did it before but he never got caught. Then he got caught that stormy night, by his own friend that went and told on him. The police came and took him away. They beat him for a while-that was the rule, if you stole you got the beating of your life. They were not your parents, and they did not care how they hit you. Mitch still had the bruises on his back. That was why he was done with parties. If it was not for his friends he never would have been in jail in the first place. But you cannot lock yourself in a room and stay in it for the rest of your life either. "What is done is done, and cannot be changed. Just don't do it again," Mitch could hear his mother's words.

"What's up bro, what are you working on?" Mitch was working on his motorcycle when his brother Russell walked into the garage. Russell was 21, and had green eyes that shone like stars. His curly hair was cut nicely and he was always wearing nice clothes. Mitch wondered where his brother was getting the clothes, because he didn't have a job. But he never really wanted to ask, because he knew he was going to hear something like, "none of your business" or "why would you care? You are just jealous" so he just did not bother.

"Not much," answered Mitch, "just trying to fix this thing so I can go to work in the morning and not be late."

"Well if you would get your alarm clock to work right you would have made it to work on time," Russell said, "but I am not going to bother you over that. I came to tell you that there is a hot party going on tonight and I was wondering if you wanted to go with me."

"Well, I am really not interested in a party tonight, and I do have to work tomorrow so I would not want to be late. Where is the party anyway?" Mitch asked. "It is Friday night and I was at work all day, and I did not hear about it. Maybe it won't be as hot as you think."

"Why don't you come out with me and find out for yourself!"

Mitch looked at his brother who was not a bad looking guy, and wondered why he did not ever bring a girl home or have a girl over. He was always hanging out with those losers he called friends. He knew that it still hurt his brother that he could not see that girl he was talking about so much, but that should not stop you from having more girls in your life. He would do this for his brother he thought to himself. Why not? It might even be fun.

"All right, I will come with you if you promise me that we will be home by eleven."

"Deal!" Russell said. "It is already seven, so go ahead and get that dirt off you and we will be gone." Mitch went to take a shower, and as he was coming out he almost ran his mom, Josephine, over. She was a hard working, single mother that had to make sure her boys had a roof over their heads and that they had clothes on their backs. She did not like the stories about Mitch, and what had happened.

"Good God child! Will you watch where you are going?," Josephine shouted. "You almost ran me over! Why are you in such a hurry?"

"Me and Russell are going to the party, and I have to be ready soon or he will leave without me."

"Who will all be there?" she asked. After all, she did not want to see her boy in jail again. To her he was still her little boy, but the one that had to learn lessons the hard way. She was asked if she wanted to take him home that night, but she wanted him to learn that Mommy won't be there for him all the time. But she said, "No!" when the police officer asked if she wanted him to stay for three days! Yes, he was her son, and she loved him very much. She hated to see those big red marks on his back, but she knew what they do in jail to the guys for stealing. She hated herself for it, but the boy had to learn the hard way.

"I am not sure who will all be there Mom," Mitch said, "but I am sure there won't be no one new that we already do not know. You yourself know that this town is so little, and everyone knows everything and everyone around here. I am not staying that long anyways, I am going to work in the morning."

"All right, just don't be too late. I am not staying up waiting for you boys all night long," she answered. Mitch had no idea what to wear for this party, he did not even know what kind of party it would be. He figured you cannot go wrong with jeans and a football shirt, after all, he really liked that shirt. He got dressed and went to go get his brother, whatever this party is, he is not staying out all night long.

Russell was planning on having a good time tonight. He had been waiting for a party now for over a week, and tonight was going to be great whether his brother liked it or not. He had many friends he wanted to go with, but he also knew if he didn't bring Mitch to the party he wouldn't get to see Marta. And it was important to him to see her, after all, they had not been seen together in a long time. Everyone should already have forgotten what happened between them. He hoped that Marta would be as happy as him when she saw him tonight.

Two months ago, Marta and he had had feelings for each other, they had even kissed. It would have been a lot more if her sister had not come in and ruined everything. Russell knew that Marta was not able to go anywhere without her sister, but he did not know she was going to tell their mother everything that was going on between the two of them. But what is done is done, he can only hope for a better change and better time with her.

Oh, how much he wanted Marta! Those sweet lips and long legs; it made his blood boil just thinking about her. But who does he get her sister to be with so he can have at least one kiss from a girl he was so in love with?

"Well, who else but my own brother?" he asked himself. "Why not? Mitch is free, he don't have a girlfriend. And he was not seeing anyone, because if he was Russell would be the first to know. They were brothers, and they shared a lot of secrets between the two of them. He was deep in thoughts when Mitch walked in, in his nice blue jeans and favorite shirt.

"How did I know that is what you were going to wear?" Russell asked. "Dude, you never go anywhere without that shirt, do you?"

"Well, it is my favorite shirt," replied Mitch. "Do you have a problem with it?"

"No, not at all," Russell said. "I was just telling you I knew what you were going to wear. You don't have to jump on me like I have really insulted you about something important, it is just a shirt."

"Well are you ready to go, or do I have to wait till tomorrow?" Mitch asked. "I just want to get this over with and be back here by eleven." They walked out together and when Mitch saw who was standing and waiting for them, he almost went back inside. "But," he said to himself, "this is for my brother, not really for me." Paul was waiting for them, one of Russell's very good friends. He and Mitch never really got along and neither one of them really tried, but they both tolerated each other because of Russell.

"Well, why did he have to go?" Paul asked, "I thought you said it would be fun, and now if he is going I am not sure I really want to go."

"Well," Mitch said, "you know where your house is. You are more than welcome to go back. Don't let me stop you."

"All right both of you. I want tonight to be fun for me *and* you guys," Russell said. "Can you get along for one night? Can't you, please, for me?"

"Fine," Mitch said, "but he started it." They were going to have fun whether they liked it or not, Russell thought, because he was going to have fun himself.

———————————

The night was cold and snowy. Ice was all over the road and

even the top of the trees were frozen, but looking out of a car it was the most beautiful site you could see. It was December and Christmas was around the corner, all the houses had lights on and the snow just made it more beautiful.

The party was in full effect when Mitch and his brother got there. From the outside it looked like there had been a lot of people there, and Mitch did not like that one bit. He knew who some of the guys who were, and he really did not care for them. One of them was his ex-best friend, Joseph, the one who told on him and got him in jail for three whole days. He could not ever forgive him for that. They had been friends since high school. They had done a lot of good and bad stuff together, and for him to snitch on him like that? There was no excuse or forgiveness.

Joseph was standing inside and looking for a dance partner when he spotted Mitch, his brother and Paul. "Oh, there will be fights tonight," he told himself. He knew what a bad temper Mitch had and how much he liked to fight, even if he was the one starting it. Joseph felt sorry that he went and told on his best friend, but what else can you do when he is stealing? What if someone else got to see it first? They would not have said he was taking only cigarettes. They would have said he was taking a lot more, and then Mitch would have been in jail for over three months and not just three days. He still cared for his friend, but tonight he would try to stay away from him because he was not in the mood to fight-he was in the mood to dance and have a good time.

Mitch had seen Joseph and the hair on the back of his head stood up, because he knew that if he even got close to him he would beat him to the ground. They walked in and so far there was no problem, Russell thought. He spotted Marta standing with her sister in the corner, and his heart skipped a few beats. God, how much he loved that girl and tonight she looked so nice. She had on tight blue jeans and a black shirt with ruffled sleeves and a v-cut neck that looked like it was made for her.

"She looks so good tonight," Russell thought, and made his way towards them. Marta was still with Jean when she saw Russell coming over with his brother and their friend Paul.

"Brace yourself," she told Jean. "We will have company in a few minutes, and if you can please try and be nice? Tonight is very important for me-so don't ruin it." Jean looked over her shoulder and saw the guys coming closer. She wanted to leave right away, but she knew there was no way her sister would want to leave. Everything started to fit in place. Why her sister did not want to go dancing, why she looked at the door all night long and why she had been so nervous. Russell, of course, was the answer. Jean knew she was the cause of them not being able to see each other and she was sorry for it, but she did not like the guy and did not want her sister to be around someone the whole city was talking about. He was the type of guy that every girl wanted to be with, but he only had eyes for her sister. Jean was not jealous, but she knew that type of guy before. They only come and use you, then leave you and never come back. What else was she supposed to do?

"Hello ladies," said Russell. "This is my younger brother, Mitch, and my friend, Paul. How are you doing tonight?"

"Fine," Marta said, "we were just waiting for a good song to go dancing, and so far there have not been one."

"Yeah, right!" said Jean. "I have heard many songs that were great to go dance, but you couldn't stop looking at the door and waiting for him." She gave Russell a disgusted look.

"Jean please," begged Marta. "You promised to be nice. Come on now, don't embarrass yourself-or me for that matter."

"She is really not this rude," Marta said to the guys. "She just had a rough day, that's all." But in Mitch's eyes it did not matter if she had a good or bad day, it mattered that she was mean to his brother and he did not like the way she looked at him.

"Well it looks to me like you are jealous," said Mitch,

9

"because if you were not, you would not be accusing anyone of waiting. What is the matter Jean? You don't have anyone to wait for, so you make it harder on your sister? Did you think I did not hear how you ran to your mommy and told her about your sister and Russell? That was very low of you."

"Who asked this monkey to speak with me?" Jean asked. "When I have something to say to you then you can talk to me. Until then, I really do not want to see your face." Jean turned around and walked out of the party.

"I am sorry," Marta said, "I will go after her."

"No," Paul said, "I will." And he gave Mitch a look that could have killed him. "Wow. I wonder why you don't have a girlfriend," said Paul to Mitch. "It must be because you don't know anything about women or their feelings."

"Look who is talking," replied Mitch. "When was the last time you even had a girl? And why are you sticking your nose where it don't belong anyways? This is between her and me. It has nothing to do with you, and if anyone should go after her it will be me. Please stay out of my way and my business," he told him and walked away.

"God, how much I hate your brother," Paul told Russell and he walked away too.

It was very cold outside and Jean forgot to bring her coat, but she did not care about it. She was so mad that a coat would just be in her way. How dare he? Jean thought. Who did he think he was talking to her like that? Like she was nothing, like she had no feelings. Her heart was beating so fast she thought it would jump out of her chest. She heard her name and did not want to turn around. If she had to walk home on her own she would. Then she would go and tell Mom where Marta was and who was with her.

"Jean, please stop! I cannot run after you!" she heard him yell.

"No!" she yelled back. "Leave me alone and go back to the

party. I don't need anyone right now. I just need to be alone, so go away Mitch."

"Please stop so I can talk to you. I am very sorry. I did not mean those things. I can just see the hate in your eyes when you look at my brother, and to me my brother is all I have I am sorry I overreacted," he told her. Jean stopped so he could catch up to her. She did not even want to look at him, because the truth was he was very attractive with those brown eyes and that curly hair of his. Mitch took off his jacket and put it around her so she would not be cold.

"Thank you," she said. "And I am sorry for all the things I said inside, too. I just hear so many stories about your brother, and that is why I do not want him around my sister."

"But have you asked him if the stories were truth?" Mitch asked. "Because in this town everyone talks, and not all the stories are truth."

"So then is it true that you just got out of jail for stealing cigarettes?" Jean asked him.

"Yes it is," he said, "but that is not something I am proud of. I made a mistake, I paid for it and I want to forget it," he told her.

The did not even realize they had been holding hands and walking slowly towards the trail everyone in town called the Love Trail. It was where all the couples would go and have their walks. The trail was so beautiful, all the young couples walked on it. The story was that one day a young boy and the girl he was seeing were walking on the side of the road what they saw there was water between four trees on one side and four on the other side the trees were leaning over it and it looked so beautiful so they walked through it and called it the Love Trail. It was so lovely at night you can sit at the end of the trail and look at all the stars. "It is even *more* beautiful tonight," Jean thought. The snow covered the end of the trees and it looked like there was ice on top of them. They stopped before they got to the end of the trail and Mitch looked at her.

"Jean, you have very beautiful eyes," he told her. "I can just lose myself looking at them. Would it be alright if I kissed you?" Her head was spinning from his words and she did not even think. All she could do was move closer to him and offer him her lips.

He kissed her very slowly at first, and she liked it. Jean was kissed before, but never like this. It never felt this right. She could not think, she could not even breathe, her heart was beating hard and she could only think of his mouth on hers.

"Well well," Paul's voice broke their kiss. "I thought you two were fighting inside, or was that just an act?" he asked them. "Because you two did a good job making everyone think you hated each other." Jean did not like Paul, he was a big guy and very arrogant. He had a bad attitude towards a lot of girls and she did not care for him to talk to her at all.

"What do you want, Paul?" Mitch asked. "We were busy. And I don't see why is it any of your concern what we do anyways."

"I think it is time to go inside and dance," Jean told Mitch. "Are you coming with me?"

"Yes I am," he said, and they walked past Paul not even paying any attention to him. We are going inside to have some fun, Jean thought. Not that what happened on the Love Trail was not fun, but they needed to be around people. And she needed to go and tell Russell she was sorry, because she was a little hard on him. Not that he did not deserve it, but she would do it for her sister and his brother she thought.

CHAPTER TWO

INSIDE WAS WARM AND NICE. Everyone was having a good time. There were people sitting, standing and dancing. Marta and Russell were dancing to a very slow song. He was holding her so carefully like she was a glass that could fall and break any minute. When Jean saw them she almost started crying, because it was the most beautiful site she had seen in a long time. Her sister did deserve a good man, and no matter what the stories were, it looked like Russell was a good guy to her. And in that moment that was what mattered, that her sister was happy.

Mitch was next to her and had seen the same thing she did. Then he took Jean in his arms and they began dancing next to her sister and his brother. Marta was very surprised to see her sister with Mitch, because a couple of hours ago they wanted to kill each other and now they were on the floor dancing.

God, how much things can change in less than a couple hours, just think what can happen in a couple of months. Marta was thinking about all the things that had been happening to her in those last two months she was without Russell. She was not herself when Jean told on her. She could not believe her sister would do something like that to her. To go and tell Mom she was with Russell, when she knew that their mother hated his family and did not get along with them. Her mom did not get along with a lot of people because they were always trying to get her out of the house, always talking how she needs a man in her life and how she is bringing two girls up all on her own. It was annoying to think you cannot go out and have fun with your friends and in the morning be the talk of the town.

By now, many people had gone home and there were only a few of them left. The party was dying down and it was time to go. All four of them were looking for Paul, and he was nowhere to be found. They found him kissing on a girl upstairs.

"What?" he asked them. All four were looking at him like they wanted to strangle him.

"Nothing loser," Mitch told him. "We were all looking for you for over an hour so we can go home. Some of us do have things to do tomorrow, and not all of us are lazy like you. Now if you want to walk home in the snow you are welcome to, but we are leaving." They all got in the car and waited for him. He sat in the car and they were on their way home, no one was really in the mood to talk. They were all tired, and they just wanted to get to bed. They dropped Paul off first, and then they were on their way to drop off the girls.

They got to the driveway and stopped the car. They had to be very quiet, because if Sophie woke up and saw the boys in the driveway there would be hell to pay. Marta and Russell were sitting in the car, and Mitch and Jean were outside saying their good byes when the outside light came on.

"Jean and Marta inside this moment!" shouted Sophie. "I do not know what got in to you girls, but do you even have any idea what time it is? And why would you be with those boys I so strongly do not want you around?"

"I am sorry, but we have to go," said Jean. "I will call you tomorrow. Come on Marta, we have to go in." Marta could not believe she was getting yelled at in front of Russell.

"No Mother," she said. "I am sorry, but not this time. I

am not a little girl anymore, and you cannot control me or my life any longer."

"Marta, what are you saying?" Jean asked. "Come on, let's go inside."

"No, let her stay with that boy the whole town is talking about. Just remember Marta, you make your own choices. And as you said, I cannot control you anymore. So as of right now, this is not your house anymore. You can come back in the morning and get the rest of your stuff. Good night." Jean went inside after her mother because she knew how hurt her mother must be. She loved both of her daughters the same and this must hurt her more than anything they could have done.

"Mom wait! She is just angry now, because she really likes Russell. And who cares what anyone is saying? Mom, you should have seen them tonight. They were dancing like they have been in love for a long time. She will come around."

"Jean, I care what everyone is saying. I am the one that is with you guys every minute of the day, and I do not want you guys to be the talk of the town. I brought my girls up to be respectable young ladies, and look what happened. I failed. After all this time that I tried to do right, and in the end I am the wrong one. I am sorry, Jean. I am going to bed now."

"I am sorry," Marta said to Russell when they were in the car. "I did not mean for you to see that. I think my mother cannot take that me and my sister are both adults and that we can make our own decisions. You can drop me off at my friend's house, and maybe by tomorrow my mother will come down and come to her senses.

"Ok," Russell said. "I will take you wherever you want to go, but don't blame your mom either. This town talks about me and my brother a lot, even though we are really not that bad. She was just trying to protect you. She does not know the truth, but Marta, I would never hurt you. I care about you very much, and I will do everything I can to keep you safe."

"Thank you," she said. Looking into a beautiful snowy night, all she could do was hope she was not going to break down and cry.

Mitch was asleep by the time the car stopped. He really wanted to just crawl in his bed, and catch at least two hours of sleep before he had to get up again. He did go to bed, but he was not able to sleep. All he could do was think about those sweet lips he was kissing a while ago, and how strong she was when her mother was yelling at her. But, he knew he would see her again. Maybe soon, maybe later, but he would definitely see her again.

It had been two weeks now Jean had not heard from her sister. She did not come home and get her clothes, she did not come to work, and she was nowhere to be found. It was not like she could have disappeared. Jean thought, "I will find her even if I have to go to the last place I ever thought I would go-Mitch's house." One day her mom thought she was working until five o'clock, but she got out early. She went to go see if Marta was at Russell's house. If not, then she would know for sure else would have to keep looking for her sister. But the truth was if she was not there, then where else could she be?

She stopped in front of the big house that looked like there were so many people living there, and she could not understand why only three people would live in a house this big. She went to knock on the door, but before she could touch it, they swung open and Mitch came out. He looked so handsome just, like in the movies Jean thought.

"Hello," she said. "I just came by to see if my sister was here. I have not seen her since the night we were at the party, so I was wondering if maybe this is where she was hiding."

It surprised him that she was right there in front of him. All he could do was stare at her, because he did not know what to say. Her sister was not there, and his brother was not home. How could he tell this worried, fragile girl that her sister ran off with his brother and they were gone far away? Somewhere no one could find them or hurt them again.

"No she is not here," he heard himself say, "they are gone, Jean. Both my brother and your sister are gone. They went to Slovenia and I do not think they're coming back. Russell has a friend that has a job there and he offered him one, and Marta left with him. I am so sorry."

Jean could not believe what she just heard. Her sister left her without saying good bye? Without telling her she would be ok? Without even seeing her one last time? She did not want to break down and cry in front of Mitch, but she could not help herself. She sat down on the ground and let herself go. All he could do was just hold her in his arms while she cried.

He picked her up, took her inside the house, lay her on his bed and sat next to her.

"Is there anything I can do for you?" he asked. "There must be something I can do." She just lay there crying. She could not talk, she could not even breathe. The one person she cared so much about left her all on her own. She was hurt, she was mad, she was sad, and she was angry. Oh was she angry with her sister who took the easy way out to deal with her problems. She ran away from her problems. From her mother and from a sister who loved her so much. She would have done everything she could to make Mom see that Marta and Russell should have been together, but no, her sister had to get up and leave. Well, she would not be thinking about her sister anymore she told herself, as she wiped her tears. Now she would be thinking of Jean only.

She got up and looked around the room, it was a typical male room clothes all over, and food everywhere. It was a mess. Mitch knew what she was thinking, and felt a little embarrassed. He began to clean up a little.

"Oh no you don't," she said. "If your room was a mess before I got here, it can wait. I think we should go out and have some fun. I know a great place to go.

"Well lets go then!" Mitch said.

They walked out and went to a little bar, not that far away from the house. He held her hand, and it felt good to both of them. He knew how hurt she was, and he knew that she might do something that was bad for both of them tonight. He did not want to make her feel like she had to do anything, but he did miss her very much. He missed her touch, he missed her lips, he missed everything about her.

They walked into the bar and it was already full of people. There were people there that they knew and some they did not know. It was Friday night and all types of people there. The music was very good, and dancing was the best way Jean knew to stop thinking about her problems. She began dancing with Mitch, while Paul watched them.

He was watching her dance, he had been watching her for a while. He knew that if he even tried talking to her she would blow him off, like she did so many of the men that asked her to dance or out to dinner. He even tried to be nice to her mother, and went to talk to her last week to ask if it would be ok to let Jean out on a date with him. But, that did not turn out good, he was asked to leave before he could even finish telling her why he came over.

The Old Witch was what he was going to call her. He really did not like her mother, but now when there is no Marta in the way he knew he could go for Jean. He also knew that the Old Witch would not let her daughter go out with Mitch, so he was going to find out why she was in the bar with him and how she got there. He wanted her next to him, and Mitch was just in the way but tonight he would fix that, too. He knew that Russell left to Slovenia with Marta, and that the news must have hit Jean very hard. All he could do was go ahead and offer her a drink.

Mitch saw him walk to the bar and order two beers. He knew what Paul's intentions were, he also knew that Paul had wanted Jean since high school. But she did not want him, and that was what mattered.

"Hi guys," Paul said. "Jean, you look very nice tonight. I bought you a beer, and Mitch I am sure you can afford your own, you do have a job."

"I have a job, too," Jean said. "Thanks for the beer, but no thanks. I am here to dance and I am in the company of a very attractive guy, so if you will excuse us Paul? We will be going to dance." And they walked away.

She will pay for that, Paul told himself. Who does she think she is? To embarrass him like that in front of Mitch? Not that he liked him, but a man an ego and she just stepped on it. She will pay for that, he promised himself and walked out of the bar.

Much later in the night, Sophia was sitting at home and waiting for her daughter. Jean should have been home right after work which was hours ago. She was worried sick and she could not sleep. She jumped when the phone rang and she thought the worst, that it was one of her daughters.

"Hello?" she said into the phone, "can I help you?"

"Yes, you can. I know where your daughter Jean is, and I know who she is with," the man's voice said.

"Who is this?" Sophie asked.

"Your daughter is out with Mitch. You should be worried if she will come home tonight or not," he said and hung up the phone.

Paul walked out of the phone booth and smiled to himself. He knew Sophie was going crazy at home, and he knew she

19

was all alone, but Jean did deserved it. He walked back to the club like nothing had happened.

In the club, people were starting to leave and it was not as crowded as it was when Paul left. It was nice he thought, now he can go and find Jean. Maybe she will want that drink he offered her earlier. He found them sitting at the table talking. He was not sure if he wanted to talk to Mitch or not, but he knew talking to Jean would mean talking to Mitch, too. He walked to their table and sat down.

"Man, don't you know when to leave people alone?" Mitch asked.

"I am not here to talk to you, so I don't see why is it any of your concern anyways," Paul told him. "Jean, I think your mother is worried sick where you might be. I think I should take you home now, so she don't worry any longer."

"And what makes you think I want to go home with you?" Jean asked.

"I am telling you that you should go, and I really think you should listen," Paul told her.

"I will go home when I feel like it," Jean said. "I don't see why is it any of your concern if I go home or not, so please just leave me alone."

He grabbed her hand and said, "I think you should listen to me and go home now."

Mitch got up and pushed Paul so hard that he fell off the chair.

"Leave her alone!" he said. "She will not go home with you. She don't want a drink from you. She don't even want to talk to you, man. Leave the girl be!" Mitch said to him, and he turned towards Jean who was standing at the end of the table.

"Mitch watch out!" he heard right before he was grabbed and thrown to the floor. Paul was on top of him, and punching him hard. There were fists everywhere. He felt them on his nose, his eyes, and his jaw. They were rolling on the ground, and Mitch was on top of Paul. Now that he saw blood he knew he should stop, but all the anger he had in him was coming out and he was taking it out on a person he did not care for. Paul was getting what Mitch held inside for a while, and he did not care where he hit him as long as he did. He hated him for everything that was wrong. For his brother leaving, for touching the girl he was in love with, for even talking to her.

"Break it up you two!" he heard the owner of the bar say. "This is not the place to fight, so get out both of you!"

Jean could not believe this just happened, that she was the cause of the fight. She went to Mitch who needed help to even walk outside. His eye was swollen shut, his lip was bleeding, he was hurt bad.

"I am so sorry," she said. "If I knew he was going to fight with you, I would have just got up and went home then you would not be bleeding now. We have to go to my house," she added, "because if we go back to yours your mother will kill us both. And you do look very bad for your mom to see you now, anyways."

"I do not care what I look like, Jean. I only care about you."

It felt good to hear him say that, but it did not feel good too look at the bloody nose that she just caused. They walked over the hill and she could see her house. She was beginning to think it was a bad idea to take him home. She knew Sophia was going to be mad when she saw him, but there was no other choice. She could not let him go home looking like that, she would just have to explain to her mom and tell her the truth.

As they walked to her house, the lights were on. Jean looked at her watch and she saw that it was 4 am. Why was her mother still up? She unlocked the door very quietly and tried to walk inside thinking her mother would be in the other room sleeping. The minute she walked in, Sophia jumped off the bed.

"Jean! My dear Jean. You are alive!" she said and went to

hug her daughter. Then she stopped herself and stared hard at Mitch. "What in the world happened to him?" she asked.

Jean had no idea what was going on, but she knew that her mother would forgive her for whatever was next. She took her mom's hands and walked her to the bed.

"Mom, there is something I have to tell you. I am sure you won't like it, but I will try and explain it to you."

Sophia just nodded her head and was waiting for the worst. In her mind she could see Marta and Mitch getting into a fight, and she could see him hurting her little girl. If that was the case, Jean did a good thing because she would kill him herself.

"Mom," Jean began, "Mitch and Paul got into a fight tonight over me, because Paul wanted to bring me home. He was rude and grabbed my hand, that is why Mitch is all bloody. He was trying to protect me from him. And there is more, Mom. Marta is not here anymore, she left to Slovenia with Russell. They are not coming back anymore, they are going to live there. Russell got a job, and that is where they are going to stay. I am not sure if they live together or not, but I do know from what Mitch told me that they are not coming back."

Sophia could not believe what she just heard. She had forgotten to tell Jean about the phone call, but now she was worried. What if the guy was talking about Marta and not Jean? She was sure he said she was with Mitch, and ,Mitch, oh dear God that boy looked like someone beat him up all night long.

"Sit here," she told him. "I am going to help you clean up. Does your mother know you got into a fight?" she asked.

"No ma'am, she does not, and I am not going to tell her till the morning when she is good on her sleep. I am very sorry you had to see me like this. I am not sure what I can do to prove to you that I will not hurt your daughter, Ms. Sophia. I am in love with your daughter and, I really would like to continue seeing her."

Jean was looking at him with her sad green eyes, and could not believe he just said he loved her. She did not care if her mother was there or not, she got up and kissed him on his lips very slowly so she would not hurt him.

"Oh my God!" Sophia said. "First Marta, now Jean. Well, there is nothing I can really do," she said. "I already lost one of my girls I am not about to lose the other one, too. Yea, Mitch you can see Jean." With that she left to get him some ice, so his swollen eye and lip would look somewhat good in the morning.

When she was gone, Jean looked at him and asked, "So what you told my mom is the truth? You are in love with me?"

"Yes I am," he said. "I have been in love with you for a long time. I just did not know how to tell you. I love you, Jean. Will you marry me?"

"Yes!" was all she could say. She had to stop herself from jumping on him, because he was still hurt. Instead, she just kissed him lightly on his lips and went to help her mother get the ice. In the morning, they went to his mother together. They had to tell her Mitch was in a fight, and they had to tell her they were getting married. Mitch knew that was not going to be good news for her because, Russell just left and now he was getting married, too. Good thing the house was empty when they got there, Mitch did not have the words to tell his mom.

Josephine was in the store and she had the feeling something was wrong, very wrong. She could not put her finger on it, but she had a feeling and those feelings were always right. She got her groceries and was on her way home, when she almost ran Paul over.

"Dear God boy! Watch where you are going," she told

him, and then she stopped talking. "What happened to you?" she asked. "Why do you look like you have been fighting with wolves?"

Paul started to say something, but he remembered Russell was his best friend, where ever he was, and this was his mom.

"No ma'am. I was not fighting with wolves, I was fighting with your son, Mitch, and he looks just like me right now. If not even worse," Paul said and walked away.

Josephine could not wait to get home and see her boy, if he was even home she thought. She was waiting for that boy all night, and he was out fighting. Just wait till she sees him! The moment she saw the porch, and Mitch with Jean on the porch, she knew what the fight was about. It made it easier to know that it was over a girl and not over alcohol or some other problems those guys had.

Paul and Mitch never liked each other she knew, but that did not give them the right to fight over a girl. Much less a girl she did not like. She knew whose daughter she was and she knew the stories, she did not care if they were right or wrong. The minute Mitch saw his mom he went to help her.

"I am glad you are alive," she said. "I see you have had a bad night, Son. I just wish to know if it was worth it. Have you looked in the mirror this morning?"

"Yes Mom, I have. I know what I look like," he said, "and I am sorry I did not come home last night. I looked very bad and did not want to scare you." They walked in the house and Mitch went to go get Jean, too.

"Mom, me and Jean have something to say to you, and we will like you to listen to us."

"Whatever it is, Mitch, just come out and say it. As long as there is no stories which your face tells me all there will be are stories how my hero son rescued a girl the whole town don't like."

"Mom, we are getting married, and she will be my wife. Please do not insult her."

"Over my dead body!" Josephine said. "You are not marrying her! Did you lose your mind in the fight last night? And, if you decide you are getting married, you can get your things and get out of my house. Because you are not living here!"

"Fine," Mitch said. "I am getting my things and leaving. There is no reason to talk to you, anyways. I tried all I could do."

Mitch went to go get his clothes, and Jean stayed in the same spot she was in.

"Doesn't it feel good to break up the family?" Josephine asked Jean. "I have heard stories about you and your sister. Why do you like to destroy my family? I have to deal with Russell gone, now you are taking Mitch, too?"

"I am sorry," Jean said. "I am not taking him away from you. It is not my fault you cannot face people that have nothing better to do than to tell stories that were not truth. No one knows me and my family better than me, and no one knows you and your family better than you. Do you think my mother likes stories about your sons? No she does not, but that will not make her throw me out like you threw your son. To you it is more important what other people think than it is to watch after your own son."

"Get out of my house!" Josephine said. "I do not know who you think you are, but in my house no one talks to me like that!"

At that moment, Mitch came out and they left. He did not say good bye to his mother, he did not even look at her. He only closed the door and left. They knew what they were getting themselves into, but they also knew now they will be together forever.

Mitch and Jean had a very quiet wedding. No one was there but the two witnesses they had to have, and they were both Jean's friends. No one really liked Mitch, but they did it for Jean. If their friend was happy, they were happy too. Jean's mom was not happy about the wedding, either, but she had her daughter home. Mitch did not go home after his mom told him he was not welcome there. They had their own room and that was all they needed. No one bothered them and they were not in anyone's way. Days passed by with just the three of them. Sophia was not working, but Mitch and Jean did, they were going to work at the same time and they were coming home at the same time.

One day, Jean did not feel good and she asked to go home early. Her boss let her go, but instead of going home she went to Mitch's work. She walked in the office where he worked and before he could see her, she collapsed right in front of his office. Robert, one of Mitch's co-workers, saw her fall and went to help her. Mitch heard people in front of his door, and went to see what is going on. When he saw that it was Jean, his blood froze and his face was so white even Robert thought Mitch was going to faint.

"Jean! Jean are you ok?" Robert was asking her..

When she opened her eyes, she saw Mitch and Robert next to her. She did not know what happened to her all, she knew was that she fell and hit her head.

"You hit that floor good, Girl. Are you all right?" Robert asked.

"Yes I am. I am fine now," she said. "What happened?"

"I don't know," Robert said. "All I saw was you faint. Do you need a doctor?"

"No, I don't. But, Mitch I came here to see if you wanted to go see the doctor with me," she said. "I have not felt good all day long."

"Yes, of course I will go with you," Mitch said, and they left.

They were in the doctor's office when he walked in and gave them the happy news. Jean was eight weeks pregnant. They were so happy and overjoyed that they had to go and celebrate. They wanted to tell everyone they were having a baby, but there was really no one to tell. Mitch's mother would just make fun of him, and say he was baby himself. Jean's mom might be happy but they would wait to tell her. They wanted to go to the bar but they knew Jean did not feel good, so they went to Mitch's friend Justin's house where there was always a party.

When they got there, Mitch recognized the car that his ex-best friend was driving, and his happy mood went sour. He would not let anything bother him tonight, he promised himself. Tonight is the night he had to spend with his wife and let everyone know they were going to have a baby.

He wished that the baby was a little girl, with green eyes like her mother and that she would be tall like him and have the same gorgeous hair her mother has. He knew their baby was going to be beautiful it didn't matter if it was a boy or a girl.

On their way to Justin's house, they tried to pick out names. If it was a girl they were going to call her Vanessa, and if it was a boy they are going to call him Alexander. Either way there baby would be gorgeous. Justin was waiting for them, and when he saw Mitch's face he knew there was big news they were going to hear.

"What's up Mitch?" Justin asked. "You look like you have something to tell me."

"Yes I do, and its big," Mitch said. "Jean is pregnant and we are going to have a baby!"

"When is the baby due?" Justin asked.

"August 29," Mitch said, "and I wish so bad that it's a little girl, but if it's a boy then I will have a son that will take my place," Mitch said.

"Oh boy! Let's celebrate!" Justin said. "Listen up everyone!"

Justin yelled when he got into the living room. "Mitch and Jean will have a baby so tonight the party is in their name."

On the other side of the room, Joseph was sitting on the couch with his girlfriend, Lidia. They were having an interesting conversation about babies when they heard Mitch was going to have a baby. Lidia knew about Joseph and Mitch's friendship, and she knew how much her boyfriend missed his best friend. They talked about Mitch once in a while, and every time she would bring up Mitch, Joseph's eyes would go dark. She knew it hurt him to talk about it, so most of the time she tried not to.

Joseph would love to go and congratulate them on their baby, but he did not know how Mitch would take that. He was sure his ex-best friend still hated him, and he did not want to mess up their night, so once again he would stay away from him. It hurt him so bad to know that after all this time Mitch never once tried to talk to him. Or asked why he did what he did. Maybe if he asked, Joseph would not mind telling him the truth. Not that he would just let all of it go, but soon he should talk to Mitch.

Everyone was happy around them, and coming to congratulate them on the baby. Mitch saw Joseph and Lidia sitting down and he felt sick to his stomach. God, he missed him so much. He missed his best friend, missed talking to him, missed having someone to talk to about Jean, missed yelling at him when he was mad. He did not know what he would tell him even if he went to talk to him. It had been over four months that they have not talked, and now Mitch had no idea what to say. Was it his fault? Was it Joseph's? He did not really want to forgive him for going to the police, but maybe that is what made him the man he was today-the dad he was going to be. He was so happy with Jean that nothing and no one could break it, but he was wrong, very wrong.

Right when they were all starting to leave, Paul came over with the Jean's best friend, Erika. Paul knew this was going to bother Jean very much, so why not? he asked himself. Now he hated her, not only did she get married. Now she would have a baby and it was not his. Paul had no idea that Mitch was drinking, and that he was really drunk. All he knew was that he wanted to pay him back for the bruises everyone saw on his face from the fight they had. And by God he would, it looked like tonight was the perfect night to cause Mitch to have a fight with him. Paul walked in and did not pay attention to anyone but Mitch and Jean he was going to say his congratulations to both of them. He had a good idea how to do it, too.

"Hey guys, I just heard the good news, so I came over to tell you both good luck," he said with a smirk on his face.

Mitch recognized the sarcasm and really did not want to pay attention tonight, he had to remind himself that the baby and his wife were more important then what ever Paul was trying to do.

"Thank you," Jean said.

"Well, I am not sure if this was a good idea for you Jean. Do you have any idea what having a child is like? Oh wait, maybe you do," Paul said. "Mitch is a child himself so it won't be hard for you to raise the other one."

Mitch struck him so hard in his face, that Paul fell to the ground. Mitch did not stop there, either. He was drunk and he hated when people called him a child. He was on top of Paul in a matter of seconds, beating every ounce of life out of him. When Paul was not moving anymore, Justin pulled Mitch off of him.

"What's wrong with you?" he asked. "Dude, you are not that boy anymore, you are not the single guy that you only have to think about yourself you have wife a and a child on the way."

Police Officer Randy was on duty that night, and he received the call. That meant he might have to rough up some guys. He knew Justin, and he also knew there were always parties there. He was called before, but for nothing major, just some fights which he hoped it was the same thing now. Just some boys having an argument about girls. He remembered last year at the same time, he was at Justin's house because a boy did not like how someone was looking at him. Kids these days, he thought, and went to see what was going on at Justin's again.

At Justin's house it was a party all right, Randy thought. There were so many cars and kids outside that is was hard not to miss. Randy knocked on the door, and Justin opened up with a grin on his face.

"Officer Randy, what a nice surprise! What can I do for you?"

"Justin, don't play dumb," Randy said. "I got a call there was trouble here. What is going on?"

At that moment, Randy saw Paul and his bloodied face. He was sitting on the couch, and Lidia was next to him. He pushed through the door to see what was going on. When he saw Mitch there, too, he had a good idea what happened but he wanted to hear it himself.

"Officer, I want to press charges against Mitch," Paul said. "He hit me out of nowhere. I was just sitting here with my girl, when he came in swinging his fists at me and I want him in jail."

Randy looked at the boy and did not know where blood was coming out of, his face was so bad that it was hard to know who he really was. Mitch knew there was no reason to explain himself. He kissed Jean and told her he would be ok. He also knew that when you went to jail for fighting, you did not get out for a very long time. He just wished he would get out to see his baby born.

He did not wait to be asked questions ,he just told Randy the truth that he did beat him. Did not try to explain why, either. He wanted to get it over with so Randy got him in the police car, and they were on their way.

"Poor Jean," she heard. People were talking about it like

they had nothing better to do. At work they were saying how Mitch beat Paul so bad, because he just wanted to get it out of him. Someone was saying how he had nothing better to do then to fight. All Jean did everyday when she got home was cry and wait. Wait for Mitch to come home and everything would go back to normal.

CHAPTER THREE

JEAN WAS GETTING BIG, SHE liked it and she didn't, but there was really nothing she wanted to change. Well, she wanted her husband home, and she wanted to share everything with him. At night she would sit at the window and cry, thinking that he should be there with her. Holding her hand every time the baby kicked, and it would be nice to have someone next to her when she went to her doctor's appointments. At her doctor's appointment next week she will know what she was having. She would find out if it was a boy or a girl. She knew Mitch wanted a girl, so she was hoping for it, too.

It had been over six months that Mitch was gone, and he had three more to go. If he was good, they said they would let him out to see the baby born, but so far he had not listened. He had two offenses already, for fighting with other inmates and for talking back to a prison guard, so it was not looking good for him

Why does he not listen? Jean wondered. Does he not want to come home and see the baby born? What is wrong with him? She had so much to ask him but she could not, he was told no visitors until the end of month. She would just have to wait and see, she would ask him all of the things she wanted when she saw him next.

Life in prison was so hard, Mitch thought one day while he was making his bed. You have to get up at the time they tell you, you have to eat when they give you food, go to sleep when someone else tells you. It was a horrible life, but he only had two more months to go and he would be done. He promised himself no more trouble, he could not live like this. His baby was coming soon, and he had to go see his wife. He lost his job because of the fight. And Paul, every time he thought of him, he hated him more and more. He was just going to stay away from him, next time there was a fight he would have to kill him, or better yet not be around him.

Mitch was thinking to himself if he really wanted to be married anymore, too. Jean was big and fat now, he thought. She did not look like his wife anymore, she did not have that sweet face, and she was mean to him. Why was she yelling at him every time she came to see him? She blamed him for the things that had happened, and he thought he helped her. They would have to talk about their problems when he got home, but for now he would be good and listen so he could go home. Where ever that was, he did not even know if Jean's mom would let him live there anymore. He missed so much of life outside of bars, that he did not even know where to start anymore.

Today is the day, Jean thought, she was going to see the doctor and find out what the baby's sex was. If it was a girl or a boy. She was hoping for a little girl, and then again as long as her kid was healthy that's all that matters. She got the news that Mitch should be home right around the time baby was born. Wow, she missed him so much. She missed the past times they had, but this time she wanted to do everything right so when he came home he would be happy.

The last time she went to visit him, he had that look in his eyes she did not like. He was looking at her like he hated, her like it was her fault he was there. She never once told him to fight, she never told him to punch Paul so he could not breathe, he did all this on his own. So why look at her like she did it? Maybe it would be better when he got home.

At the doctor's office it was nice and quiet, there were not that many patients and she was next. Jean was very nervous to find out what she was having.

"You are having a girl!" the doctor said. "I hope you are ready for it!"

Jean started to cry. She was so happy and sad at the same time she, knew how happy Mitch would be if he was there, so there was even more reason to be sad than happy. When he called her next she would tell him about the baby girl they were having.

Time passed by and Jean was bigger and moodier, the baby was coming soon she knew. One night while she was sleeping, she felt a bad pain and like she had to go the bathroom. She got up and found that her water had broken. She knew that she was going to have to go to the hospital. She woke up her mom, and they went together. The nurses gave her some medicine and let her rest. She wanted Mitch there so bad, but he wouldn't be out until the next day.

The pain came stronger, and the doctor said, "Jean you are all ready to have this baby girl!" As soon as she heard her cry, she forgot everything else. It was the sweetest voice she had ever heard. The doctor put the baby in her arms, and as she was held the beautiful baby girl tears were falling on her cheeks. Her mom was next to her crying, just like she did. The baby was named Vanessa, since that was what her dad wanted. It was too bad that he was not there, but would see his baby as soon as he could.

Morning came and Jean did not see Mitch. She heard he was out, and then she also heard he was drinking with his buddies. Wow, she thought to herself, what was all that talk about having a baby? He was not even around; to him it was more important to drink.

Mitch came in three days later to see little Vanessa, even when he came to see her he was drunk.

"Wow," he told Jean, "you were so big and look how little this baby girl is. At least she has your eyes, everything else is mine. Sorry I cannot stay, but I have to celebrate. Your mom will take you home, you will be all right, you understand don't you?"

Jean could not believe what he was saying to her.

"No!" she said. "I do not understand! If you were going to make kids, you can at least see her for a little bit longer. You just got out of jail, can you not stay?"

"Well I could if I really wanted to," Mitch said, "but I am not sure I really want to. My buddies are waiting for me, bye!"

"This was supposed to be my happy day," Jean told her mom. "So why does it feel like there is nothing to be happy about? Yes, I just had a baby that I love more than anything on the world, but my world is crashing on me."

"Everything will be fine," Sophia said. "He was not out for a long time, and now he has to have some fun. I am not saying it is ok for him to do what he is doing, but you do have to give him some time."

Mitch was at home waiting for them when they got there. He went to help them, but Jean really did not want him around her -when she needed him around he was not there! Jean was very hurt when he did not want to come and see Vanessa , she did not care about his excuses, whatever they might have been.

"Hello gorgeous," Mitch said to his little girl, "How are you today?"

"She cannot talk yet," Jean said with a smirk on her face, "and if you really wanted to know how she was, you would of been there the minute she was born. I wonder where you have been all this time. It has been five days since Vanessa was born, have you done *anything* for her?"

Mitch looked at Jean, and at that moment he really did not see anything in this woman. He asked himself many times why he married her and now he had no idea.

"I am sorry," he said. "I was out with my friends. I had just got out of jail. I was there for nine whole months. Can you not understand that I need some time?"

"Well I could understand if it was not your baby, and if it was not that important, but I just cannot understand how you could say you loved me, or the baby, so much and not be there when it was the most important for both of us."

"I don't see a point of talking to you," he said. "I am going out. I might be back, I might not, and if I do come back we are not going to live like this. I am not going to fight with you for the rest of my life. I know I married you, and I know I am stuck with you, but that does not mean I have to listen to your complaints every minute of my day. I am going to look for a job, and when I get back we are going to talk about this," he said and left.

———————————

Days passed, she did not see or hear from Mitch. She had things to take care of, a little girl to look after. The bad part was she did not have a job, and he did not either, it was not like he was home for her anyways. It was a good thing it was spring she thought, there were apples, pears, tomatoes, and she would never go hungry. There were days that she only had tomatoes to eat, or apples, but that was all she had. She did not have a job and was not able to work.

Mitch came home seven days later, and had nothing to

show for the days that he was gone. He went to look for a job, Jean thought, and how come he does not have one yet?

"I found a job," was the next thing that came out of Mitch's mouth, "I am going to work in the new factory that they just opened up."

It looks promising, Jean thought. Then they talked and they got their things taken care of. There were no more fights and everything was just fine-well at least for a while. One night while Jean was sleeping, tired of being always up with the baby, Mitch came home late. He laid next to Jean and fell asleep.

Vanessa must have heard him and she woke up, started crying, and wanted someone to hold her. Jean thought maybe for once, he could get up and give her a bottle, after all, he was her father. For the five months that she had been born, he had not once changed her diapers, not once fed her, or given her a bath. Vanessa was crying loud, and he just laid there.

"Aren't you going to do anything about the baby?" he asked her.

"Well I am sorry," Jean said. "Aren't you her father, too? Don't you think you should maybe get up and give her a bottle? Maybe change her diaper?"

"No," Mitch said, "you do not have a job, you do not do anything ,at least what you can do is change your baby."

"My baby?" Jean asked. "I thought it was ours, not just mine."

"Fine," Mitch said. "Now it is just yours." Then he got up and left.

He was gone for a week, no one saw him or heard from him. He walked in the house one day while Jean was taking care of Vanessa. He was covered in bruises and looked like there was nothing left of him. Jean felt sorry for him, went to him, and tried to ask what happened.

"Nothing happened to me," he said. "I got into a fight with one of your good friends, and he did this to me; well not him

37

the police did." Jean could not believe that he just got out of jail for fighting, and he was in it again.

"Mitch are you ever going to change?" she asked. "Am I always going to have be here alone, waiting for you? Am I ever going to have a normal life with you in it?"

"I don't know," he said. "I do not know what is wrong with me, but I will try to change for you and Vanessa. I will try to do anything and everything I can."

It worked for a while, for about almost two years, when they found out they were having a baby again.

"God Jean," Mitch said, "why are you not more careful? We cannot even take care of Vanessa, how can we take care of the other baby?" but he was secretly happy inside. "I am sorry" he said. "I should have not said that. I do not know what I was thinking. Maybe after having this baby, we wont have as many problems as we did."

They had a boy and named him Alexander. Mitch was not there for his birth, either, because he was in Slovenia helping his brother finish a job. To Jean that was important, because it meant he was doing something to better his life, and to have things for her and the babies. But he was wrong, the baby came and the problems continued. He was out a lot, he was drinking all the time, more and more every time he left.

One night while he was gone, Jean was thinking to herself why don't I just leave him? What good my life with him in it? Tomorrow morning, I am leaving, and I am never coming back. There is no reason for me to be here. Morning came, and Jean took the kids and left she went to her cousin's to stay there, and think about her marriage and her problems. Alexander and Vanessa were older now, but she still needed to think about them even, without Mitch in it, they were her babies and she would do anything for them.

Mitch came home to an empty house; he had no idea where they went, and Sophia would not talk to him. She had nothing to say to him all, she said was if it is so important to you, then maybe you should of been there when she needed you the most. He just wanted to beat her to the ground, but he knew if he put one hand on her and he would be in jail for the rest of his life, and that was not worth doing.

"I will find her," Mitch said, "and when I do we do not want you in our life."

"Well there is one thing you are forgetting, Mitch. This house is not yours or Jean's it is mine. I live here I worked for all this. What have you done?" she asked.

"I am going to get Jean," he said. "I have a good idea where she is. When we get back, you better be gone, because you do not want to cause your daughter any more problems. If you are not gone, I will be. If you are the one who will take care of my kids for me, then you can stay."

He went to her cousin's, and she was there with kids. He begged her to come back, and Jean knew she could not live there forever, so she went home with him

When she got home, the house was empty. All she found was a letter to her:

Dear Jean,
You are my daughter I love you more then the world. I will do anything for you, but as long as Mitch is in my house, I am not coming back. I will be in Slovenia with Marta, I really am sorry, but maybe you should think about you and your family. Don't worry about me, I will be fine. Just take care of those cute kids, and I will come and visit you whenever he is not around. I am sorry.

Jean dropped the letter to the floor, sat down, and cried like a little baby. She loved her mother very much, her mother has done everything for her, but now she has to choose who to spend her life with. would it be her husband or her mother? God how hard that was, but she also had two kids with Mitch. She had to think about them, too, and maybe he could change.

In Bosnia there were no divorces, and no matter how miserable you were, you had to stay with the same person. When you said till death do us part, it was till death do us part. Mitch felt bad for Jean, he knew she missed her mother, but really what was there for him to do? He did not like every move he made to be watched.

———————————————

Days passed, followed by months and years. There were times when Mitch did not come home for months, and Jean never once asked him where he was. She found herself a job while the kids were at school, she worked long hours, just so the kids could have something nice.

Very often Jean and Mitch would fight about what clothes she bought the kids, mostly he wanted them to wear old clothes, and nothing really new. He would always say that the money she was spending on the kids could be used for their school, or something else. They had to remodel the house, and there was finally money for it this time. One day, Jean gave Mitch all the money they had saved up to remodel the house. He left and did not get back home for seven days. When he got home, there was not stuff for the house.

"What happened?" Jean asked. "I thought you went to go get the things, and it took you seven days? I see you are back, but where is the stuff?"

"I got robbed," Mitch said. "I was robbed, and I did not want to come home, because I was afraid you would yell at me. Please don't look at me like that," he said. "You are looking at me like you want to kill me."

"Damn right I do!" Jean screamed. "I have given you every penny of my money, and what do I have to show for it? You were robbed? Yeah right. I wish I could believe you, Mitch, but

I really cannot. How many times have you lied so far? I guess we just cannot have what others have."

He did not really care what she had to say, he was off the hook, and he just wanted to sleep. The next months followed with him not wanting to do anything with the kids, or the house. The neighbor kids were more important than his own it seemed.

One night they had a get together with the neighbors, and little Igor was sitting on the floor playing with Alexander. Mitch came by, and did not like what Alexander had to say to Igor, so he hit him.

"Wow," Alexander said, "Dad, you like Igor way more than you like me, I wonder if he is your kid." Alexander was eight, and he was sick of being treated like a dog, like he was not his son. He would always do the right things for his father, but never got any love for it.

Vanessa was different, Alexander thought, she would never really get yelled at, or in trouble for some reason. Dad always thought more of her then him, and he hated him for that. Even though he was just a little boy, he still never wanted to be around his father, or to be near him. Every time he would try to get close to him, Mitch would go away, or have to do something that had nothing to do with Alexander.

He was always getting into fights at school, and he was always getting beat up. He hated his life, and mostly he hated his father. His father never had anything nice to say to him, so he could not ever tell him how his days at school were, he was always scared that he would get yelled at or hit.

One day Vanessa and Alexander were doing their homework, when Mitch came home drunk. He wanted to see what they were doing, and how their homework was. Of course, he found something to yell at Alexander about.

"Your homework is horrible!" he yelled at him. "Don't you have any brains in your head, or were you just born stupid" Alexander thought that his dad was drunk, so he did not want to get into a fight. He just took his work from him and put it away.

"So you think you are done?" Mitch yelled.

"Yes I am."

"No, you are not! Not till I say you are! Bring your work back, and I will show you what it means to be smart," Mitch told him.

Alexander brought his things back to the table, but by the time he came back, Mitch was all ready passed out. Yes, he did not like his father, he did not like the way he was treated, but he was still his dad ,so he always had to do what he was told. His mother was everything to Alexander, he loved her with all his heart, he just did not know or see why she would stay with a person that treated her so badly like his father did. He was ten years old but he all ready knew when he grew up he would not treat any woman like his mother had been treated.

Vanessa had been much luckier then Alexander. Their mother was always nice to both of them, but their father was nicer to her than to him. Alexander sometimes wondered why that was. What had he been doing wrong that he always got hit, pushed, or punished, and Vanessa was always let go with just little punishments? One night while their dad was out with his friends, Alexander wanted to know why his dad was better to his sister than to him, so he asked his mom.

"Alexander don't be ridiculous!" Jean said, "Your father is just harder on you, because he wants you to grow up to be a respectful man, that's all."

"Oh yeah," Alexander said, "why don't he take his own advice and reaccept you? Mom, why do you take so much from him! I know I am just a little boy, but why do you let him walk all over you?"

"Boy, that is my problem, not yours. I am trying everything I can to be a great mother to you and your sister, and to be a good wife. There is no reason you should even be worried what me and your father do, that is our business and please stay out of it!"

"Yes Mom, whatever you say!" He knew he had lost this fight.

Alexander and Vanessa never really had any friends. In school, kids never wanted to play with them, or be their friends because they lived far away. All the kids that were in their classes lived so close to school, that all of them were friends at home, too. Alexander had one or two friends at home, but he never wanted to play with any of them, because he was always picked on. He just mostly went where ever Vanessa was going, which he did not know why she got so mean whenever he went places with her and her friends. What he did not know was that Vanessa was twelve, and she was interested in boys her own age, and playing with her brother was just plain embarrassing.

Vanessa was still small for her age, she did not grow as fast as her friends Lidia and Tina did. Lidia was the same age as her, and Tina was the same age as Alexander. Lidia had gorgeous brown hair that was past her shoulders, and smoking brown eyes that, even though she was twelve, every boy that looked at her lost himself. Vanessa was jealous of Lidia, but she never said anything to her friend, because that would just be mean. It was not her friend's fault that she was so gorgeous, and Vanessa was not. Lidia had everything she wanted, she had a bigger house, better parents, she had a sister and not a brother, something Vanessa did not want. Tina was very pretty, too, she was short little girl; that is what everyone called her. She had the cutest smile in the whole town, and pretty brown eyes.

Sometimes she wanted her brother to go away, to stay home and not come out with her, but for some reason it never worked. Her mother would always say, Vanessa you know if he cannot go, you cannot either. She had to take her brother everywhere with her, and sometimes she would not go just because he did.

Vanessa, Lidia, Tina, and Alexander were always together. They made saved their old wrappers from chocolate, candy, and everything else they could find, and they played grocery store at Lidia's house almost everyday. They did not go to the same school, so one day when Vanessa came home she wondered why Lidia was not waiting for her. She went to her house, and her mom told her that Lidia was out shopping with her dad.

How much Vanessa wanted to hear her dad say, let's go shopping, or let's do anything that was fun, but nope. Not at their house, they never went anywhere, but to school and home. There were times that their parents would go out at night, and Vanessa and Alexander would stay at home alone. They did not really care, but they still wanted to be a part of the family and go places.

Lidia got home late that night, and she and Vanessa did not get to play at all. Vanessa was still upset, when her mother went to say good night to her and her brother.

"What's wrong?" Jean asked her.

"Well, I did not get to play with Lidia at all today, and I am just a little sad," Vanessa said.

"Honey you cannot always play with Lidia, they have a different lifestyle then we do."

"Yeah, I know," Vanessa said. "They have everything we can only wish for." She looked at her mom with those big, sad green eyes and said, "Mom, are we ever going to have what they do?"

Jean's heart was breaking to see her daughter like this, and to know that her daughter might never have what others did. She did not know how to explain to her that she don't know what life would bring.

"Vanessa, honey, for right now we have what we have, maybe later on all this will change, but for right now we have to do with what we have. I am sorry," Jean said and kissed her softly on the cheek.

That night Vanessa dreamed of a big house, and Lidia in

it. She saw Lidia and her parents playing outside, and she saw herself outside of the fence looking in. When she woke up, she wondered if one day she might have a big house just like in her dreams.

Time went by, and Vanessa and Lidia became best friends, there were times that Jean would let Vanessa go by herself without Alexander, those were the best times, Vanessa thought. She did not have to worry about someone following her the whole time and saying, come on I am ready to go home it is boring, and I want to go home now.

Those were some good times, Vanessa thought one day while she was cleaning the house. She was lost in her thoughts, and she did not hear the knock on the door. When the door opened, she dropped the plate she was washing and screamed so loud, that Lidia could hear her two houses away. She did not only scare her self she scared the mailman, too.

"I am sorry," he said. "I was knocking, but you did not hear me."

"Oh, I am sorry, too," Vanessa said. "What can I do for you?"

"Here is the letter, make sure you give it to your parents as soon as they get home," he said. "It is very important, and you have to make sure you give them this."

"Ok," Vanessa said, "I will do it."

Lidia came over right after she seen the mailman leave, she walked into the house and gave Vanessa a weird look.

"What was that for?" Vanessa said. "What did I do?"

"Nothing, but you scared me with your scream. I heard you all the way at my house. What were you doing that you did not hear him come in?" Lidia asked.

"Oh nothing, I was just cleaning and thinking, so he just scared me, that's all."

"Why was he here?"

"He got this letter for my dad, and he told me it is very

45

important; to give it to dad and mom as soon as they get home."

"Well, let's open it," Lidia said.

"No!" Vanessa said. "I do not open my parents' mail and it looks very important. I am not even going to try."

"Oh well, I tried," Lidia said. "I am going home now. Tomorrow after school, let me know why you scared me so bad with your screaming."

"Ok, I will if I can hear anything between Mom and Dad tonight. I will let you know tomorrow for sure."

"Ok, bye," Lidia said and left.

Vanessa was wondering if she should open it, and see what was in it, if or she should just leave it alone. Well if it was not so important it would not bother her so much, she thought. That's ok, I will find out from Mom and Dad, anyways I am ok without being punished for one letter. She went out and forgot about the letter, and how important it was.

CHAPTER FOUR

THAT NIGHT WHEN THEY WENT to bed, Vanessa could not sleep, she opened her door so she could hear her mom and dad talking.

"Oh my God!" Jean was saying. "Did it really come to this? I had heard the news, and I knew it was bad, but I did not know that they were going to call all of the guys in our town to go fight. It is not even our fight."

Vanessa could not believe what she was hearing. Her dad had to go to war? She had heard many kids talk about it at school, but she never thought her dad would have to go. Vanessa was only twelve, she did not know what war was; she only knew what she heard about it. She had heard many stories about war, and that not many people come home alive, and she was very scared.

Mitch was sitting on the end of the couch, just staring at the letter. He knew he had to go because every guy in town was going, but he really did not want to go. This was his home, his wife, his kids, and now he had to leave it all behind and go to war and fight, even though he did not know what he was fighting for.

Morning came and they had to say good bye to their father, even though they were not close they had to say good byes, and it was not easy. Vanessa knew where her father was going, but Alexander did not. That morning before they went to school, Alexander asked his sister:

"Where is dad going? Looks like you know, you and mom both know, but no one will tell me," Alexander said.

"He is going away for a while," Jean said, "he will be back as soon as he can."

"Is he going to work?" Alexander asked.

"No, he is not," Vanessa said, "stop asking questions that you will not understand answers to."

"Vanessa, be nice to your brother," Jean said. "Go get ready for school, or you will be late."

They were at the bus stop waiting to get to school, and Alexander just could not help himself.

"Vanessa tell me, where did dad go this morning?"

"He went to war," Vanessa said, angry. "He might be back, he might not, happy now? You asked, and I told you, now leave me be."

"What do you know anyways?" Alexander asked. "You don't know anything, and if he went to war, how come I did not hear about it? Don't tell your stupid lies to no one, or they might think you are crazy," Alexander told her.

That day, many kids came to school and talked about how their fathers had to go to war that morning, and how they might not be back. It was a very sad day, not just for Vanessa and Alexander, but for many other kids, too.

———————————————

They were watching the news every day, and praying that they would not hear bad news, because their mother once told them, no new is just like good news. The war in Kosovo was going stronger and stronger every day, there were many people around town talking about it, it was the very big news of town. There are no men left in a town, Vanessa thought one day when she was going home. Everyone is gone, all these house only have women and children in them, there is not one man in town.

Vanessa was still very good friends with Lidia and Tina, and she was there more than she was in her own house. Vanessa did not have a television, but Lidia did, and that is where she watched all the horrible news about Kosovo. All the people that died each day, and many fathers that were not coming home.

Time passed, and there were nights when they went to sleep praying that maybe tomorrow Mitch would come home, and everything would be the same. It was very bad not to have a father at home. When he was home they were not afraid of anything, and now when he was not there, every little noise scared them. When Mitch was home there was food, too, Jean thought. He was not a great husband, and he was not a great father, but he was a person that provided food for them, and now he was gone. There were many times when Jean had to go and work at the next door neighbor's all day long just to get some food, or to get bread and milk so she could feed her kids.

She knew the kids didn't understand why there wasn't any food and they did not understand why she was out all day working in the sun just to bring them milk and eggs or some bread. One day they will understand, Jean thought, or at least she hoped they would. Vanessa saw that her mom was working all the time, and all they had was breakfast or dinner, or sometimes just an apple or orange or some tomatoes. She knew her mom was trying, and she also knew no matter what, her mom would always be there for them.

It has been over four months now they had not heard or seen their dad, and they were really worried. They could see their mom she losing weight and not getting any sleep. Many nights Vanessa would wake up to go get some water, and her mother would be sitting in the bed, praying for Mitch to come home safe.

Vanessa and Alexander were walking home from school one day, and it looked like many of the guys were back. Some of the guys they knew. and some they did not. They were ran home, hoping their dad was there waiting for them, and that he was all right. Vanessa walked in the house first, she almost ran Mitch over.

"Dad! You're back!" she screamed. "Oh Dad, how much I have missed you!"

"Slow down, Vanessa," Mitch said. "I am not going anywhere anymore. I am here to stay with you guys." He hugged all three, and it felt so good. Alexander thought this was what he had always waited for. He waited to be hugged by his father, to see his dad hug his mom, and for all of them to be happy again. It was, after all, a very happy moment in their life.

It took them over a week to get used to Mitch being back, and to have all four of them home again. It was not much that they had, but at least this time they had all four of them, and it was nice. No one yelled at anyone ,and it was a happy time.

One day while they were coming home from school, Vanessa noticed that something was bothering her brother, he was not his usual annoying self. He was not talking and that was very strange.

"What's the matter Alexander?" Vanessa asked him. "Why are you so quiet, and how come you have not said a word since we left school?"

"Nothing is wrong with me," he said. "I think I am just very tired, and as soon as I get home I am going to lay down., I have a headache, too."

Vanessa knew he was lying, but she was not going to say anything to him. She would talk to mom when she got home. They walked in the house, and Vanessa went straight to find her mom. She knew where to look because her mother was always working in the yard, making sure the tomatoes and peppers grew good, and that they would have food over the winter.

"Hey baby girl," Jean said. "How was school?"

"Well it was ok," Vanessa said, "but I think something is wrong with Alexander. He is not talking, and he went to sleep as soon as we got home. Maybe he is sick or something, but I think you should come with me, and see it for yourself."

"Ok," Jean said, "let's go inside and see what's wrong with your brother."

They walked in on Alexander throwing up. Jean went to him, and sat next to him. She was massaging his back and his head, so he would feel a little bit better. She also noticed that he had a very high fever.

"Did you eat something different at school today, Alexander?" she asked. "I know what I sent to school with you, but did you eat or drink something that did not belong to you?"

"No Mom, I did not," Alexander said. "I think I am just very sick. I got sick right after we played outside."

"So you might have gotten sick from too much sun," Jean said. "Let's get you to bed, and you can have some rest. I am going to make you some soup, and I hope you will feel better by the time your dad comes home from work."

Mitch came home, and Alexander was still not feeling good. They had to do something very fast, because he was getting worse by the minute. They did not have insurance, but they knew if they did not take him to the doctor he could get much worse.

They went to the hospital, and Alexander had food poisoning. The doctor said if they did not bring him in when they did, it would have been deadly. Alexander later explained to everyone that one of his friends brought in some food that he never had before, and he wanted to try some, that is how he got very sick.

Life had been good, Alexander thought one day. There

were no fights at home, his mom and dad were getting along better then they ever had, and it was a happy house.

———————————————

One Saturday morning while they were sleeping, Lidia came over screaming. Vanessa was trying to calm her down so she could at least understand what she was saying to her.

"My dad. My dad," was all Lidia could say.

"What happened?" Vanessa asked. "What happened to your dad?"

"He is dead! He died last night working at my uncle's house."

Lidia's dad worked cutting trees and making them ready for winter. Carl, Lidia's dad, went to work that day, and never came back home. He died after he was hit with a tree that fell on him. Vanessa was trying to talk to Lidia, but there was no help. She was very upset, because Carl was everything to her. They did everything together, from shopping for a prom dress, to going out to eat just two of them.

Vanessa had never had that. She never went out with her dad alone anywhere, they were just not that close, and she could not really understand why Lidia was so upset. Lidia knew Vanessa never had that with her father, but she was her best friend, and she ran away from home just to be away from all the sadness. She knew she had to go back sometime, but not today. Today she was going to stay away, she knew there were going to be a lot of people, and that everyone would feel sorry for her mother and her sister, but no one really understood how they felt. They lost someone that was everything in their life.

Jean went to see Lidia's mom, Monika, and to be there for her. She also told her where Lidia was, and Monika understood. Carl was the best father there was, the girls adored him, and he loved them so much. Why did he have to go, Monika thought.

Why did he leave her behind with two girls that were growing up so fast?

Monika had family, and they all lived close. Her mother and her brother were there for her, too. Carl's mother, his sister, and his brother were at the house, also. There were so many people there, all Monika could do was sit there and not move. She really did not have anymore tears left. Everyone knew that Carl and Monika were happy, but no one knew the real truth, no one but Monika and Carl, and now it was just Monika.

She had been seeing someone else, they were going to get a divorce, but they did not know how to tell the girls so they decided to live in the same house. Now Monika thought he left her alone to tell the kids about someone they had never met. Today was a sad day for everyone, Monika thought she would not say anything until all this calmed down, then she might tell the girls. She just hoped they will forgive her.

She knew that this was very sad time for the whole town, because Carl was everyone's best friend. He was a great guy, and whenever someone needed something, he was there to help no matter what. The funeral was huge, Vanessa thought, there were so many people, it seemed like the whole town was there. She was there for her best friend, even though she was only twelve she was not stupid. She saw a guy that was standing next to Monika's brother, and she did not like the way he was looking at Monika. He was looking at her the same way her father looked at her mother, maybe she was just mistaken, she thought.

During the next couple of weeks, she would see a car parked in Lidia's drive way. One day she went there to ask if Lidia could play and she saw the same man that she had seen the day of Carl's funeral. That's strange, she thought, this man was not family, so what was he doing here lately? She had only seen family come to Lidia's house, and like every other kid, she was curious to know who the man was.

"Hi," he said, "I am Darko, and you are?"

"Vanessa," she said, "nice to meet you I. was just looking for Lidia, so I can play with her. My mom let me out for a while, before I have to go do my homework is Lidia here?" At that moment, Monika came out of the room all dressed up.

"Oh wow, Miss Monika," Vanessa said, "you look beautiful. Where are you going?"

"We are going to dinner," Monika said. "Lidia is in the other room, if you wanted to go see her."

Vanessa said her good byes and walked to Lidia's room. She opened the door, and found Lidia lying on her bed and crying. Lidia was a very tough girl, and she never cried for any reason. She hated when people saw her cry.

"Get out!" she told Vanessa. "I don't want you here, get out of my room!"

Vanessa had no idea what was going on, but she walked in the room and closed the door.

"What's wrong, Lidia?" Vanessa asked. "What happened, and why are you crying?"

"I told you to get out of my room!" Lidia said. "I want you out of here. How hard is that to understand?"

"I am not leaving until you tell me why you're crying," Vanessa said. "I am your best friend through good and bad, and I want you to tell me what is wrong with you."

Lidia could not talk, she was crying so hard. Vanessa went and sat down next to her on the couch, and just held her hand.

"It will be ok," she said. "Whatever it is, I am your best friend, you can always tell me. I will never tell anyone, I swear."

"I know you won't," Lidia said. "My dad has been dead a month, and my mom is all ready going out on dates with that stupid guy, Darko. I have no idea what is going on, but how could she do this to our family? Did my dad not mean anything to her? Were they not happy? What did I miss?" Lidia asked.

"I am sorry, Vanessa said, "but your mom does have to move on. She is a grown woman, and I am sure if your dad was alive he would want her to, don't you think so?"

"Who's side are you on?" Lidia asked, and looked at Vanessa, very angry. "This is my dad's house! How dare he come into my dad's house! Who does he think he is? I am glad my mom is gone, but she will have a lot of explaining to do when she gets back."

"Ok you need to calm down," Vanessa said. "Why don't we go down to your basement and play for a while, because my mom did let me out only for a little bit. I have to go home, and do my homework," Vanessa said.

"Ok, but I am not going to leave this alone, if that is what you are thinking," Lidia said.

Darko and Monika were sitting in the quiet little restaurant, and Darko noticed that Monika was very quiet. There was something bothering her, but there was something bothering him, too. He did not know how to tell her what was on his mind, but he knew he had to get it out soon, or he would go crazy.

"Monika," he said, "there is something I have to tell you. All I am asking, is that you do not hate me for the rest of your life, all I need you to do is listen to me." She did not like the tone of his voice one bit but she nodded at him.

"You remember that day that I was at your house with Carl, and when we were talking outside?" he began. "Well, that day we talked about going to his brother, and getting all that wood cut off." Monika's blood froze, she was not going to cut him off, she was going to listen to him until the end.

"Well," Darko began again, "the night he died, I was there with him. We were cutting the same tree, and my end came up short. I did not know what to do when the tree fell on him, I tried to help him, I really did, but the tree hit him right in the head and I was not able to do anything. Please believe me," he pleaded, "I wanted to save him. Yes, I love you, but I would not want Carl dead just to be with you."

Monika raised her hand, she was not about to talk, she did not know what to tell this man. She thought she loved the man, but he knew about her husband's death and he had not told her right away.

"Are you all right?" he asked.

"Don't talk right now," she told him, "right now you listen to me. How dare you come to my house. How dare you talk to me. You lied to me for a whole month! You knew all this time, and you never told me anything?" How could you? I want you to take me home, right now. I never want to see you again. Never."

They left restaurant, and were on their way home. It was a nice summer night, and all Monica could think was, how dare he?

"Why did you not tell me this earlier?" she asked.

"I don't know, I was scared what you would say. I was scared you would think I did it."

"Oh really?" Monica asked. "You were scared, so it is ok to lie for a month, and not tell me, right? Then you take me out so my daughter can hate me, and then you tell me you were there? Does everyone know you were there, or did you only hide it from me?"

"His brother knows I was there, and his brother knows I tried to save him."

"Stop it! she screamed. "Stop lying to me I cannot and will not take your lies! I do not need you in my life anymore, so do not come around me or my family. To me you are dead."

He knew he had lost her forever, and that nothing could get them back together again, so he just did what she wanted, he drove her home. When she got home, Lidia was still up waiting for her. Lidia wanted to say something, but her mother had a face that told her not to say anything.

"Mom what happened to you?" Lidia asked.

"Nothing Honey, nothing for you to worry about. Why are you not sleeping? You have school in the morning," Monika said.

"Are you sure nothing happened?" Lidia asked again.

"Yes Honey, I am just tired," Monika said. "Can we talk about this in the morning? I am beat now, and I would like to go to bed."

"Sure Mom, but can I ask you something?"

"Sure go ahead."

"Did he hurt you?"

"No Honey, he did not, and you have nothing to worry about. He will not be coming around here anymore. Ever," Monika said, and walked into her room.

Lidia could hear her mother cry very late into the night. She knew her mom was hurting, she just did not know what happened, but in the morning she will find out she promised herself. In the morning, Lidia went to go look for Vanessa, and talk to her about her mom.

"Hey you are up very early," Vanessa said when she saw Lidia.

"Yup, I am up, and something is wrong with my mom, but she won't tell me," Lidia said.

"What do you mean, something is wrong with your mom?" Vanessa asked.

"She came home last night, and she cried all night long. She also told me I will not have to see that jerk again."

"Maybe they had a fight," Vanessa said. "You know how grown ups are."

"Yeah, but why would my mom cry all night?" Lidia asked. "Well I just wanted to tell you that. Now I have to go and talk to my mom. I will find out what happened, and if he hurt my mom in any way, I will hurt him myself."

"Ok, let me now if I can help you," Vanessa said.

"Yeah right," Lidia said, "like we can beat up a grown man."

"But we can try," Vanessa said.

Lidia came home and her mom was up sitting at the table, she could see her mom's eyes very red, and that she was crying even when she woke up.

"Hi Mom," Lidia said.

"Hi Honey," Monika said and cleaned her eyes, "how did you sleep?"

"I slept good, Mom, but I know you did not. Why did you cry all night?" Lidia asked. "What happened last night?"

"Nothing, Honey, that you have to worry about. I am going to be late for work, and I want you to go to school. All you have to do is forget that anything happened, and that we adults do stupid and crazy things sometimes."

"Mom, why will you not talk to me?" Lidia asked. "I am twelve, but I am not stupid. I can talk to you I talked to Dad about everything." That is when Monika broke into tears. "Oh Mom, I am sorry," Lidia said. "I did not mean to make you cry."

"Come here," Monika said. She hugged Lidia hard and cried on her shoulder. Lidia was confused and scared for her mom, she really wanted her mom to tell her what happened.

"Last night," Monika began, "when I went out to dinner with Darko, he told me something that he kept from me for a long time."

"What did he say?" Lidia asked.

"Honey, this is very hard for me, and I really do not think you should know about it," Monika said.

"But Mom I want to know - I need to know - did he say something to hurt you? Because if he did, I will go and hurt him right now."

"No! He did not hurt me physically," Monica said. "He told me he was there when your father was killed by a tree. Lidia had to sit down.

"What do you mean he was there? Like he killed Dad, or he was just there with him?"

"I don't know," Monica said, "he told me he was there, and he tried to save Carl, but for some reason I do not believe him. Lidia there are things you do not know about me and your father. There are things that we did not tell you and your sister, because we did not want you hurt."

"What things, Mom, what don't we know?"

"Well, me and your dad were going to get a divorce, but we did not know what to say to you guys, so we were not happy. I was seeing Darko even though your father was with us, and I am sure he was seeing someone else. That is why there were nights he was late, and not home most nights."

"No. No!" Lidia screamed. "This cannot be true! Dad and you were in love. How could this be happening? How long was this going on, that I did not know?" Lidia asked.

"I am very sorry, Honey, but it is true. This is what happened, I cannot take it back or make anything better. I can just tell you the truth."

"But Mom, you and Dad lied to me! I do not even know who my real parents are anymore!" Lidia said and stormed out of the house.

It is better to let her calm down on her own, Monica thought. If I go after her, I will just make her more angry. This way she will come back to me, at least, she hoped it wouldn't be long before she did.

Vanessa was cleaning her room when Lidia stormed in and sat down on her couch.

"Hi to you, too," Vanessa said.

"I am not in a mood for small talk," Lidia said. "Did you know that my mom and dad wanted to have a divorce, but they did not do it because they thought they were going to hurt me and Tina?"

"No, I did not," Vanessa said.

59

"Well, my mom just told me that, and she also told me my dad must have been seeing someone else, just like mom was."

"I am sorry," Vanessa said. "I am sorry this happened to you, but, Lidia, you still have a great mom. She told you the truth."

"Yeah, she told me the truth," Lidia said. "A month late, a whole month, Vanessa, my father was everything to me, and he lied to me, too."

"I am here for you, if you need me for anything," Vanessa said. "I am very sorry this is happening to you."

Jean heard the girls talking, and went in the room.

"Hi Lidia," she said, "what's going on with you today?"

"I will tell you what is going on with me," Lidia said. "I have had two parents at one point, and both of them lied to me, so I hope you never lie to your daughter, because it hurts really bad Mrs. Jean. It hurts like someone is sticking a knife in your heart."

"Honey it will be ok," Jean told Lidia. "You do have to go home and talk to your mom, because I am sure she feels just as bad as you do."

"No she don't," Lidia said. "If she felt bad, she would have not lied to me. I wonder what else is there that I do not know about."

"I understand you are very upset," Jean said, "but so is your mother. This was very hard on her, and she told you things she did not have to, but she still did.

"What do you mean she did not have to?" Lidia asked. "She is my mother, he was my father, and they both lied to me."

"They had their reasons," Jean tried to explain, but the more she tried the harder to get it through to Lidia. The girl was very upset, Jean thought, maybe it would be better if she just left it all alone for now. Maybe it would be safer to talk to her later. Jean was getting ready to get out of the room and go on with her housework when Lidia asked:

"Mrs. Jean, will you ever lie to your daughter about getting a divorce, just to make her happy?"

"I would do anything for my daughter and my son," Jean said looking at Vanessa, "but sometimes there is just no way of telling how you can hurt a child. Lidia, you might think that your mom and dad hurt you, but they only tried to protect you. That is all they tried to do, and don't blame your mom, she was left alone to explain to you why things did not work out with her and your dad. If your dad was alive would you be as mad at her as you are right now, or would you forgive him and let it be?"

"I don't know," Lidia said. "I don't know how I would feel if Dad was the one who told me that things did not work out, but my mom did tell me, and why did she have to wait a whole month?"

"Honey, no one has the answers for everything. I sure don't. I am sorry," she said and went out of the room. Poor girl, Jean thought when she left the room. She is torn between her father gone, and her mother telling her the truth about her dad and mom not wanting to be together. I hope I never have to tell my kids anything that would hurt them. She was deep in her thoughts when Mitch walked in the door.

"What are you thinking about?" he asked.

"Oh nothing, Lidia was here, and Monika told her everything about her and Carl and the divorce, and I was just thinking how horrible it must be for a twelve year-old girl to find out the truth at the wrong time that's all."

CHAPTER FIVE

TIME PASSED AND EVERYTHING CALMED down. Lidia and Monika worked through their problems, and Vanessa was there for her just like promised she was going to be. She would always say that is what friends are for, and she never wanted to lose a good friend, and Lidia was her best friend in the whole wide world. She never wanted to lose Lidia, no matter what. She was a friend with her sister, too, but she and Lidia shared a lot of good memories, and a lot of secrets just the two of them knew.

Vanessa was spending a lot of time with Lidia, and no time with her brother. He was getting annoyed. Whenever he asked her to go do something, she would always say the same thing,

"I cannot Alexander, I am going to see Lidia."

He started to hate Lidia, because he wanted his sister back. He wanted to play ball with his sister, he wanted to go places with his sister, but he never got to because she was always busy with Lidia, Alexander thought with disgust. Vanessa and Alexander were walking to school one day, and he just could not help himself anymore,

"Vanessa, what do you and Lidia do when you guys are alone, and why are you always with her?"

"She is my best friend," Vanessa said, "you will understand that when you find a friend, like I did."

"Well I have friends, too," Alexander said, "but I do not spend every waking moment with them. Why can't I ever go out with you? Why can't I ever be there with you at Lidia's house?"

"I am sorry, Alexander," Vanessa said. "I know you miss going out with me, but right now Lidia needs me. We have a father, she don't. Think how it was when we did not have a dad at home."

"Well, we did not have him at home, but I did not see Lidia with you the whole time dad was gone," he said.

"Well her dad was gone, too, at that time, remember? All of them were. Why are you arguing with me over this, anyways? I thought you said you have friends. If you have friends, why would you want to be with me and not with them?" Vanessa asked.

"All of my friends are bad," Alexander said. "They all like to skip school, and go fishing, and I am not sure that I want to do that."

"You better not," Vanessa said, "Mom and Dad would kill you if you do."

"I never said I was going to do it," Alexander said, "you asked about my friends, and I told you what my friends are like."

"Ok," Vanessa said, "you do not have to get all angry. I will see next time I go to Lidia's to take you with me, happy?" Alexander took his sister's hand and they went inside the school.

They were close, and they loved each other very much. They were brother and sister, they did not have what other kids had, but they had each other. Alexander walked in his classroom, and all his friends were there,

"Hey Alexander!" Mario called. He was one of Alexander's friends, but he was the kind of boy that always got in trouble.

He tried to be good, too, Alexander thought. It just seemed that he was always around the wrong group of kids. He was a follower, whatever they wanted, Mario did.

"Hey Mario!" Alexander called back. "What are you guys doing?"

"Well, we are going down to the pond after school to fish. Would you like to come with us?" Mario asked.

"I cannot," Alexander said. "I am going home with Vanessa today, and if I tell her I am going to the pond, she will not let me."

"She is not your mom," Mario said. "Why do you always have to be around her? She is your sister, and that is all."

"Well I like my sister," Alexander said, "and I cannot go with you guys today."

"He is a wuss, that has to be home right whenever his mommy and daddy tell him," one of the kids said behind Mario.

"I am not a wuss! I just don't like to be in trouble," Alexander said. I just like to be at school because I have to, and then go home, do my homework, and play."

"Ooh, you mean you like to be a good boy for your mom and dad, right?" Milan asked.

Milan was a boy that no one really liked. He was very bad at school, he always caused fights, and for some reason he liked to pick on Alexander a lot. He would always take his lunch, or he would take the money that his mom gave him so he could buy his food.

Alexander did not want to fight with him, or with anyone else. His mom always said how much she hated when kids fight. He also heard stories about his dad always fighting, and he did not want to be anything like him. If that meant getting a punch here and there he would take it.

Milan was Paul's son, and Paul and Mitch never got along. Alexander wanted to know why they never talked, but he never asked. He could not ask his dad, because he would just tell him that it was the past and to leave it alone.

Milan was always fighting, his dad was always at school for something. Alexander remembered one day, that Milan's dad was at school, and that he was yelling at the teacher. Telling her she did not know how to do her job, and that his son is perfect in every way, and he would never do anything wrong.

"See? What did I tell you?" Milan said. "I am going to the pond today. Mario, you're coming, right? Alexander is a wuss, and he cannot go, so why don't we leave now? What is the point of waiting till the end of school?"

"Ok, let's go," Mario said, and gave Alexander a look that pleaded him to go with them.

"Alright you guys wait, for me," Alexander said. "I will go with you guys, too, but only for today, and we have to be back here before the bell rings, so Vanessa would think I was at school all day."

"Ok we will do it," Mario said. "I will make sure you come back on time."

They left school with out anyone knowing they were gone. They went to the nearest pond, and they found a free placc. It was only going to be just them, having fun, not thinking about school, or any of their other problems.

Alexander liked it there, he did not have to study. School was really not for him anyways, it was boring and he had to think a lot. It was not like his dad would notice that he was not at school. His dad does not notice anything that has to do with him. Why would he notice that he did not go to school?

They were all getting along, even Alexander and Milan. They were having fun, throwing things in the pond and catching fish. Mario and Milan had been there before, they had all the stuff ready for fishing, they even had food. They dug up some worms to feed the fish, so they could catch them. It was about time to go back to school, when Mario noticed two guys watching them from the shore.

"Do you guys see them?" Mario asked.

"Yes, I see them," Alexander said. "They could be teachers from our school, and now we all are going to get in a lot of trouble."

"Don't worry," Milan said, "we just have to find a different place tomorrow, and they will not even know we were here."

"What do you mean tomorrow?" Alexander asked. "I thought we were only doing this today. I am not missing no more school, my mom and dad will kill me if they find out."

"How will they find out if you do not tell them?" Mario asked. "Watch yourself, because if you do tell them, and I get in trouble, you are a dead person."

"Fine. Fine," Alexander said. "I won't say a word, but can we go now, before school lets out? Vanessa will wait for me."

"God, you re such a scaredy cat," Milan said, "she is your sister, not your mother."

"You do not know his sister," Mario said. "If she knew where he was today, and that he was not at school, she would go straight to their parents, and tell them all about us and we all will get into trouble."

"Then we better get out of here, and go to school."

They got to school a few minutes before bell rang, and they waited for Vanessa outside. There were other kids that came out of their classes, and just gave them dirty looks. To Alexander, the other kids did not matter, only his sister did. As long as she did not know about it, everything would be okay. She was the only one who could go and tell his mom and dad, and then they would have big problems. Mom and Dad don't even understand how bad school can be, Alexander thought.

"Hey!" Vanessa said. "How was your day today?"

"Oh, it was ok. You know how teachers are, Alexander said.

"Are you ready to go home and study some more?" Vanessa asked.

"Nope! When I get home I am not even going to look in

my book. What is the point? I have to do the same thing I did at school, and I will have to do it again tomorrow."

"All right, well let's go home," Vanessa said. "It has been a long day for me, too."

The next day, when they went to school, Milan and Mario were waiting for Alexander at the door to the classroom.

"You ready?" they asked.

"Yup, let's go," Alexander said.

They did not notice that there was a teacher, still in the hallway, looking at them when they walked out the door.

They went to a different pond this time. This one was closer to school, and they knew it was not going to take them as long to get back. They liked this spot, and they were going to continue coming here, since the other one was being watched. They did not know if the people were waiting and watching them, or if they were looking for someone else, but they were going to stay away from that place just in case.

This was Alexander's second day, but Mario and Milan had been missing school for over two weeks already. There were no phones, so they knew that their parents would never know if they were skipping school or not. They got back to school that day right on time, and Alexander went home with his sister, so no one really knew anything.

It had been over two weeks now, that Alexander did not go to class, and he was starting to worry that someone might tell his parents. Someone other than his sister, because for all she knew he was there with her every morning and went home with her, too.

"Are you guys sure no one will find out that we were missing school?" he asked one day when they were going back.

"Well, I don't really care," Mario said. "I am sure I will fail this grade, so what is the point of going?"

"I don't care, either," Milan said. "I have not been in school for over a month now, and my parents still don't know what is going on. Now if you do get caught, don't you tell them we were with you. If I get punished by my parents, I will make your life a living hell."

"I am not going to say anything!" Alexander exclaimed.

The next day, when they went to school, there was a teacher at the door waiting for someone.

"Oh no," Alexander said.

"What's the matter?" Vanessa asked.

"Who is that teacher, do you know?"

"That is your teacher for third period," Vanessa said. "*You* should know. Alexander, are you okay? You are as white as a ghost."

"Yeah, I am fine. Just not feeling too good," he said.

They went inside, and where Mario and Milan always waited for him, they were not there anymore. He had a bad feeling, but he went inside the classroom. When he did not see the guys there, he thought they just did not go to school. When the class began, someone knocked an the door.

"Come in!" his teacher called.

When the door opened, Alexander's heart froze. It was his principal; Mario and Milan were with her.

"Hi," Mrs. Watkins, the teacher said, "what can I do for you?"

"I need one of your students," Principal Owen said. "I need Alexander to come with me. May he be excused?"

"Of course," Mrs. Watkins said. "Alexander, you can go."

They walked out of the classroom, and all three boys were thinking it was one of them that snitched on the others, otherwise they would not have been caught.

"Sit down, all three of you," their principal said. "I am going to call your parents, and then we all will talk about why the three of you have not been in school for over three weeks."

She walked out of the office. Mario and Milan turned towards Alexander.

"I hope you did not say anything," Mario said, "because if you're the one who talked to the principal, I swear to you, that you won't know how you will walk home. I will break every bone you have in your body."

"I never said anything to anyone," Alexander said, "I swear. I did not even tell my sister I was not at school, so I don't know how the principal knows."

"You are very quiet." Mario turned to Milan, "Did you tell Principal that we were missing school, because if you did that would be stupid. You were with us and you would get in to trouble too."

"Well I would not get in trouble, because my parents don't really care if I am at school or not," Milan said, "but I did not say anything to principal. However I did talk to one of the kids at school, where they asked when we go that we are not in class. I told him he should come with us, but he said, 'no thank you,' so he could be the one."

"Why would you do such a stupid thing?" Alexander asked. "Just because your parents don't care, mine do, and I am dead meat when I go home!"

"Well, you should have thought about that way before you went with us," Milan said with a smirk.

"You know what," Alexander started to say, but at that minute the door opened and the principal walked in.

"All right boys!" she said. "How about I hear from you, what happened when you three have not been in school. I know all three of you have been together!"

"We went to the pond to fish, Mrs. Owens," Alexander said.

"So you don't think we know how to teach you students in this school, so it was more important to go fishing, than study right?"

"No ma'am, it is not," Alexander said.

"So the three of you just decided that is better not to come to school for three weeks, and no one would ever know about it? Do your parents know Alexander?" she asked.

"No ma'am, they do not."

"So what do you think will happen to you when your mother or father come to school today?"

"I am sorry, I do not mean to be rude, but we don't have a telephone at home, so I was wondering how will they know."

"Oh don't worry," she said, "they will know. I all ready called your father's company, they are sending him this minute to come and pick you up."

Alexander knew he was in big trouble. He wouldn't be able to sit down after his dad was done with him, but he did not know what else he could do. He was caught and there was no excuse.

"I am sorry," Mario told Alexander. "I know we will be in big trouble, and I know I was the one who got you in to this. If it was up to me, we would walk out of this mess without any trouble, but we both know we are dead meat."

Alexander gave him a weak smile, it was all he could do.

Mario's parents, Alexander's dad, and Milan's dad were all in the principal's office at the time school let out. Vanessa was waiting for the boys to get out of class, when one of the girls that was in class with them told her all of them were at the principal's office. She knew it was not good, but she thought they were fighting like those boys always did they were always at each other's throats for something.

She waited by the office, and she could hear voices, she could hear her dad's voice in there, too. Good god, she thought, what did he do that Dad had to come down to school? Their dad was never at school for anything, so this must have been something big.

The door opened and all of them walked out, Alexander, Mitch, Mario, his mom and dad, and Milan with his dad.

"Let's go," Mitch said, "we will talk about his at home, we are not going to talk abut this in the hallway."

Alexander gave Mario a weak smile. "Hey dude, I will see you tomorrow," he said.

"Yeah, ok," Mario said, "if we can talk."

They started walking home, and for a long time no one said anything. Alexander would rather get the beating of his life than take the silence from his dad.

"Dad," he said, "I am sorry. I know you are mad, but I did not really want to go to school, that is why we were at the pond fishing."

"For two weeks?" Mitch looked at him. "For two whole weeks? While I am trying to put clothes on your back, and give you school books, you were going to fish? So you don't think that school is important do you? That it won't do anything for you?

"Look at me, Alexander! This is the job I am doing because I have to, because I did not have a mother or a father that wanted to work hard to send me to school. I had to learn to read and write on my own. No one ever took time out of their life to send me to school, or to give me a reason to go. Do you think I would be working at the factory if I had any kind of schooling?"

Alexander did not know what to say, he never really talked to his father like this, and his father never explained to him what his grandparents were like. He knew his dad was in and out of jail, but he never knew why.

"And you," Mitch turned to Vanessa, "did you know about this?"

"No Dad," Alexander said, "we would be back at school right before the last bell rang, and no one would know we were missing."

"Oh wow," Mitch said, "you guys are smart, but not as smart as your principal. She got all of you guys together and the stupidest one of all of you guys was Milan, for telling that kid where you guys were. I am not going to do anything about this. You are going to write fifty times in your book what you did and why, and that would be your punishment. This is your last time ever to do something stupid like this, next time I will not be so nice about it!"

And that was the end of it, Alexander thought. His dad has turned into this person that he never knew, Mitch did not tell Jean why he went to school, either. He just told her that he was at school, and that he picked up the kids, and then they all came home together.

Later, Alexander learned that you cannot hide anything from his mom. She found out and made him clean his room for a whole month without any help. That was not really bad, he thought. He had received bigger punishments than that, but thank god he did not.

When he went to school the next day both boys were there. They were excited to see him and ask what his punishment was.

"Well," Milan said, "so what happened to you? Your dad looked very mad yesterday."

"And yours did not?" Mario asked, "Your dad looked like he wanted to eat you alive, and I thought you said your parents don't care."

"Well they care for some reason, but I did not get punished. I got twenty belts and I am off the hook," Milan said.

"Well, I got five with the belt, and a whole month of cleaning my room," Mario said.

Alexander looked at them and said, "I did not get the belt."

"Huh?" the boys asked. "What do you mean you did not get the belt?"

"Well I am telling you my dad made me write fifty times what I have done and why, and I have to clean my room for a whole month, but that's all."

"How come you did not get the belt?" Milan asked. Me who never gets the belt for anything I do. I got it, and you did not! How is that fair?"

"I have no idea if it is fair or not, but I am not going to go home and ask my dad why I did not get a beating. That would just be crazy, so I am off the hook and my punishment is easy, but I do know I am not cutting school anymore."

"Either am I!" Mario said.

"You both are cowards," Milan said. "I will find someone who will go with me. I don't need you two."

"Good luck with that," Mario said. "I am good just like this.

"Me too," Alexander said, and they walked in the classroom. At school everyone already knew why the boys were called into the principal's office, so they did not bother the guys and ask any questions. At second period, Milan came back to class.

"What happened?" Mario asked. "I thought you re going to go to the pond and fish."

"Go away!" Milan said, with anger in his voice. No one wants to go with me, because everyone is such a chicken and scared of their parents."

"What did you expect?" Alexander asked. "We are in fifth grade, and no one can live on their own. We all still need our parents to have a roof over our head!"

CHAPTER SIX

EVERYTHING WAS GOING GOOD AT home and at school, Vanessa thought, one day while she was walking home. How easy it was to be her, there were many kids at school who did not have what she had. Yes true, she did not have much, there were kids that had more than her, but just today at school one of her friends told her that she had not eaten for three days already and that there still was nothing she could find to eat. Vanessa thought of giving her the last of her food, but Dina did not want it. Vanessa did not understand why.

"If you are hungry, and you did not eat for three days, why don't you want to share with me?" Vanessa asked her.

"Because you did not eat any either, and I know you are hungry too," Dina said.

"Well yes, but I can share with you," Vanessa said, "we'll share it and neither one will be full, but neither one of us will be very hungry, either."

They shared the food, and they were both still hungry, but it made Vanessa feel better about herself. She knew that Dina did not want to eat the last of it, but Vanessa had food at home, and she was told by Dina's friends, that Dina had nothing at all.

Her mom and dad were not working, her dad was in

the war when Vanessa's dad was, but he did not come home the same. He had many problems when he got back, he was not able to sleep, or to eat right. He was always having bad nightmares if he would try to sleep, so he was awake most of the time.

Dina was the same age as Vanessa, she was only thirteen, and was not able to work anywhere, even though Vanessa heard she was looking for a job already. No one in their right mind would hire a kid to do anything, maybe she would able to help a neighbor, like Vanessa's mom did, so she could get some food. Vanessa thought about telling her this at school, maybe it would work out well for her.

The next day, Vanessa went to school. Dina was not there like she always was, Vanessa thought maybe she was already in class. She would just wait and see when she walked in, but Dina was not in her seat, either. Hmm, Vanessa thought, I wonder where she could be.

The teacher walked in, and on her face there was a lot of sadness. Everyone noticed that something was wrong, but no one wanted to say anything. After the bell rang, the teacher told them that Dina's mother had died the night before. She was shot in the head by her seven year-old son. Dina's father had brought a gun home, and never bothered to check if it was loaded or not.

It was very sad to hear, Dina was Vanessa's friend. Vanessa did not know where Dina's house was, and she was not able to go to the funeral, either. A week later, Dina came back to school. Everyone felt sorry for her, but that is not what she really needed. She just needed a friend to talk to.

"I am sorry," Vanessa told her, "teacher told us what happened to your mom, and I did not know where you live or I would have been there for you."

"It is ok," Dina said, "I am sure you would have been there, but it was sad. It was just family and close friends. My mom and dad did not have many friends, so it was just neighbors."

"So do you mind telling me what happened?" Vanessa asked.

"We lost electricity, and my mom and me were laying on the couch, while my brother was playing on the floor. We did not know he was playing with the gun, we thought he was playing with one of his toys. The gun was under the couch, and he somehow got it. When the gun went off, it went right through my mom's head. Then right after that, the electricity came back on and I had to see my mom's blood all over me," Dina said, and burst into tears.

"I am so sorry," Vanessa said, "I did not mean to make you cry."

"You did not. It is just so fresh in my mind, seeing my moms head like that, and I was laying right next to her. That could have been me, and I wish it was," she said. "Now I have to be older sister to my brother, and a slave for my dad, who has no one left but me."

Vanessa really felt bad for Dina, she did not know what to say to her. There was nothing she could say, or do.

"I am here if you need me," Vanessa told her. "I can talk to you anytime, and you can come to my house sometimes, too. My mom would love to meet you."

"Well thank you," Dina said, "but I won't be going anywhere but home. That is where all the chores are waiting for me, and I have to do so much. I am not even sure if I will be going to school anymore."

Vanessa thought about that, how her life would be so different if she would lose her mom. Her mom was everything to her, but sometimes Vanessa was not fair to her mom or to herself. She wanted to see what it felt like to be out on your own, and to work for money. She never had any, so all she wanted was to get out of the house and live on her own. Now when she heard Dina's side of the story, she did not really want to go anywhere else but home to her parents. Thank god she still had both of them.

Vanessa came home from school that day, and hugged her mom right away.

"What was that for?" Jean asked. "Don't get me wrong, I love hugs from my kids, but I am wondering, what did you do wrong?"

"Nothing, Mom," Vanessa said, "I am just glad I have you to talk to, and I have Dad."

"Well I am glad you have me to talk, too," Jean said. "Is there something you want to talk about right now?"

Jean looked worried, she thought that her little girl was becoming a women, and that this was time for the sex talk. God, she did not want to talk to her about that. Not now, not till she was eighteen, that was the age that girls should date and have boyfriends. She still had five years to go, but she did not know if that was what Vanessa was hugging her for or not.

"Mom it is ok, sit down," Vanessa told her, "you have that worried look on your face. All I said was that we needed to talk, not that I did, or will do, anything bad or stupid. I was talking to Dina today, you know the girl that her brother shot her mom a week ago? I was just wanting to hug you, because I am glad I have both of my parents. I know I have not been that great of a kid, and that I have made problems for you and Dad, wanting to go on my own, and all the things I said. I am sorry. I don't want to go anywhere, I want to stay here with you and Dad, and make sure you guys are okay."

"Vanessa, honey, you are thirteen, not thirty, and you cannot go on your own, even if you wanted to," Jean said. "You have to stay here until you are eighteen, like it or not. But for Dina's mom, I do feel very bad, is there anything we can do to help her?" Jean asked.

"Nope she don't want anyone's help. She only said she will be now doing all the chores, and she will have to be a big sister to her brother, and a slave to her dad who cannot work. I just hope she don't do anything stupid and quit school. Today she was talking about not going to school anymore, so she can stay home and work."

"She cannot have a job anywhere," Jean said, "she is still a kid. No one will even give her a chance. I am thirty, and I cannot find a job, what makes her think quitting school and going to look for a job will do her any good?"

"I don't know, Mom. That is what she was saying today at school," Vanessa told her.

"Well tomorrow, try to explain to her that going to look for a job will be very stupid, and that no one will hire her, because she is too young."

"I will try my best," Vanessa said. "But Mom, I am really glad that we had this little talk. I feel closer to you."

"I am glad, too," Jean told her, "but I would like to talk to you about something else."

"Ok," Vanessa said, "I am listening."

"Well you know your body's changing, and you will be a women before you know it, right?"

Vanessa nodded her head, not knowing what her mom was really trying to say.

"Well," Jean began, "I was hoping that I could talk to you about sex."

"Sex!" Vanessa cried. "Why do I want to talk about that? And with my mother, over so many friends I have?"

"Well, Vanessa you are thirteen, and your body is changing. I just wanted you to know to be safe, and that it is your body. You can do with it whatever you want. I will support you with everything you do, just be very careful. Guys will say anything to get you to bed with them, and then they will leave you."

"Mom, you do not have to worry about that," Vanessa said. "I don't even have one guy that likes me at school. There is many of them that I like, but I do not know one that likes me."

"I am glad for that," Jean said, "because you are so young, but don't be so naïve. I am sure there is someone that likes you, and I am also sure that if there was anything you wanted to talk about you would not come to me. You would go to Lidia, and talk to her about it. But, I want to make sure that you know what you are doing at all times."

"Yes, mother," Vanessa said, "how did this talk come anyways? I just came here to give you a hug for being there for me, and all of the sudden I am getting sex talks. If I knew this was coming, I would not give you a hug. I am going to see Lidia, I will be back soon," she said as she walked out the door.

"I knew it," Jean said, "after I try to talk to her about something serious, she has to go and tell Lidia or whoever. Fine don't be late," Jean called after her, and closed the doors. The kids these days, she thought, and then went back to making dinner.

In her thoughts, she knew Vanessa was a good kid and, that she would always think before she did something, but she also knew guys. God, these days kids were getting into trouble way easier than when she was younger. When she was younger, she wanted a boy that would give her everything she asked for. But since that is not what she got, she at least wanted that dream for her daughter. If Vanessa tried very hard she could get it.

She was so deep in her thoughts when Mitch came home, that she did not even hear him.

"Hey, he said, "why do you have that look an your face?"

"What look?" she asked.

"The look that says one of our kids did something, or I did something."

"No one did anything," she said, "I just had a talk with Vanessa about sex."

"Oh boy," Mitch said, "how did she take it?"

"Like every thirteen year-old girl, she thinks she knows everything."

"Don't you think it is a little too early to talk to her about sex?"

"Too early? What do you think kids do these days? It is never too early to talk to your child about sex, crime, stealing, or anything that is very serious," Jean said.

"Okay, all right," Mitch said, "I can see how the talk went. She did not want to hear it."

"Oh, she heard it, and then went to talk to Lidia about it."

"I am sorry, I know how our kids can be, they think they know everything. Don't let it bother you, she will come around," Mitch said.

"Yeah, she will," Jean said. "I just hope it is not too late."

"It won't be, Vanessa is thirteen, she will be all right. She don't look like she even found a boy she likes."

"She told me there are so many of them she likes, but she said there is no one that likes her."

"Maybe, because she has a bad attitude," Mitch said.

"Vanessa does not have a bad attitude," Jean said. "She only tells everyone what is on her mind, and to you, that is having a bad attitude."

"Hey, don't take this out on me," Mitch said. "I came home to eat dinner, and go to bed. I did not come home to get in trouble, because our daughter did not want to listen to sex talks from her mom."

"Yeah, go always be a big hero!" Jean cried.

"What do you mean by that?" Mitch asked.

"Nothing, really, it is just always easier for you to think the kids are only my priority. That I have to always worry about them, and talk to them when it comes to things like this."

"I never once told you to go and talk to Vanessa about sex, she is way too young to be talking about sex."

"Don't you yell at me," Jean said back. "I know what I am doing with my kids."

"Well, I am not sure you do, because you are talking to a thirteen year old about sex."

"Oh yeah? If I was you, I should wait until she is eighteen and already has two kids, right?"

"That is not what I am saying," Mitch said. "I am just telling you it is too early, that's all. Come on, why are we arguing over this, anyway? We know Vanessa and Alexander are smart kids, and they will do what is right."

"I hope you are right," Jean said. "I am just worried that's all."

"Well don't be," Mitch said, "everything will work out just fine."

———————————

That night, when Vanessa came home from Lidia's, she asked her mom if she could get some food and take it to Dina, because Dina did not have any.

"Well, we can start tomorrow by asking all of our neighbors if they have any extra," Jean said, "but for right now, you need to sleep."

In the morning, Vanessa went to school and told Dina her plan, but for some reason Dina did not want to hear it.

"What is wrong with you?" Dina asked. "I asked you to be my friend, not someone who will go door to door, and ask people for food to give to poor me, who doesn't have any."

"Well, I thought that is what friends are for," Vanessa said.

"No that is not what I want. I don't want your help or anyone else's. This is my last day at school, I am going home, and staying home. I don't need no one and no one's help, either."

"Oh come on," Vanessa said, "you cannot be serious. You are thirteen, what will you do?"

"Why does everyone think that I cannot do anything?"

Dina yelled. "I can do a lot more than any of you think. Ever think of having sex for money?"

"Dina, that is so stupid," Vanessa told her. "You are too young for that."

"Well, yes, so? That is what guys like. They like young bodies, and I don't have any other choice."

"Yes you do," Vanessa said. "Stay in school, let us help you, and you will have a choice."

"Listen Vanessa," Dina said, "I know you are very good person, and you are trying to help me, but did you ever think what would happened to you if you did not have your mom?"

"I already talked to my mom," Vanessa said. "I am sorry, what happened to you is horrible, but don't quit school. This should make you stronger, would your mom want you to do this to yourself?"

"Don't you dare talk about my mom! You do not know anything about my mom," Dina said.

"I am sorry, I did not mean anything bad."

"Well, just leave me be, and don't talk about my mom or about me. I will do whatever I can to have a better life then I already have. No one can stop me," Dina said, and walked away.

Vanessa thought about going after her, but what would that do? Nothing really, she knew that Dina's mind was made up, and that nothing she did would change that. She wanted to help her, but she did not know how, so she just left her alone.

Later, Vanessa heard some kids talk about Dina, and how she was standing on one of the corners in her mini skirt, waiting for guys with nice cars. It made Vanessa very mad. Another day, when they were in class, she overheard two popular girls talking about Dina.

"Well, she does not deserve for us to even look at her, after what she is doing," one of them said.

Vanessa could not hold it in anymore, she turned around and looked at the girls.

"What are you looking at, nerd?" Michele, one of the girls asked.

"Oh nothing," Vanessa said, "I am just looking at two very sorry people sitting behind me, who don't have nothing better to do than to talk about people they do not even know."

"Oh yeah? Well, maybe if you felt so bad for your friend, you should have helped her, so she would not be selling her body to strangers."

"I tried to help her," Vanessa said. "Which is a lot more then I can say for you two sorry people. You have everything you want, you have a house full of food, you have both of your parents, you have nice friends, and you have everything. Well, I am sorry, you can have everything, but to me you have nothing if you have the heart to talk about a person that just lost everything. You don't even know what she so going through. You are nothing to me, but just two very sorry girls that don't know any better, than to talk about other people."

Vanessa was so mad. First, no one calls her a nerd, and second, who do they think they are, to even think they can talk about Dina like that? They did not know her, they did not know what she was going through, they only knew how to sit there and talk about her. To Vanessa, no one was more poor then those two, because they could have everything they wanted but they did not have heart.

When the teacher walked in, Vanessa made the excuse that she was sick, and that she had to go home, then she left the classroom and went to look for Dina. She was going to ask her if she could come to her house and talk to her mom, maybe her mom could stop her from doing whatever she was doing.

When she stepped out, she saw Dina on the corner and she started to walk towards her, but then some cars pulled up. No matter how loud Vanessa yelled Dina's name, she did not or would not hear her. That was the last day that Vanessa, or anyone else, heard from Dina. Many people came to school asking for Dina, and if anyone knew where she was, but everyone, including Vanessa, could tell that Dina was gone. They did not know where she was.

Some time later, Vanessa found out that Dina was dead, and that her body was found in the same pond that her brother and his friends were fishing just six months earlier.

CHAPTER SEVEN

THE TIME PASSED, AND EVERYONE already forgot that Dina was ever at school with them. No one cared about her being gone, most kids were thinking about how to get out of school, go home, and have fun. Vanessa thought about Dina sometimes, and she missed sitting next to her at school. Dina was gone, and Vanessa had to go on with her life, and make sure she got good grades, so she could become something in her life. She always wanted to be a hair stylist, and to have her own salon someday. She wanted to work hard towards that goal, but something always came up to tear those dreams down.

One day while Vanessa was in class the math teacher came in and told them that there would be no school today, and that they all had to go home. All the kids of course went running toward the door, to get out before the teacher changed his mind.

That day, there was news on the radio that Bosnia was entering into war. In Banjo Luka, where Vanessa lived, there was only talk about the war, and about Sarajevo and Vukovar. In Vukovar, there were mostly Croatian people, and their war was as bad as it was with Sarajevo. There was no food before and now it was even harder to find.

There was a lot of talk of guys going to war, either in

Sarajevo or in Vukovar. If Vanessa's dad went, he would have to go to Vukovar to help.

One night, Vanessa's parents were sleeping in their room, and Vanessa and Alexander were sleeping in theirs. A noise outside woke them all up. As Mitch came out of the room to see what was going on, a very loud knock came from outside. Mitch told everyone to stay inside, that he was going to see what it was.

He went outside, and came back to tell his family there were three men in uniform outside. He was told to put pants on and get back out. He did not know where they were taking him, but he had to go. Mitch grabbed his pants, and left the house.

When morning came, many wives in town were left without husbands. No one knew when they would see them, or if they would see them at all.

On television, there was always bad news in Sarajevo. Jean thought maybe that was where Mitch went. Many times she watched television just in case she might see him, or hear where he was, but they had to try to live their lives with or without Mitch.

School was only out for a week, and then all was back to normal. What you saw on television, you were not aloud to talk about at school, or even on the playground. When you were on school premises, the only thing you were there to do was learn.

School for Vanessa and Alexander was not the same anymore. They were teased before, but now they were harassed. Whoever was Croatian would talk only to Croatian kids, and the Serbs were talking among themselves. It was very clear who was whose friend. If kids were friends before the war, some were not friends anymore.

There were many more fights at school now than before the war. Teachers and the principal did not know how to react, when parents of those children were the ones teaching them that at home. Many kids were taken out of school by their parents, because they did not allow them to be friends with a different race than their own.

Vanessa and Alexander did not have money for the bus, so they always had to walk home. Most of the time they were left alone, and they would pray to come home before anyone would see them walking. One day, when they were going home from school, they were not so lucky. Vanessa and Alexander got out of class, and started their walk home like they did everyday. Milan who was Alexander's friend, or so Alexander thought, came over to talk to him.

"Hey," Alexander said, "I have not seen you in class today. What have you been doing? I hope not fishing again."

"Nope," Milan answered, "I was making sure I do not go to this rotten school that lets everyone in."

"What do you mean, 'lets everyone in'?" Alexander asked.

"Well lets see, how can I explain this to a kid that is as stupid as your are? Do you know who goes to this school?" Milan asked.

"Yes, of course I know," Alexander said. "I do, my sister does, half of my friends do. What's your point?"

"My point is that I am a Serb, and very proud of it. You are, well, a Croatian. That is not welcome anywhere where we Serbs are."

"Well that is what you say," Alexander said. "I go where I feel like going, not where you tell me."

"Oh yeah? Well let's see if you will be walking home today, on my roads that my grandparents built."

"I have been walking on these roads since I was a little boy," Alexander said, "and who will be the one stopping me? You? I don't think so. I am so sick of people like you," Alexander said as he walked away.

Just as he turned to see where his sister was, Milan came around, grabbed him by his jacket, and threw him on the floor. When Milan threw him against the wall, Alexander felt a sharp pain in his head. He touched the spot and saw that he was bleeding, but even though he was hurt he would not let a bully like Milan take him down that easily.

Blood was all over them both, but neither wanted to stop the fight. All the kids gathered around, most of them were cheering for Milan. No one wanted to cheer for Alexander he was a different race. They did not want to end up like him, with a bloody head.

The principal entered the hallway, grabbed them both by their jackets and stopped the fight.

"Both of you, in my office! Now!" he yelled.

They walked in, Alexander and Milan had their heads and noses all bloody, and their clothes were ripped.

"What's the problem?" the principal asked. "Why are you two fighting?"

"Alexander told me that I was a Serb, and that I should not be in his school," Milan began.

"No, that is not true," Alexander said. "You told me I should not be walking on your grandparents roads, and that *I* do not belong here."

"Well it is true. You don't, your sister does not, or your parents. I am sure your dad is already dead, because my dad killed him."

"Stop it, both of you," the principal said. "This is a school, a place where you should be learning how to respect each other, and others around you. Because neither of you knows what respect is, both of you are suspended for three days now you may go. And Milan, if I see you anywhere near Alexander again, you will be in very big trouble. After this suspension, both of you need to report to me everyday!"

When they got out of the office, Alexander went to go look for his sister, and Milan went back to the classroom. Neither of the boys wanted to get suspended from school, so they stopped their fighting.

When Vanessa saw her brother with all his clothes ripped, and his head bleeding, she knew was up.

"What happened?" she asked.

"Me and Milan got into a fight. I am suspended from school for three days, and so is he. We got into a fight over who can walk on the roads, and who cannot."

"You know better then to fight with Milan. Are you out of your mind? Do you know what Mom will do to you? Suspended? How crazy!" Vanessa bombarded him with questions.

"Hold on," Alexander said, "so you do not think I should be fighting with him, because he tells me where I can and cannot walk, where I can and cannot talk, you think what they are doing is okay?"

"No, I do not," Vanessa said, "but I do know that no matter what we do, we are out numbered. We have to do what they tell us to, Mom will tell you the same thing when we get home."

Seeing her son and daughter walk home from school was very hard for Jean, she wanted to give them money for the bus, but she only had money for food, and they needed food more then a bus pass. When she saw Alexander covered in blood, she almost passed out.

"What happened to you? She cried.

"Nothing, Mom, I just got into a little fight."

"Little fight? What were you fighting for? What did I tell you about fights?" Jean asked.

"I was fighting with Milan, and I am suspended from school for three days."

"Oh my god!" Jean exclaimed. "Come on now kids, don't I have enough to worry about already? I have to worry if your dad will ever come home, I have to worry what will happened to you at school every day, I have to worry what you will eat. Why can't you just control your anger and let it be?"

"He started the fight, Mom!" Alexander cried. "He told me I cannot walk on the same road he does. What was I supposed to do, let him talk to me like that? It is not his country live, we here, too."

"Child of mine," Jean said, "can't you see that we are a minority here, and we have to do what they tell us? We have to go anywhere they tell us. Do you want to be dead? I am sure you don't, and I want you to do whatever they tell you to."

"But, Mom!" Alexander started to say.

"No Alexander," Jean said, "you will do what I tell you. You will stay away from Milan, and all the other kids that make trouble for you, is that clear?"

"Yes, Mom," Alexander said, even though he did not want to. He knew he had to do what his mother told him.

He did not go to school for three days, but Vanessa had to. She did not have anyone to walk with, she had to walk by herself she hated every minute of it. She turned around at least ten times to make sure no one was following her, and that there were no cars coming. If there was a car coming, she would find a little path, and get inside it until the car passed, and then get out. She did not want to be found on the road alone, maybe nothing would happen, but she still did not want to risk it.

The second day, she went to school by herself and on her way back, she was so lost in her thoughts that she did not hear a car coming. When the car drove by and stopped, Vanessa froze. What should she do now? Should she run in the other direction, or keep going?

When she walked by, the door opened and a very nice young man, in the passenger seat, asked her if she wanted a ride home.

"No, thank you," she said, "I am not supposed to ride with strangers."

"But, I am not a stranger," the young man said. "I know you, I have been going to school with you for the past seven years, and I know where you live. Come on in, I will give you a ride home."

In the car there were three people, the driver, the young

man, and a girl in the backseat. They all had funny faces on that Vanessa did not understand. It was very strange that this boy knew her, but never before now, did he stop to ask her for a ride.

"Ok," she said, "if you know where I live, it can't hurt." She got in the car, and felt really strange like she had made a very big mistake.

"My name is Joey," he said, "that is Cassy, and this is our neighbor Joe."

"Hi everyone, my name is Vanessa."

On that, all three of them looked at each other with a strange look in their eyes.

"Oh," Joey said, "you are not one of us, then."

"One of you? What does that mean?" she asked. She knew what it meant, it meant she was not the same race as they were. Now she was very sorry she got in the car with them.

"You know what I mean," Joey said. "I am sorry, but you cannot ride in the car with us. We only ride with our own kind. And, I would really advise you not to ever sit in a car with strangers, because if I was not nice, we could do so much to your body, and then we could sell you. Just make sure you do not walk on these roads alone anymore."

"Yes sir," she said, "thank you." She got out of the car, and thanked her lucky stars that Joey was nice and that he did not rape her, or do something even worse. Thank god it is over, she said, and she paid a lot of more attention to the cars so she could hide while they passed. She never wanted to see the looks on peoples faces, like she just did in that car. She would go home, and she would not mention this to anyone, not her mom, not her brother, or her friends.

Thankfully, she still had Lidia, and she could talk to her about everything, but she wouldn't tell her about the car! Lidia was mixed race, not like Vanessa was. Vanessa's mom and dad were both Croatian, while Lidia's mom was Serbian and her dad was Croatian. Lidia's mom and Vanessa's mom were still very good friends, and no matter what, they would stay that way. Everyone in the town was changing. she was just hoping that Lidia's mom wouldn't change, too, because then Vanessa would not have anyone to talk to, or hang out with.

When she got home that day, she went to see Lidia. Before she could walk in the house, she saw the same car that stopped to take her home. Hmm, she thought, who could that be? Maybe it was not anyone she knew, she hoped it wasn't. She walked in the house, and saw Joey sitting on the couch with Lidia.

"Oh you are here," Lidia said. "I want you to be the first one who meets my new boyfriend, Joey."

Vanessa almost wanted to say she had already met him, and didn't want anything to do with him, but she knew her friend would ask many questions, so she gave him a quick smile and said, "Hi Joey, nice to meet you."

Joey smiled back, and said, "Same to you."

Vanessa knew that he was not glad to meet her, and he only said that because of Lidia. She made an excuse to go home.

"Why do you have to leave so early? You just got here," Lidia complained."

"I know, but I have a whole bunch of homework I have to do. I just came by to see how you were doing, that's all. I see that you are busy, so I will just leave you be, and I will see you later. Nice to meet you, Joey," she said with out looking at him, and walked out. Vanessa went home and laid on the couch, she really did not plan to feel sorry or cry, but the tears were came on their own.

What happened, she asked herself. Why is it that I cannot even go see my best friend, and feel weird about a guy she is with? What can I do to change all this? No matter how I feel about this guy, no matter what he really is, there is no way of telling Lidia what I know about him.

What did she know? The only thing Joey said to her, was

to get out of the car before something would happened. He did not touch her, no one did, so maybe she wouldn't say anything for now. She would just go to school like she had been, when she saw Joey's car in front of Lidia's house she just wouldn't go there. If she had to tell Lidia about his car, then she would do it later, when all this blew over.

Vanessa was hoping that the time would not come, when she have to tell her best friend that her boyfriend threw her out of his car. To Vanessa, that was mean and rude, but things could have been much worse! She was sitting in her room, deep in her thoughts, when Lidia came over.

"Oh my god," Lidia said, "do you know what Joey just told me?"

"No, but I am not even sure I want to hear it," Vanessa said.

"Well anyways," Lidia went on, "he told me that there was a girl they picked up today on their way to my house."

Oh no, Vanessa thought, here it comes.

"Joey said he asked her to get out of the car, because she was very dirty and very nasty."

"Oh really?" Vanessa shrieked. "Do I look dirty and nasty to you? Because, Lidia, that girl was me. Do you know what your sweet, lying boyfriend told me? He said, 'get out of the car before something bad happens to you, because you are not one of us.' That is why I left your house today, as soon as I saw him."

"No that cannot be true," Lidia said, "Joey would never lie to me."

"Ok then, you believe your sweet Joey, and don't believe me," Vanessa said. I don't have any reason to lie to you, and I have no idea why he would, either. But, as of right now, if you believe him over me, then you can just go get your sweet boyfriend, and we will not be friends.

"Fine then," Lidia said, "but before I go, just so you know, no one is ever more on your side then I am. If I go now I am never coming back, and I cannot believe you would call my boyfriend a liar."

"Bye Lidia," Vanessa said, "don't let the door hit you in the behind."

Lidia walked out and almost ran Jean right over.

"What happened?" Jean asked, "Are you two girls all right?"

"Ask your daughter," Lidia yelled, and walked away.

Jean walked in the room and saw Vanessa crying.

"What happened?" she asked. "Did you two fight?"

"Mom, there is nothing to talk about," Vanessa said, "I have nothing to say. We disagreed on something, but other than that, there is nothing.

What could she do? She couldn't tell her she got in a car with three strangers. That one of them was Lidia's boyfriend, and that he told Lidia they picked up a nasty girl. How dare he? Just wait until Vanessa saw him again!

Jean walked out of the room not knowing what to say. She knew there was more than Vanessa was telling her, but if she was not willing to talk, Jean was not going to press her.

Vanessa could not wait to go back to school the next day. She wished more than anything to see Joey, and ask him what kind of lies he told Lidia and why he did not tell her the truth. She did not see him in school for a while. She thought to herself how typical of him, first he lies, then doesn't show up at school so she can ask him what his problem is.

Time passed by, Vanessa was starting to wonder if she was going to see her dad anymore. Month after month passed, the only news was that he was gone with a bus full of people from their town. They at least hoped all of them were together. In November Mitch came home, everyone was happy to see him.

When he was home, he had horrible nightmares. He never explained them, never wanted to talk about them, but he had them every night. One night after they went to bed, Vanessa heard her dad cry. She got up and went to her parents' bedroom door, hoping she could hear why her father was crying.

"It was horrible!" she heard Mitch say, "They made us stand and watch when they would rape a girl Vanessa's age, and then they would blame it on one of us. Who ever got blamed would get beat so much that you did not know if they were alive or dead. Then, they would pour water on that guy and person would come to."

Vanessa was frozen at the door. Oh my god, she thought. What did my dad have to go through? She hoped it was over. She wanted to hear more, but all her dad did was cry. She heard her mom cry with him, and there were many nights when both of them did nothing but hold hands and cry.

Many times Mitch would come home from work, and find all kinds of notes on the door:

"GET OUT OF HERE!"
"THIS IS NOT YOUR COUNTRY!"
"GO BACK WHERE YOU WILL BE
WITH YOUR PEOPLE!"
"WHY ARE YOU STILL HERE?"
"YOU DO NOT BELONG HERE!"

He ignored the notes, many times it was kids just walking by the house. Mitch knew those notes must have come from their parents, because that is the only way kids learn. He was worried about his own kids, he was trying not to bring up the subject with them. He did not want to have to answer questions he did not know the answers to.

Alexander came home from school one day, when Mitch was home early from work.

"Hi Dad!" he said. "I have something I want to talk to you about."

Oh boy, Mitch thought, here goes the talk.

"Don't look like that," Alexander said, "it is not the sex talk if that is what you were thinking."

"Oh thank god," Mitch said, "you are only eleven, I am not sure you are ready for the sex talk."

"Well I might be, or I might not be, but that is not what I want to talk to you about."

"Ok, then what is there that I can help you with?" Mitch asked.

"Well I was wondering why all the kids tell us we do not belong here. You are back from war isn't it over?"

"I don't know why they are telling you to get out," Mitch said, "but I do know that if anyone tells you that you do not belong here, don't fight with them. Don't even say anything. Just ignore it, because if you ignore it there will be no fighting."

"But Dad, that is not the answer I was looking for. I want to know why I cannot sit and eat with the people I used to before this war started. I cannot just ignore it. They were my friends, and now they do not even talk to me. They look at me like I do not belong here. I do not want to go to school anymore, I do not see the point," Alexander said angrily.

"All I can tell you is to be who you are, and what you are is my son," Mitch told him. "That is how your mother and I raised you, and that is what I want you to be. Don't pay attention to them, and what they are saying. I want you to stay in school, I want you to finish, and be something I never was."

"Alright Dad," Alexander said, "but that still is not the answer I was looking for."

"That is all I can give to you," Mitch said. "Now go get your homework done, and don't you ever think about quitting school."

"Yes sir, whatever you say," Alexander said, and walked in the house.

Mitch sat down on the ground, and did not know what to think. What is this world coming to, he thought. His son did not have any friends, none of his neighbors talked to him, no one came over anymore. It was very strange, but he did exactly what he told his son to do-nothing.

Before the war started, they were slept with their windows open. Now, they had to lock their doors at night when they went to sleep. Now, there were not just notes on the door, there were writings on the door, the window, and even the roof. It would always be the same, "GET OUT!", "YOU DON'T BELONG HERE!" They had nowhere else to go. Mitch grew up here, he raised his family here.

Many neighbors had already left to Croatia, but what did they find there? In Croatia they did the exact same thing they did in Serbia. Serbians would throw Croatians out of their homes, and Croatians would throw Serbians out.

As long as I stay here on my land, Mitch thought, I don't care who is going where, or who is doing what. I was born and raised here, and if I have to, I will die here, too.

In March, everything changed for Mitch and his family. It was the same as every other day, he came home from work and tried to get some rest before dinner. They ate and went to sleep. At about one in the morning, they heard a very loud knock coming from outside. Mitch got up and told his family to stay inside. He did not want them in any danger. He opened the door, outside were four uniformed men with guns.

"Good evening," one of them said, "you are Mitch, right?"

"Yes I am," he said. "Can I help you?"

"All you have to do is go inside, and get your family. You do what I tell you, and no one will get hurt."

Mitch had heard these words many times when he was in the war. The Serbians would say exactly the same thing to all the people they took outside and killed. He walked inside and told Jean and the kids to get dressed, and come outside.

It was very dark outside, Vanessa could not see anything, or anyone. The man ordered them not to look at the men, and to get on their knees and be very still and quiet. Then one of the men went behind them and tied there hands.

"This is how this will work," the leader said. "I am going to ask questions, and anything that I do not like to hear, Mitch will get hit for, and after that his son. If anyone makes any noise, or screams, we will kill all four of you. Is that clear?"

When no one said anything, he went over and hit Mitch in the head, then leaned toward Jean and said, "I asked you a question."

"Yes sir, that was clear."

"I would like to know why you are still here," he asked Mitch.

"Because this is my land, I was born and raised here," Mitch said. "This is my house, my land, my family. That is why I am here."

"Wrong answer," the man said, and one of the guys went over to Mitch and hit him in the face.

"There were many notes on your house, your doors, even on your roof. Why didn't you leave?"

"Because I did not think I should leave my house," Mitch answered.

"Man, you really do not know any right answers to my questions, do you?"

He ordered two guys to pick Mitch up so he could hit him. He beat him so badly that Mitch lost consciousness. When they saw he was not awake, they took a bucket of water and poured it on him. When he came to they hit him again.

Finally, Alexander could not take it anymore.

"Stop hitting my dad!" he screamed. "If you want someone to hit, why are you not going to fight for your country? Why are you bothering us?"

"Oh well, well, look at this," the leader said. "I thought I told you, little shit, to shut your mouth, or I will kill you all."

He put the gun to Alexander's head, and said, "I would love to pull this trigger, but then I would have to kill all of you. I do not want to have your rotten blood on my conscience, but while I am here I can beat you, too. So you can join your daddy.

The leader hit Alexander in the head with his gun, and when he did not make any noise or cry, he hit Alexander some more. When Vanessa started crying, one of the men went to her and put his hand on her shoulder.

He said, "Don't worry little girl, nothing will happened to you, as long as you do not make any noise. If you are going to cry, I want you to do it very quietly."

The man then leaned down to Jean and touched her face.

"Why didn't you leave?" he asked, "None of this would have to happen if you would have just listened.

"I don't know," Jean said. "I didn't think I had to."

"See what you all have done? Because you would not leave, now we have orders to kill you. Do you want to die?"

The leader went over to Mitch, and put his gun to Mitch's head. He said, "This is what I have to do." He pulled the trigger, everything around them went blurry. They could not see or hear. The gun shot was so loud, Vanessa was not able to even talk afterward.

They could see Mitch's blood all over them. Jean finally screamed.

"If you killed him, why cant' you kill all of us?"

"That was not our plan," the leader said. "You should have

listened. He would be alive. Don't blame us for something you did to yourself." After that, they left.

There was blood everywhere. It was starting to get lighter outside, they could all see that Mitch was not with them anymore. The men had killed Mitch, and badly bruised Alexander. They had not, however, touched the women. Jean wondered why they would kill Mitch, and beat Alexander, but they did not touch them.

The neighbors were beginning to leave for work. One of them, Eva, was walking that morning. The weather was nice, so she wanted to get some fresh air, but the air did not smell fresh. The air smelled like blood. She walked out of her house, and a chill ran up her spine. This is not going to be a good day, Eva thought, something will go very wrong.

Eva was a doctor at a nearby hospital, and this morning she had gotten a call saying many people had come in throughout the night. She did not have to go in until later, but she wanted to go and help out. So she stepped out, and started walking. Halfway down the road she saw some people outside of Jean's house.

"Hmm," she said, "I wonder why Jean would be out this early. It is not even six in the morning yet. I better go and check if everyone is okay."

She came to a sudden stop when she saw that they were all on their knees. She ran to Jean and checked her, she was still breathing. Then she did the same with Vanessa and Alexander. She could see there was no help for Mitch, he was covered in blood. They were alive, but the three of them were unconscious, she needed to do something fast.

Eva went to untie them, and see what else she could do. she untied Jean, and put her slowly on the ground. When she got to Vanessa and Alexander, she heard Jean's very low moan. She ran over, and when Jean opened her eyes she saw Eva right by her side.

"Mitch, can you check on Mitch?" Jean whispered.

"I am sorry," Eva said, "he is gone, Jean. Do you know who did this?"

Jean did not know what to say, she did not know who the man were last night.

"All I know is that they were in uniform, and they had guns. I did not get to see their faces. They told us to have our heads down and be quiet, and nothing would happen. I should have yelled, screamed or done something."

"But, you did not know if they would have killed you, too," Eva said.

"I wish I was dead. I am as good as dead now," Jean said. "Look what I have--nothing! I have two kids, I have to take care of all by myself. Who knows? They might be back again."

"Did they say anything to you?"

"Yes, they said they warned us, and asked why we didn't get out when they told us to."

"What do you mean, they warned you? Did you get anything in the mail, or something like that?" Eva asked.

"Well, we got papers thrown at the house that said, 'get out of here', 'why are you still here?' or things like that. We never were *really* warned by anyone to get out, so I did not know we had to."

"It is okay," Eva said, "you are fine now. I am sure they won't be back, but you have to be strong for your kids, Jean. You have to be there for them. Like you said. you are all they have now."

Jean looked over at Vanessa and Alexander, who was all bruised from getting beaten up all night, was sitting in his own blood, and his father's blood, too. It was a horrible scene, and she could not watch it anymore.

"Eva, will you help me get the kids inside?" Jean asked. "I have to get something to cover Mitch, so the kids won't be looking at him."

"Sure, I will, but you have to be the first one to get up."

Jean got up very slowly, she had been on her knees all night. As soon as she stood, she had to sit down again. Everything in front of her eyes went black, she was on the ground in a minute.

"Okay, you sit there," Eva said. "Let me go see if I can get the kids inside, and then I will be back for you."

"Thank you, Eva," Jean said. "Thank you for everything. I do not know what I would do without you."

CHAPTER EIGHT

As Jean stood alone outside, she looked around, and all she could see was blood. Oh my god, she thought, look at my husband. I have nothing anymore. I have a house, and the kids, but I don't have anyone to come home to me anymore. I have no one to be there for me at night when I am sad. Why in the hell did we not leave?

Out loud, she asked, "Mitch, why didn't we go? You would be alive now, and we would have our family, the way we always planned. Those bastards broke my family up. They took what was most important to me, they took you!"

She got up and went over to Mitch, he was covered in blood. She did not want to look at his head, and the hole she had seen. She just wanted to touch his face one more time. She had to see if, just maybe, he might open his smoky brown eyes, look at her one more time, and tell her everything would be okay. That she had nothing to worry about.

But that did not happen, his face was so cold, his eyes were shut and his whole body was cold. Who would ever have thought that she would be alone at thirty-five? She wanted to spend the rest of her life with Mitch and only Mitch.

Eva came out and saw Jean sitting next to Mitch.

"Come on, honey," she said, "let's get you inside. I got

this blanket to put over his body until we get someone to take him away."

"Take him where?" Jean asked. "Where do I take him?"

"We'll see about that in a little bit. You have to get dressed, and make sure the kids are ready to eat something, or whatever you want to do. I am going to call someone here to be with you and the kids, I have to go to work."

"Thank you for everything," Jean said. "If it was not for you, then I would not be able to do any of this."

"Don't worry about it," Eva said, "I just want to help as much as I can."

They covered Mitch's body, and went inside to check on the kids. Vanessa was sitting on the couch, and Alexander was in the other room looking for his clothes. Vanessa walked over to Jean and gave her a big hug. They both burst in to tears.

"What are we going to do now, Mom? We have no one anymore. Are we going to have to leave our house?"

Vanessa had so many questions, and Jean had no answers.

"I don't know, honey," Jean said, "we will do whatever we can. We are still a family, and we will always stick together no matter what happens. From now on it is just me, you, and your brother.

Alexander came out of the room, and saw his mom and sister hugging and crying. He walked over to them, it was the most beautiful site Eva had seen in a long time.

Eva went outside to see if she could find anyone to stay with Jean, she had to get to work, she was already much later then she told her boss she would be. She walked to Jean's first neighbor, and knocked on the door. When no one answered, she went to the next neighbor. No one was home there either, Eva was beginning to think no one would help her. She was getting very frustrated.

On her way back to Jean's, she saw two people walk from behind the house and go inside. She wondered who it could be. When she walked in, the two people that were with her were her first neighbor, and the other one that Eva just came from. They were both leaving for work, when they saw Mitch laying outside.

"We were going to work," said Rick, Jean's next door neighbor, "and we saw that something was not right. That is why we are here, what about you?" Rick and Steve both turned to Eva.

"I was doing the same thing," she said, "I saw all of them outside laying on the ground. That is why I am here."

"Yes," Jean said, "Eva helped me get the kids inside, and got something to cover Mitch with."

"I was just at your house, Rick, to see if you would come over, because I have to get to the hospital. I did not want to leave her alone. Are you both going to stay with her?" Eva asked. "I really have to go."

"Yes, I will stay," Rick said.

"So will I," Steve said. "You can go ahead and go."

"I will be back after my shift to check on you, Jean," Eva said.

"Thank you very much for everything. I really mean it," Jean told her. "I will see you later then."

Eva left Jean alone with Steve and Rick, they had both been her neighbors for a very long time. She used to be able to tell them anything, but now she was not really sure. She felt she could not trust anyone anymore. She was alone with her kids, and she needed to be very careful.

"I am going to see who I can call to get Mitch out of here," Rick said, "and get him to the hospital so he can be checked. Then we'll see what else is there to do."

"Okay," Steve said, "I will stay here and see if there is anything more I can do to help Jean."

"Thank you both," Jean said, "I don't know what I would do on my own."

"You have nothing to worry about," Steve said. "I will do everything I can to help you figure out the next step."

They both walked out at the same time, that was very suspicious to Jean. Why did they both have to go outside, when only one of them had to find out what to do with Mitch? Rick walked away, and Steve went back inside.

"Jean, we will have to get you and the kids ready," he said. "You guys can go and stay at my house for now."

"I am not going anywhere," she said. "Thank you for the offer, but I have to stay here. This is my house and I have to stay in it."

"Okay," he said. "I just wanted to help you. I thought maybe you wouldn't want all the memories of last night to play in your head."

"Steve, no matter where I am, I will have those memories in my head. I am willing to go through those memories, maybe I will remember the voices or something else about the men. I'm not sure how much I can do, but I want to see if can remember anything."

"Thank god you and the kids are okay!" Steve told her.

"Yes, thank god," Jean said, with tears in her eyes.

"Oh Jean, I am sorry. Did I say something to make you upset? If I did, I really did not mean to, I am very sorry!"

"It was nothing you said. Don't worry about it, I was just thinking. Yes, me and the kids are okay, but my husband is not. I don't have him anymore, Steve. Do you know how that makes me feel? It makes me feel like I have nothing. My husband is gone, he is not coming back. I have to get everything done on my own now. Don't get me wrong, I know I can, but I have to live alone. Now, I don't even know if we are going to stay here or not."

"What do you mean, stay here or not? Do you have somewhere else to go?" Steve asked.

"No, I don't have anywhere to go, but I do not want

someone else to come and kill me. Where will my kids go then?"

"No one will come here anymore," Steve said, "I am sure."

"How do you know they will not show up anymore?" Jean asked. "They were here last night. I don't know what stopped them from killing me and the kids, too. They should have."

"Stop it! Don't let me ever hear you talk like that! You have your life, and your kids to worry about, you have to concentrate on that. And I am here," Steve said, "I will help you as much as I can, and so will Rick and Eva."

"Yes, you guys will be here for me," Jean said, "throughout the day. What will happen to me during the night?"

"Nothing will happen," Steve said. "If I have to, I will guard your house at night, so you are not all alone."

"Thank you for that," Jean said. "Thank you for your kind words, and everything else."

"That is what neighbors are for," he told her, "now you will have to get dressed. Do you have anyone you want to call and stay with you, while I go see how Rick is doing?"

"Yes, I will call Monika, she will come and stay with me," Jean said. "You just go ahead, I will be fine."

Steve left, and by the time he got back, Jean had a full house of people. There were a lot of neighbors with her, Mitch's mom, Josephine, was there, too. Steve saw that he was not needed, and went home. When he got there, his answering machine was blinking. He went to check it, and it was his girlfriend, Megan.

"Steve, honey, I do not want you over at Jean's house anymore. If her husband was killed, you could be killed, too. When you get this message, call me back!"

He picked up the phone and called her, Megan was not home, so he left her a message telling her not to worry, he would find out what happened, and who did it. When he hung up the phone, he heard his doorbell. He went to open the door, and saw Rick there.

"So, have you taken care of everything?" Steve asked.

"Yup, I got it all done for her. She won't have to do anything. The only thing she will have to do, is make sure all the expenses are paid."

"Who do you think did this? Do you have any idea who could of done it?"

"This is a very safe neighborhood. Why would anyone want to go around shooting people?" Rick asked.

"I am so disgusted, I have no idea what to think anymore. I never would have expected this to happen, much less a house away," Steve said. "I have no idea who did it, but also, how come I did not hear the shot fired? I did not hear anything, and I was home all night long."

"Don't blame yourself," Rick said. "I live two houses from them, and I did not hear anything, either. We should go over and see how she and the kids are. I am sure she has other people there, but I also know that news travels fast, so there must be people she don't even want there."

They walked to Jean's house, there were many people inside. Most of them were neighbors, but Josephine was there, too. She was standing outside when Rick and Steve got to the house.

"How are you holding up?" they asked Jean.

"I am doing good now," Jean said. "I am sure I saw Mitch's mom, I should go and say hi to her."

"She is outside," Steve said.

Jean walked outside and saw Josephine sitting down by the spot that Mitch was shot. Josephine heard foot steps, but she did not turn around. She did not care to know who was standing there. Her son was dead, and there was no one to blame, or was there?

Of course there was. If Jean had not taking him away from her all those years ago, her son would still be alive, and maybe with someone who was there for him no matter what. What kind of wife could not protect her husband when the bad times came?

"Mom," Jean said softly, "are you alright?"

"How dare you ask me that!" Josephine said. "My son is dead. My baby boy is gone, and you are standing there asking me if I am alright? Of course I am not!"

"Mom, I was just asking you if you are alright. He was your son, he was also my husband. We both lost someone that was dear to our hearts."

"What do you know about me and my heart?" Josephine asked. "If it was not for you, my son would still be alive. You killed him, if you ask me!"

"How dare you! How dare you come to my house, and accuse me of killing my own husband? He was my everything. He was my kids' father, he was the man I loved for fifteen years! Who do you think you are? I want you out of my house!" Jean screamed. "I don't want you anywhere near my house, or my kids. I want you gone."

She turned and walked inside the house. She did not dare look at Josephine any longer, she did not want anything to do with that woman. Josephine got up and walked inside after Jean, she grabbed her by the hand, and looked her right in the eye.

"How dare you tell me to leave! This was my son's house. I am not leaving. Those kids are not just yours, they are his, too. If you tell me not to see them, I am not going to listen to you. They are my grandchildren."

"And how many times did you see them when your son was alive?" Jean challenged. "You can count it on your fingers. You came to the house twice, mother in law. And, yes, I can tell you that you cannot see my kids, because I am now all they have. So if I was you, I would let go of my hand before you make an even bigger scene than you already have."

Josephine looked around, and saw everyone staring at

them. She let go of Jean's hand, and walked outside. Alexander ran after her.

"Grandma, wait!" he called. "I don't know what you and Mom are fighting about, and I do not care. You are my grandma, and I will see you whenever I want. No one can tell me if I can or cannot!"

"Thank you, Alexander," she said. "I love you, just like I loved your dad. I am not sure if me and your mom will ever be on the same page, but I do have to ask her to see you. After all, this is her house."

"Well, don't go anywhere for now. Stay with us, Grandma. I know Mom needs you, but she won't admit it. She would love to have her mom here, too, but she is far away and very sick."

"Okay Alexander, I won't go anywhere, just because you asked me. Honey, did you know that you have the same eyes as your father? You look a lot like my Mitch. God, how much I wish I had made things right with him. I never spent any time with him, not even when he was little. I miss him," Josephine said. "I miss everything about my Mitch."

"I know, Grandma. I know you miss Dad. I miss him, too, but we cannot do anything about it. We have to stay here, and live, like Dad would want us to."

Jean went to find Alexander, and found him with Josephine.

"Oh, I am sorry," she said. "I was just looking for you, Alexander."

"It is okay," Josephine said, "we are done talking. Maybe you and me should take a walk, Jean, and talk about things. There are a lot of things that you will need help with. If there is anything I can help you with, just ask and I am here."

Jean did not know what Josephine and Alexander talked about, but it seemed to work. After many years, Josephine was finally talking to her, and not yelling.

"Okay, let me tell someone inside to keep an eye on the kids," Jean said. "Then we can go and talk."

She asked Monika to watch the kids, while she talked to Josephine.

"You want someone else to go with you?" Monika asked.

"No, I will be fine, she won't do anything to me. It looks like Alexander got her calm, maybe she will be civil."

Jean returned from her walk with Josephine to find an envelope on the table with her name on it. She was afraid to open it. What if it was another one of those letters that said, "get out" or "you don't belong here"? She took the letter to her room to open it, where she could open it alone. She sat on the bed, and opened the letter carefully. As soon as she opened it, she closed it right away. The letter was from her sister in Slovenia.

Dear Jean

Sorry I have not written to you in so long, but as you already know, Mom was very sick. I tried to tend to her, but having two kids and a sick mother is a little hard to do all on your own. I am sure you already know this from having to take care of two kids when Mitch was in jail.

Mom died a week ago. I had no way of contacting you. and I was not sure if you wanted to be here when we buried her. I am sorry that I was not able to let you know sooner. We already buried her, she wanted to be buried here. I did all that, I am not asking anything from you, I am just telling you our mother is gone. I hope you and the family are doing good, and I will talk to you later.

Marta

Jean threw the letter, and buried her head in her pillow. Wow, she thought, not only did I lose my husband, but I lost my mother, too. No one even thought that I wanted to be there when she was buried. Nope, no one thought of me. Well, I have to pick myself up, and be with my kids. Not only is this hard for me, but it is hard for them, too. I am their mother, I have to be strong, and there for them.

Vanessa came into the room to see if her mom was okay, and found the letter on the floor. Before Jean could stop her, she read the letter and burst into tears.

"Honey, it will be okay," Jean said. "We will be fine, this will take some time to get used to, but we are going to be fine."

"If I hear one more person tell me we are going to be fine, I am going to scream," Vanessa said. "Everyone has been telling me that today. 'Oh Vanessa, don't worry you, and your family will be fine.' I am so sick of people thinking they know how we feel. Not only did we lose Dad, we lost Grandma, too. What else can go wrong?" She looked up to the sky.

"Dear god," Vanessa said. "Why are you doing this to us? What have we done that was so bad? What are we paying this high price for?"

"Vanessa, stop that," Jean said. "It is not God's fault that some people are just stupid, and want to go on a killing spree. We have to be grateful that we are alive, and thank God for that. Now, dust yourself off and let's go outside and show people that we are not weak. That we are a strong family, and no matter what, that we can take care of ourselves. I am here for you, Vanessa, and for Alexander. No matter what happens, I am always here for you," she said as they walked out to the living room.

There were so many people, and Jean suddenly wanted to be alone. She wanted to tell everyone to go home, but she knew she could not do that. She was sitting on her couch, when two men, she had never before seen in her life, came in. They asked someone where she was, and then walked straight for her. Jean froze, thinking they could be the ones that were there last night. She would soon find out.

"Hi Jean," one of them said, "I am Jeremy, and this is my associate, David. We have to talk to you. We are sorry for your loss, but we have to talk to you about Mitch."

Jean thought the worst. She thought that they were going

to tell her they were the ones who killed Mitch, and they wanted to kill her, too.

David began, "You see Jean, a couple months ago we were playing poker with Mitch. He lost a big amount of money. Five thousand dollars, to be exact. (So you killed him, Jean thought.) We are here to ask if you know of any place that he might have hid the money.

"Are you asking me to look into whatever my husband was doing, to give you money that I do not even know he lost? I am sorry gentlemen," Jean said, "but I cannot help you. He is dead and I do not know about any money."

"I am sorry, but we will need the money in two months. We are giving you two months to come up with the money."

"Are you out of your mind?" Jean asked. "Where will I find that kind of money? I do not gamble, and I was not the one who took it from you in the first place. I do not know what to tell you, but I wish you would just leave."

"We are leaving right now," David said, "but remember we are coming back in two months. You better have the money, or you will end up like your husband. We will be back, Jean, we promise!"

Could this day get any worse? Jean thought, anything that could go wrong did. I don't have anymore energy to deal with more problems. As she was thinking, Paul came in. Oh no, she thought, what does he want? She had not seen Paul for over ten years. Why was he here now?

"Jean," he said, "I am sorry for your loss. If there is anything I can do for you, just ask and I will be glad to help."

"There were two gentlemen here just a minute ago," Jean said. "They said they will be back in two months. I need a lot of money, can you help me with that?"

"Anything you wish," Paul told her, "I will be glad to help."

CHAPTER NINE

Jean managed the humiliation of asking Paul for money so she could pay Mitch's debt, and stay alive. She did not want to end up like Mitch. She had two kids to think of, and now she was the only one that could help them and be there for them.

Vanessa and Alexander returned to school after three days. Vanessa thought that her mother did not look good, but she did not know how to help her. Her mother was all alone, and she did not want anyone's help. Vanessa wanted to help her mom, and be there for her, but she also wanted to be at school, and had to study. She wanted to finish high school, go to college, and be a hairdresser, but it did not look like that was going to happen. She knew her mom needed her, and she would have to be there helping her. Every time Vanessa wanted to talk to her mom about college, something else came up.

When the subject of school came up one day, Vanessa told Lidia and Tina that she might not be going to college after all.

"Why not?" Lidia asked. "How can you not go? You are doing so good, you really should go."

"And who will be there to help my mom? She has no one but me and Alexander. I cannot leave her and go anywhere."

"You do not have to! You can stay here, where we are, and still go to college from home. There is a school just little bit from us, and I know you will do great!" Lidia said.

At the end of the school year, she went to talk to her teacher about school programs.

"What school would you like to go to?" Mrs. Edwards asked. If anyone could help Vanessa get a scholarship, it would be Mrs. Edwards. She was always cheering for the kids to go on to college, and work hard to get what they wanted in life. Mrs. Edwards knew about Vanessa's life, she knew that times were very tough for her.

"Well Mrs. Edwards, I would like to go to college to become a hair dresser, but I am not sure I will be able to afford it. I also have to help my mom," Vanessa told her. "What can I do?"

"I can see that you think a lot of your mom, and that you want to help her, Vanessa, but you also have to think about your future. There are times to help your parents, but there are also time you just have to think about yourself."

"If I do go to school, and I cannot afford it, what happens then?"

"You should get a full scholarship, because you have good grades. But, you do know if you quit your classes you will have to pay everything back."

"Well, let me talk to my mom first, and see what she says. Then I will come and see you, thank you Mrs. Edwards."

"Vanessa, just remember that you have to have your application done, and you have to be enrolled by the end of next week. If you take to long then I can't help you."

Vanessa went home that day, and promised herself that she was going to talk to her mom. She came home to find Jean working on dinner.

"Hi Mom, are you having a good day?"

"Yes I am," Jean said. "Nothing bad happened today, and

one of our neighbors said I can start working in the farmers' market. That is good news."

Vanessa saw a good opportunity to talk to her mom about college.

"Well, Mom, I talked to Mrs. Edwards today, and she told me there is a good chance that I will get a scholarship if I commit to college."

"That is great news," Jean said. "Are you sure you will be able to do it?"

"Yes, I am sure, Mom, and if I get this college done, then I can have a good job. I will be able to live well."

Jeans heart was breaking, her daughter wanted to go to college so she could start working and help around the house. Vanessa was still a child, she wanted her to enjoy her life, not think about working to support the family.

Alexander was ready to finish school, too. He could go to college but the way his grades looked, that was probably not possible. Unlike Vanessa, his grades were not that good, he was barely getting by. Alexander did not even care if he was at school or not, he went because his mom always bothered him about it.

"Alexander, you have to go to school. It is for your future," he would always hear her say.

"Mom, I am only going because you want me to, that's all."

One day at school, Mario came up to him.

"Hey dude," he said, "how about after school we go over to my place?"

"Why?" Alexander asked. "You never asked me to your place before. Why do you want me to go now?"

"Well, because I am going to be home alone, and I hate to be bored. Maybe if you are there I would feel better."

"Okay, well, I guess we can go now," Alexander said, "school is about to be over, anyways."

They were walking to Mario's house, when they saw a

car pull over, they thought something was wrong, and maybe someone needed help. The guy driving had on the same uniform as the men that came to Alexander's house, and killed his dad. Alexander froze, he did not know what this guy could do to them. Or, if he was one of the guys that was at his house.

"Be careful! This guy looks like the guys that were at my house when my dad was killed," Alexander told Mario.

They both went to the driver's door, and saw that the man was not alone. He had a little girl with him. The little girl looked very scared, the boys saw tears in her eyes.

"What are you doing?" Mario asked.

"Nothing," the man answered, "why don't you two boys go back where you came from, or go your own way. If I was you, that is what I would do."

"But you are not us," Mario said. He leaned over to see the little girl better, he noticed that her nose was bleeding and that her eyes were bloodshot. "Are you okay?" Mario asked the little girl.

The little girl did not say anything. She just sat there and looked at the man who was watching her. Mario and Alexander did not know what to do. They were wished that maybe someone would come and save that little girl. They knew they could not go up against him. He was a big man, and he had a gun. They both saw it when he told them to get lost.

They saw a car coming their way, and thought it was the best chance they had to save the little girl. Mario went out to the middle of the road and Alexander followed him, both were hoping the car would stop, would help save the little girl. The car seemed to be slowing down, Mario and Alexander were relieved to see that it was Rick, Alexander's neighbor. When the car stopped, Rick got out of the car, and walked toward the boys.

"What in the name of God are you two doing? Are you trying to get killed?" He saw that both of their faces were white as ghosts, and that they were scared, but he thought that was from almost getting run over. He stopped talking when he saw a car pulled over just a little up the road.

"What happened here?" he asked. "Is there anyone in that car?"

"Yes, there is a man, and he has a gun. He also has a little girl that looks very scared, her nose is bleeding and her eye looks swollen. That is why we were on the road. We're trying to stop people so they can maybe help her," Alexander said.

"You boys stay right here, and no matter what happens, stay here." Rick walked towards the car, he saw the little girl just as the boys told him. He gave her a little smile, and went to the other side of the car, where it looked like the man needed help.

"Is there anything I can help you with?" Rick asked.

"Yes, get the hell away from my car!"

"I cannot do that," Rick said. "You and the little girl look like you need some help, and I am here as long as you let me."

"I have a gun, and I know how to use it! So, I am going to ask you one last time, to step away from my car!"

Rick saw an opportunity to get his hands on the gun, and to make sure that he wouldn't get shot. He grabbed the gun, and turned to Mario and Alexander still standing where he told them to.

"Come here, both of you, and get the girl! I have the gun pointed towards your head," he told the man in uniform. "You move, and I will kill you."

"What made youth think I can move?" the man asked. "If I could move I would have all of you dead by now. The little girl is mine, don't you dare take her away from me."

"What do you mean, yours?" Rick asked. "Yours as your daughter, or yours as you took her from someone?"

"Mine, you idiot," he said, "means my daughter."

"Well, I will find out if she is your daughter, from her,"

Rick said. "Right now, don't you move, because one wrong move, and you won't have a head anymore."

Rick walked to where the boys were standing with the girl, he knew it was going to be hard to get the girl to tell him anything.

"What's your name? I am Rick, and I am not going to hurt you."

"E-Ella," she said. "My name is Ella, and that is my dad. We were at my mom's house, but some men came around and tied us up. Then they made my dad put that uniform on, and made us drive away. That is why we were pulled over, and that is why my nose was bleeding."

"Okay Ella," Rick said, "how old are you?"

"I am seven," she said. "My mom and my sister are not doing good, either. They took my mom inside, and then told my dad not to ever come back. I want to go home and see my mommy. Can you take us home, please?" She looked at Rick with her gorgeous blue eyes, and little bruised nose.

"I will do everything I can to help you and your dad," he told her. "Boys, stay here with her, I will be right back."

Mark walked over to the car, he had a good idea what could have happened. He heard what was going on, but he was not quite sure that it was the same thing as what happened to Jean. He hoped it was not. He went back to the car where the man was laying on his seat.

"Please, I just want my daughter. She is all I have left!"

"What happened?" Rick asked. "How did you get all the way here? Why are you here? Where do you live? Maybe I can take you home."

"How do I know you are not one of them? How do I know you are not trying to talk me into giving you directions to my house, so you can take my daughter away from me?"

"I don't have any kids myself," Rick told him, "but I do have many nieces, and I can see you care a lot about your daughter. My name is Rick, and I just want to help you! I don't want anything from you, and I sure don't want your daughter."

The man looked at him with his sad eyes and started to cry. Rick did not know what to do, he sat next to him and just touched his hand. "Let it out, just let it out," Rick said.

"What has happened to this world? Why can't we live like we used to? Why do we have to be so afraid to live in our own houses? How long is this going to last?" He was asking so many questions that Rick did not know the answers to.

"I don't know," Rick said. "I don't know, but I do know that I want to bring you home, so you can check on your wife and your other daughter."

"How did you know about my wife and daughter?"

"Your little girl told us her name, and that someone took your wife and other daughter."

"No one took my wife," he said, "she is already dead. I heard when they killed her. Before they put me and my daughter in the car, and told me to go far away, never look back, or come back again."

"Do you know who did this?" Rick asked.

"No, I have no idea! This morning around 4:30am, I heard loud knocks on our door. I went to open it, and as soon as I opened the door, one of the men hit me with his gun. I fell to the ground, and they went inside, they brought my daughters and my wife outside. They tied us all up and began to beat us. After they were done beating me, they put this uniform on me to look like I was one of them.

"After they could not beat me anymore, they untied my wife and older daughter, and took them inside. I heard my wife screaming for me, but I was barely able to see, because I was on the ground, rolling in my own blood. I tried to get up, but every time I tried, I got hit with a gun.

"They raped them and then brought them back outside, so I can look at them doing it again. They spared my little girl, but every time she tried to say something, they would hit her.

That is why she has all the bruises on her body. My name is Eric, and I live in town. I don't know where I am, or how I got here, but thank you for stopping and helping me."

"Don't thank me," said Rick, "thank the boys, because they almost got ran over. I think they thought you were trying to hurt your little girl."

"If you had a gun, why didn't you use it on them?" asked Rick.

"I would have, but I was caught off guard. I was sleeping, and when I opened the door, I did not take my gun with me. I wish I had, my gun was in the car. I just took it out little bit ago. But I will show you where I live, if you want to take me home. I can check if maybe my daughter is still alive. I know my wife is dead, I heard the gun shots," Eric said.

"How many gun shots did you hear?"

"I am not sure, I think it was two or three, but I am really not sure."

"Okay, tell you what we are going to do. We are going to take these boys home, and then I will take you and your daughter home. Is there anyone you want to call to tell them what happened this morning? It is after noon, I am sure that people are looking for you," Rick told him.

"We can do that. I will just leave my car here, because if they see my car, they will come back again."

"No problem," Rick said, "you can just leave your car here. We can come back and get it later, if it still here. I am not sure of anything anymore."

They all got in to Rick's car, and Rick told the boys he was going to drop them off first.

"No way!" Mario said, "I want to go with you. Look what they did to this little girl."

"Mario!" Rick said. "I told you I was dropping you off, and I am going to drop you boys off. After I go to his house and check things, then I will be back to see if you boys are good.

And don't even think that I forgot about your school, either. I will be talking to your parents later about that."

"Oh come on, Rick," Alexander said. "You know my mom will kill me! Do you have to tell her?"

"Boy, you only have one mother, and you are not listening to her. Do you know what you are doing to her when you skip school, or don't you care? We will talk about this when I get back. Until then, I want you both to stay at Mario's house, so I can find you."

"Alright! Yes sir!" the boys told him, and got out of the car.

"Thank you," Eric said, "I know how much the boys would like to come, but I am not sure I want them to see what we might see."

"No problem," Rick said, "I am just glad that you and your daughter are okay. I hope your wife and your other daughter are good, also. We'll just have to wait and see when we get there."

When they got to Eric's house, from the outside everything looked normal.

"Will you stay in the car with my daughter?" Eric asked. "I am going inside by myself, so if there is the worst, then she won't have to see it."

"Yes, I will stay here. You go ahead, if you need me, just call."

Eric got out of the car, and he began getting sick to his stomach. He was not able to walk very fast, but tried to make it inside the house. Maybe his wife and daughter were still alive. When he got to the door, he saw the blood where he was laying earlier this morning, and he saw his younger daughter's shoes.

He walked inside very slowly, and when he opened the door, he saw his daughter laying on the floor. He saw blood all over her head, and knew she had been shot. He also wanted to check and see if his wife was anywhere. He did not find her in the kitchen, or in the bedrooms. He was beginning to think that someone took her.

He walked in the bathroom, and saw her laying on the floor, naked and covered in blood. Her face was blue from the beatings the night before. On her left breast there was written in blue ink "I TOLD YOU TO GET OUT! THIS IS NOT YOUR COUNTRY, IT IS OURS!" On her right breast were Serbian signs in big letters, and underneath, it said "WE RULE THIS COUNTRY!"

Eric felt sick, and walked outside. When Rick saw him run out, he told the girl to stay in the car. He ran over to Eric.

"Did you find them?" he asked.

"Yes, I found them. They are both dead, one in the kitchen, and the other one in the bathroom. What do I tell my daughter now? How do I tell her, her mother and her sister are both dead?"

"I am so sorry for your loss," Rick said. "I will be here as long as you need me."

CHAPTER TEN

ERIC WAS OUTSIDE TALKING TO Ella, when two other people came by. They looked at Rick, and told him that they were the next door neighbors, Nancy and Robert.

"Eric, is everything okay?" asked Robert.

"No, my wife and my daughter are both in the house. They are both dead."

"Oh my god," Robert said. "What happened? Do you know who did it?"

"No, I don't know who did it," Eric said. "Do you think I would be standing here talking to you if I knew who took their lives? No, I would be out looking for them, because it is head for a head. If I ever find out who did this to my family, I will kill them with my bare hands!"

Robert turned and noticed Rick standing with Ella. "Who are you?" he asked Rick.

"Don't talk to him like that," Eric told Robert. "If it was not for him maybe, me and Ella would be dead, too. He and two boys found me and Ella, and brought us back home so, I can make arrangements to have my wife and daughter buried."

"Do you need us to do anything?" Nancy asked. "We are here if you need anything."

"I have to go and take care of some things. Will you guys watch Ella, and make sure she eats something? We won't be able to sleep here tonight. We will stay at my mother's until everything is taken care of."

"No problem," Nancy said, "anything you need we are here to help. Where is your car, anyway?"

"Oh, I crashed it. That is how these two boys found me. They thought I was kidnapping Ella, so they stopped Rick and almost got themselves killed, because they were in the middle of the road."

"Oh," Nancy said, "I did not know what happened. I was looking for your car this morning, and when I did not see it, I thought you guys just went somewhere."

"Come on, Eric," Rick said. "I will take you where ever you need to go.

"No, that's okay," said Eric, a little too fast. "I will have someone from my family come and take me where ever I have to go, but thank you for everything," Eric told him.

"If that is what you want, then no problem," Rick said.

"Thanks for everything. I am sorry you had to be here, but please tell the boys thanks for everything, too."

"I will, and don't worry. Everything will work out. I am very sorry about your family."

"Thank you again," Eric said, "you saved me."

Rick was not married, but he knew if he had a wife he could never be that calm. Eric did not cry when he saw the bodies of his wife and his daughter. Rick thought that was very suspicious. But there was nothing he could do. He had to go and talk to the boys to see why they were out of school so early, and why were they walking home.

He got to Mario's house and boys were playing outside. When they saw him walking, they both stopped playing and ran to him.

"So what happened?" Mario asked.

"Did you beat him?" asked Alexander.

"Why would I beat him?" Rick was confused by Alexander's question.

"Because I thought he was lying. The little girl did say he was her dad, but she also stayed with us, and when we found him he was not acting like her father. He was acting like he took her from someone. How did everything go at their house?" Alexander asked.

"It was fine," Rick said. "You guys saved the little girl." But even now he was not sure if he did the right thing. Did Eric really steal that child? He did not cry for his wife and the other girl, but everything else fell into place. Even the neighbors knew who he was. Rick would just go home, maybe he would hear something about it later. If he didn't hear anything, then good. He did save the girl.

"I am very tired guys. Alexander, you are coming with me, so I know you got home and your mom won't be looking for you. If I was not so tired I would tell her about school, but I am way to tired to even think straight."

"Thank you, Rick," Alexander said. "I know I did a bad thing skipping school, but we just wanted to be away. Today was just not my day. And think, if I stayed in school, we would not have seen the little girl."

"Well, about that," Rick said, "you both have to swear to me you won't tell anyone about it. You know how much people in this town can talk."

"We promise," they both said.

Rick went home and straight to take a shower. Eric's face was playing in his head. He did not know a man that did not have any emotions. He did cry in the car, but he did not when he was home, and to Rick that was so strange. How could a man not have any feelings, and not cry when he saw his wife and kid dead? Rick did not have any kids, but if one of his nieces would die, he would die with them, too.

Unless that man hurt his wife and his kid. What if that was not his kid and his wife? What if Rick helped him take a little girl away from her real father? Nothing was making sense to Rick, so he got out of shower and was going to check on Alexander. And ask him why he thought that Ella was not Eric's daughter.

Before he left he, made sure to lock his house and all the windows. Yes, he was a Serbian, but no one liked him because he would talk to Croatian people. He did not want to come home and have someone already take his house over. Everything always had to stay locked.

He walked to Jean's house, and before he could knock, he heard voices inside. It sounded like Jean and someone else were yelling. He stopped at the door. Rick knew that it was spying, but he did not want to interrupt whatever the yelling was about.

"Mom, I did not know!" he heard Vanessa say.

"If you did not know, then how did you find out?" Jean screamed back.

"Alexander and Mario were talking outside of the house today. I heard them say that they saw a girl in someone's car, and that they did not think she was his daughter. So, I went and asked them about it."

"And they said what, Vanessa?" Jean demanded. "They told you that the father took the little girl , and killed mother and the other girl. What I heard today does not match what you just told me."

"What did you hear?" Vanessa asked.

"I heard that whoever rescued the little girl and the man, is in some real trouble, because they are looking for him. The guy that claimed he was her father, was not. The people that said they were the neighbors, were not. Whoever was so close to getting that little girl from the monsters, let her right back into their arms."

Rick's blood froze. He was not able to open the door, he could not walk, he could not feel his arms. So Alexander was right, the guy who called himself Eric, if that was his name, was not little Ella's father. He was the guy who killed her family and now he had her. He was so blinded by trying to help him get home, and save the little girl, that he did not even think of that. He thought something was wrong, and now he knew what it was! Rick turned to walk back home, and at that moment door opened.

"Rick!" Jean said. "What are you doing here?" Jean saw his face, and knew something was wrong, very wrong. Rick never had a sad, or even worried face. He was so brave and helpful when Mitch was killed!

"What happened to you?" Jean asked. "Come on in, and let's have a talk. I am sure I can help you. Whatever it is we will work together to fix it." Jean had no idea what could make Rick look so scared and worried, but she was determined to find out. She wanted to help him, and be there for him, as much as he helped her.

Rick was still not able to talk, so he just sat there looking pale in the face. His arms started to shake and he needed some water-or air.

"May I get some water?" Rick asked finally.

Jean got up and gave him a glass of water. He drank like he had never seen water before.

"Rick, are you going to tell me what's wrong with you?" Jean asked.

"Yeah, give me a second," he said. "Vanessa, may I ask you to go and find your brother? Can you do that for me? As soon as you find him, please bring him back. Both of you come straight home, do you understand me?"

Vanessa wanted to argue and tell him no. She wanted to stay home and see why her neighbor was acting so strange, but she knew better and left.

"Jean I did not want to listen to what you and Vanessa were talking about, but I heard what you said. I was the guy that thought he rescued the little girl."

"Oh Rick!" Jean said. "There are guys looking for you. I hope they don't know what you look like."

"What did you hear? Where did you hear it from?" he asked.

"I was at the store today, and Emily was talking to Ed. He was asking her if she heard shots last night. I did not really pay attention to what they were talking about, because you know how Emily likes to make things bigger then they are, but when Ed said shots, I was confused and wanted to know what she would say. Emily told him that she heard three shots and someone yell. It sounded like they were yelling outside, so she looked out her window and saw a guy in uniform carry a little girl with him, the guy did not see her, but she saw him take the owners' car and she also saw him hit the little girl.

"Ed asked why she didn't call for help. Emily told him he was crazy and she did not want to die. I am sure Emily was able to call for help, but she refused to because she was scared for her own ass.

Rick swallowed hard, "Go on," he said.

"By this time, I was right next to Emily and she wanted to stop talking. I asked her what the story was about and she said, 'Oh nothing, just something I witnessed last night.' Then she turned to Ed and said, 'I also saw some guy come in today with the same dude that left last night with the little girl and he was there for a while, then the other two people came out of Marie's house.'

Rick grabbed her hand, "What do you mean Marie's house? The lady said her name was Nancy, and her husband's name was Robert."

"No Rick, that is not what Emily said. She said all those people were at Marie's house. And when they walked out, the guy who brought the little girl and the other guy left. She don't know who it was, she could not see him very good, but other neighbors are looking for him. They think he might have something to do with Ella's kidnapping, too."

"What did Vanessa tell you?" Rick asked.

"She told me that she overheard Alexander and Mario talk about a guy and little girl, and that Alexander did not think that he was her father."

"The kids were right. Oh my god, Jean, I let little Ella go back into the monster's hand."

"You did not know. If you knew, you never would have done that. Come on Rick, think if someone other then you stopped to help the boys, he would do the same thing. You cannot trust people around here anymore at all."

"What do I do now?" Rick asked. "Where do I go? Who do I talk to? I have to tell someone what I saw, what I know. Those bodies are probably still at that house, and no one has gotten them yet."

"Oh no, they got them," Jean said. "Emily told us that Marie went in and saw the bodies. Face it, Rick, there is nothing you can do. The little girl might be dead by now. The best thing to do is stay low, and don't tell anyone anything."

"What if someone notices me, and recognizes me, then what?"

"Nothing," Jean told him. "Trust me, when something like this happens here, no own really cares anymore. I am still waiting for the night when they come back for me."

"Jean, no one is coming back. It is over they got Mitch. They are not coming back for you."

"I would not be so sure. I heard that they have been going back to houses and stealing and taking whatever they want. Like I said, Rick, people talk in this town way too much."

The doors swung open, and Alexander, Vanessa, and Mario ran in.

"What happened?" asked Alexander.

By Rick's face he knew it was nothing good, but he still wanted to know.

"You were right, Alexander," Rick told him. "The guy was not little Ella's father, and they took her. I let you down, and I let everyone else down. Most importantly, I let that little girl die when I could have saved her."

"I am sorry," Alexander said, "but don't beat yourself up over it. No one could tell that he was not her father, she even told us he was. He probably made her say that."

"Bastard! Bastard! I want to kill him myself!" Rick yelled. "I am sorry, I have to go. I don't know where I am going ,or what I am doing but I have to get out."

"Rick, don't go!" Jean pleaded. "Please stay here with us!"

"Are you sure?" Rick asked. "I would not want to impose. I just need some air. I will be back."

Rick never came back, he never went home. He just disappeared and no one ever saw him again. Jean heard many stories about Rick. She heard he went to find the guy that took the little girl and they killed him. She heard he never made it passed his house, he was struck by a car. They said he could not live with the lie.

Rick was the only person Jean knew that was full of life. She felt very sorry for Rick, and waited every day for him to come back home. but he never did. Some new people were living in his house, and they were not friendly at all. They never said hi, and they gave her the same looks that she was getting used to. Every time she would go to the store they would look at her just like the others. Like she didn't belong there. She grew up with these people, they used to be her friends. Now she began to wonder if she even knew these people.

One night while they were eating dinner, someone knocked on the door. Jean got up, and when she opened the door, two little girls stood there. One of them was Nikki, she did not know the other one. The girls were only seven years old, Jean thought maybe their parents had sent them.

"Can I help you girls?" Jean asked.

"I hope you can," the little girl with green eyes and blonde hair said. "I am Emma, and this is Nikki we are very hungry.

We did not eat in, like, forever and no one is home. Do you have any food? And promise us you won't tell our parents."

"We happen to be eating dinner right now, and we have a lot of food left over. Come on in, and have some," Jean told them.

The girls walked in and sat down to eat. They were almost done when someone knocked on the door again.

"We are very popular tonight," Jean said. "Let's see who that is."

When she opened the door, two very angry people were standing on her steps.

"Are Emma and Nikki here?" the woman asked.

"Yes, we are Mom," Emma said. "I was just sitting here, and Ms. Jean gave us some food."

"Get out of this house, right now," her mom said. "What did I tell you about talking to them, much less to be in this house?"

"But, it was okay with me," Jean said.

"I don't like your kind here," the woman told her. "I wish you would just pack your stuff and leave. Why don't you understand you will never be liked here, ever. If I was you, thank God I am not, but I would be gone before something very bad happened to you and your kids."

They took the girls and left. When they were gone, Jean looked at her kids and said, "I think it is time for us to leave. We have no one and nothing here anymore."

"But, Mom, where are we going to go?" Alexander asked. "What are we going to do?"

"I don't know," Jean told him. "Many people are leaving next week with the busses, and I heard there is place for us, too. If they have somewhere to go, so do we. But make sure you only tell your friends that we are leaving, and no one else. Understood?"

CHAPTER ELEVEN

JEAN WAS WORRIED ABOUT HER kids telling other people they were leaving. She did not want anyone knowing what they were planning to do, because leaving this hell hole was the most important thing now. She did not have anyone, or anywhere else to go, but she did decide on leaving. She wanted to make sure her kids stayed alive and it looked like staying here would not do them any good.

Jean knew Vanessa still wanted to go to college and here that was not possible. She might not have to pay, for it but she knew that going to school here would destroy Vanessa. Vanessa did not talk about going to college anymore. She only thought about it once in a while.

Last night her mom was talking abut leaving, but was she really serious about it, or was she just thinking it? Vanessa went to talk to Lidia, and to say her good byes.

"Leaving! What do you mean, leaving?" Lidia was pacing the house like she was going to fly away. "You mean leaving this town, right?"

"Yes, my mom told us last night that we are leaving, and to tell our friends. So I came to tell you and Tina that we are leaving, so here I am."

"So you think leaving will do you any good? Let me answer

that for you. No, it wont! Where are you going to stay? Who will be there for you? How will you get to know people?"

Lidia was asking so many questions, and not even waiting for Vanessa to answer. She was just way too upset, so Vanessa did the best she could, she did not say anything.

"See," Lidia continued, "the way I see it, it is best for you guys to stay here. Where did you think you will find friends like me?" That made Vanessa laugh.

"Why are you laughing? Did I say something funny?" Lidia was giving her the evil eye, and Vanessa thought then that she should just not say anything.

"Sorry," she said, "I know this must hurt you, and I won't be here very time you need me, but we will write to each other and we'll talk on the phone, and we'll do everything we can to keep in touch."

"Yeah okay," said Lidia, "whatever you say, but I know better. If you leave this town, we might never see each other again."

"And if I stay," Vanessa said, "are you going to protect me from getting killed? Are you going to be there when they put signs on my house that tell us to get out? No, you wont. You do not know how hard this life is for me." and she walked out.

She was so upset with Lidia. She came over to tell her, like a good friend, that she was leaving, and Lidia gave her a whole speech about staying. Lidia was not the one who had to be so scared every night. She was not the one people looked at so meanly. She wouldn't be the one leaving, either. It was very hard for Vanessa to look at all the houses and her neighbors, because it might be the last time she saw them.

For so long she wished that maybe one day she could have her mom's house, and maybe raise her kids there. No one would give them evil looks, but now they had to leave it all behind.

She did not mean to cry, but the tears just came pouring down her face. So many people had been mean to them. Their dad was dead, and she did not have any other relatives. And now Lidia was mad, too. Vanessa thought she heard Lidia calling after her, but she did not turn around. Lidia was very rude and mean to her, so why would she?

It took Lidia only a minute to realize what she told Vanessa was mean. She knew Vanessa heard her, and she also knew Vanessa was very stubborn. She was mad at Lidia and she was not going to stop.

Lidia was mad at herself, too. It was not fair of her to blow up at Vanessa like that. But she was her best friend on the whole world, and now she is leaving.

"Vanessa, if you don't stop this minute, I am going to catch you and beat your butt!" she yelled.

"Oh yeah?" Vanessa yelled back. "Well just try, little miss, and see what Vanessa can really do!"

"Come on, Vanessa, stop! I am not going to run all the way to your house! I am sorry, so stop!"

Lidia caught up to her, and grabbed her hand.

"I am sorry," Lidia said, "I know this must be hard. Sorry I have been so selfish. I know you will write to me, and we will talk as much as we can. We can even visit and stay as close as possible. There is so much we have to do before you leave, though."

"Just make sure no one knows about me leaving. We would like to be alive by the time we leave." Vanessa said.

"Okay, I won't tell anyone, but Mom and Tina, that you guys are leaving. Is there anything I can help you with before you leave?"

"I don't know yet," Vanessa said. "I have to see when we are leaving, and what my mom will say. She is not home right now, when she gets back I will ask her."

"That means you're not going to college like you wanted to, huh?" Lidia asked.

"Yup, it means I am leaving this hell hole, and not coming back."

"When you say it like that, it makes me want to move, too," Lidia said. "I know how much you go through, but I also know it is a lot easier on me, than it is on you. Just promise me that you will always think about me, and that you will write me, any free time you have."

"I promise!" Vanessa said. She hugged Lidia, and they both cried. Neither of them knew if they were going to see each other again.

Monica watched the girls from her bedroom window. Her heart was breaking for both of them. Jean told her this morning that they might have to leave. Jean did not know where they were going, or how she would get there, but she did not want to stay here anymore. Monica did not blame her, she would have left long ago. Monica thought Jean was doing the right thing, because she was thinking of her kids and their future. Monica always thought about Jean and her kids, but Jean never told her how her life has changed for the worse after Mitch died. Jean kept it to herself. No one really knew how hard it was for her.

This morning, when she and Jean were talking, Jean told her all about the knocking on her door, people walking on her roof, her dog and other animals were poisoned. Jean had chickens, a rabbit, little cats, and a dog. Now she had nothing, because two nights ago someone went to her house. And in the morning, Jean found everything dead. Monica felt very bad, but no one ever really bothered her because she was Serbian. Maybe she could talk to Jean, and ask her to stay at her house.

Jean saw the girls on the road, too. She knew Vanessa had told her friend they were leaving. There was nothing else she could do, she tried to stay as long as possible, but anymore time here and they could all end up dead. She had to do this.

"God, please help me," Jeans said. "I don't know where I am going, or what I am going to do when I get there, but my kids deserve so much better.

She was outside looking around her house, her yard, her land, and her heart grew heavy. All this was hers, but any day now someone could come in and take it over. It was not even called home anymore. Home should feel good like you want to be there and spend time alone, or with your kids, but that is not what this felt like. It felt like she was going to hell every time she went to her house.

She had to leave, staying here was getting worse by the minute. She told Monica she was leaving, and that was all, she had no one else to tell. Monica seemed to understand her leaving, and she was happy about that.

Alexander went to talk to Mario, and tell him he was leaving. He knew Mario was going to be upset, because Alexander was the only friend Mario really played with. Mario was at home with his brothers when Alexander came over.

"Hey," Alexander said, "do you think we can go somewhere we can talk? I have something important to tell you."

Mario thought Alexander was talking about girls, so he told his brother that he was going for a walk.

"And if Mom asks us where you are?" his brother asked. "What do I tell her?"

"Tell her I went for a walk with Alexander, duh. Exactly what I am doing!" Mario told his brother.

Alexander and Mario found a tree to sit under. Something was bothering Alexander, Mario could see it. He had a feeling this was not about a girl anymore.

"What's up, man?" Mario asked.

"Well, my mom told us last night that we are leaving, and we might not be back."

"Leaving? What do you mean, leaving? Where are you going?"

"I don't know anything," Alexander said. "I know we are leaving, but I don't know where. I just thought your should know before I leave."

"When is this happening?" asked Mario.

"I am not sure of that either. Just make sure you don't tell anyone, because Mom said if less people know it would be better for us."

"Don't you think that is very selfish of you?"

"What? What's selfish of me?" Alexander was taken back by Mario's question.

"You, your mom, and your sister are leaving and going away. You are leaving all your friends behind, for what? Do you really think there is anything better out there?" Mario asked. The minute he said that, he saw Alexander's face change. He was not so sure it was a good idea to say that.

"Selfish? How could you even say that to me?" Alexander asked him. "Me and my family have gone through hell for the past two years, because of all the war things going on. We have not done anything to anyone, but still my dad was killed. I am always getting beaten up by someone for something someone else did, and you are telling me I am selfish? Have you ever gone one day with out food?"

Mario knew he made Alexander very angry, but he was angry, too.

"No, I have not," Mario said. "But I know some people that have, and they are not going anywhere. It just makes them work harder."

"So you think I should work harder to stay here?" Alexander asked. "Okay since you are so smart, where should I work? Mario, what should I do? I am eleven years old! What can I do, to make sure my house is not taken over by some big guy with a gun?"

"Nothing," Mario said, "you don't have to do anything. You have a mother, right? she should."

"Really? My mom should do what, Mario? Fight with every guy that walks through our door telling us we have to get out, we do not belong here? Who will give her a job? Let me tell you who, no one. No one wants us to work. No one wants us here. Everyone will be so much happier when we are gone."

"I want you here!" Mario yelled back. "This is where you grew up! you are my best friend, and I want you to stay." He looked at Alexander and said, "I am sorry that you won't be here when I get married, that you won't be here when I have kids. I am sorry that I ever became your friend, because now you are leaving, and I am staying here all alone. Thanks a lot." And he walked away.

How did this come out to be my fault, Alexander thought. Why do I have to explain where I am going, or what I am doing? He got up and started walking back home. I don't care anymore, he told himself, but he knew he was sad for all the things Mario said. He knew they were true, but his mom said they were leaving.

He was walking home, when he saw some guys in the middle of the road just talking. Kids he did not talk to, or like. They saw him, too, and now it was too late to turn around back to Mario's house. Mario did not want to talk to him anyway. Whatever, Alexander thought, he would just walk passed them. If they said something he would keep walking, he didn't need or want to get into a fight.

He walked a little closer, and saw Milan was one of the boys. He knew how much Milan hated him, and how much his dad hated Paul. Paul was happy his dad was dead.

"Hey Alexander," Milan called. "Where are you going?"

"I am going home. Why?" Alexander said.

"On these roads? Have you forgotten that you do not belong here, or that you are not allowed to walk around here at all? This is our town, our roads, and I am sure you just forgot, right?"

Alexander wanted to tell him that the roads didn't have his name on them, but he also knew that saying anything would cause him to fight. All the boys and Milan stood on the road, and were holding hands so Alexander was not able to walk through.

"So now what?" asked Alexander.

"Now you tell us why you are on our roads," Milan said.

"Well I did not know they had your name on them," Alexander said. They were not going to let him pass, so what was the point?

"Oh, you're a really smart boy, huh? So, smart boy, how about you come here, so I can show you this is my road."

"No, I am okay," Alexander said. "I can stand here all day. Someone will walk by, and I will be able to get home."

"Home! What home? You don't have a home. You know that house you live in is mine, too. Before you ask if it has my name on it, I am going to tell you that it does. It has all of our names, all of them but yours."

Alexander was getting very tired of Milan talking to him like that, because that house was never Milan's that was his mom's house.

"Don't think you are smart," Alexander said. "Don't think I don't know what you are trying to do. You're trying to make me fight, and I am not going to do that."

"Oh no?" Milan asked. "So if I spit on you, and pull on your clothes, you won't do anything?" He walked over to where Alexander was standing, and spit in his face, then tugged on his shirt until it ripped. All the other boys were cheering him on. Milan looked at Alexander with so much hate.

Alexander just stood there. He knew if he tried anything, all those boys were going to gang up on him. He knew he could take Milan by himself, but not five guys at the same time.

"What's the matter?" asked Milan. "Are you going to cry? Oh no, you won't, right? Because you think you have to be a hero, like your dad was."

"Shut up!" Alexander yelled. "You do not know nothing about my dad!"

"Well, maybe not, but I do know that he just sat there while he was getting beaten up by my guys."

Alexander could not take anymore, you could talk about

him all you wanted but don't you dare talk about his dad. He loved his dad and he would not stand there and listen to Milan insult him. He hit Milan in the mouth, and the next thing he knew, he was on top of him, beating him with both fists. He had so much anger in him, and Milan was the perfect person to take it out on.

Milan's buddies were standing there watching him get beaten up by Alexander. When Milan started bleeding, to Alexander that was the sign that he should stop, but he did not. He hit him in his nose, eyes, jaw, everywhere that he could find an opening he hit him.

He could not hear what Milan was trying to say, but the next thing Alexander knew, he was being grabbed by two guys and thrown on the road. He remembered getting kicked in his side, his face, and all over. He saw Milan's bloody face get on top of him, and that was the last thing Alexander saw.

Mario was at home and feeling very bad. He knew he should go talk to Alexander, now that he was calm. As he walked a little up the road, he saw five guys kicking someone, and he had a bad feeling who it was. When he got a little closer, he could see it was Alexander. Without thinking, he jumped in, beating everyone he could. He took Milan off of Alexander and punched him in his mouth.

"Get the hell out of my sight!" he yelled. "All of you, get the hell away from here!"

He could see that Alexander was bleeding badly, and thought that he wouldn't be able to wake him up himself when he heard Alexander moan very low.

"It is okay, buddy," Mario said. "I am here now. It is okay, just try to open your eyes."

His eyes were stuck shut, and his ribs hurt, he could not move his jaw and he was not able to talk. They really beat him up good, Mario thought. If he had not told him that he was mad, and if he had not walked away from him, none of this would have happened. Now he had to do something about him, no way was he going to take him home like this. Jean and Vanessa would kill Mario if he brought him home bleeding but he really needed some help.

He saw someone walking towards him, but he could not tell who it was. When the man came closer, he saw that it was his neighbor, Joey.

"What are you doing, Mario?" Joey asked him. Then he saw Alexander laying on the ground. "Oh my god, what happened to him?"

"I was coming to talk to him, when I found Milan and four other guys beating on him. Will you help me take him to my house? If his mom sees him like this. she will kill me for not saving him."

"But you did save him," Joey said.

"Yes, but they won't see it that way! So will you please?"

"Okay let's take him to your house. Where is your mom?"

"Not home," Mario said. Thank god, he thought, she would kill me, too.

They brought Alexander to Mario's house. When Alexander started to move, Mario told him to stay still. Mario gave him some medicine, even though it was hard for Alexander to swallow. Alexander did, and he felt a little better.

"You did not tell my mom yet, right?" Alexander asked.

"No, I was afraid she or Vanessa would kill me, so I did not say anything. What happened?"

"Well, I was walking home, and Milan told me I was on his road, and that I should not be walking on it. Then he said my dad was a cry baby, that is why he got killed. I did a good number on him, too."

"I know, I saw it," Mario said. "Now it is going to be hard to take you home. You mom will be so pissed. And I am sorry, too. I wish I did not get angry with you. Now I see why you say you have to go."

"It is okay. I was angry with you, too. I should not have

been. About my mom, let's tell her I fell out of the tree, or something, so she won't worry so much," Alexander said.

"No way, dude I am not lying to your mom. Let's tell her you were riding a bike, and you fell."

Alexander looked at him and started to laugh, but then he was in so much pain that he had to stop.

"Okay, so falling out of the tree is a lie, but falling off a bike is not? Right."

"Okay, so what do you want to tell your mom when you go home?"

"I don't know," said Alexander. "We'll see when we get there."

Jean saw them walking, and she saw Mario almost carrying Alexander. She ran to them to see what happened. When she got closer, and saw Alexander's face she lost all words.

"I know it looks bad, Mom, but don't worry I fell off the bike. I did not want to come home right away, so Mario cleaned me up."

"Alexander, don't you lie to me. Who did this to you?" Jean asked.

"If you don't tell me, Mario will. So you better start talking, right now."

"Okay, I will tell you, if you promise you won't go talk to their parents. Promise me you won't, Mom."

"Fine, I promise," Jean said.

"Milan, and some other guys, told me that Dad was a crybaby when he was killed. And that the road is under Milan's name, and so is this house. That is why I got into a fight with him. He got some punches from me, too, but they were not as bad as mine."

Jean was so angry, but she promised she wouldn't go to the boys' parents. That was when she did not know who did it. Now that she knew it was Milan, she would wait until her son was asleep, then she would go to take care of that little child herself. But not before she talked to the parents who raised him like that. She owed Paul for so much, now she was going to give it all back. Just wait until her kids were safe in bed.

"Mario, can you stay here with Alexander? Don't do anything stupid, I have to go talk to Monica, and I will be right back."

"Mom, remember you promised you wouldn't do anything."

"Yes, I know," she said, and walked away.

She went to Monica's house, and when Monica saw her, she knew something bad had happened. Jean looked like she wanted to kill someone.

"What happened?" Monica asked.

"I need you to watch my kids tonight, I have to go and talk to Paul."

"But you hate Paul," Monica said. "What do you want to see him for?"

"Because I hate him, that is why I want to see him. Look are you going to watch the kids for me or not? I do not need twenty questions now!" Jean told her.

Monica could see that this was very serious, and did not want Jean to do anything stupid.

"I will watch them for you, if you tell me why you want to see Paul."

"Okay," Jean said. "Alexander just got home. Milan, Paul's son, and some other kids stopped him, and now Alexander cannot see out of his eye. He is all black and blue, and I want to see Paul and ask him, if he didn't know how to be a parent, why had he have kids. If he doesn't know how, I will show him."

CHAPTER TWELVE

PAUL AND HIS WIFE, KRISTEN, were setting the table for dinner, when Milan and his friends came in. They did not go in the kitchen, they went straight to Milan's room, which was very strange to Paul and Kristen. Paul went to check on him. When he opened the door, Milan covered his face, and asked, "Don't you ever knock?"

"I don't think I need to knock, this is my house," Paul told him. "Why are you covering your face?" He walked to Milan and saw that the covers were bloodied. "You got into a fight again, didn't you? What have I told you about fighting? I thought I told you if you cannot beat the person, don't fight. If you look like that, I am sure the other person looks just fine, huh?"

Milan looked at his dad. He was always on his side, he did not understand why his dad was making fun of him now.

"Dad why are you making fun of me? It is not funny. Alexander did this to me."

Then Paul burst into laughter, "Alexander, Mitch's little boy, that Alexander?" Paul asked. "The little boy anyone can take on, did this to my boy? Wow, I really thought you could do better."

"He was not moving when his friend saved him," Milan said, that got Paul to stop laughing.

"What do you mean he was not moving? What did you do Milan?"

"Nothing, just beat him up a little."

"Who was with you?" Paul asked.

"All of us," Milan said. "We were all on top of him right away. He got on the bottom, and then he did not move anymore."

"I am so ashamed of you," Paul said. "You are eleven years old, and you cannot fight your own battles. You have your friends do it for you!"

"I thought you would be mad at me for fighting, instead you are making fun of me?" Milan asked.

"Oh, I am mad. I am very mad! First you get into a fight with someone you never should have. Just because he is little, and you think you can beat him, does not make you any stronger."

"Dad it was Alexander. We have always fought, and I always win. I don't know what happened this time. Where did he get the energy to fight like that? And how did he get so strong? He beat me up, I can honestly say I will not mess with him anymore."

"And I can tell you, honestly, that you are never to fight again--with anyone. I don't know what to tell you, but your mother is almost ready for dinner. I don't know what you are going to explain to her, but I would not even tell her you were fighting if I was you. You know how your mother gets. You better hurry up and get clean," Paul said and walked out.

"Dude, what was that about?" one of the boys asked. "If it was me, and I got home like that, my dad would kill me. And I do not even want to talk about my mom."

"You all know we're in this together, right?" Milan asked.

As soon as he said that, the boys had to go home for

dinner. Milan went to clean himself up and think of a lie to tell his mom. She would be nothing like his dad.

"What was all that about?" Kristen asked when Paul came to help her.

"I am going to tell you, but you have to promise that you are not going to yell, or scream. You are going to wait for him to come down, so we can see what he came up with. I am sure he won't tell you the truth."

"What happened?"

"Well our son was in a fight today, and he was fighting with Alexander." She immediately wanted to go and check on her boy, but she promised she would not. She also wanted to see what Milan would tell her. Why wouldn't he leave that poor boy alone? Kristen knew Milan was always picking on Alexander, he was always coming home saying he did this, and that. He was told a million times to leave the boy alone, but he just did not seem to get it.

"That little boy got our son very good this time, though. Maybe he learned his lesson."

"What do you mean? Is he hurt? Is Alexander all right?" She kept asking him questions, but they both had to wait and see what there son would say.

"Don't worry, I am sure he is okay. Milan just had a few bruises." he did not mention all the sheets were bloody, that their son might not be able to see in one eye, and that his jaw was broken. The less he told her, the more Milan would have to.

Milan got out of the shower and looked in the mirror. He was not as bad as he was when he first got home. He looked at himself one more time, and worried about telling his mom how he got his swollen eye and bruises. But he still did not know how little boy like Alexander could mess him up so bad. If his buddies were not there to fight with him, maybe Alexander would have won. The boy had been asking for it for a while now.

He thought very hard about what to tell his mom, he did not go anywhere with bike all day, but he could tell her they were playing with a scooter at Joe's house. His mom would believe that for sure. Yes, that was what he was going to tell her. He got his story straight, and walked down to dinner.

He walked in the kitchen and his mom was carrying plates to the table. When she saw Milan, she almost dropped them.

"Milan, what happened? Are you okay? Oh, poor baby, why did you not come and see me right after you got home?"

Milan looked at his dad, who gave him the go ahead for his cover up story.

"Me and the boys went to Joe's house, and we were all on the skateboard. I went on it last, and then somehow I fell off and got very hurt."

Good lie, Paul thought, but to bad it won't work. But he wanted to see how far the boy would go with his lie.

"I am sorry, baby? Are you ok?" Kristen asked.

"I am fine now, but the sheets have to be washed. I kind of got a lot of blood on them. I was just cleaning my face, so I would not scare you."

"Are you hurting anywhere else?" Paul jumped in.

"No. I am fine guys. Really. I just stepped wrong on the board, and then when it went under my feet I hurt myself."

"And you only got your face. How strange," Kristen said "I thought you would have gotten your body more than your face."

They sat down to eat dinner, and as soon as they were done, the door bell rang. They all looked at each other. Milan looked at his parents with a scared look in his eyes. Paul got up to see who it was, and Milan stayed glued to his chair. He was not able to get up or look at the door when his father opened it.

Paul opened the door, and Jean was standing there. She did not wait for him to talk, or to invite her in. She walked in the house, and stormed into the kitchen. Paul just stared after her. She never once came to their house, not even when he asked her to. He had good idea why she was here tonight.

He closed the door, and muttered, "Hi Jean, come one in."

Jean went inside. She wanted to see little Milan, and tell him what she thought of him. But when she saw the way Milan looked, and his bloodshot eyes, she could not find the words that she wanted to say.

"Can we help you?" Paul asked. "It was nice of you stop by."

"Don't give me that crap," Jean said angrily. "Do you know what happened to my son today?" She looked straight at Milan.

"No, I have no idea," Milan said, looking at his mom and dad for help. But they were not going to help him.

"Really? Well, then did you explain to your parents how you go those bruises, and why your eye is swollen shut?"

"Yes, I have. They both know what happened to me today."

"They do? Well, how about I hear what happened to you? maybe we didn't hear the same story."

"I was at my friends house, and we were playing with skateboards, and I fell. That is how I got the bruises."

"Really Milan? Is that really what happened, or would you like me to tell them I heard? I am sure they would want to know the truth," Jean said, and walked over to where Paul and Kristen were standing, watching their son try to cover up his lie.

"I got into fight with Alexander today, Mom and Dad. I did not want to tell you, Mom, because I knew you were going to be mad. Even though we all know this is not their town, they should not even be living here. They should go far away," Milan said.

"Are you done?" Paul asked him. Paul saw the hurt in Jean's eyes. He saw that whatever Milan was saying, hurt her deeply. Paul and Kristen looked at each other, and were not able to say anything. They knew that Milan learned these things from school, but they also knew there was no excuse for the way their son was behaving.

"Go to your room, Milan," Kristen told him. She turned to Jean, who was standing there looking like she was going to pass out.

"Sit down, Jean," Paul said. "I've wanted to talk to you for a long time, but I was not sure if you were going to listen to me."

"What is there to listen to?" Jean asked. "I can see that even your son does not want me in this town. I don't see why I should be here anymore."

"Because you grow up here," Paul said. "Don't take what other people are telling you personally."

"Paul, do you have any idea what Alexander looks like? He is all beaten up. He has bruises all over. If Mario did not show up, he could have died. I cannot do this to my kids. I am going to be leaving here in a couple weeks. I hope your son is happy when we are gone. I have helped every single person in this town, and I cannot believe that they are all looking down at me because I am a different race.

Paul and Kristen both knew she was telling the truth, and they were lucky that they were not her. They could see how people were unfair.

"Is there anything we can do for you?" Kristen asked. "Anything at all? Just let us know and we'll do it."

"Just please talk to your son, and tell him we are not bad people. I know he and Alexander don't get along. Paul and Mitch never got along either, but they did not almost kill each other."

"We will talk to him, and I promise he will not bother Alexander anymore. We will tell him not even to look at him," Paul said. "I will make sure of it, I promise you."

"Thank you, thank you both," Jean said, and walked out.

Paul went up to the room to talk to his son, while Kristen cleaned up after dinner. Kristen felt very bad for Jean. She hated that her son was like that. If it was up to her he would not even go to school anymore, because school is where he got all his crazy ideas.

Milan was laying on his bed, reading a book, when Paul walked in the room. Milan pretended that his dad did not even walk in the room, and was still looking at his book when his dad kicked his bed.

"Hey son! How about you put that book down so we can talk?"

"Talk about what, Dad? Don't you see I am reading here?"

"Yes, Milan. I see what you are doing, but this is what you are going to do. As of this moment, you will never talk to Alexander, not even look at him. When you see him someplace, you are going to turn the other way. Do you understand me?"

"Why are you friends with them, Dad? They are not our race, they don't do the same things we do, they are just them. So many people don't like them, why do you?"

"Milan, you listen to me very carefully now. I don't care what race they are, who they talk to and who they go see. I have known Jean since she was a little girl, and I am not going to be like other people and turn my back on her now, when she needs me the most. For sure my son will not be the one who will tell them where they can and cannot live. Do you understand?

"As of right now, you are grounded. you are not allowed to see any of your friends and you are not going to school for a week. At home, you will go out and work with me in the sun. So get ready, son, the morning starts at five o'clock."

Paul walked out of his room and started down the stairs

when he heard the phone in Milan's room ring. He walked back, and unplugged it.

"You won't be needing this any more, either."

Milan hated Alexander even more now. He hated that because of a stupid boy like Alexander, he was grounded. But that's okay he would see him again. This time when he saw him, he would make sure Alexander wouldn't be able to talk at all.

———————————

Jean walked back home, and Alexander and Vanessa were both still awake.

"Why are you two still up?" she asked. "You should have been in bed hours ago."

"We were wondering where you went," Alexander said. "Where did you go, anyways?"

"I went to talk to Milan's parents."

"Mom, are you crazy? Are you really crazy? Do you know that now I won't be able to show my face at school any more?"

"Well that's good, because you are not going to school anymore. Today was your last day, neither you or your sister are going to school. I will go to school tomorrow, and tell your teachers why."

"Mom, we only have two more weeks of school! I really have to finish! It is my last school year, and if I do not finish now, it will be harder."

"Fine. Then, Vanessa you can go, but Alexander is not going anymore."

"Good for me," said Alexander. "I don't like school anyways."

"You're also not going to Mario's anymore, or anywhere that you could be seen by Milan. I am sure he is even more mad now than he was before, so it is best if you stay away from him."

"Mom, how long are we going to stay here for?" Vanessa asked.

"I don't want to go anywhere, but I can see that we have to. I will deal with it, and tell you how long we will be here."

Jean was getting ready for bed that night, and could hear dogs barking outside. She knew that someone must bean in the road or around her house, because the dogs only barked like that if someone was there. Jean looked out the window, and saw two men standing in the road, nd looking directly at her house. She was afraid they were going to come to the door, but after a while the dogs stopped barking. She knew she was safe, at least for tonight.

Jean must have fallen asleep, she suddenly heard a very loud noise coming from the top of her house. Alexander and Vanessa woke up, too, and she signaled them to be quiet. Maybe the people would go away if they did not make any noise. They heard very loud stomping on the roof. There must have been three or more people up there. After a while, they started shaking the doors and windows, too. Vanessa thought about going to the window, and seeing who it was, but she was too scared to get up.

When the noise stopped, Jean looked at the clock. It was four in the morning. She felt that it was safe to go to sleep. There would be other neighbors awake now, and no one should bother her.

In the morning, she went to school and talked to the principal. She explained to her Alexander would not be coming to school anymore, but Vanessa was going to finish. Jean was very afraid for Vanessa, so she decided to take her to school, and pick her up for the next two weeks. On the last day of school, they had to get Vanessa's diploma, but the principal told Jean that she should be back in a week because that was when graduation was.

Jean had heard people talk about busses that were going to Croatia at the end of the week. She was getting ready to pack and at least take their clothes with them. While Jean was packing their clothes, she heard a loud knock on the door. It was late at night and she did not want to open the door. She thought maybe if she did not open the door, they would go away. After a minute, she heard more loud noises from outside. Vanessa and Alexander came out of their room.

"Mom, are you going to open the door?" Alexander asked.

"I am not sure I want to," Jean told him. "You two just stay here, I will be right back."

They knew better than to let their mom open the door by herself, so they were right behind her. When she opened the door, two men in uniform were standing there.

"Do you not hear us knocking?" One of them asked.

"I heard you," Jean said, "that don't mean I have to get up and open it as soon as I hear you, now does it?"

"Well, yes it does," the other man said. "We are here to tell you, that as of right now, you do not own this house anymore. So, we will give you one hour to get out. If we come back and you are still here, it won't be good for you or your kids. I suggest you move out before your hour is up."

"And where exactly do I have to go?" Jean asked. "Are you going to find a place, or something? Or are you just going to throw me out of my house, and not worry about it?"

"Ma'am, we have nothing to do with that. we were told to come here and give you one hour to get out, that is all we know. Now, it is up to you if you want to leave, or not. But we might not be the ones coming back. You should think really hard if you want to risk being in this house."

They left her with those words, Jean did not want to be at the house longer then she had to.

"Get your clothes on, and your shoes," she told Vanessa and Alexander. "We are gong to Monica's, and we are staying the night there. Tomorrow morning we are leaving this house, and this place, We are never coming back here again."

They went to Monica's house, ate dinner, and got ready for bed. Vanessa and Lidia were in the room getting ready to go sleep, and Alexander was in the living room, while Jean and Monica were cleaning up after dinner."

"Are you sure you know what you are doing? Monica asked Jean. "This is something you really have to think about."

"I already thought about it long and hard," Jean said. "And there is no reason for me to be putting my kids through hell every day and night. If I was in that house tonight, who knows what could happen? That is why in the morning, I am leaving and not turning back. The only bad thing is, my kids will never find friends like they have here. Lidia and Tina are Vanessa's best friends, and they have been since they were little. I am not sure what this will do to them ,but I have to go."

In Lidia's room, she and Vanessa were laying on her bed and talked about all the things they've done, together and all the times they stayed up all night talking about school, boys, and their parents.

"Who do I talk to now?" Lidia asked.

"I don't know. I am sorry that I have to go, and that we won't see each other probably ever again, but I cannot stay here. You should have seen those man tonight they were serious about us leaving and not being there when they come back. I am sure my mom knows what she is doing. We will be fine."

"Yeah, you will be fine, but what about me?" Lidia whined. "I won't have a best friend to talk to anymore, and if I have a problem with boys you won't be there for me to run to and complain."

"I am sure you will find a different friend. And I know you have many friends at your school you hang out with."

"Vanessa we have been friends since we were born. No one other than you knows me better."

"I know, I am sorry. I am just trying to make it easier. I

know anything I say, or do, will not help the pain. Yours or mine," Vanessa said, and went to hug Lidia.

Lidia hugged Vanessa tightly and they both cried, they had been best friends for thirteen years and now they may never see each other again.

It was very late when they went to sleep. In the morning, Lidia and Vanessa got up and went to pack the little bit of food that Monica gave them. Lidia went with them to the buss stop. The last thing Lidia told Vanessa was, please stay in touch and don't ever forget me.

CHAPTER THIRTEEN

JEAN AND THE KIDS GOT to the parking lot where all the busses were waiting, along with all the other people who were thrown out of their houses the night before. Jean did not dare talk to anyone, because the people might be the same ones that told her to get out.

The busses came, the driver told them all what to expect. It was a day of driving and they might have to stop many times and be checked by Serbian guards. No one was allowed to leave unless they said so first.

The driver also told them it was his third trip to Croatia, and he had seen a lot of bad things happen to a lot of good people. He said every time he stopped, and Serbian guards were checking people, if they were wearing very nice jewelry, the guards did not let them go because they had money. No one ever heard from those people again because the guards killed them after that.

Jean thought that something like that could happen to her and her kids, but she really had nothing on her that was worth any money. So she really was not that worried, the only thing she was worried about was Alexander. He was a young man that the Serbians could use in their war. Many times Alexander had to hide when the Serbian guards were around so they would not see him. Jean thought about her son a lot, she did not want nothing bad to happened to him.

The busses loaded, and Jean looked around. There were a lot of people going away, mostly older people and women with children. There was not one male that was not over sixty on the bus. They all knew if there was anyone younger, the Serbian guards would not let them cross to Croatia. Six busses filled up with people that were ready to get out of the hell that they were living in for a long time. All of them were sick of the war, they all just wanted to get out.

It was July, and very hot outside. Most people did not have any luggage with them, because they were thrown in the middle of the night. Many of them were older couples, and most of them were sick. Many of the older men were complaining that they would not have gone anywhere, if it were not for their wives. One of the men told everyone he really wanted to stay and fight, but his wife made him leave.

They had been riding for over four hours. Vanessa and Alexander were really hungry, but they both knew there was no eating on this bus. If they took out the sandwiches that Lidia made for them, everyone would want some, and they only had four. They would have to starve themselves until everyone else was sleeping.

"Mom," Vanessa said, "I am very thirsty, can I get something to drink?"

"I am not sure if we have anything, but let me check," Jean said. She took out a bottle of water, and gave it to Vanessa. "Here," she said, "drink this fast and give some to your brother. If anyone sees you, they will take it and then you will have no more."

Vanessa drank fast, and so did Alexander, they were lucky that no one saw them.

The busses stopped, and they all looked outside to see what was going on. Everyone was so quiet that you could hear the flies buzzing. Outside they saw fours cars, full of guards, waiting for the busses. Jean and the kids were in the third bus, they saw four guards walk onto the busses in front of theirs. They could see people moving on the busses in front of them, but they could not tell what was going on. They did see the guards take four people out from the first bus.

They took them off the bus and then put them it, they told them something and the guards walked away to the second bus. From the second bus, they took three girls, then walked onto the third bus where Jean and her kids were.

All four men walked onto the bus. Two of them stayed at the front of the bus, while the other two walked from person to person. One of them walked passed Jean, then turned back around and stopped right in front of her.

"Do you think where you are going is better than here?" he asked Jean.

"I am not sure where I am going, but I am sure that it will be better than here," Jean answered without even looking at him.

"Did your mother teach you,, when you talk to people, you have to look at their eyes?"

"Yes sir, I just don't see people around that I have to look in the eyes."

Jean wanted to say so much more, but knew anything else might get her in trouble. Or worse, it might get her kids in trouble. The guard looked at her, and when she did not say anything more he went on towards the end of the bus. Vanessa was holding her breath when he walked passed them. When they finally walked off of the bus she started breathing normally again.

They waved the buses through, and the people they took off were never seen again. Jean was happy no one from their bus was taken, but she also wondered what would happened at the next stops. They had four more to go before they reached Croatia.

The bus driver told them to get ready, They were getting

stopped again. This time there was six guards, and they had uniforms on, but not hats. Their hair was long, and they also had long beards. They stopped all three buses at the same time, and this time they did not take any one from the first or second bus, which was a good sign. There was one more bus to go through. What if no one was taken off bus number three, Jean thought. That meant their bus was next to have people taken off.

All six men walked on the bus. Two of them stayed in the front, two went in the middle, and two all the way to the back. Jean and her kids were in the back. The men walked through, from all the older people to all the younger ones.

"Is there anyone that has a heart condition?" one of the guards in the back asked. No one answered him, and when he saw that no one was stepping forward he got very angry.

"Well since no one wants to tell me they are sick, then I am going to pick people I want to be sick." He went passed Jean and picked the lady that was sitting right next to Alexander.

"You!" He said. "I want you at the front of the bus!" Her husband got up from where he was sitting and stopped his wife from going forward. Another guard stepped forward, and hit man the in the face with his gun. The man fell down in front of Jean.

"Don't just stand there," the guard said. "Help him. I am sure you have some water or food. Give it to him so he can come back to us, and have some smart ideas."

No one moved, and that seemed to make the guard even more mad. He went to where Jean was standing, grabbed her by the arm, looked her in the eye, and pushed her forward.

"Why is it so hard for you people to listen? If you would have listened, this never would have happened to you."

Jean almost fell on the man still lying on the floor, but she was not going to help him. She did not know him, and what if the guards only wanted to see who could help so they would take them off the bus? She was not going anywhere without her children. She looked over to where Vanessa and Alexander were standing, and prayed that neither one of them tried anything.

"Why are you just standing there? Are you deaf?" The guard grabbed Jean's ear, pulled it hard, and yelled in it, "Hello? Can you hear me good?"

"I can hear you," she answered. "Can you see he is coming back? So why should I help him?"

"You are very lucky," the guard said. A girl started to cry, and the guard left Jean to see why the girl was crying. Alexander went to his mom.

"Go back, Alexander. No matter what happens, you or your sister do not talk, or even move, from that spot. You understand me, right?"

"Yes, Mom," Alexander said, and went back to stand with Vanessa.

"Are you okay?" Jean asked the man on the floor.

"I am fine. Where is my wife?" he asked.

"She is off the bus, standing right there. It looks like there are more people with her, mostly girls." Jean told him.

"They are not taking my wife from me! If I have to die today, I will, but that is my wife. I go where ever she goes." The man got up off the floor, and one of the guards saw him.

"Well, look who decided to join us! Did you have a nice nap?" the guard asked.

"Where is my wife? What did you do to her? I swear if anything happens to her, I will kill you myself!"

"I would not make threats if I were you!" the guard yelled at him.

"I just want to be with my wife! Is that so much to ask? If you have to take me outside to be with her, I will go! You are a person, just like I am. I am sure if someone took your wife, you would not just stand there and let them take her, now would you?"

"But no one took my wife. I took your wife, because when

I asked who was sick, or if anyone was sick, no one answered. You left me no choice."

"My wife is not sick, so why did you take her? Come on man, bring her back! All we want is to get the hell out of here!"

"If I don't bring her back, there is nothing you can do about it," the guard told the man.

"Oh, watch me!" the man yelled, and started to walk passed the guard. He did not get far before he was hit in the head again. He fell to the floor, but he did not black out. He laid on the ground and waited. He was not going to let them take his wife, he would die before they took her away from him.

The guard that was at the front of the bus saw what happened, and went to see if the old man needed help. But when he got near him, the man pushed himself up. He surprised the guard, who fell to the floor. Before he know what was going on, the old man had his gun in his hands.

"Move and I will shot you!" the man said. "I am going to get my wife, and no one will stop me!"

Just before he stepped off the bus, someone fired and he fell to the ground. He was shot in the chest. Blood sprayed all over the driver and on the front windows. Everyone started to scream. When one of the guards came back on the bus, everyone stopped screaming.

Vanessa and Alexander were very scared, but knew going to their mom would make things worse, so they stayed where they were. They could only see blood, they could not see the man. He just gave his life to help his wife, and now that he was dead there was no one to help her anymore.

More guards showed up and took people from the front of the bus to clean up the mess and get rid of the old man's body. His wife was next his body screaming, and hitting everyone that came near her. No one could calm her down.

"If you don't shut up, I will shoot you too, so you can join him!" One of the guards said.

"Shoot me then! I am as good as dead without him!" the woman screamed back.

"Don't tempt me, woman! It's not my fault he pushed a guard and tried to take his gun. See what happens to you people? I take that back, you are not people. You are animals!"

They started walking away from the bus, and Jean thought that they were going to leave. But was she wrong, they were only getting started. Three of them got back on the bus, one in the front and the other two in the back.

"My name is Mr. Jelovic," the guard in the front said, "and the other two gentlemen are Mr. Bogdan and Mr. Davor. If you need anything, or any help, they will be happy to help you. What you have seen here today is just the beginning of what will happen if you do not listen to us."

"Why do you people do this to us?" Jean asked. "We only want to get away. Why do you have to stop us, even when we are trying to leave? Isn't that what you all wanted in the first place?"

"Mom! Be quiet!" Vanessa hissed. "Why do you always have to be the one that is saying something? Aren't you scared?"

"Yes, I am," Jean said. "I am scared to death that I might be the next one taken off this bus, and that I might never see my kids again, but someone has to speak for us. Can't you see that there is no one else?"

"That's right," Mr. Bogdan said. "No one is talking, because they know better. We have guns, and we know how to use them."

"And that makes you a man?" Jean asked. "I am sorry, but that guy you just killed is more a man than you will ever be!" Before she could even finish her sentence, Mr. Bogdan was next to her. He took her under her arms and started dragging her along with him. Before he could walk away with Jean, Alexander threw himself down on his knees.

"Please don't take my mom from me!" he pleaded. "She is all I have, and if you take her away I won't have anyone at all." Someone stood up in the front row, and tried to pull Alexander away, but he would not let go.

"Tell your idiot son, if he don't move, I will have him shot outside with you!" Bogdan yelled.

"Alexander, go stand next to your sister," his mother told him, "I will be okay. I will be back, I promise."

They took Jean outside. Everyone ran to the windows to see what they would do. Mr. Bogdan hit her in the face. When she just stood there, not crying, he hit her again. Vanessa and Alexander both wished there was something they could do to help, but they knew they were too young to make a difference.

"Are you all just going to stand there?" Vanessa asked. "They are going to kill my mom! She spoke for all of you when they killed that man."

"Yes," someone said, "but we cannot do anything other than just stand here. We are the same as you. Helpless. We cannot do anything if we want to stay alive."

They saw Jean coming back to the bus, and both Vanessa and Alexander ran to her. Jean's nose was bleeding, someone handed her a napkin so she could wipe it.

"Both of you go back and sit down," Jean told her kids. "Why didn't you listen to me? You could have gotten yourselves killed! I had to watch your father get killed. I do not want to see my kids die, too."

"Sorry, Mom," Vanessa said, "we are just glad that you are okay! Are you?"

"Yes, I am fine. They might be back again, so we just have to sit down, and not talk anymore."

"Are you going to be quiet this time?" someone asked from the front row.

"I did it for all of us, not just for me. But, since none of you know how to defend anyone except your own selves, yes I will be quiet."

Mr. Bogdan walked back on the bus, looked at everyone, and said, "I want to see everyone's hands, and who ever has earrings. If you take forever to get your jewelry off, I will help you."

The way he said it, everyone on the bus knew he was not talking about helping them in a nice way. Everyone that had rings and earrings were taking them off. For some it was not easy, their rings had been on their fingers for maybe twenty years. They were hard to take off, but they were doing everything they could.

Bogdan did not wait, he went to the first lady with her ring still on. He saw she was having trouble, and took out his knife. Vanessa had a good idea what he was going to do, and she closed her eyes. Jean put her hands over both kids' eyes, so they would not see what was about to happen.

Bogdan took the lady's hand, looked it, and said, "Looks like you're having trouble taking this off." Then he slid his knife under the ring, and cut her finger off. The lady passed out, either from the pain or from the blood that was spraying everywhere. People were screaming, some people stopped when Bogdan yelled again.

"Did you think I was kidding? I don't care how hard it is to take off, I don't have all day. So, hurry up!"

When one of the girls could not take her earring out, he did not wait for her. He yanked it off so hard that not only her earring came off, but half of her ear, too. The people on the bus were terrified, there was blood everywhere. The people that cleaned the windows, and got rid of the old man's body, had to clean all this blood, too.

When he came near Jean, he saw that her nose stopped bleeding. He looked at her, and pulled her by the ear.

"I see your husband never cared about you, you don't have

any rings or earrings, poor you," Bogdan whispered in her ear. Jean wanted to tell him that it was none of his business, but she just looked him, with a look that said if she could, she would kill him with her bare hands.

When he was done taking everyone's things he looked at them and said, "It was nice doing business with all of you. Now you can go!" With that, he stepped off the bus.

CHAPTER FOURTEEN

JEAN LOOKED AROUND TO SEE if anyone there was that could help the woman missing her finger. She really wanted to help the girl with only half her ear, too, but Jean did not have any schooling as a doctor. So she did not know much but she found some gauze and gave it to the poor girl. She was in and out of consciousness, because she was in so much pain. Jean tried to help as much as she could, but there was no help from anyone else. They were all more worried about their jewelry.

She heard a young girl tell her mom that she would miss her earrings. She heard someone else say that those were there rings, and they didn't know how they were going to live without them.

"I am sure you will be fine," Jean told the little girl. "I am sure you can buy yourself new earrings, and I am sure all of you can get your ring back. But, this lady and this girl cannot get their ear or finger back."

"Not our fault," the little girl said. "They took my earrings. Do you know how much they were worth?"

"I am sure they were cheaper than your ear, now weren't they?" Jean asked her.

The bus stopped again, and everybody froze. They looked outside, they had almost made it. They had to pass through one more city, then they would be out of the Serbian guards' control. No one would bother them anymore, now they just had to get there.

When they got off the bus, they saw a doctor and ambulance waiting for them.

"How did they know?" Vanessa asked her mom.

"I don't know, but as long as they are here to help. That is all that matters."

The doctor heard Vanessa asking Jean. "This is the fourth bus today," he told her, "so far your bus has been the luckiest one. We had two busses before yours that had people without four fingers, or that both ears were ripped apart. We also had people that had no fingers at all on their hands. They killed over ten people on the other busses, how about this one?"

"There was one person killed that I have seen," said Jean, "and there are five missing. The wife of the man they killed, and the four people that cleaned up the blood. Why are people so stupid? Why do they have to kill to get their point across?"

"I wish I had the answers for you," the doctor told her, "but I can tell you that all of you are very lucky. Now you are free, there will be no one bothering you anymore. You can have a good life! I hope you can forget what happened on that bus, I am sure it won't be easy."

There was food and water for everyone. Many babies were playing around, and kids were running and playing. It was nice to see people happy, but Vanessa was not. She missed her friends, and she knew Lidia and Tina were missing her, too. She also knew she was never going back again, she left all that behind. It was time to make a new life, she just hoped that she wouldn't have to go through any more bad things today.

Their new bus came around, and it was very nice and comfortable inside. They had lots of room and the seats were much nicer, too. Jean, Vanessa, and Alexander sat in a seat that was big enough for all three of them.

"Mom, I am very tired," Vanessa said. "Do you think it is safe to sleep?"

"You sleep," Jean told her, "if anything happens, I will wake you up."

Vanessa laid her head on her mom and drifted off to sleep. It did not take long, she was very tired. She dreamed of her house and her dad. They were playing around then Lidia came over and hugged them. She leaned over to Vanessa's ear and very quietly whispered the last words Vanessa heard Lidia say. "Please, don't ever forget me." Then Vanessa woke up.

When she woke up, she started to cry. Jean did not know why Vanessa was crying, but she held her tightly just the same. Her daughter had been through so much, but she knew she had done the right thing by getting her kids out.

"What's the matter, Baby?" Jean asked, once Vanessa had calmed down a little.

"I was dreaming of Dad and Lidia," she said. "Lidia told me never to forget her, Mom. What if our life turns out to be better then hers? What if one day I *do* forget about her? Do you think she will forgive me?"

"Baby, don't think like that," Jean told her. "You will always think about Lidia, no matter what. She will always be your best friend, and you will never forget her or your dad."

Vanessa knew her mom was right, she wouldn't ever forget her friends or her dad. She might make some new friends but she would never forget Lidia and Tina, or any other friends she ever had in Banja Luka. They would always be her friends.

Vanessa was so deep in thought, when the bus stopped she did not even notice. Everyone was afraid to get off the bus, when the doors opened and two men in uniform came on everyone stopped talking. They saw that their uniform was different, they did not know if that was a good thing or not.

"We are here to help you," one of them said. "I am Morgan, and this is Raul. If we can help you with anything, let us know. This is the fourth bus today, so we did not get many things ready for you guys. Tonight you will sleep at the school, and tomorrow you can find yourselves a house."

"No one will hurt us, right?" Someone asked.

"No, this is your home now. No one will ever touch you again," Morgan said.

They all stepped off the bus, and walked toward the school. In the school, there were many people lying on benches and little beds. There were all kinds food and drinks that Vanessa and Alexander never had before. They were hungry and thirsty, so they got some food before they found a spot to sleep.

They ate their food and laid next to Jean on the floor, because there were no more empty beds. No one wanted to turn the lights off because they were still scared, even though everyone had been so nice.

It was hard for Jean to fall asleep. Everything that happened that day kept going through her mind. She thought that it was very stupid of her to stand up to those guards. She could have been killed, but someone had to do it and no one else even tried. Jean thought about the house she left behind, the people still there going through the same thing she did for the last three years. There were so many things to think about, but at least she was safe.

She saw that Vanessa and Alexander were sleeping, she decided to get out of the room and see where she was. When she walked out of the room, someone's hand touched her. She jumped, Jean did not realize anyone else was awake.

"Is there something you need?" Jean asked the person that touched her.

"No, I cannot sleep," they answered. "Where are you going?"

"Just outside," Jean said, "I cannot sleep, either. Did you want to come with me?"

"Sure! I am Maria, nice to meet you. Sorry that I scared you."

"I am Jean, and it is okay. I just did not know anyone else was awake. I thought I was the only who could not sleep."

"Oh no," Maria said, "it has been a long time since I have slept, but tonight I cannot sleep because of all the things that happened on our bus. I am just little worried."

"Where are we going ladies?" one of the guards asked them. "Are you hungry?"

"No, we just cannot sleep, and we did not want to bother anyone," Jean said. "That is why we are out here. We are just talking, that's all."

"Oh, you are not a bother," he said. "My name is Marko, and if you need anything, don't hesitate to ask. I am here to help. I will be guarding you guys all night, so don't worry you are safe here."

It had been a long time since they had been free, and it felt good. Maria and Jean went outside, the view was beautiful. It was a warm summer night and it felt like they had no wonders in the world. Tomorrow they would worry what house they were going to get, who they were going to live with, and if they were going to have all the things the others told them they would.

"Do you think we are really safe here?" Jean asked.

"I don't know. I have not felt safe in over a year, I am not even sure how that feels anymore. Who is here with you?" Maria asked Jean.

"Just me and my kids," Jean told her. She did not want to go into details why, so she just left it at that. Before she could ask Maria who she was there with, Marko, the guard, came back to tell them that Vanessa was awake, and looking for her mom.

"Sorry," Jean said, "I have to go inside and see if she is okay."

"Oh, no problem," Maria told her. "I will be outside for a while yet, but if you don't come back I am sure we will see each other some other time."

Jean walked inside, and Vanessa was still awake.

"Where were you?" Vanessa asked her angrily.

"I was outside talking to Maria. Why does it matter? You were sleeping, and I was not able to sleep."

"I had a bad dream, and when I woke up you were not here," Vanessa told her mom. "Then when I called your name, you were not around, either, so I was scared."

"It is okay," Jean said, "I am here now. Nothing to worry about. Now, you can go back to sleep. I won't leave again, I promise."

Vanessa fell asleep again, and Jean stayed awake looking at both of her kids. As kids they never had anything, everything always was passed on from someone else. Maybe now she would be able to afford new things for her kids.

Jean woke up to kids screaming, and running around. She looked around to see where her kids were, luckily they were still sleeping. Jean got up and went to find some breakfast for them, when they woke up they would be hungry. In the hallway were tables full of food, everything looked so delicious. She filled her plate, then did the same for Vanessa and Alexander.

The smell of the food woke them both up, they saw more food this morning than they had in their whole lives. Maybe this is a new start, Vanessa thought, maybe we won't starve here and have a lot more then our friends back home. She burst into the tears.

"Honey, what's the matter?" Jean asked her. "Is something wrong with your food?"

"No Mom, I am just thinking about all of our friends that don't have any food this morning, and us here eating all this. I am sure many of our friends would not even think about us if they were here, and if we were back where we came from. I just cannot help but to think that, for once in our lives, we have something other kids don't."

That brought tears to Jean's eyes, too. She and her daughter were hugging and crying when Maria came over to see them.

"What's going on here?" she asked. "Why are you two crying?"

"Just remembering all the things we went through," Jean said. "Now we are somewhere miles and miles away. And, on our first day, we are eating food and drinking drinks we have never had."

"Oh come on," Maria said, "that is no reason to cry, that is a reason to be very happy."

The guards came in and told them that breakfast was over, and that they would have to go out and look for a house. He also told them not to worry if they did not find something right away. It was only Friday, they had two days to find a house. School would be open on Monday for all the children that came in on the busses, and for all the ones that still lived in town. Many people had left their houses here, just like Jean had left hers.

For now they were safe, there was no one to tell them to leave anymore. Maybe someday they would have their complete freedom.

CHAPTER FIFTEEN

Vanessa wasn't having the best of days when she looked outside, and saw that all of her chores were still waiting for her. It was Friday, and she wanted to go out badly. She wanted her mom to tell her she could go, and that she could stay out later then eleven.

Vanessa remembered when she came to this town. When there was nothing, and no one around. Now there were so many people, and they kept coming. It was not bad having people around, but many of them were people coming back to the houses that they had left only a year ago.

Since her family arrived in town, a lot of things had changed. There were many houses without doors and windows or roofs, that were all fixed now. At first they lived with Maria and her daughters. Maria's daughters did not like Vanessa at all, and she really did not like them, either. They wanted everything from everyone but they did nothing in return. One day, Vanessa asked Maria if she could borrow her daughter's shoes. When Emily got home, Vanessa overheard her talking to Maria.

"Mom, why would you give her my shoes?" Emily asked.

"They are just shoes, Emily. She needed to wear them. What's wrong with that?"

"Well, I don't like her, and I don't want her to wear my things!" Emily screamed, and shut the door in Vanessa's face.

"Oh, I cannot wait until I am out of this house!" Vanessa cried.

Jean was looking for a house of their own, but was having trouble finding one where they would not have to walk very far just to get to a store. Vanessa didn't care if she had to walk all day, just so she could be away from Emily.

They found a house not far from the city. As soon as they moved in, all three of them started in on it. From the outside, it did not look that bad. It had all the doors and windows, and a roof in place. It did not look like there was a lot of work done to be on the house. It had more rooms, and looked a lot bigger then the one they left behind.

On the first level were two rooms, the kitchen, and a bathroom. They had to go outside to get to the upstairs where nothing was done, it just look liked a giant storage room. All three of them had to wear masks before they could go inside to clean. All the furniture in the house was old. The kitchen sink was full of dishes that had been sitting there for about six months. It smelled so bad, everywhere they turned was dirt.

Vanessa was there to help her mom, and did not mind it. She went to the storage room on the lower level. When she walked in, it smelled like an animal had died in there. There was a big refrigerator in the room. There was no electricity at the time, so Vanessa did not want to look inside. She guessed everything that was in the fridge would have to be thrown away. After Vanessa opened the fridge, she ran to the bathroom and vomited. The meat that had been left in the refrigerator had maggots all over it. But, if they wanted to live in this house they had to make it livable.

Jean found a job in the city cleaning the post office. She was getting money for enough food which was a lot better than in Bosnia. Every day when Jean came home from work, Vanessa had lunch ready for them, they would eat and Jean would take a nap. After her nap, all three of them would work outside until dark.

Going to sleep now did not include waiting for someone to walk on the roof, or someone coming to tell them to leave. Those times were done. Now they were trying to work and have a better life. Vanessa was still young, but she helped the people around her, and they would give her a little money. She tried to help her mom as much as she could.

Vanessa had many friends here, too, but they were nothing like Lidia. No one could ever take her place or even come close. She wrote to Lidia once or twice, and she got a letter and a picture from her but that was all. Vanessa sometimes wondered what her life would be like if her dad was still with them. Would they be here in this town, or would they have even left Banja Luka yet?

Since Jean was working, Vanessa and Alexander got up early in the mornings to make sure the animals were fed, and the cows were milked. They also had land where they could grow all kinds of vegetables. Vanessa wanted to work outside, but couldn't because every time she tried to tell her brother to clean up inside, he wouldn't.

"Come on, Alexander!" Vanessa yelled at him one day. "It is nice out, let me go take care of the outside and you take care of inside."

"Are you crazy?" Alexander asked. "None of my friends work inside their houses, and no one even helps with dishes. That is a woman's job!"

"A woman's job?" Vanessa screamed at him. "What do you mean 'woman's job'? Then what is a man's job?"

"To work and provide for the woman!" Alexander said, like he really believed it.

"Listen boy, I am not sure who told you what a woman's or a man's job is, but we both know we are all mom has. If we don't help her, no one will. Now, get in the kitchen and do the dishes, or get out and do the outside work. I don't care what you do," Vanessa said, "but do something!"

Alexander gave her a despising look and went to do the dishes. If he didn't, then not only would he hear it from Vanessa, he would have to hear from his mom, too. He could not stand that his mom always used guilt on him. Alexander was almost done with the dishes, when someone knocked on the door. He opened it, and there was an old woman standing in front of him.

"Can I help you?" Alexander asked.

"Yes, son, you might be able to. I live in the house up the hill from this one, and I was wondering if you could come on over, and help me do some things around the house."

Alexander was about to say no, when he heard his mom say, "Yes, he will be there. How soon do you need him?"

"Any time he is free," the woman said. "My name is Anna, and I live right up the hill from your house. I am alone and old, and I cannot do things myself anymore. I was wondering if you could also come, and help me clean up my house."

Alexander smiled now, because not only did he have to go, his mom had to go, too.

"Yes, Anna, I will be there after I rest a little from work. I just got home. Let me eat something, and I will be there."

"Well, I did not eat today," Anna said. "Is there enough cooked so I can eat here, too?"

This lady never quits, Alexander thought, now she has to eat at our house, too.

"Come on in," Jean said. "I am not sure what Vanessa made, she cooks and cleans while I'm at work." Alexander started to say something, but he closed his mouth when his mom went to the sink where he had just finished doing dishes. "And Alexander helps her around the house, whenever she needs it."

"You have good kids," Anna told Jean. "My kids are older, and they never come to see me. When they were younger, I was there for them all the time. Now when I am alone, no one comes to help me. I am old and alone, and I don't have anyone. I don't know what to do," Anna said and started to cry.

"Oh, Anna," Jean said, "it will be okay. We are here if you ever need any help. If I am not home Vanessa and Alexander are always home. Just ask them, they will help you."

"You are such a sweet family. The people that were here before you did not want to help me at all. I always asked for help, and they never wanted to. Thank goodness they are gone."

"Where did they go?" Jean asked.

"They left for Serbia," Anna said. "I did not have anywhere to go, so I stayed in my house. God knows I was scared to death, but there was no one I could go with. No one wants an old lady on their back that they have to worry about, so I stayed. So, can you make me dinner tonight? I have not had a cooked meal in over a month."

"I can," Jean said, "just let me get some rest. After lunch, I will be there to help clean up the house and make food."

Vanessa came inside after she was done with all her chores, and found Anna sitting on the couch and talking to her mom. Alexander pulled her aside as soon as she got in the door.

"What are you doing?" Vanessa screamed at him. "I have to talk to Mom and see if she is going to let me go out tonight. Why are you pulling me? Who is that old lady anyways?"

"That's why I am pulling you," Alexander told her. "She is so creepy. She came over to ask Mom if we can help her around the house. Her excuse is she is old, and she cannot do it herself."

"Alexander!" Vanessa said. "You can see that she needs help. Why not help her? If she just wanted our help, why is Mom making her a plate?"

"Because as soon as Mom said we were going to eat, she invited herself to eat with us. I don't see this coming out good," he said. "I think she just wants to use us for something. I am not sure we can trust her."

"Oh come on, what can an old lady do, anyways? I am going inside to talk to Mom, and see if I can go out tonight."

"Oh, about that," Alexander said, "I am going to ask if I can go, too. I did not do dishes for no reason."

"You can go," Vanessa said, "but not with me. I am going with Danielle and Alex, and you are not going with us."

"Alex, who is he?" Alexander asked. "Do you really think you can go with him without talking to Mom first? I am going to tell her he is going with you, since you won't let me go."

"Fine, say whatever you want," Vanessa told him. "I am not scared of you, or your threats. Just remember, if Mom doesn't let me go, you are not going, either. I would be very careful what I said to her if I was you."

They all ate lunch, and then Vanessa and Alexander cleaned the table. As they were getting ready to go feed the cows, Anna asked if they could come over after they were done.

"We will be there when we are done," Vanessa told her.

Anna finally went home. It took her a good four hours to leave after lunch. She asked a million questions about Jean and her family. When Anna left, Jean was exhausted. She wanted to take a nap, but instead she went to see what Vanessa and Alexander were doing, and find out why they were so quiet during lunch.

Jean was very quiet as she walked back to the kitchen. She heard them talking, but could not make out what they were saying. She walked a little closer, and she could hear Vanessa clearly.

"Come on, Alexander. If you ask Mom to go with me, and she says no, then you cannot blame me," Vanessa said, "plus why would you want to go with me, anyway?"

"Vanessa, I am going no matter what you say. You should stop fighting with me, and work faster so we can talk to Mom before she takes her nap. You know how it is when she lays down. If we start asking questions then, she won't let us go for sure," Alexander told her.

"I don't want to go if you are going to bother me the whole time," Vanessa said. "What fun would that be?"

"I am sorry. I am going to tell Mom who is going, and then she won't let you go, either."

Jean decided it was time to go in, but at that moment the door opened, and Vanessa came out.

"Mom!" she cried. "What are you doing here?"

"I live here," Jean answered. "Didn't you know that?"

"No Mom, not in this house. Right here at this door, is what I meant," Vanessa said. Vanessa could never hide anything from her mom, Jean knew right away that something was bothering her.

"What's going on, Vanessa?" Jean asked. "If you have something to ask me, now would be a great time to do so, because I am about to go take my nap."

"Well, I wanted to go out tonight," Vanessa told her mom. "I was wondering if I could stay out a little bit later then eleven. It is Friday, and you do not have to work tomorrow."

"Who are you going with?" Jean asked.

"I am going with Danielle and Alex, they will be here at seven to walk with me. We were going to get Monica first, and then we will go to a disco club. They opened one last weekend."

"And I did not know about this, because?" Jean asked.

"I did not want to bother you until I knew for sure we were going," Vanessa answered.

"And, don't forget me," Alexander added. "I want to go, too."

"Who are you going with," Jean asked him.

"I am going with Vanessa. If she can go, I should go, too."

"Yes, that is true, but you are younger than she is. Don't

you have any of your own friends? You know if she stays out later, you cannot. You have to be home at eleven."

"Mom! How is that fair?" Alexander whined. "I never get to stay passed eleven. I always have to go with someone other than her. Why are you guys so unfair to me? Is it because I am the only guy here? That's it, isn't it?"

"Oh Alexander, don't be such a child," Vanessa said. "You just have to find some of your own friends, and you will be just fine. I have my own friends, and you hanging out with me does not really work."

"And why is that?" Jean asked. "Is there someone I should know about?"

"Yes," Alexander said.

"No," Vanessa said, "I don't think so. He is my friend. Alex and I are just friends, and that's it. Why is it every time I have a guy friend, you guys always think he is more?"

"Maybe because you talk about him all the time," Alexander answered.

"So? You can talk about your friends," Vanessa said angrily.

"All right, stop it both of you!" Jean interrupted. "Vanessa, you can stay out until midnight. Alexander, you can only stay until eleven. If you guys break your curfew, either one of you, you will not go again. Do I make myself clear?"

"Yes, ma'am," they said, and walked towards the house.

None of them knew that Anna was watching them. She knew if she did not say something, they would go inside to play and never come to help her. She was old, those rotten kids. How could they do that to her? If she had to she would knock on their door again.

Anna hated kids, they were nothing but trouble. Her own two never came to see her. She did everything in her power to bring them up right, and to give them everything they ever wanted. Now, she had to beg other kids to help her.

"Hey guys," she called. "Are you done with your things? How about a hand?"

"Oh no," said Alexander. "The witch saw us. Now we have to go there and help her."

"Alexander be nice," Jean scolded. "They are going inside to change their clothes. They will be there as soon as they are done with that," she called to Anna.

"Do we have to?" Alexander looked at her with sad puppy eyes.

"You want to go out tonight, right?" Jean asked him.

"Yes, but that doesn't mean I want to slave over at the witch's house all day, just to have some fun. I don't even slave at my own house, Vanessa does."

"I do not slave," Vanessa said. "I help Mom, so she doesn't have to do everything herself."

"No," Alexander said, "you do things so Mom will let you go out at night."

"You are such a jerk," Vanessa told him. "Do you see now why I don't want you to go places with me? Because, all you ever do is embarrass me!"

The kids went inside to change, and Jean stayed home to work on dinner while they went to help Anna.

"Do you think her house is very dirty?" Alexander asked Vanessa.

"I am not sure. I hope not, because it is already five. She better not have a lot for us to do. I would like to be ready by seven," Vanessa said.

Walking to Anna's house didn't take them long. As they got closer, they both started to get a bad feeling. They were in for a messy surprise at Anna's, and they did not even know the half of it.

CHAPTER SIXTEEN

As soon as they walked in, they both knew they would be there way past seven. Anna's house was a mess, nothing more than a trash can. Something Vanessa had not seen since they moved there a year ago.

There was garbage everywhere. Her furniture was full of clothes. Her dining table was full of dishes, her dishwasher was broken, of course. There was junk all over the floor.

"Oh thank you," Anna said. "I have not seen such kind kids like the two of you around here. All these other kids don't like to think about older people."

I would not either, Alexander thought. Dear God has she ever cleaned before? Anna's voice interrupted his thoughts.

"How about some help with the yard when you are done in here?" Anna asked. Alexander could not hold back anymore.

"I am sorry," he told her. "We are going to do your clothes, and then we are going home. We might be back tomorrow to finish up, but tonight we are going out with our friends.

"Oh," Anna said, "that's okay, you can just come back tomorrow, and finish the rest. Thank you for coming."

They walked outside and almost threw up their lunch.

"Have you ever seen a house this dirty? I don't ever want to go back," Alexander said.

"Don't worry," Vanessa told him, "I don't either. We'll just tell Mom how bad it is."

"I hope she don't make us go."

"She won't," Vanessa reassured him. "Not after we tell her how horrible it was."

"How was it?" Jean asked when they got home. "Was it as bad as I thought it was going to be? She is old, so I assumed her house was a disaster."

"Mom are you making fun of us?" Alexander asked. "Because if you are, not only do we get to stay out longer, you get to go clean it tomorrow. If you knew how bad it was, and did not tell us, that would not be nice." Alexander gave her his puppy eyes, and Jean just laughed at him.

"No, I did not know that it was bad, but by the look of two of you, I can assume that it was. But so was this house when we moved in, and you both survived."

"Yeah," Alexander said, "we had to. This is the house we live in. The one that old witch lives in, we have nothing to do with. Not only that, she wanted us to work on her lawn."

"But it is dark outside," Jean said. "Why would she want you to work outside in the dark?"

"I don't know, I told her we have things to do, and we could not stay to long."

"I am going to get dressed," Vanessa said. "I think you should do the same, Alexander." She gave him a look that told him she did not want him to go with her, and Jean saw it.

"Remember Vanessa, he don't go, then you don't, either."

"I did not say anything," Vanessa said.

"You did not have to. I am your mother, and I know what your looks mean. Now, go get ready before I change my mind."

As they were changing their clothes and getting ready,

they heard a knock on the door. They knew it could not be their friends because it was too early.

"Where are those kids of yours?" They heard Anna yell. "Where did they go?"

"Why? What is the matter?" Jean asked.

"They took my mother's watch that was on my couch. It was there before they came in, and now I cannot find it. I am sure your no good son took it!"

Alexander stormed out of his room before Jean could even say a word.

"Excuse me?" he asked. "I did not take anything from your filthy house. I cannot even believe you could find clean clothes in your house, much less your mother's watch. Me and my sister went to help you, not to take things from you. Who are you calling no good?"

"Alexander, calm down," his mother told him. "I will take care of this, you go and get dressed." She turned to Anna, "I can assure you that my kids would not take anything from your house. Alexander and Vanessa are very good, and honest, kids. They do not lie, or steal. That is not how I raised my kids, but if you believe they did, we can go through their pockets and see if they took your watch."

"Oh no you don't!" Vanessa said. "You will not go through our pockets. I do not care how good it will make her feel."

Vanessa gave Anna a dirty look, and looked back at her mother. "Mom, we did not, and will not, take anything from her. If she does not believe us, that is her problem."

"See? I think she took it," Anna said. "If she did not take it, then why would she have a problem going through her clothes?"

"Mrs. Anna," Vanessa said, "I would not take anything from your house, and tomorrow you can call your own kids to clean your house, because me and my brother will not be coming anymore."

"Fine," Anna said, "I am going to call my kids, and they

will be here in a minute. Don't think that I don't know what race you are."

"I do not need this!" Jean said. "I came here so I would not be threatened anymore. Get out of my house!" Before Anna could even say another word, Jean closed the door in her face.

Oh, she will pay for that, Anna thought to herself. I only wanted to scare her. I never even had a watch, but now I am going to find some thing that I can bother them with every day. They will buy me a new watch if I need them to. I know who they are, and what race they are. This is still my town. I am the only person that stayed here, and I will protect what is mine. She cannot tell me to get out of a house that is not really hers.

Jean was sitting at the table when Vanessa and Alexander came out ready to go.

"I am not saying either one you took anything, but if you even saw a watch, and maybe picked it up I need to know about it, now."

"Mom, there is no way you can even see the couch, much less a watch," Vanessa said. "It is all dirty with clothes all over the place. Her dishes were so nasty that it took us the whole time just to wash them. No one went near her couch. She is mad, because we did not finish her house, and we did not do her lawn."

"I guess don't worry about it. I am sure she will be back with something else in the morning," Jean told them. "Now you two go out and have fun. Don't stay passed your curfew or you don't get to go out next weekend. I am serious about it this time, Alexander."

"Why do you say it like it is only me?" Alexander asked. "It is not like Vanessa does not stay out passed her curfew, too."

They left the house a little after eight o'clock. It was later then they wanted, and it was all thanks to the witch that lived next to them. But they were going to forget about her tonight, and deal with her tomorrow. Who knew what else she would find missing in her house.

"We are going to Marina's house first," Vanessa told Alexander. "After that, can you please find your own friends to hang out with?"

"Wait, why are we going to her house? You know I do not like her, and everyone knows she hates me. Do I have to go?"

"Well, if you want to go home with me, you will. Otherwise, I can tell Mom I lost you, and I spent the whole night looking for you."

"Why are you such a witch?" Alexander asked. "All I want to do is have some fun. Why is it so hard for you to get along with me?"

"Maybe because you talk too much," Vanessa said. "Only talk when you are being talked to tonight. That is all I ask."

"That is going to be a little hard," Alexander told her.

They got to Marina's house, and knocked on the door. Marina was one of Vanessa's best friends, and she always took forever to get ready. Vanessa knew Marina was probably not ready, but she hoped she had at least started to get dressed. Marina opened the door, and the moment she saw Alexander, her face changed.

"Vanessa can't you ever go out by yourself?" she asked.

"Well, not this time," Alexander said. "Sorry to spoil your night, princess, but I am coming with her. I am going to stay with her most of the night, and if you try to get rid of me, I will tell my mom and she won't be able to go anywhere next week. Maybe even the week after that!"

"Jerk!" Marina said. "I remember why I don't like you, maybe because you talk too much."

"Sorry, but I am not a fan of you, either. If I were you, I would try to be nice to me, if you want to see your friend more then once a month."

"Fine," Marina said, "come on in. I am not ready to go yet."

"What's new?" Alexander asked. "Do you really need so much make up? I have news for you, if a guy really wants you, then he don't care what you look like. Not that any guy would want you."

"Vanessa, could you please tell your idiot brother to shut up? I do not want to hear him babbling anymore."

"Alexander, be quiet!" Vanessa told him.

"Yes, Mom," he said, and walked in after the girls.

Marina lived in a big house, with her parents and her older brother. He was very cute, but very taken by one of Vanessa's other friends, Amanda. Amanda always got what she wanted, when she wanted, and Vanessa hated her for that. Vanessa wanted the same things, but for some reason could never get them.

"Is Amanda here yet?" Vanessa asked Marina.

"What do you think?" she answered. "She has been here all day with my brother."

"Does her mother not ask where she is?" Vanessa asked. "Mine would send the police after me if I was not home right when she said."

"I know, tell me about it," Marina said. "All they did all day was stay in his room. They only came out to eat, and then went right back in."

"I wonder what they were doing," Alexander said, and made kissing sounds.

"None of your business. You are still a child," Marina told him. "You are what, two now? And probably still wearing diapers? What do you know?"

"Listen-" Alexander started to say, but Vanessa stopped him.

"Come on now guys if we want to go out and have fun, then you two need to stop."

"Fine," Alexander said, "I will be outside waiting. Don't take all night."

"Why does he always have to go?" Marina whined after

Alexander walked out. "You know none of our friends like him. They all make fun of you for it, too. I am almost ready, I just need a little more lipstick."

Vanessa never wore any make up, because she did not own any. Marina always made sure to put some on her, though. "You have to look good for all the guys that want you," she would tell Vanessa. She did not complain, she let Marina go ahead and experiment on her.

Marina was done, and they were not far down the hall when Darko's door opened, and Amanda came out half naked.

"Oh! I did not know you were here," she said without covering herself. "I am just going to the bathroom. We are going out, too. You guys should wait for us."

Vanessa was so stunned that she just stood there staring at her.

"Why don't we go?" Marina said, as she pulled Vanessa along with her. "I think Vanessa has seen a ghost, I should take her outside."

"Oh, alright," Amanda said. "I hope to see you at the disco! Don't wander around too much, I have someone that I want you to meet Vanessa."

As they walked out, Marina pinched Vanessa's arm.

"Ouch!" Vanessa cried. "What was that for?"

"What is wrong with you?" Marina asked her. "Haven't you ever seen a naked person before? You were just staring at Amanda!"

"Well, she was half naked in your hallway! I did not know what to say," Vanessa said.

"I know that, but you could have looked away. You were just staring at her like you had seen a ghost or something. Good lord, you act like you have never seen a naked person before."

"Who is naked?" Alexander asked.

"None of your business, little boy," Marina told him, "Let's go."

"You know, you keep calling me little boy. It makes me think you want me," Alexander said.

"Only in your dreams," Monica told him.

"Whatever," he said to her. "So who was naked?" he asked again. "And why is my sister so quiet?"

"She saw Amanda *half* naked, and she got scared. She just kept staring at her," Marina said.

"I did not get scared," Vanessa said defensively. "I guess I was just surprised. Look, it is already eight-thirty. We are never going to make it to the disco, and back home by midnight, if we keep standing here talking about Amanda. Let's go have some fun.

They walked to the disco quietly, each of them thinking to themselves. Wow, Vanessa thought, now I know what she was doing in his room all day. She was not even ashamed when she saw us! she just kept talking like she did not even see me. I wish I could be like that, and not get embarrassed about anything.

When they got to the club, it was full of people, smoke, and music. Even though Vanessa was only fifteen, and Alexander was thirteen, no one asked them for an id, so they just walked in. Inside it was too loud, so they had to walk back out. When they did, they almost ran over Darko and Amanda.

"Oh! Hey guys," Amanda said, "I was just going in to find you, Vanessa. I have someone I want you to meet."

"Who?" If it is your boyfriend, I've already met him, and I would gladly take him if you are giving him away, Vanessa thought to herself.

"This is Goran," Amanda said. "He is new to town, and I thought maybe you would like to show him around a little."

"Me?" Vanessa asked in shock. "I don't know where to go in this town, even though I have been here for a year. Why not Marina?"

"I see you are not interested," Goran said, "you are trying to pass me to Marina, now."

"I am not trying to pass you to anyone," Vanessa told him. "I am just saying that Marina knows a lot more about this town than me."

What are you trying to say? Just because I know some people, does not mean I know everyone," Marina said, and she walked back inside.

"Oh, no matter what I say it is never right," Vanessa said.

Goran knew Marina from Bosnia, and did not want to be around her that much, but he could use her to find out things about Vanessa, because it did not look like she would be saying much any time soon. He would make Marina tell him all he wanted to know about her friend, even if it took him all night.

"Are you going to talk to me?" Goran asked Vanessa. "Are you always this quiet?"

"Yes, I am around new people," she told him. "What would you like to talk about?"

"Well, that is more like it," Goran said. "How about where you live?"

"I live about fifteen minutes from here. We came here a year ago from Banja Luka, me, my mom, and my brother. How about you?"

"I live the same, but in the opposite direction than you," he told her. "I was Darko's and Marina's neighbor before. They got out before my family did. I came here just a month ago, with my mom, dad, and two brothers. Anything else you want to know?"

"I have a brother, too," Vanessa said. "His name is Alexander, and I wonder why he is not here right now. My mom won't let me go anywhere unless he goes, too. And he won't let me talk to anyone without him around. It is very embarrassing to say that, but that is how my life goes."

"It is okay, I am sure I will meat your brother soon," Goran said. "Do you think we should go inside, or should we stay here and let Marina and Amanda come and look for us?"

"That would be too much fun," Vanessa said, "but I do have to go look for my brother. I will see you later." With that, Vanessa walked inside.

That girl is very interesting, Goran thought. I have to find out more about her, but it looks she won't be telling me anything. I'll have to go to my one and only source, Marina.

Vanessa walked around looking for Alexander for over fifteen minutes, and could not find him. What was even more strange was that she could not find any of his friends, either. It only meant one thing--Alexander was somewhere getting himself in trouble. If Vanessa wanted to come out again next week, she would have to find him. Damn it, why did Goran have to show up? Usually Alexander was the one keeping an eye on his sister, now Vanessa was the one looking for him. Where could he be?

When she found him they would have to go straight home. It was already ten forty-five, and by the time they got home it would be passed Alexander's curfew. Where is that boy at, Vanessa wondered. She had looked everywhere, and now she was beginning to worry. She spotted one of Alexander's friends standing outside, but by the time she made it out there, he was gone, and Vanessa didn't know where to look next.

CHAPTER SEVENTEEN

WHILE VANESSA WAS GOING CRAZY looking for her brother, he and two friends, Jacob and Joseph, were walking up the hill to the old witch's house. No one would say that Alexander took something from them if he did not. He wanted to go talk to the witch all night, but he did not want to do it alone. And as long as his sister and his mother did not know where he was he would be okay.

"So she said you took her watch?" Jacob asked. "Are you sure your sister did not take it?"

"Dude, my sister would not do that. No matter what anyone did to her. You know Vanessa, she gets scared if someone says her name wrong. Imagine if the police were looking for her because of a stupid watch."

"Well, you never know. Your sister is so quiet, and those are the worst ones. They are like snakes, and when they bite you, then you die."

"My sister is not that bad," Alexander said. "I can handle her, but I cannot, however, handle my mom yelling at me. We will have to be very quiet, and no one must know about this."

"I won't say word," Joseph said.

"I won't either," Jacob added.

They walked up the hill, and saw a light. The old witch was still up.

"This won't be easy," Alexander told his friends. "Since she is still up, make sure you don't show yourselves, or she will make our lives a living hell."

The boys walked up to the house, and peeked through a window. Anna was sitting on her couch watching television. She was not really paying attention to the show, because she had the strange feeling that she was being watched. She looked out the window, but she did not see anyone. The feeling she was being watched did not go away.

Oh well, she thought, who ever is outside will knock on the door if they really want to come in. Anna had lived by herself for way too long to be afraid of anything. She learned long ago, if someone wants to break in, they will do it. No matter what locks you have on your door. But the feeling was not going away, she got up, went to the window, and peeked outside.

"Get down!" Alexander whispered. "She is coming to the window!"

They laid in the grass, and barely breathed, while Anna looked out the window.

"Hmm," she said, "no one out there. I am just going to bed." Anna turned off the tv, and walked to her room. The feeling she had earlier still did not go away. She put on her robe on and locked the room.

"I bet it is just some rotten kids trying to scare poor, old me," Anna said to herself. She laid down in bed and listened carefully for noises from outside. She heard nothing.

"It don't matter who is out there," she said. "I am going to sleep." She touched the gun under her pillow. This will protect me, or kill me, she thought.

The boys were still laying in the grass when the light in Anna's bedroom turned off.

"I thought she would never go to sleep," Alexander said. "Now let's go have some fun!"

"Dude, she is not sleeping yet, and I heard she has a gun. I am not sure I want to go through with your plan," Joseph told him.

"Then why did you come with us?" Alexander asked. "You knew what we were going to do."

"I did not think you would go through with it!" Joseph said. "I see now that you will, so I am out of here."

"Let him go," Jacob said, "we can do this without him."

"Yeah, but all of us came here to do this together," Alexander said. "He is going to tell on us."

"No he won't" Jacob said. "I will make him cry like a baby if he does."

"Never mind let's just go. We'll do this some other time."

"Are you forgetting that she lied about you today? She said you stole a watch from her," Jacob said.

"Dude, you do not have to remind me, I already know," Alexander said. "I am just not so sure we should scare her right now. Since Joseph left, our plan would not work anyways. Let's go and come back next week. Maybe this way she won't know it's us, because it will be a while after she accused me of stealing her watch."

The boys walked to Alexander's house, and he looked at his watch.

"Oh, it is eleven now. I am so good, and not grounded," Alexander said.

"What about Vanessa?" Jacob asked. "What will happen to her?"

"Well, that is where you come in," Alexander told him. "You are going back right?"

"Yeah, so?"

"You could tell her you walked me home."

"Why would I do that? What makes you think she will believe me, anyways?" Joseph asked him.

"My sister believes my friends," Alexander told him. "Just tell her what I told you, and everything will be fine, believe me." then he turned and walked in the house.

"Great," Jacob said to himself, "what did I get myself into?" He walked down the street, and when he spotted someone walking towards him, he froze.

Vanessa had looked everywhere for her brother, now she had to get home and tell her mom that she could not find him. She had already forgotten that she had met Goran tonight. If Alexander was home she was going to personally kill him. She had wanted to stay at the club with her friends and not think about my brother.

She was on her way, when she saw someone walking towards her. She kept walking, and so did the other person. She could not tell if it was a guy or a girl, or if it was a grown up or a child. Vanessa was hoping it was just someone going out. When she got a little closer, she could see that it was Jacob, one her brother's friends.

"What are you doing, walking down this way?" she asked. "Have you seen my brother? Please, tell me you have."

"Slow down!" Jacob told her. "Your bother is safe, I walked him home. We had some fun, but he said he had to be home before eleven, so I walked with him. We saw that you were busy with that new guy, so we did not bother you."

"Oh crap," Vanessa said, and blushed.

"You don't have anything to be scared of," he told her. "I know you were thinking your brother would not see you, but he did. Since me and Joseph were with him, we left you alone. Aren't you glad we are his friends?"

"Where is Joseph?" she asked. "I thought you said he was with you."

"What is this, twenty questions? I am late, and I have to

go home. Good night, Vanessa. Talk to you later." Jacob passed by her and continued walking.

Something is up, Vanessa thought. Why would he take Alexander home? He never goes home without me, and he is always interested in anyone I meet. Something is not right, but I will find out what it is. Then, I am going to hurt him for making me worry so much.

Vanessa walked in the house, and Alexander was sitting at the table eating, with a big grin on his face. Seeing his sister when she walked in the house was worth waiting for. She looked like she was going to kill him, but she walked passed and went to her room.

Vanessa was changing when she heard a light knocking on her window. It scared her. Who could be knocking on her window at this time? Vanessa was wondering if she should open the window, or just wait until they went away. But her secret visitor was not going away. Instead they knocked a little louder. Vanessa worried that it might wake up her mom, or might attract Alexander, so she opened the window. To her surprise, Goran was standing there looking as beautiful as ever. It was raining outside, but that did not stop him from coming and knocking on her window.

"What are you doing here?" she asked, half to herself.

"You left without saying good night, so I had to come and say good night to you."

"How did you know where I live?" Vanessa asked him.

"Darko told me. I did not want to come to the door, because I did not know how your mom would feel about that."

"Good thing you did not," Vanessa said. "Now, I am saying my good night and want you to leave. If my mom or my brother hear that you are here they are going to eat you alive!"

"Okay, but can I get a good night kiss?" Goran asked.

Vanessa had never kissed a boy before, and she did not know how to, either. when she was little, she and Lidia always talked about kissing boys. Which Lidia had probably tried many times by now.

Goran looked confused when Vanessa leaned down, and gave him a peck on his cheek.

"Now you can go," she told him. "I gave you your good night kiss."

"No," Goran said, "that was a friend kiss, like you would kiss your brother. Let me show you a good night kiss." He pulled her down to him, their eyes locked, and everything around them disappeared. Vanessa did not think it was possible, but even the rain seemed to slow down.

Goran's lips touched Vanessa's and she jumped. She let go of her thoughts and it was as if she were not there anymore. She could hear Goran breathing very slowly, and then as the kiss got deeper his heart pounded louder. The kiss only lasted a couple minutes, but it seeed like forever to Vanessa. She did not want it to end. It felt amazing and warm on her lips. Lidia was right, it felt like nothing else she had ever experienced, but at that moment, Goran pulled away, still looking into Vanessa's eyes.

"Well, that was some kiss," he said finally. "I knew you could do better than just a peck." Goran smiled at her.

He is gorgeous, Vanessa thought, and a lot of trouble.

"Okay, you got your kiss, now you have to go," she told him. "My mom will wake up if she hears any noise, and I am surprised that Alexander is not in the room already."

"When can I see you again?" Goran asked.

"I might go out tomorrow, I have to see what my mom says. My mom is nothing like Marina's mom. She won't let me out if she even thinks you are in the picture."

"Well, make sure you don't tell her," Goran said. "I will wait for you tomorrow at the same place, at the same time. If you are late, I will come knocking on your window again. I will miss you." Goran walked away.

Oh wow, what a night, Vanessa thought. She almost forgot she was mad at her brother. She will have to wait until morning to tell him how mad she was. Not only did the kiss calm her down, it did something inside her that she had never felt before. Vanessa had never been kissed before, and she wondered if Goran was that good with all girls. It made her uneasy to think about it.

Vanessa told herself tonight she would think about the kiss and nothing more. As she fell asleep she could see Goran's gorgeous brown eyes winking at her. Soon she was dreaming.

She was at her house waiting for someone, but she did not know who. There were very loud noises outside, she went to see what it was. But it was so dark outside whatever or whoever was making the noise was not clear to her. Then she felt a hand on the small of her back. She slowly turned around and found Goran. He was standing and staring at her. There was anger in his eyes, but she did not know why. He tried to explain it to her, but she could only see his mouth moving. No sound was coming out of it.

She started to scream at him, now she was angry, too. She sensed someone else in the room with them, someone who should not be there. Vanessa turned and saw Marina by the door, smiling. She was grinning and talking to Goran, Vanessa could not hear what they were saying.

Marina walked very slowly to Goran, took his hand, and put it to her cheek. Vanessa was not able to move, even though she wanted to very badly. it was like someone was holding her back. Marina waived to Vanessa, and then disappeared with Goran.

Vanessa woke up kicking and screaming. She was so loud that Jean heard her in the other room. Jean ran to Vanessa, and so did Alexander. When Vanessa saw her mom and her brother, she knew it was just a dream. She also knew not to say anything about last night, because that would just upset her mom.

"I am okay," she said. "I just had a bad nightmare."

"Well try to sleep some more," Jean told her, and walked back to her room. Alexander looked at his sister, gave her a little smile, and walked out, too.

She could not go back to sleep. Every time she closed her eyes, Goran and Marina were there in front of her, holding hands. What does that mean, she wondered. Marina introduced us, and if she wanted Goran to herself, she would never have told me about him. It was three in the morning, and she knew she had to be up to feed and milk the cows and, so she had to go back to sleep.

She woke up to her alarm clock, and touched her lips. It felt like Goran's kiss was still there. She could still smell him, and see his wonderful bright smile.

"Who cares about the dream?" Vanessa asked herself. "I am going to make sure Mom lets me out again tonight, so he don't have to wait for me." Vanessa got dressed, and as usual her brother was still sleeping.

Her regular chores were to feed the cows and milk them, to give the pigs their food, and to make sure all the chickens were fed too. But this morning she wanted to do extra, she made coffee for her mom, and was very quiet when she left the house. It was a little after nine when she got back inside, and every one was still sleeping. She wondered if she should wake her mom, or just leave her be and go on with the rest of the chores.

Jean woke to the smell of coffee, and got dressed. She wanted to let Vanessa sleep in since she had such a rough night, but it was too late. Her daughter was up and about getting all her chores done. It was Saturday, and that was what Vanessa always did so she could go out. Alexander was still sleeping like he had no worries in the world, and Vanessa was washing dishes when Jean walked in the kitchen.

"Morning," Jean said. "I see you got up early, and got all the chores done. You must have a date tonight.

"I don't know what you are talking about," Vanessa said. "I am trying to help you, so you don't have to do it all by yourself. If I was lazy, like my brother, then I would not have done anything."

"Why are you people up so early?" Alexander asked, walking into the kitchen.

"Maybe because it is already ten o'clock," Jean answered. "And maybe because the cows and other animals cannot wait until *you* are done sleeping to eat." Alexander looked to see if Vanessa was still mad at him. He knew she was mad because he left without her. Good thing she did not know where he went.

"What is on your mind, Alexander?" Jean asked.

"Nothing! Why?"

"Maybe, because your face looks like you did something wrong," Jean answered.

"I don't know what you are talking about."

Alexander was trying his hardest not to look suspicious. So his mom and sister would not know something was going on, he got up and went to take a shower. Maybe they would forget about it.

"Mom, were you up when we got home?" Alexander heard Vanessa ask as he walked away.

"I was up when Alexander came home," she said, "but I did not hear you come in. Did you two get separated somewhere?"

"I was with my friends. I don't know where Alexander was." It was not easy for Vanessa to lie to her mother. She would have to find out how Alexander got home before her.

CHAPTER EIGHTEEN

ANNA WOKE UP EARLY, AND went out to look for signs of anyone at to her house last night. There was a reason she did not want her yard clean, and she did not have anyone to do it for her, anyway. She walked to her window. Where it looked like there were shoe prints, and the grass was messed up.

I wonder what they wanted, Anna thought to herself. Maybe I will make my way down to Jean's house. she might know something, or maybe heard who was there. Anna went inside to get ready. She wanted those rotten kids to come over and clean her house again, too. She knew Jean would make them, no matter if they wanted to or not. The girl was okay, but that boy of hers! She did not like him and did not try to hide it, either.

Maybe today when they came over, after her house was clean, then he could help her with the yard. If he didn't help, then she would tell his mom about her watch again. Anna did not like lying, but she would to make sure her house was clean. She walked to Jean's house, and did not see anyone outside, or hear any noises from inside.

Anna looked all over, but it looked like no one was home. Where could they be at ten in the morning? She walked back home, and vowed not to move from her window. As soon as she saw them come home, she would be back so those rotten kids could help her.

Vanessa was getting ready to go to the store when she saw Anna coming. As soon as she spotted her, she told her mom, and they hid in her bedroom. They hoped that Alexander wouldn't come out of the shower, letting Anna know they were home. After yesterday, Vanessa did not want to even think about Anna's house, much less go there to help her again. Vanessa had more important things to do at home. Alexander was finally done with his shower and dressed, now they only had to get out without Anna seeing them.

Alexander walked out first, and looked around. He did not see anyone so Vanessa and Jean came out, too. Half way down the driveway, they heard Anna yell.

"Where are you guys going?"

"So close," Alexander whispered.

"We have to go shopping," Jean answered. "We'll be back later."

"Well don't take all day," Anna called. "I have to have my house clean, too."

"Well, then clean it," Alexander said.

"Alexander, stop that!" Jean yelled at him. "Keep walking, and don't think about her. "We'll be back soon," Jean yelled to Anna, and waved to her.

Anna was mad now. Not only did she not catch them coming out of the house, but they were home when she knocked and did not open the door for her. Anna walked back inside her house to wash the dishes herself. Maybe cleaning my own house is not such a bad idea, she thought. She would clean her house, then call those rotten kids over to see that her house could be clean without their help.

As she was about to wash a glass, someone knocked on her window. It took her by surprise, and she dropped the glass. It broke all over the floor. Great, Anna thought, now there is more cleaning for me to do. She went out to see who it was, but there was no one there. She was beginning to think either someone was playing games with her, or she was going crazy. She walked back inside to clean up the glass.

Anna was afraid of blood and she did not want to cut herself, so she just left it all over the kitchen floor. She would blame it on the kids when they got there. Instead, she sat down to watch tv.

She suddenly saw a shadow on her wall that was not hers. It looked like there was someone at her window again. It did not look like an adult, it looked like a small child. Anna pretended she did not see anything and got up to go to the kitchen. She walked quickly to the door to find out who was playing in her yard. Why didn't they knock on her door?

As she walked out, she saw little Joe running away from her house. Little Joe was a good child. He was one of the kids Anna liked, she was surprised to see him run away. She wondered what his parents were going to say when she went over to ask what was he doing in her yard. But Anna walked inside her house to finish her show, maybe she would go later.

Anna was not going to forget her broken glass, someone would have to pay for it. She was sorry that someone would be little Joe, but he had to get what he deserved. Joe was only eleven and he was Anna's favorite child. He was always there to help her, even when she did not ask for it. It was sad for her to think he would come and knock on her window, but he would not go inside.

Her show was over, and Anna was about to go see little Joe's parents, when he knocked on her door. It scared her, but she managed to yell, "Come in!"

Joe walked in, and saw all the glass. "What happened?" he asked.

"Well, when you knocked on my window, I dropped the glass and it broke. Can you pick it up? I am afraid I will cut myself. What are you doing here?"

"I am sorry," Joe said. "I was scared that maybe someone else was here, and I did not want to come in."

"So you knock on my window, and then run away? It don't matter, just please get the glass off my floor."

While Joe was helping Anna take care of the glass, Alexander was shopping with his mom and sister. It was nice outside after last night's rain. They were just getting a few things for the house. Alexander was jealous that most of his friends always had what ever they wanted, but he did not. For some reason, today it did not bother Vanessa. She was in a happy mood, and Alexander wondered why she was up way so early. She had all the chores done before he even got up, and did not ask for any help. What happened last night that his sister was in such a good mood?

They were looking at meats when Goran walked in, and when Vanessa saw him her face turned bright red. Now I see why my sister is in a good mood, Alexander thought. Goran looked at Vanessa, and gave her a little wink before he walked out. Jean noticed it, but she did not say anything.

"So when were you around Goran?" Alexander asked on the way home.

"If you were there last night, you would have seen it," Vanessa told him sharply.

"So really, Alexander, why did you come home before your sister?" Jean asked. "I thought I told you both to stay together."

"I have friends, too," Alexander said. "I don't always have to be her dog."

Well that was a first Vanessa thought. But she saw that Alexander's face had turned red. There was more to it than him wanting to be with his friends.

Alexander was trying to think of answers, but he knew

if he kept talking, his mom would figure out what he was up to, and wouldn't let him out again. He wanted to scare Anna again for lying about the watch.

"Alexander and Vanessa," Jean said, "I can see that you are both trying to hide something. I am going to find out what that is, even if I have to wait. But just so you know, when the truth comes out, you are going to be grounded. Now, we are done talking about it. Let's get home and try to get inside so Anna don't see us right away."

Both Vanessa and Alexander knew that their mom was right. When there was a secret they could never keep it up from her long. And when she did find out, she really would ground them.

They walked home, and made it inside the house unnoticed. It was a big relief that they did not have to go and work for the old witch. They put the groceries away, and sat down to watch tv before they had to go and tend to the animals. The three of them wondered why Anna didn't see them come home.

Maybe something happened to her, Alexander thought with a smile. He did not like her before she lied about the watch, now he really hated her. Maybe she wouldn't bother them anymore, and she would leave them alone.

———————

Marina was in her room cleaning, and thinking about going out that night. She did not bother her brother, because his girlfriend was still there. When she was there, her bother never came out of his room. What did they do all day in his room?

Marina and Darko were not close, but they did not fight, either. Many times Marina wished she could be like her brother, but she more wished she could be like his girlfriend, and have her own boyfriend and never be home. A knock on the door woke her up from her thoughts, and she jumped.

"Come in," she called.

Goran walked in and looked around.

"Where is your brother?" he asked. Goran was her brother's friend but she did not mind his company. She liked him to stay in her room and talk to her once in a while, but as long as Darko was home that was not going to happen.

"He is in the room with Amanda, he's been there all day," Marina told him.

"I will just go and bother them, then," Goran said.

"Before you go, there is something I want to talk to you about," Marina said looking at him. She really liked his brown eyes, and his nice arms.

Goran stopped in his tracks, turned around and looked at her. He had an idea that Marina liked him, but she was his best friend's sister. You don't go after your buddy's sister. Goran and Darko had been friends since Banja Luka. They had been together in many shelters running, from the people that tried to killed them.

"What would you like to talk to me about?" Goran asked.

He sat on the other couch, facing Marina. She was a very attractive girl, and any guy would be happy to talk to her. She had gorgeous, green eyes and blonde hair to her shoulders. She always wore jeans that were a little too tight for her body, but Goran thought, if the girl liked that, then there was no reason that he could not.

"I saw you talking to Vanessa last night," Marina said.

"Yes, I was, she is a very cool girl. I had fun with her, I just hope she gets to come out again tonight."

"I am not sure she was going to," Marina said.

"How do you know? Have you talked to her?" That took Goran by surprise. He saw Vanessa at the store, and wanted to ask her if she would be out that night, but he did not want to get her in trouble with her mom.

"I just know how her mom is," Marina said. "She doesn't

get to go out every night, like we do. She has to work and earn it." Marina walked over to Goran, and sat next to him. He froze. He was not afraid of her, but he was afraid of what might happen to him if Darko was to walk in the room. Marina touched his hand, and Goran jumped like she hit him.

"I am sorry," he said. "Marina, you are a very attractive girl. I would be the luckiest person ever if I was with you, but we both know that Darko is my best friend, and you just don't date your friend's sister." Goran stood up and walked out. That went well, she thought. Next time I won't let you get out easy, Goran.

Goran knocked on Darko's door and did not even wait for him to answer. He walked in, and he wished he hadn't. Amanda was struggling to cover herself, and Darko was smiling.

"What the hell Goran?" Amanda yelled. "Don't you wait until someone tells you to come in?"

"No, I don't," Goran said. "I didn't think you would be naked in the middle of the day, either." He walked to Darko and gave him a high five.

"Dude, you really should have waited," Darko said after Amanda slapped him hard on his chest. Darko and Goran were friends, but Darko was the one to have girls with him all the time and Goran was one waiting for the right woman.

While Amanda tried to stay covered up, Darko and Goran talked about the events the night before. Goran told them about meeting Vanessa, and how he thought she was gorgeous and wanted to going out with her.

"Oh come on," Amanda said, "you don't think you can find anyone better than that?" Amanda knew Vanessa way before Goran did. They had lived together, and she claimed to be her friend, but she did not like Vanessa's brother.

Darko must have heard her thoughts. "You know Goran, if you want to have her in your bed all day, like me and Amanda are, then you will have to bribe her brother away. I hear he is always with her."

"He did not bother us last night," Goran told them. "And no, I don't want to have her in my bed all day. Even though that would be nice, I just met the girl, and I don't think like you do."

"Suit yourself," Darko said, "but I think this is life." He leaned over to kiss Amanda, who was still lying in bed.

"So you are going to ask her out tonight?" Amanda asked with arrogance in her voice.

"What is it to you, if I go out with her or not?" Goran asked her.

"It's not," she answered. "I just know that if you want sex, you are going after the wrong girl."

"And what makes you think I am like that?" Goran asked. "I want her to get to know me, not my bed. And I want to be with her. Not that the bed is a bad idea, but I like her for who she is. I can find a girl for one night all over this place." Goran walked to the door.

"Oh by the way, Amanda," he said, "your brother was looking for you last night. I told him you were with Darko, and he was not surprised. He was asking everyone if they saw you. Have you even gone home?"

"No, my mom knows where I am," she said.

"Well, I am going home. When I came back, you two better be dressed, too," Goran said and left.

"He is crazy if he thinks Vanessa will go for him," Amanda said. "She is so quiet, and stubborn, he doesn't know what he is in for."

"Why don't you let him find that out himself?" Darko asked. "And maybe you should go home, if Ivan was looking for you. I would not want your mom or dad to find you in bed with me."

Amanda went to the bathroom to get dressed. She heard voices from Marina's room. She did not want to go inside, but she wanted to know who Marina was talking to. When she walked a little closer, she heard Vanessa.

"His kiss felt so good to me."

There was something Goran forgot to mention to me and Darko, Amanda thought. She leaned closer so she could hear more.

"Why did you go home with out him?" Marina asked.

"I was worried about Alexander," Vanessa told her. "It was too hard for me to ask Goran to take me home, so I just went by myself. But when I got home, he knocked on my window. He kissed me, and I thought I would melt in his hands. His hands were rubbing my back and it felt so good. When his hands moved lower down my back I thought, oh wow, Goran, you have not even finished with the top part, why you are in such a hurry to get to the bottom?"

Amanda was done listening. This girl is stupid, she thought. Just because his hands were on her back did not mean that he was going to bed with her. She walked to the bathroom, got dressed and was going back to Darko's room when Vanessa and Marina came out.

"Where are you two going?" Amanda asked.

"We are going to eat," Marina said. "I am not sure what you are still doing here, but since I am sure you were with my brother all day and night I won't even ask."

"Better for you," Amanda said, and walked in Darko's room.

"Was that Marina?" Darko asked when Amanda sat down.

"Yes it was. And guess who was with her. It was Goran's girl, and while she was talking to Marina. I was listening. I told her he hardly even kissed her yet, but wanted to sleep with her."

"I don't think Goran would do that," Darko said, "but I will ask him when I see him. We are all going to be here at my house tonight.

To Marina's surprise, Vanessa talked the whole time they

were eating. Usually Vanessa didn't talk much, but today she was just a chatterbox.

"So do you think he likes me?" Vanessa asked.

"He kissed you, didn't he? That means something," Marina told her. She was not a jealous person, but maybe that was the reason Goran jumped this morning when he talked to her. Marina was better looking than Vanessa, she thought to herself. Vanessa was her friend, and Marina had known Goran way longer, but Vanessa had already kissed him. That was something she would change tonight, she thought.

"You know we are all going to be at my house tonight," Marina said.

"Yes, I know. You told me last night," Vanessa told her. Vanessa thought maybe Marina wanted her to shut up about Goran, and talk about something else. But what was more important than the one guy she kissed? He was her first, and she wanted to share it with her friend. Who else can she tell other than Marina? But talking to her made Vanessa think that her friend might have feelings for Goran, too. Every time Vanessa said Goran's name, Marina would flinch. Walking home from Marina's house, Vanessa thought of how Amanda could stay at Darko's all night and not get in trouble. She wanted to be the same, but then that would mean her mom did not care. Vanessa's mom cared a little too much at times. She heard footsteps behind her, and when she turned around, Amanda was right next to her.

"Do you hear when people call you?" She asked.

"Sorry I did not hear you, I was thinking."

"Thinking about Goran a little too much, aren't we?" Amanda teased.

"How did you know I was thinking about him?" Vanessa asked.

Amanda forgot that she was not in the conversation between Vanessa and Marina, and now she had to explain how she knew about Goran. What better way than to lie?

"I talked to Goran today," she said. "And he was telling me and Darko that he was kissing you last night."

"I don't see why he would go and brag about that," Vanessa said. "It is not like we were kissing all night, it was only one kiss."

"Well, that one kiss must have been good, when you cannot even hear someone calling your name. Come on, I am your friend too. Tell me about it," Amanda urged her.

"I'd rather not," Vanessa told her. "I don't want this thing to turn into something that might not even happen. I am not sure why everyone always thinks they can get into my business. I will have a word with Goran to see why he would go around and brag to people."

"Why are you so arrogant?" Amanda asked. "I have been with Darko for almost a year, and I don't see why you would blame a guy for talking to his friends. I think it would be better if you don't say anything to him. If you do that just might upset him."

"Upset *him*? And if I am upset, who cares right?"

"I don't see why you would be upset. He did not tell your mom or your brother, because that could be bad. Everyone knows about your mom and brother, how protective they are." Amanda was now trying to cover her lie. If she did not, Vanessa would tell Goran, and he would be mad at her. Not that Amanda really cared about him, but she cared about Darko, and those two were really good friends.

"Fine," Vanessa said when she got to her house, "I won't say anything to him, but if this happens anymore I am not going to talk to him at all."

"Thank you," Amanda said, and walked back to her own house.

Not only did they not pay attention behind them, but they did not see Emily who was planning to break up Goran and Vanessa, and to make Vanessa think it was Amanda fault. Emily was not friends with either of the girls, but she liked

Vanessa least because she wore her shoes when they were living together, and she kind of liked Goran. Not that he was going to pay any attention to her, but Vanessa did not need to be with him, either.

Amanda was just full of herself, and never thought anyone was as good as she was. Everyone in town knew that Amanda and Darko were dating, you could always see them walking hand in hand. They did not cover it one bit. The kids were in love, the only problem was Emily did not have any one to be with.

She would definitely see that Vanessa and Goran did not take things far. She saw the kiss that happened last night outside of Vanessa's window, and thought about going and talking to Jean. For now, Emily was going to find Goran and talk with him. Maybe after that, she could talk to Darko and see if she could make a deal to be over at Darko's house tonight. It would be so great to see Vanessa's face when her plan came to life.

Emily walked inside, and called Darko. On the third ring he picked up.

"Hello," Darko said.

"Hey, it is Emily," she said. "What are you doing?"

"Emily who?" He knew who she was, he did not think she would ever call him. He did not like the girl, and he did not want to have anything to do with her.

"Oh come on Darko!" she said. "You have known me for as long as we have been in this town! Why do you always talk to me like this?"

"Like what?" he asked. "Like I don't like you, and I don't want anything to do with you? Well, let me tell you, I don't like girls that only go after guys that have money, and you are one of them. Your sister and your mother are nothing better. So just to make myself clear, I really don't want anything to do with you!" Before she could even say anything, he hung up!

"Oh, some men!" Emily said. "I might just have to break

up him and Amanda, too. If not tonight, I will make it happen soon."

But her first worry was Goran, and she was going to find him, and see what she could say that would make him not want Vanessa. Then she remembered Marina. She would call Marina and see if she would invite her over to the house. She tried calling her, but she did not answer the phone. So Emily went straight to Marina's house. When she did not find anyone at home, she went back to her own house to make a plan. It didn't have to be at Darko's house but it would work. Oh boy was she going to make trouble, not only would Vanessa hate Amanda, now she would hate Marina, too.

CHAPTER NINETEEN

"ALEXANDER!" YOU COULD HEAR JEAN yell down the street.

When Alexander walked in he knew why she was yelling, and he tried to think of a plan fast. His friend, Joe, and Anna were standing in the kitchen talking to his mom. He tried to play cool for now, but he was going to have a long talk with his friend later.

"What?" he asked. "Why are you calling me, and why are you yelling?"

"Joe told Anna that you guys were underneath her window last night. Do you have anything to say for yourself?" Jean asked.

"I was never with Joe," Alexander answered. "I was with Josh, and I don't know why Joe would say I was with him."

Joe looked like he was going to pass out. His cheeks were red, and his eyes were half shut, his mouth was turning blue, and he was shaking. Anna standing next to him looked like she wanted to eat Alexander.

"Joe?" Jean turned to the boy. "I don't know why you would tell Anna that Alexander was there, if he was not. I am not sure what is really going on here, but Anna I assure you that Alexander will be punished for all this." Before Alexander could say anything, she added, "After I talk to Josh.

"I am sorry you were scared last night," Jean said. "I am sure it was horrible, but I really have to get my house cleaned. The kids won't be able to come and help you today, because there is so much that has to be done here."

"Not even when they are done here?" Anna asked.

"No, Anna, my kids are not slaves. If they have to work at our house, they don't have to work at yours. Have a great day," Jean told her and opened the door for her to leave.

"You did not cook any food today?" Anna asked.

"Yes, I did, but we already ate lunch, so there is nothing left. Sorry."

Anna walked out with Joe, who was still shaking.

"Joe, are you sure what you told me was truth? I do not mind Alexander getting beat, but I just want to make sure you are still my favorite kid."

"Yes, Anna, it is true. I don't know why he lied, but I am sure Josh will be on my side."

"I hope so," Anna said and they walked away.

When they were left alone, Jean turned to her son and looked at him.

"Alexander, even if you were there, and Josh tells me you were, there is something in your eyes that tells me you are lying. This is not over yet. Now go and get ready, so we can feed the animals.

They walked out where Vanessa was already cleaning after the animals and getting ready to milk the cows. Vanessa was in a strange mood today, too, Jean thought. Ever since they got back from the store, she had bean working nonstop. That was nothing new, but normally Jean still had to tell her which things had to be done, but not today. It must mean she wanted to go out again.

"Vanessa!" Jean called out to her. "I want tot talk to you. Come inside!"

Oh great, Vanessa thought, now what have I done? She walked in and saw Alexander's face was red, and his eyes were looking straight at her. He was trying to tell her something, but she was not sure what.

"Do you remember why you came home alone last night?" Jean asked.

"Because Alexander was with Josh, and when I saw Josh going home from here, he told me the same thing."

"Okay, that is all I wanted to know," And just as Vanessa turned around to walk out, Jean asked, "Why have you been slaving all day?"

"I have not," Vanessa said, "I am just doing things that need to be done, so I can-"

"Go out," Jean finished for her.

"Yes, go out," Vanessa said.

"You know you don't have to be a slave just to be able to go with your friends," Jean told her. "All I ask is that your chores are done before you leave."

"Yes, Mom," Vanessa said.

"What's up with mom?" she asked Alexander when he joined her.

"I have no idea. Anna and Joe were here little bit ago," Alexander said.

"I heard Mom yelling at you. Did you do something wrong last night?"

"No I did not. I came home with Josh. When mom asks him, then she will know that Joe was lying."

"Alexander, why would he lie?" Vanessa asked. "He is your friend, or at least I thought he was. I did see all three of you hang out last night. Either you are lying, or something funny is going on."

As Vanessa and Alexander were finishing up their chores, and the sun was beginning to set, Amanda came over to see if Vanessa was going out to Darko's tonight.

"You know who is going to be there, right?" Amanda said, teasing Vanessa.

"Who?" Vanessa asked, knowing Amanda was thinking

of Goran. Just because Vanessa knew he was going to be there, did not mean she had to go.

"Goran, dummy," Amanda told her. "I have something to give you." And she handed Vanessa a letter.

The letter was addressed to her, so she opened it. She had to sit down to read it. She read some of it, and glanced over to Amanda. She wore a smile that meant trouble, and Vanessa knew, even though the letter said that it was from Darko, it was not. She read the letter, but she did not have to play along.

Dear Vanessa,

I did not know how to tell you this before but I am very attracted to you, and I would like to know if you would go out with me. The reason Amanda is the one giving you this letter, is because we broke up and she knew that I liked you. Many nights when I am making love to Amanda, I think of you and I would love it if you can come to my party tonight.

Always,
Your Darko

Vanessa looked over at Amanda and thought to herself, I know your game little girl. There is no way in hell that Darko would ever send you to ask me to go out with him, but I will play along with your little game.

"I am almost ready to go," Vanessa said.

"You are going to Darko's party?" Amanda asked, panic in her eyes.

"Yes, I am going. Didn't you read the letter? It said for me to come, and I am going." Vanessa knew that it was not Darko's handwriting. The letter was Amanda's doing so Vanessa would stay home, and not see Goran tonight.

Why was it so important to others if she was going out with Goran, or not? Why couldn't they live their lives, and let Vanessa live hers? Not only did Marina act weird about

Vanessa going out with Goran, but now so was Amanda? What does Goran have over these girls?

It did not matter, she was going out tonight, and she was going to dress to impress. She put her jacket on, so her mother would not see what she was wearing, and they left the house. Alexander did not go out, he stayed home waiting for Josh, and he needed to talk to their mom anyway.

"You look good," Amanda told Vanessa.

"Thank you," Vanessa said. "I feel good tonight, too. Mom said I can stay out longer since I did all my chores today."

Amanda was very quiet the whole way to Darko's house. Vanessa knew why, so she did not ask. Many times when Vanessa would say something about Goran, Amanda rolled her eyes, so Vanessa decided to be as quiet as Amanda. She did not care if Amanda talked or not, she was better off listening to the birds singing, than to Amanda telling her how Goran was so wrong for her.

"Vanessa," Amanda said suddenly, surprising her.

"Hmm?" Vanessa was thinking of kissing Goran in front of everyone that night.

"I have to tell you something, and I hope you don't hate me." Here it comes, Vanessa thought.

"Go ahead, I don't know why I would hate you," Vanessa said. "I know it is not me that Darko broke up with you for.

"We did not break up," Amanda said. "I made it all up. I wrote you that note thinking maybe you would not come to the party tonight."

"Why? Why is it so important for me not to go?"

"Groan is like a brother to me," she said, "and I don't want to see him hurt. He does not know how your mom is, but we all do. When he wants to see you, and your mom does not let you go, it will hurt him. And I cannot stand to see him hurt."

"I thought you said the note was from Darko, not from Goran."

"I know you don't like Darko, so I wrote it thinking that it might make you not want to go" Amanda told her.

Think again, Vanessa thought, but she did not say anything to her. They made it to Darko's house, and there were people already there. Vanessa walked away from Amanda, and went to find Marina. Maybe *she* wouldn't give her a hard time about seeing Goran tonight.

When she knocked on Marina's door, there were noises coming from inside and the door was locked. That had never happened before, her door was always open. Vanessa waited for Marina to open the door, and when she finally did, Vanessa was sorry she even knocked. Marina's shirt was all messed up, and Amanda's brother, Ivan, was trying to zip up his pants. Vanessa looked at both of them and giggled.

"What's so funny?" Ivan asked. "I am sure you have seen a man zipping up his pants?"

"I don't think I really want to," Vanessa said.

Marina pulled Vanessa into the hallway, and pushed her towards the bathroom.

"Why are you pushing me?" Vanessa asked. "I have not said anything but the truth. You already know how I feel about him!"

"Yes, I know!" Marina said. "Will you please not saying anything to anyone about me and Ivan? I don't care if they know, but I don't want him to feel uncomfortable tonight."

"Don't worry," said Vanessa. "Why would I say anything? It is not like you did not tell me that I talk to much about Goran."

"I am sorry. What you and Goran do is your business."

"And did you just figure that out, or was it because you need me to keep my mouth shut?"

"Vanessa, I know how Goran is, and I don't want to see him hurt."

"Why does every one think I am going to hurt Goran?

What if Goran hurts me?" Vanessa asked and walked out of the bathroom, almost knocking Darko on his ass.

"Sorry!" Vanessa said. "I did not mean to run you over."

"It is okay," Darko said, and flashed her one of his smiles. He looked good, but he smelled even better.

"Have you seen my sister?" he asked.

"Yup, she is in the bathroom, and I am leaving."

"But you just got here," he said. "You know it is my birthday, so will you stay? For me, please?"

Vanessa could not say no to that smile.

For a second, she wished he had sent her that note. Amanda had tried to play her like a fool, and Marina wanted just her to keep her mouth shut. Vanessa decided to try to have a good time, and maybe she would get to see Goran.

She walked out the front door and sat down on the steps. the night air felt so good. The sky was full of stars, and the wind was playing with her hair, but Vanessa was mad. She did not know if she had anything to be mad about, but she was mad. She did not have many friends, and the ones she did have seemed to think that they could use her. Marina only talked to her when she needed something, and Amanda was thinking about Goran.

"Is anyone ever going to think about me?" she asked out loud.

"I will," Groan said from behind her. "I could think about you day and night, if you let me."

Vanessa jumped up, startled.

"I am sorry," he said, "I did not mean to scare you. Marina told me you walked out, and I thought I might find you here. I was thinking maybe we could take a walk before party the starts and talk a little bit. We did not get to do that last night."

"Alright," she said. Goran took her hand, and a spark shot through her.

"So how was your day?" Goran asked.

"Other than everyone telling me that I am going to hurt you, it was good."

He stopped and looked at her. "What do you mean, you are going to hurt me?"

"I don't know, but Amanda and Marina told me that they are only thinking about your feelings. If we go out, I am going to hurt you because my mom is very strict. There will be nights that I won't be able to see you, and according to Amanda, that will hurt you. She will just hate to see you hurt."

"I see. It that why you have ran out of the house?" he asked. "It is okay, Vanessa. There will be times that I won't be able to see you, because I will be working. It doesn't mean that we cannot see each other some other night, or that I cannot come to your house when your mom won't let you go out. As long as we both agree that we can see each other, then others don't matter."

He is so sweet, she thought. He smelled so good and it was nice to be in his arms. They walked around the corner to a school park. They sat down and Vanessa looked at him. Goran's gorgeous brown eyes were looking right back at her. How many times had she wished for this in her life. And now it was right in front of her, and she did not know what to do.

"I know you are nervous," he said. "I am nervous, too. I did not walk with you here so we could make out, I walked with you here so we could talk."

She just kept looking at him, not able to say anything. She did not want this moment to end. He leaned in and kissed her lips. She melted in his arms. All the things the other said today were gone. There was nothing in this moment, but her with him. She wrapped her hands around his neck, and she felt him slide his tongue inside her mouth. It felt weird, because this was her first time, but she still wished it would never stop.

"Well, well," a familiar voice said from behind them. They both turned to see the person standing there, someone neither one of them liked.

"Oh, don't stop because I am here," Emily said. "I liked watching you two make fools of yourselves."

"Just don't talk to her," Groan said to Vanessa, and they got up. They were about to go back to Darko's party hand in hand, something that, to Emily, should not happen.

"Goran!" she yelled, disgust in her voice. "Do you know who you are kissing? Do you know what will happen if her mom finds out where she is and what has she been doing?"

"Listen Emily," Groan said. "I don't know what you want, or why you are even here, but we are going back to the party where you are not wanted. I know what I am doing, and who I am doing it with." They walked off, leaving Emily by herself.

So what, she thought. It is okay, my Plan B will work for sure. Emily walked after Goran and Vanessa. Plan B could not fail, or she was going to be very angry.

The music at Darko's house could be heard a mile away. His parties were always the ones people talked about. His parents never cared if he had them, as long as they stayed under control.

When Goran and Vanessa got back, they went to look for Marina. When they found her, she was with Ivan, Amanda, and Darko.

"Oh look who showed up!" Marina said. "Where did you two go?"

"We went down to the park," Goran told her.

"I hope you guys had a good time," Darko said and winked at Goran.

"We had a good time, but we were interrupted by Emily. I think she is on her way here," Vanessa said. "I am not sure you want her here. I know many people here don't like her."

"Tell me you did not invite her," Amanda said and looked at her boyfriend.

"No. She called today, and I hung up on her," Darko said.

"I had a phone call from her today, too," Marina said,

"but I did not answer it. I am not sure if she is going to show up, or not."

"Too late," Amanda said when she saw Emily coming over. She was with one of her friends, Jamie, who no one liked, either. The two girls were nothing but trouble.

"Hey guys," Emily said, walking up to them. "This party is great!"

"I thought I told you that you were not invited," Darko said to Emily. "I want you to leave *now*!"

"Oh don't be a party pooper," she said. "I am just here to have some fun. Didn't you know Marina invited me over? Isn't that right?" Emily winked at Marina.

"No, that is not right," Marina said. "I never invited you, and I did not talk to you today."

"It does not matter who invited you, I want you to leave," Darko said.

"I will leave as soon as I tell you why I am here," Emily said and looked right at Vanessa.

"What's there to tell us that we don't all ready know?" Darko asked.

"Oh, so you know that Goran was at Amanda's house today? And that they spent half of the day alone?" she asked. Goran was holding Vanessa's hand, and he squeezed it when he heard his name.

Amanda and Ivan looked at each other, and both started laughing. That took Emily buy surprise. Darko turned around to look at her, he had pity in his eyes.

"Emily, if you don't know anything about people, I would suggest that you don't go around accusing. Goran is my best friend, he is also Ivan's best friend. So if Amanda spent half the day with him, it is because her brother was there. Why is this any of your business?"

"If you came here to start something," Amanda said, "you came to wrong place. We are here to have fun. And, as Darko already told you, there is no place for you."

Emily turned to Vanessa and looked straight in her face. "So I guess you like this tramp then?" she asked Goran.

"Watch how you talk to her," Darko warned. "This is my house."

"Why do you think I am tramp?" Vanessa asked Emily.

"Because I saw you kissing him in the park."

"I don't care what you think," Vanessa said. "My mom trusts me, and I have the right to be with whoever I want."

"I just wonder what your dad would say," Emily said.

That made Vanessa jump from her seat, and if Goran was not holding her back, she would have jumped right on top of Emily and beat the hell out of her.

"No one *ever* talks about my dad," Vanessa said. "If I was you Emily, I would count my lucky stars that you are at Darko's house. Anywhere else, and you would be mine. I would watch my back from now on, though."

Vanessa turned and walked away with Goran by her side.

"I know she hurt you," Goran said, "and I am sorry."

It does not bother me when people talk about me, my mom, or my brother, but don't ever talk about my dad. My dad was everything to me, and when he died, something inside me died, too," she said.

Vanessa did not want to cry. She hated when people saw her cry, but the tears rolled down her cheek. Goran stopped and wiped her face. He felt bad for her. He did not like seeing her cry, and he knew Emily really hurt her with her cruel words. All he could do is be with her.

"Do you want me to take you home?" he asked.

"No, I don't want to ruin Darko's birthday. I just need a minute to get ahold of myself, and then we can go back. It is not his fault Emily doesn't know how to control herself. Maybe buy the time we get back, she won't be there anymore."

"I hope so," Goran said.

They walked back to the party, and it looked like everyone

was having a good time again. Everyone but Emily, who was still watching Vanessa from around the corner. She was not afraid of her, no matter what her threats were. But she would make sure Vanessa would never threaten her again.

CHAPTER TWENTY

"WHY ARE YOU ALL ALONE tonight?" Jean asked Alexander when Josh did not show up.

"I don't know," Alexander told her and went to his room. What's going on, he wondered, why is he not here yet? Josh should have been at Alexander's house an hour ago. As Alexander lay on his bed thinking, he heard a knock on the door. He got up, thinking his mom did not hear it, but he was wrong. Jean opened the door, and Josh came in the house.

"Hello, Jean," he said, "is Alexander ready to go?"

"Yes he is," she told him. "Come in, I have some thing I want to ask you."

Josh looked at Alexander, who was trying very hard to tell him something with his eyes. Whatever it was, Josh could not tell, so he did not know what kind of trouble he was in.

"What did you and Alexander do last night?" Jean asked Josh.

"Nothing, we went to the disco, saw who was there, and then we went walking around. We saw Joe, talked to him little bit, and I walked Alexander home. When I was on my way back, I saw Vanessa coming home, and I said hi to her."

"Are you sure that was all?" she asked.

"Yes ma'am, that was all."

"Well, Joe was here with Anna today, and he said that you three were at Anna's house underneath her window peeking in."

"I don't know why he would say that, but we were nowhere near that creepy old woman's house."

"Are you sure?" Jean asked again.

"Yes I am sure, there is no reason to lie to you."

"You guys can go," Jean told them. "Alexander, don't bother your sister, and be home at eleven."

"Eleven, Mom? Josh came an hour late, and I still have to be home at the same time? How is that fair?"

"I am sorry, son," she said. "Life is just not fair!"

"Fine, I will come home at eleven, but tomorrow night I am staying extra late!"

"We'll see if you even go out tomorrow," Jean said. "If I were you, I would go now, before I change my mind."

The boys left, and halfway down the road, Alexander saw someone walking their way. He knew it must be Joe, and he had something to say to him.

"Do you think that is Joe?" Alexander asked Josh.

"It could be," Josh answered. "Why?"

When they got closer, they saw that it was not Joe, but Emily.

"Where are you two losers going?" she asked them.

"Out, if you must know!" Alexander said. He hated Emily not only because she fought with his sister, but because she thought she was better then everyone else. Many nights when they lived with Emily's family, Alexander and Vanessa would talk about how mean she was. And how she was always telling lies, trying to start trouble, or trying to get someone else in trouble.

Tonight she was walking with her friend, Jamie, who was not much liked, either. The two girls were good for each other, because no one else wanted to be near them.

"Are you going to look for your slut sister?" Emily asked.

"Watch how you talk about my sister," Alexander said.

"Or you will do what?"

"Nothing. I won't do anything," he said. "Just watch how you talk about my sister."

"If you see her before I do, tell her I would not walk home alone at night anymore."

"Are you threatening my sister?"

"And if I am?" Emily asked, and stepped in front of him.

"Come on, Alexander," Josh said. "We are already late. She is not worth it." Josh pulled Alexander with him, and they left Emily standing there.

Emily's plan was not working, but the next part would for sure. There was still time to Darko and Vanessa. But of course first she needed to make sure Vanessa's mom knew where her daughter was.

"Are you sure you want to go to Jean's house?" Jamie asked.

"Are you scared? Let me know now, because my plan has not worked all night. If you cannot handle it, then don't go with me. I will go by myself!"

Emily continued on her way to Jean's house, and as she suspected, the lights were on in her room. The old woman did not sleep when her kids were not home. Maybe she should scare her, so then she would not let her kids go out anymore, and Emily could have Goran all to herself. Instead she decided to knock on the door so she could see Jean's face when she told her where her daughter really was.

"I am not going to the door with you," Jamie said.

"Fine, then go back, and don't come see me anymore!" Emily walked away and left Jamie standing in the middle of the road all by herself. Jamie was scared to be alone, but she was not about to go knocking on Jean's door.

Jean was getting ready to watch her favorite show, when she heard a light knock on the door. She waited a minute or so and it came again. Jean got up, expecting to see Anna at the door, but instead she found Emily.

"Hi Ms. Jean," Emily said.

"Hi Emily! Is something wrong?" Jean knew that Vanessa and Emily could not stand each other, and she had no idea why Emily was at her house.

"I just came by to tell you where Vanessa is," Emily told her.

"Save it, Emily," Jean said. "I already know where Vanessa is. I was the one who let her go in the first place."

"Well, do you know who she is with?" Emily asked.

"All of her friends, of course," Jean said, annoyed that Emily was asking so many questions.

"Well do you know that she is with Goran?" Emily asked. She saw Jean's face change color and she knew she had hit a button.

"I don't care who she is with!" Jean said, noticing that her voice had risen, and she was practically yelling at Emily. Jean did not know why, but this girl just got on her last nerve.

"I just thought you might want to know that I saw them kissing in the park tonight. If you want to come with me, I will show you where she is." Emily looked at Jean her eyes begging her to come with. When Jean spoke nothing but kindness came out:

"Emily, I am going to ask you to leave, and never come back ! If you don't want me to talk to your parents, you will leave and stay away from my children."

Before Emily could say anything else, Jean closed the door and turned off the porch light.

What a bitch, Emily thought. She turned and walked down the road. My plans have not worked all night. There must be something I can do to change that. Emily turned to look for Jamie, but she left her to deal with Vanessa by herself.

Emily had to have Goran tonight. She just had to, there

was no question about it. She would have to go back to Darko's and see what they were doing. Maybe there was still time to break up Goran and Vanessa.

Emily pictured Vanessa and Goran in a corner of Darko's room, sitting and talking, maybe sharing a kiss or two. Knowing Vanessa, there is nothing else that would be happening.

"Fool!" Emily shouted out loud. "If I had a guy like Goran, there would be no kissing and talking. I would have him all to myself. He could touch any part of my body, he could have what ever he desired, and I would give him what every man deserves."

Emily had been with many boys before, even with two married men. She knew a lot more than Vanessa, and tonight Emily would show Goran what she could do, and how much better she was than Vanessa. After tonight, Groan would ask, "Vanessa who?"

Jamie got back to Darko's house just in time for a slow dance. She looked for Ivan, but did not see him. She saw Vanessa and Goran dancing, and Vanessa saw her. Vanessa shot her a look that told her not to come any closer, but the only reason Jamie was there was to find Ivan. She wanted to dance with him, maybe talk to him, or even kiss him. The thought of Ivan kissing her made her palms sweat, and her cheeks began to feel warm. But when she found Ivan, he was not alone. Ivan was dancing with Marina.

Since when did he like her, Jamie asked herself, I guess there is no room for me. Good thing only Vanessa saw me. Jamie turned around to leave, and almost ran Emily over, who was standing right behind her.

"What are you doing here?" Jamie asked. "How come you are alone? Did you decide not to talk to Vanessa's mom, or did she tell you to go away?"

"What are you? A police officer?" Emily asked. When Jamie stood there staring at her, Emily knew she had to tell the truth. "The old bitch told me to go away, or she would tell my mom what I was trying to do.

"And what have *you* been doing here?" Emily asked Jamie. "Why are you even here?"

"I came back to talk to Ivan." When Emily looked like she was going to burst into laughter, Jamie quickly added, "Don't look at me like that, and don't you dare laugh at me! What is *your* plan now?"

"I don't know yet," Emily said, "but I am working on one. As soon as I have a plan, I will let you know. Are you with me? Because if you are not, then you might is well go away."

"Goran was never your man," Jamie said to her.

"You don't have to remind me, but after tonight, he will be," Emily said.

The girls were so busy thinking of a plan, that they did not notice that the music had stopped. Everyone was now standing around Darko, singing happy birthday. Darko blew out his candles and cut the cake. When he gave the first piece to Amanda, Emily made a gagging noise. Everyone turned towards her and Jamie.

"Good going," Jamie told her. "We were invisible until now."

"Shut up scaredy cat," Emily said.

"What are you two doing back?" Darko asked. "I thought I told you both to leave."

"Well, we could not go without singing you happy birthday first," Emily said. "But now, since we have, we will leave." They walked away to a corner of the house, and sat down on the ground.

"Now we wait," Emily said.

"What are we waiting for?" Jamie asked.

"Why did you want to talk to Ivan, anyways?" Emily asked, changing the subject. Jamie did not know how to explain to Emily that she had been waiting for Ivan to ask her out for almost two weeks now.

"I was waiting for him, so we could dance," she said after a long pause.

"Why would you want to dance with him?" Emily asked puzzled. Maybe she did not know Jamie as well as she thought she did. Jamie was her best and only friend, and she did not tell her she had feelings for Ivan.

"Why didn't you tell me, or ask me for help?"

"I could see you are trying to steal Goran away from Vanessa," Jamie said. "I did not want to bother you with my problems."

"I am not trying to steal him. I am going to have him tonight," Emily said with arrogance.

"Do you have any idea how you are going to do it?" Jamie asked.

"I am still thinking, but since we are talking about stealing boyfriends, let's figure out how you can get with Ivan. We will make sure he doesn't want anyone but you."

"I thought he was free," Jamie said sadly.

"You did not know that he and Marina have been sneaking around for over a week now? If Darko knew that, they would not be such good friends anymore. Darko does not like his little sister with his best friends. That is why Goran asked Vanessa out. I am sure he wanted Marina in the first place. Why would he want Vanessa? Why would anyone want Vanessa?" Emily asked.

Jamie did not tell her that she was sick of always hearing about Vanessa, and how much Emily hated her.

"Why are you so quiet?" Emily asked. "Are you thinking of a plan to get Ivan for yourself?"

"No," Jamie answered, "I am thinking of how to get away from here. I am a fool for even coming back tonight."

"You are not leaving me here alone, are you?" Emily asked her with panic in her voice.

"I don't know what to do, Emily. I don't want to stay here

and cause trouble. It is Darko's birthday. I just want to go home and go to bed."

"Don't go! I promise you will have good time," Emily said.

"What are you planning on doing?" Jamie asked her. she knew that she was going to regret asking, because Emily had that look in her eyes. The one she got when she was thinking something of evil to do, which was a lot.

"Don't worry, we will make them regret the choice they made," Emily said.

"They? Who are they? I don't think I want a part in this," Jamie said.

"Well, do you want Ivan, or not? If you don't want him, then walk away. I go after what I want," Emily told her. "I want Goran, and I am going to have him tonight."

Vanessa knew the girls had not left. She knew Emily pretty well by now, and she knew that Goran had something to do with it. Every time Emily wanted something, she did not let go easily. But tonight, Goran was with Vanessa and she was not going to let him go.

Vanessa looked all over to see if Emily was still there, but she could not find her. Vanessa knew something was going to happen, but she did not know what. Goran broke her thoughts when he came up behind her, and put his hands on her back.

"You look worried," he said. "Are you sure you are fine?"

"Yes, I am okay," Vanessa told him. "Don't worry about me, I am just wondering why Emily and Jamie are back again."

"It does not matter," he said. "What matters is that we are here, together, at Darko's party, and no one can make any trouble."

Goran looked into her eyes, and when she looked back at him, she knew he would never let anything bad happen to her. Vanessa shook off her bad feeling, and determined herself to have fun. No matter how much Emily tried to bothered her.

Marina and Ivan excused themselves to go get some more

drinks, which was suspicious to Amanda. She wondered why Ivan and marina needed to go and get drinks together. Amanda told Darko that she had to go to the bathroom, but she really wanted to go and spy on Ivan and Marina. As she walked up the stairs, she could hear them laughing.

"Do you think they fell for us getting drinks?" Marina asked.

"I hope so, because I have been looking at your lips all night. I just want a taste of them."

"Well, now you can have them all you want," Marina told him.

At the moment their lips met, Amanda walked in the room. Marina pushed Ivan back so hard that he almost fell off the couch.

"What are you two doing?" Amanda asked.

"Nothing that you need to worry about," Ivan told her.

"It did not look like nothing it, looked like you were going to kiss," Amanda said.

"Why is that any of your business? You are always here with my brother," Marina said.

"Because if your brother knew that you two were kissing, he would not be his friend," she said and pointed at Ivan.

"Just relax," Ivan told her. "If Darko has a problem, I am sure he would tell me."

"If Darko has problem with what?" Darko asked walking into the room.

They all stared at Darko like they were seeing a ghost.

"Why are you all in here, when there is party going on?" he asked.

"Come on," Marina said, "let's go." She grabbed Ivan's hand and walked out.

"What was that about?" Darko asked Amanda. "There was full room of people, and now there is just you and me!"

CHAPTER TWENTY-ONE

SOMETHING STRANGE IS GOING ON, Darko thought while he danced with Amanda. Vanessa and Goran were normal, but Marina and Ivan were looking at each other differently. It was almost as if they wanted to escape. Amanda was acting very strangely, too. She had been staring at Ivan and Marina since they came back downstairs.

Tonight is my night, Darko thought, and I will not let anyone spoil it. Just then, the music stopped. He looked at his stereo, and saw that Emily had turned it off.

"Listen up everyone," she said loudly, "I have something to say."

"We don't really want to hear it," said Darko.

"Oh no but this will be very interesting, especially for you, Darko."

"Make your point fast," he told Emily, "because we have a party to get back to."

"As you all know, it is Darko's birthday," Emily began and everyone started laughing at her. This is not going well, she thought, I need plan fast. Jamie came out, and stood next to her.

"Tonight it made me think about how badly I have been behaving towards everyone," Emily said. "I would love to have a boyfriend or even friends like Goran, Ivan, and yourself, Darko."

The boys looked at each other, knowing it would never happen. They said nothing, and just waited for her to finish.

"I just came back to say that I am sorry for ruining your birthday earlier, Darko, and that I will try not to bother anyone anymore. I have decided to work on my behaving, and I promise I will try to get along with everyone.

"We forgive you," Darko told her. "Right guys?" He turned to find everyone staring at him like he was a crazy person.

"Speak for yourself," Vanessa yelled from the back of the room. "I don't want to have anything to do with her, or Jamie. I won't forgive her now, or ever."

"Oh, of course," Emily said, "the only one that won't forgive me, is the only one that doesn't really matter. What matters to me, and Jamie, is that the others forgive us. You don't really have to."

Darko looked at Vanessa to see her reaction, and froze. She was staring at Emily like she wanted to rip through her. The best thing to do is keep them apart, Darko thought.

Tonight had been great, everyone had laughed, danced, and even kissed. But the way Emily and Vanessa were looking at each other, it don't look like the night was going to end on a good note.

"Vanessa," Darko said. "I am sure you want to hurt Emily, and you are mad she is even here, but it is my day. Please, don't make me be mean to you."

Vanessa looked at him, and then noticed that everyone else was watching her and Emily.

"I am fine," she told Darko. "I will not start anything. Not only because it is your day, but because I do not start fights."

"Well, maybe not," Emily said, "but I know someone in here that would love to protect you!"

"And who would that be?" Vanessa stepped forward with Goran by her side.

"Ivan," Emily said as she turned to look at him. "Why don't you tell us all who *you* think would be the one protecting Vanessa?"

Ivan looked lost. "I have no idea," he said finally.

"Marina, how about you?" Emily asked. "If you were to get into a fight, who would be there for you?"

"I think that's all I want to hear from your mouth," Marina answered and walked towards Emily. Vanessa and Amanda were right behind her. The girls did not want to fight, but they were tired of listening to Emily talk.

"Before you guys make you way up, to take me down, I want to say the real reason why I am here," Emily said.

"I knew you could not be here for anything good," Darko said.

"Darko, your sister and Ivan are an item. Amanda, your girlfriend knew about it. And Vanessa, Goran is not what he tells you he is. He stays in Marina's room all night long without Darko knowing about it!" Emily finished.

The three girls froze, and looked at Darko at the same time. That was a lot to take in, Darko thought. That explains why my sister and Amanda were acting very weird. It also explains why Goran has been in my room very early in the morning. Whatever Emily was doing, worked on Darko. He just stared at all of them.

"Thank you, Emily," Darko began, "but if I may, ask how do you know all this? Why didn't you come to me before with this? Why on my birthday?

"And for that matter, why on the second try? If there is something you, want you got it," Darko told her.

He turned to Ivan and Goran, they had frozen like the girls. That told Darko that Emily was telling the truth, or at least part of it. He was determined to find out what was truth and what was a lie.

"The first time I wanted to say something," Emily began, "but Vanessa walked away with Goran, and now I have a microphone. I can tell you all of your friends, including your sister and girlfriend, are lying to you. There was no other way I could tell you, because you would not listen. Even when I called you today, you hung up on me."

"Is that why you called?" Darko asked.

"Well yes, and I wanted you to invite me, but you would not," Emily said smiling at him.

"Well what is your price?" Darko asked her.

"Price?" Emily looked at him, not knowing what he meant.

"When someone tells me they know something that I do not, they usually want something in return. You just told me a lot I did not know about, so what is your price? What do you want, Emily?"

"Goran," Emily answered, "he is the one I want. He is the one I have been after for a long time. You think you can give him to me?"

Darko looked at Groan who did not know what to say, or how to react. Before Goran could talk, Darko responded for him.

"Emily, money, shoes, and things are what I can give you. Goran is his own person, and I cannot give him to you." Then he looked at Groan and Ivan and asked, "So boys, is there something you want to tell me?"

"There is no truth to what she said," Goran told him. "I spent one night in your sister's room. That was the night we all had too much to drink. I fell asleep on the floor, and you were in the next room with Amanda. When I woke up in the morning, I came into your room at, like, seven and I figured you would know I spent the night, because I have never been at your house that early unless I spent the night.

"As for you Emily," Goran went on, "you and me will never happen. Not only have I never wanted you before, now I want you even less. You want to know why?" He stopped to take a breath before he went on. "Because you are a conniving little bitch that is so stuck on what she wants, that you will hurt anyone just to get it.

He looked at Vanessa and said, "I hope you believe me. If not, there is nothing I can do to change your mind, but even if you believe her over me. I will never be with her, you are the one I want."

Vanessa just stared back at him. There were no words she could find. Emily shocked her with everything she had to say, but not only did Amanda know about Ivan and Marina, Vanessa also knew about them. But it looked like Emily did not know that.

"I guess it is your turn," Darko said, looking straight at Ivan. "Is it true what she said about you and Marina?"

"Darko, that is my business," Marina said from behind him. "No matter what this tramp here said." She looked at Emily, "I will do what I please, with whoever I want!"

"I did not ask you," Darko said to his sister. "Ivan, I am still waiting."

"Yes, it is true," Ivan told him. "We are seeing each other, and have been for over three weeks. The reason we did not tell you, is because we did not want you to overreact. Yes, I like to spend time with Marina, and she likes to be with me. I am sorry you had to hear it from that trash," he said looking at Emily.

"Save it!" Darko yelled, angry. "So not only did my sister lie to me, you lied to me, too. You are my best friend! I would expect this from Marina, but not from you! I want you to leave now. I don't want you here, or near my house. And the last thing I ever want to see you around my sister."

Ivan looked at him, and without a word, he turned around and started to walk out.

"And you," Darko turned to Amanda. "You knew about all this? he asked. "And you did not tell me? Why?"

"I just found out tonight," she said I did not know how to tell you, or how you would react. now I see that you don't want my brother around your sister, which makes me wonder who I spent my last two years on. If you cannot accept them to be together, how can you accept me?"

"They have nothing to do with us," Darko said. "But I am sorry, I cannot have a girlfriend that will lie to me. You had time to tell me about this. You could have told me the truth when we were standing around. I would not have been mad as I am now.

"Not only am I mad at Ivan and Marina for lying to me, I am mad at you. too. The one person I thought I could trust, now I know I cannot."

"Then I am leaving," Amanda told Darko.

"Good night," Darko said and turned to walk to his room. Suddenly Emily came out of no where him and put her hand on his shoulder.

"I know this is very hard to deal with, but I am here for you," she said to him.

"No thank you," Darko said. "I think you have done all the damage you came here to do. I hope you are really happy."

"I have to go after him," Groan told Vanessa. "I hope you can forgive me for not telling you I spent the night in Marina's room."

"When was it?" Vanessa asked.

"I cannot tell you about it now, but I will after I check on Darko. Please don't leave!"

He kissed her lips, and left her standing with Emily and Jamie. Marina walked after Ivan, and Amanda had walked home right after them. Vanessa was stuck with the two girls she did not like all her friends were gone.

"How does it feel to be all alone?" Emily asked from behind her.

"I hope you feel better after you just destroyed a friendship and a relationship," Vanessa told her.

"Oh, I don't feel better yet. Now, when I have Goran to myself then, I will feel so much better."

"Jamie, why are you with her?" Vanessa asked. "There are so many other people that are not as bossy and bitchy as she is."

"I am sorry about all this," Jamie told her. "I did not want to come back, and I did not want her to do this. I have no part in it. If I knew she was going to do all this I would not have come back. Well, now I know what kind of person she really is. I am sorry I was your friend," she told Emily and walked away.

"Well," Vanessa said, "now what will you do? You are all alone. How does it feel?"

"Oh shut up, bitch!" Emily said. "Jamie will be back when she sees that Ivan is free, and that she needs me."

"What do you mean, 'when Ivan is free'?" Vanessa asked looking at her.

"I want Goran, she wants Ivan. Is there something you don't understand, stupid?"

"I think you better lay off those insults," Vanessa warned her, "before something I don't want, happens."

"And what's that?" Emily asked. "Are you going to hit me? Or are you going to call your boyfriend for help?"

"I am just asking you to stop insulting me," Vanessa said. "I don't want to be the one ruining Darko's party."

"That's a little too late. I already did what I came for."

"So, you did not come here to tell everyone you are changing. You came here to break up a friendship and a relationship and be gone. Well, you have done your part, now why don't you leave?"

"I am not done yet," Emily told Vanessa. "Goran is still here."

"Yes he is, but he is with me. Did you not hear him when he said, stay here, don't leave, I will be back? He said that to me," Vanessa said. "You must have problems hearing."

"Oh, I have no problem hearing anything. I am just waiting

for him, because he is still here, and he will change his mind once he finds out how your mom and brother are."

"And how exactly are my mom and my brother?" Vanessa asked.

"Well your mom is a control freak, and your brother is a geek that follows you around, because he does not have any real friends."

"Emily, you are pushing it. This is your last warning."

"What's the matter? Cannot take the truth? I know more about you than you think."

"You don't know anything about me."

"Oh really? Like your mom is not lazy? She comes home from work and you have everything ready for her, plus have to do all the other chores just to go out at night."

"My mom is not lazy. I do all those things by choice, not because she tells me to."

"Don't try to cover it up, Vanessa, we all know you will do anything just to go out at night and see Goran. Goran is someone who will not be with you for long," Emily told her. "He likes girls with class and you don't have any. You are poor white trash, you came here with nothing, and you never will have anything.

"What makes you think Goran even wants to be with you? He only wants some ass, but he does not know he won't get it from you. As soon as he finds out, I will be there to comfort him. And I will give him anything he wants and he wishes for."

Vanessa just could not listen to anymore. She could not let this girl, that thinks she knows everything, ruin her chance with a great guy. Not only that, she was not going to let *anyone* call her white trash!

"Emily, I am asking you nicely, don't talk anymore or I will be forced to punch you."

"Oh, and you think you can?" Emily asked. Emily was smaller than, Vanessa but she knew how to fight.

"You really think you can punch me?" Emily asked again, coming closer to Vanessa.

"I am telling you to stop calling me and my family names, and do not to talk to me."

"And if I don't stop?" Emily asked.

Emily was right in Vanessa's reach. One more move, and she would be right in Vanessa's face. Vanessa told herself she would wait, she would wait until she was provoked. She would wait until she could not take it anymore. She would not lose her temper on this girl. Maybe she should just walk away. Right then she got sucker punched in the jaw.

Vanessa had never felt that kind of pain before. She was shocked, it knocked her off balance, and she stumbled. She could feel blood in her mouth, and Vanessa felt something hard beating her teeth. She spit and blood and a few of her teeth came out.

"This is not what I wanted to do but you asked for it," were Vanessa's last words to Emily. She would remember them for a whole week. Vanessa jumped on her in a split second, punching her all over her face and body. She did not care if she used her hands, knees, legs, or her head.

Vanessa was bleeding very bad, but so was Emily. Vanessa did not talk, she did not think, she did not know what came over her, all she knew was that all of her anger was going to be used on this girl.

Someone was trying to grab Vanessa away from Emily, but she punched that person and went right back to the person that started it all. The music stopped, and people gathered around them. Someone yelled, "Go tell Darko there is a fight! He needs to be here now!"

Vanessa heard Darko's name, but he would just have to be mad at her now. Emily asked for this. She was on top of Emily, not even trying to see if she was moving. All she knew was that Emily started it, and now Vanessa would finish it.

Vanessa knew she was missing teeth, because she could

feel the space and she saw when she spit them out. Her eye was swollen, and her vision was blurry, but that did not stop her from punching blindly. Emily had her arms around her head, trying to protect it, but there was no way of saving herself. Emily thought she was going to die.

"Why is everyone standing around?" someone asked. "Help Emily!"

Thank God, Emily thought, someone will help me.

Vanessa was not fat, but she was heavy. Emily felt like she would lose her breath any time now. Her jaw hurt, her head was on fire, she did not even know if she had bones left in her that were not broken. Emily blacked out after one of Vanessa's punches to her head. She did not feel anything anymore.

Guys were yelling, girls were screaming. There was blood all over Vanessa's hands and face, all over the floor.

"I don't want to talk to anyone," Darko said when Goran walked into his room. Darko was so mad he had already punched a hole in the wall, and he was getting ready to kick his door.

"I know you don't, but Marina is her own person. You really cannot be mad at her or Ivan, they were not telling you to protect you. And, you have had some great times with Amanda, you should not throw that away because some crazy person told you a bunch of crap. I am sure they were waiting for the right moment to tell you," Goran told him.

"Whose side are you on?" Darko asked through his teeth.

"Yours," Goran answered, "but I am telling you, Marina is your sister, Ivan is one of your best friends, and Amanda is your girlfriend."

"Not anymore," Darko told him.

There was a knock on the door, and it flew open. Jacob, one of Darko's friends, walked in completely out of breath.

"What is it?" Darko asked.

"Vanessa. Emily. Fight," Jacob tried to say.

"Oh God," said Goran, and he ran out before Darko could.

All three boys went running. They did not understand why everyone was just standing around, and not helping Emily. They all hated her, but that was no reason to stand there and not help her.

Goran ran to Vanessa who was still punching Emily's side. He pulled her off, and held her close to him. He was wearing a white shirt, and now Vanessa's blood was all over it. Vanessa did not see who pulled her off, because her vision was so blurry.

Darko called 911, and they heard sirens within minutes. Darko checked Emily's pulse and saw that she was still breathing, but she was knocked out. Vanessa passed out before help could arrive, and Goran laid her on the floor. Ambulances, fire trucks and police cars all showed up.

"Give them room to pass!" Goran heard Darko yell at the crowd around the girls. The paramedics strapped Emily and Vanessa onto gurneys and had them in the ambulances in a matter of seconds. Then they were off again.

"I will be right there," Goran told one of the paramedics.

"Are you her relative?" the man asked.

"No, I am her boyfriend," he said, looking at Darko as he said it.

"Someone has to go tell their parents," Darko said. "It was my party, so I will."

"No one is going anywhere," police officer Johnson said.

Jacob Johnson was a friend of Darko's, Goran's, and Amanda's families. He was glad he was one of the officers on the scene. He also knew both girls.

Vanessa was Jean's daughter who would never hurt a fly,

but the apple doesn't fall far from the tree, he thought. He had heard the stories about her father when he was younger, and how he always wanted to fight. There were also stories about Emily, and how she was a troublemaker. But tonight it was different, tonight it was Vanessa who was the troublemaker. He just hoped that both girls were going to be all right.

CHAPTER TWENTY-TWO

IVAN, MARINA, AND AMANDA WERE walking home when they heard the sirens coming, they all thought of Darko at the same time.

"Do you think we should go back?" Marina asked.

"I am going back," Amanda said. "No matter how mad he is at me, if he needs me, I am going to be there for him."

All three of them turned around just as two ambulances drove passed them.

"Why two? Was there someone in both of them, or did they just send two? What happened?" Ivan asked very quickly.

"Slow down," Amanda told him. "We don't even know if it happened at Darko's house. Let's just go back, and see what is going on. It could be nothing." Amanda had a strange feeling in her stomach, the one that always told her when something was wrong.

They were not far away, when they saw all the police cars and fire trucks in front of Darko's house. They walked in, looking for Darko, and hoping he was not the one on his way to the hospital.

Darko was in the middle of answering Officer Johnson's questions when he saw them. He was mad, upset, and scared all at once, but when he saw Amanda all those feelings faded away He was glad to see her, he really needed her right now.

Nothing like this had ever happened to him before. He had never had to deal with the police. This was supposed to be his day, now not only was he betrayed by his best friend and his girlfriend, he also had to deal with two girls on their way to the hospital. How was he going to tell the parents their daughters were in the hospital?

"So, you don't know what happened?" Officer Johnson asked again, looking at Darko.

"I told you a million times, I don't know what happened. I was not there," Darko told him.

"But this is your birthday party, right?"

"With all do respect, Officer Johnson," Darko said. "I know this is my birthday party, but I can't be everywhere all the time. I already told you I was in my room with Goran, and that the girls were out here."

"Were they arguing tonight?" Johnson asked.

"Yes, they did. In fact, everyone was on the edge tonight," Darko said, "including me. I don't know what else to tell you. I don't know who started the fight. I was not out here, I don't even know why they were fighting. All I know is that I came out of my room, and there was blood everywhere."

"Don't go anywhere," Johnson told him. "I am going to talk to Goran. If I have any more questions I will be back!"

"What happened?" Amanda asked Darko after Officer Johnson left.

"I went to my room, and Goran went after me. Next thing I know, Jacob rushes in telling us the girls were fighting. When I came down, all I could see was blood. Goran pulled Vanessa off of Emily, who was bearably breathing. They both are in very bad shape."

"Is that why there were two ambulances here?" Amanda asked.

"Yes," Darko answered. He looked at her, "Why did you come back? I told you to stay away. I thought we broke up?"

"Even though we broke up, I knew someone was in trouble. I had to come back and make sure it was not you. I still love you.

"Did you want me to go?" Amanda asked after a short moment.

"No, I would really like it if you would stay. I am sorry I was a jerk tonight. It was just all Emily said hit me hard, and I was not sure how to deal with it."

"Your sister and my brother are together, and you know you cannot stop them from seeing each other," Amanda told Darko. "You know damn well if someone was telling me to stay away from you, I would not listen. I know you would not, either."

Darko looked at her with sadness in his eyes.

"I know," he said. "I behaved like a jerk tonight, and I have to apologize to them, too. Did they come back with you?"

"Yes, they did. I think they were looking for you, but I don't know where they are now."

Darko hugged her, and it felt right. Goran was right. For once in his life, he had the right girl, and he was not letting her go. He was angry at Emily, and he had taken it out on everyone else. Darko and Amanda were standing on the steps when they heard someone talking behind the house.

"Stay here," Darko told Amanda.

He went around back to see who was there. He could see two people, but he couldn't tell if they were boys or girls.

"What happened here?" a man's voice asked.

"I know Vanessa beat up Emily bad tonight, and I think you should be the one to go and tell Jean," a girl's voice answered.

"If anyone is going to tell Jean what happened here tonight, it will be me," Darko said walking up to them. Jamie and Sasha jumped when they heard his voice.

"We were just thinking that the police will take really long before they can go tell their parents," Sasha said. Sasha was Jamie's brother, but they were nothing alike. Jamie was always with Emily causing problems, while Sasha had a job and did not bother anyone. He was older and much wiser than his sister.

"Thank you for your concern," Darko said, "but I will be the one who will go. If you guys have anything to say, feel free to talk to the police. They are right in front of the house."

"We'll leave you to it," Sasha said and pulled his sister with him.

Goran had not moved from the spot where Vanessa was laying just ten minutes before. Everything happened so fast. If he would have just stayed with Vanessa, and let Darko go everything would have been fine. She looked so awful, he thought. Her eyes were swollen shut, her face was bleeding, and he was sure she was missing teeth.

Why would Vanessa fight? What caused her to do this? What did Emily say? The questions kept running through his mind. Knowing Emily, she must have provoked Vanessa somehow. Why didn't anyone stop the fight? There were so many people there that could have pulled Vanessa off. Goran was still deep in thought when Officer Johnson walked up to him.

"Goran," he said, "I need to ask you some questions."

"Sure," Goran said, still looking into the ground.

"What happened here tonight?"

"I have no idea. I was not there. I was talking to Darko, when Jacob ran into his room, and told us the girls were fighting. I am not even sure what they were fighting about, but I do know that Emily was looking for someone to fight with all night."

251

"What makes you say that?" Officer Johnson asked.

"She had already tried to get Vanessa to fight earlier tonight. This was the second time. I don't know what she was thinking, but Emily told Vanessa she wanted me."

"Are you and Vanessa going out? He asked.

"We are, and we are not. I don't really want everyone to know about us, because I know how strict her mom is. Her mom would be very mad, because she won't allow her kids to date until they are eighteen."

"If you know all this, why would you date her in the first place?"

"I like her," Goran told him. "I am not going to be asked who I am, or am not dating. You are here to find out what happened to Vanessa and Emily, not to give me the third degree about who I am dating."

"Watch it boy," Officer Johnson warned him. "I am a friend of your family, but tonight I am a police officer who has a job to do. We can do this here, or I can take you to the station. It is all up to you."

"I did not do anything wrong, and you cannot take me anywhere because I was not around," Goran said.

"Well, tell me how it started, and do not leave anything out."

"They were fighting tonight, and Emily started it by provoking Vanessa. When Vanessa tried to walk away from her, she followed her around talking bad about her father, her mother, and just insulting her in every way she could. I am sorry, but that is all I know," Goran told the officer.

"Just stick around," Johnson said. "If I have anything else I need to know, I want to be able to find you."

"Yes sir," Goran said.

Why do they need me to stay Goran wondered. It was not as though he made them fight. Poor Vanessa's mom, her daughter was in the hospital covered with cuts and bruises. He knew it would be a lot easier to tell Maria, Emily's mom, than

Jean. Emily's family was not as worried about her, because she was always causing some kind of problem. No one wanted to think that her mom gave up on her, but most of the time Emily did whatever she wanted.

Goran shook his head and stood up, ready to go look for Darko. He was sure by now Darko was with Amanda, and maybe Marina and Ivan. When Goran found them, they were talking to Officer Johnson about Jamie and her brother, Sasha.

"So what did she say exactly?" Johnson was asking.

"Jamie was telling Sasha that he should be the one to go and tell Jean that Vanessa beat up Emily tonight," Darko said.

"When did this happen?" Goran asked.

All of them turned around and looked at him.

"Why does it matter to you?" Johnson asked. "No matter what happened here, no one will go tell their parents but me, and maybe one of my officers, but none of you."

"Why can't we go tell her?" Goran asked. "She knows us,m and it would be easier for her to hear it from one of us than it would be to hear it from you guys."

"Because it is my job!" Johnson said, and walked to his car.

"Do you think if we go around, and take the short cut we would make it there before he does?" Amanda asked.

"No, we'll have him do his job, and we will do what he told us, nothing," Darko said.

"Does any one else feel guilty, like I do?" Goran asked.

"I don't know what I am feeling," Darko answered. "It happened here, and Jean will hate me and my family now, but we didn't do anything."

"Maybe that is why *we* should go tell her," Marina said. She was holding Ivan's hand in front of her brother, and she did not care. She was Vanessa's best friend, and she wanted to be the one to tell her mom.

"Okay then, who all wants to go with me, and tell Jean that her daughter is in the hospital? Darko asked.

Everyone raised their hands. The kids walked behind Darko's house, and left without being noticed. While the police were still questioning the others, the five of them headed straight to Jean's house. They knew that Officer Johnson was almost on his. If they wanted to get there before him, they had to come up with a story and move fast.

"We'll just tell her the truth," Darko said.

"And that would be?" Goran asked looking at him.

"I don't know what to tell her," Amanda said. "I was not there, but I will try to explain to her that it was not Vanessa's fault."

"Does anyone know where Alexander was tonight?" Darko asked.

"I have not seen him at all tonight," Goran answered.

"I thought he went everywhere with his sister?" Darko asked.

"I saw him around with his friend, Joe," Marina said. "I am not sure he was with him all night, though."

"I guess they will all find out soon," Goran said.

They walked up to Jean's driveway and paused. There were no lights on, they were certain she was sleeping. All of them were scared to tell her, but they knew they had no choice. They saw someone else walking up to them from the other direction, they hoped it was Alexander.

"What are you all doing here?" Alexander asked. "Where is my sister? I thought she was with you, Goran?"

"Alexander, we have something to tell you and your mom, but you have to stay calm."

"Who do you think you are, to tell me I need to stay calm?" he asked.

"We have something to tell you, but we cannot do it if you are going to yell," Darko said.

"Well hurry up, because I am late and I have to go in."

"Your sister was in a fight tonight, and she was taken to the hospital," Darko told him.

"What do you mean, she got in a fight?" he asked quietly. "Who was she fighting with?"

"She and Emily got into a fight, and both of them were taken to the hospital. We wanted to tell your mom before the police showed up," Darko told Alexander.

"Oh wow," he said, "my sister was bad enough to bring the police here?"

"Listen Alexander," Goran said, "I know she is your sister, and that you two are very close, but she did not do this by choice. She was made to fight with Emily.

"How do you guys know she was made to fight?" Alexander asked.

"Emily tried to fight with her earlier, but I took Vanessa for a walk," Goran said. "The second time, I was not around."

"What do you mean, you were not around?" Alexander asked him.

"That is not important," Goran answered. "We are going to tell your mom where Vanessa is, and then we will be on our way to the hospital, so we can see how she is."

Jean was watching them from the window. She could not make out what they were saying, but she could see not only Alexander, but other people, too. She thought she could see Darko and Amanda. Maybe Darko was taking her home, and Marina was going along because Ivan was. But why was Goran there, and her daughter not? I guess I will have to go and find out the answers, Jean thought as she got dressed. Either way, her kids were both in trouble, it was way passed their curfew.

"My sister *is* my business," Jean heard Alexander say.

"We know," Darko said. "We are not here to argue, we are here to tell your mom about Vanessa."

"And where exactly *is* Vanessa?" Jean asked.

Everyone jumped, and their heads turned towards Jean's voice. She had surprised all of them.

"Mom, what are you doing outside?" Alexander asked, stepping next to her.

"Well when there are six people in front of my house yelling, I figured I had better come outside and see what is going on," Jean said. "Where is my daughter?"

"We are sorry, Jean," Darko said.

"What are you sorry for?" Jean asked. She suddenly got a bad feeling. Her stomach tied in knots, and her motherly instincts kicked in. Something was wrong with her daughter.

"Sorry I am late," Alexander told his mom. "Just so you know, what happened tonight, I had nothing to do with."

"Are you all just going to stand there, or am I going to hear where Vanessa is?" Jean asked nervously.

"Vanessa got in a fight," Alexander said before Darko could even open his mouth.

"Fight?" Jean asked. "Vanessa does not fight."

"She was provoked by Emily tonight, and they started fighting," Darko told her. "Vanessa is in the hospital, and so is Emily. The police are on the way here to tell you, but we thought, since we are her friends, you should hear it from us."

Jean had to sit down. She took her kids out of a war zone so they would not worry about dying. Here they were, two years down the road, and her fifteen year old was in the hospital.

They heard a car coming, and they turned. When officer Johnson got out of the car, he looked at the kids and then at Jean.

"I guess they told you where your daughter is," Johnson said.

"Yes, they told me."

"Are you okay?" he asked.

"Do you know how she is right now?" Jean asked through tears.

"Mom, don't cry," Alexander said. "Maybe she just has some scratches, she will be fine."

"Son, people don't go to the hospital for scratches," Jean told him.

"I am going to tell Maria, and then I will come back if you need a ride to the hospital," Johnson told her. He turned towards Darko and the rest of them standing there.

"You know I could take you to jail tonight? I was looking around for all of you, and you decided to flee the crime scene."

"My house is not a crime scene," Darko said. "We thought we were doing the right thing, coming to tell Jean ourselves."

"You all should go home now," Officer Johnson told them. "There will be nothing you can do for Vanessa tonight, maybe you can visit her tomorrow."

CHAPTER TWENTY-THREE

VANESSA WOKE UP TO SOMEONE asking her if she knew where she was. She had no idea, all she knew was that her body hurt like hell. She did not know which was worse, the pain in her face, her mouth, or her ribs.

Vanessa could hear voices around her, but she could not make out who they belonged to. Many of them kept asking her if she was okay, and if she was able to talk. How was she going to talk, when she could not even feel her mouth? She tried opening her eyes but they hurt too bad. When she managed to open her left eye, she could see only lights, and they were blurry.

"You are awake," someone said to her.

She tried to say yes, but she could not talk. Instead, she managed to groan in pain.

"Well, I am Doctor Gordon, and I am going to give you some medicine for your pain. It will make you feel better. You have no serious injuries, but you have lots of bruises. Your teeth will have to come out. There are four teeth on your left side that we'll have to take out, because they were chipped but not knocked all the way out. Just relax, and we'll take care of you."

Vanessa looked around, but could not say anything to

him. She wanted to ask how Emily was. Where was Goran? Her mom? Alexander? Where were Marina and all of her other friends?

A nurse came in and gave her some medicine that made Vanessa doze off. While she was asleep she had a dream that the police came and took her, they locked her in a dark room all by herself. She screamed for help, but no one heard her. When the door finally opened, Emily walked in and looked at her with pity in her eyes.

"See? Goran did not save you," she said to Vanessa. "Hell, even your own mother did not come to see you. Looks like you are a worthless piece of shit that no one wants around." Emily walked out and left Vanessa crying.

The door opened again, and Vanessa hoped that she would see Goran, or her mom, but instead her dad walked in. He was supposed to be dead, but here he was, right in front of her.

"Vanessa, honey," he began. "What did you do? Why did you do it?"

"Dad?" she said. "Is that really you? I thought you were dead, but I am so glad you are here."

"I am here for you," he said. "I know you must have had a reason to fight, but you are my daughter, and I want the best for you. I don't want you in jail, or the hospital. You know how other families are, they are not like ours. I am watching all of you, Vanessa. I want my family to stay strong, and be together. You all have been through so much in your life."

"She started it, Dad! She hit me first! Do you remember when you told me not to hit first? I never have, but she was talking about you and Mom, and I just could not take it."

"Vanessa, baby, there will be many people that will try to get you to fight, but you have to stay strong. Not just for yourself, but for your mother, too. You know that your mom is everything you have, and you kids are all she has. No one can take that away."

"Dad, why did you leave us?" Vanessa asked.

"I had no choice," he answered. "It was my time to go. But, I am with you in your heart. Whenever you need me, I will be there with you."

"How long can you stay with me?" she asked.

"As long as you need me, baby girl. As long as you need me."

He sat next to Vanessa and hugged her. She had the warmest feeling in her stomach, and for the first time in a long time, she knew she was going to be all right.

"Vanessa. Vanessa, wake up," she heard a voice saying.

She looked to her dad, and he looked at her.

"I guess it is time for me to go again," he said.

"No Dad! I can stay here with you!" she said. "It is okay, they can call me all they want. I don't want to go, anymore. Please let me stay with you!"

"No," he said, "you are way too young to stay with me. I will see you again one day, I promise. Now you have to wake up, and take care of your mother. Tell her and Alexander I love them very much."

"Vanessa! Vanessa, wake up," she heard the voice say again. She opened her eye and saw the doctor next to her.

"Good morning, sunshine," he said. "How are you feeling? Better, I hope."

"I. Am. Feeling better," she tried.

"That's my girl," Dr. Gordon said. "You will be all right. We have to take you for x-rays, and then we will see if your family is here yet."

She wanted to ask if anyone had called, but she could not. She just nodded, and closed her eyes again. Vanessa was hoping her dad would come back, but he did not. When she fell asleep, no one was there, she only felt pain.

She had her x-rays done, and went back to her room. No one was there yet. They will be here, Vanessa thought. She did not know how she was going to face her mom. She had been in a fight, and she knew that was going to hurt her mom.

She had never done anything to hurt her before. Vanessa fell asleep again, and hoped when she woke up someone would be there.

"Vanessa can you hear me?" she heard. She knew that voice, but it was not her mom. She slowly opened her eyes, to find Office Johnson sitting next to her.

"Hi," he said, "how are you feeling. The doctors said you cannot talk yet, so I won't bother you much. Your mom and brother are outside waiting."

"Can I see them?" she asked.

"They will be in as soon as I leave. Vanessa, I have lots of questions for you. I am going to see how Emily is doing, and give you time with your family."

Officer Johnson left, and Vanessa's family walked in. When Jean entered Vanessa's room, she did not know what to expect. As soon as she saw her daughter, she started to cry.

"I left the war for my kids to be safe, and now you are in the hospital. You look worse than if you were in the war! What happened to you?"

"Mom, don't cry," she said. "I know I look bad, but don't cry. I will be all right."

"Why did you fight? Why would you do this? What happened to my sweet girl?

"Never mind," she said when Vanessa tried to answer. "Just rest now, you will tell me everything when you can. For now, just know that I am here for you, and rest as much as you can."

God, Jean thought, her father was a fighter, too. I just hope she don't turn out like him, and always come home beat up. Vanessa fell asleep again, and Jean took her hand in hers and prayed.

She prayed that her daughter would be okay, and that she would not be charged with murder. The doctor had told her that Emily was still not awake, and that it did not look good for her. Why had this happened? Jean felt a light tap on her shoulder and she turned around. It was Officer Johnson.

"Can I talk to you outside?" he asked. They walked out of Vanessa's room, and by the look on his face, Jean knew it wouldn't be good news.

"Emily is in critical condition," he said. "She is in a coma right now, and they don't know when, or if, she will wake up. If she doesn't wake up in the next forty-eight hours, Vanessa will be charged with attempted murder and she will have to go to jail."

Jean fell into the chair behind her. "What are you saying to me?" she asked him. "That my daughter might go to jail for the rest of her life? Did you not see that she was beaten up, too? It was not like she started it either."

"Jean," he began, "I am sorry I have to be the one to tell you, but if Emily does not get better, we will have no choice."

"Let's just hope she gets better," Alexander said.

Maria was standing behind them, and listening to Jean cry. She felt bad, not only because Vanessa might go to jail, but because her daughter was the one who put her there. Maria walked towards them, and when Jean saw her she stood up.

"I am sorry," Jean told her, "I don't know what came over my daughter, but I heard that Emily is in bad shape."

"Yes, she is in a coma, and we don't know for how long. Jean, you are one of my friends. I know our kids do not get along, but I also know that if my Emily dies, I will have no other choice than to make sure your daughter is put in jail."

This surprised Jean, because not only did she know how Maria was with Emily, but because they were friends.

"Let's just hope everything works out," Officer Johnson said. He had seen the look on Jean's face. He knew she had been through hell and back. Now was someone telling her they were going to put her daughter in jail.

"I hope so," Maria said. "My daughter is unconscious,

and it is Vanessa's fault. She can talk to her mom, but Emily cannot. I really hope she wakes up, because if she doesn't, I will make sure Vanessa is in hell for what she did to my Emily."

"Now wait a minute," Jean said, "why would my Vanessa be in jail, when Emily is the one who started the whole thing? Maybe she deserved what she got. And where were you?" Jean asked Maria. "Who were you with, while your child was fighting with mine?"

"It is none of your business where I was. Your business is to take care of your daughter, and make sure she doesn't became what your husband was."

"And what was he?" Jean asked, stepping right up to Maria's face.

"Ladies," Officer Johnson said, stepping in between them, "I know this is a very stressful time for both of you. The best thing for you to do is pray that everything goes well for these girls, and that they will both be home soon.

"I hope so Maria said. "I hope so not only for your sake," she looked at Jean, "but for your daughter's sake, as well."

"You pray for your child," Jean told her, "and I will pray for mine."

Jean and Alexander walked back to Vanessa's room. She was still sleeping, and Goran was sitting next to her bed, holding her hand. He was talking to her in a very soft, sweet voice, it gave Jean chills all over her body. This boy really cares about my daughter, Jean thought.

"Hello Goran," she said "how is she doing?"

Goran let go of Vanessa's hand and looked at Jean. His sad look told her that he was not able to talk to her yet.

"She will be okay," Jean told him. "You will see, she will be just like new." Jean started to cry.

"Oh Mom," Alexander said, "are you going to cry all the time? You heard the doctor, she is fine. She's just resting. You should be more worried about if she will go to jail for the rest of her life."

"Jail?" Goran asked. "Why would she go to jail?"

"Emily is in a coma," Jean said. "If she doesn't come out of it, Vanessa will be charged with attempted murder and sent to jail."

"But Vanessa was provoked!" Goran said. "It is not like she was the one who started it. Emily wanted to fight with her all night long, and then she got what she deserved."

"Don't talk like that," Jean said. "I know you care about my daughter, but don't wish bad on other people, either."

"I am sorry," he said, "but I know she wanted Vanessa to fight with her for a long time, but Vanessa always refused to do it. Now, when she did it, they want to blame her and put her in jail? Over my dead body."

"That is sweet to heat," Jean said, "but you should not say that. They will do everything they can for both girls. You should go home and get some rest. I will stay here, and call you as soon as she is better."

"No ma'am," he said. "I am sorry, but I am staying here till she wakes up."

"Mom," Vanessa said quietly.

"Yes Honey? I am here," Jean answered, and walked to her bed. "How are you feeling?"

"Like all of Croatia ran me over," she said.

"Well I can see your sense of humor is back," Jean said. "Vanessa I don't want to worry you, and I probably should not tell you this, but Emily has not woke up yet. She is in a coma, and if she doesn't wake up soon, I don't know what will happen to you."

"It is okay," Vanessa told her mom, "Dad told me she will wake up, I am not worried."

"Dad?" Alexander asked. "Call the doctors, she has lost her mind."

"No, I have not," Vanessa said. "Dad came and talked to me in my dream. He told me everything will be all right, and I believe him."

"As long as you believe him," Jean said with tears in her eyes, "I am sure your dad is watching over you."

Goran was watching them from the back of the room. He did not want to interfere on their family moment, but he hoped he would get to talk to Vanessa soon.

"Someone is here to see you," Jean told her, as if reading Goran's mind.

"Goran," Vanessa said, "I heard his voice. I knew he would come. Can you guys leave us alone for a minute?"

"Sure honey, I will be outside if you need anything," Jean answered.

"I will. Thank you, Mom, for everything," Vanessa said.

"She is all yours," Jean said to Goran as she walked out of the room. "I will be close by, so if you need me, just call."

"I will," he said. Goran walked to Vanessa's bed, and sat down next to her.

"How are you?" he asked.

"I am better now that you are here. Did you hold my hand, or was that a dream, too?" she asked.

"Yes, I was holding your hand. Your mom asked me to go home and get some rest, but I did not want to miss when you would woke up."

"Thank you for staying," Vanessa told him. I don't remember much about the fight, but I do know she punched me first. You believe me don't you?"

"I believe you," Goran said. "I hope everything works out, so you won't have to suffer anymore. Right now you need your rest, I will be back to see you tomorrow."

He bent down, and kissed her on the cheek. Little butterflies in her stomach made her think of him coming back tomorrow, and she fell right back asleep. Goran left her room, and went to find Jean and Alexander to tell them he was leaving. He found them in the hallway talking to Officer Johnson. They all had very serious faces, and Goran wanted to know what was going on.

"So she is pressing charges?" Jean asked.

"She is Emily's mother, and she can do that," Johnson said. "As soon as Vanessa feels better, she will go to jail and be there for three days, after that she can go home free. That is only if Emily gets better by that time. If not, then Vanessa will stay as long as the judge decides."

"What do you mean, she is going to jail?" Goran asked from behind them.

"This is for family only," Johnson told him. "I am sorry Goran, but you have to leave."

"I am not going anywhere. I do not care what you say, I want to know what is going to happen to her."

"Vanessa is only fifteen, and this is her mother," Johnson said. "When I am done telling her, then she can tell you. But, as far as I am concerned, you have no right to be here."

"Fine," Goran said. "Miss Jean, I am going home for the night. I will be back first thing in the morning. Will you please let me know what is going on when I am come back?"

"Yes, Goran, I will," Jean said. "Be careful, and I will see you in the morning."

He left without looking at Officer Johnson. As far as Goran was concerned, Johnson could kiss his ass. Outside, Darko and Marina were sitting in the car, waiting for him.

"How is she?" Marina asked.

"She is better, but Emily is still in a coma. they don't know if she is going to wake up or not. Her mother is pressing charges against Vanessa, and when she is better, she will have to go to jail. If Emily dies, Vanessa will be in jail for the rest of her life."

"That won't happen," Darko said. "Don't worry. Vanessa will be fine. That girl has been through some rough stuff, she will get herself out of this, too."

"Darko, you have not seen her. She is all bruised up. Her eyes and her face are all blue, and they will still send her to jail. Don't they have a heart?"

"I promise you, everything will be okay," Darko said. "You need to go home. This has been a long night. We'll be back tomorrow morning, and I am sure all this will be better."

Goran arrived home, went to his bed and prayed that everything would be better in the morning. He fell asleep and dreamed Vanessa was standing in his room, talking to him. He felt her hands on his, and she smiled when he kissed her. It seemed so real, it woke him up. He looked at the clock, and saw that it was only five am. Too early to go see Vanessa. Goran went back to sleep, and dreamt about her again. This time Vanessa was in jail, talking to him through a window. She looked very pale, and she was asking him to help her.

"I will do everything I can," he said. "I promise, Vanessa, I will take care of you!"

"Please, help me," she begged.

"Goran woke up with a pain in his stomach. His palms were sweaty, and he had tears in his eyes. He got up, and went to find his parents. Maybe they would help him to help Vanessa. They were not home, so he went looking for Darko and Marina, instead. Just his luck, he ran into Emily's mother.

"Hello Goran," she said.

"Hi Maria. How is Emily today?"

"Don't pretend like you care about my daughter," she said.

"I am sorry I even asked then," Goran said, and walked passed her.

"Spoiled little shit!" she yelled after him.

He turned around looked at her, "Maria, the apple does not fall far away the tree. Your Emily got into a fight because of her words. She started it."

"My Emily only wanted you to like her. Was that so hard for you to do?"

"Even if someone gave me a million dollars, I would never be with your daughter."

"Not even if that would help her wake up from a coma?" she asked.

Goran looked at her, confused. "What are you talking about?"

"Well, I think if you spend a day or two with her, then maybe she will wake up. Please, Goran, this would mean so much to her. I am sure it will work. All she ever does is talk about you."

"I am sorry, but you are out of your mind," he told her, and started to walk away.

"Please, Goran," Maria begged. "I really need this from you. My daughter will die if we don't try it."

"What makes you think this will work?" he asked.

"It is worth a try. All I am asking is that you try."

"You know I am dating Vanessa, right? How do you think this is going to make her feel?"

"Do you think I care about that little shit?" Maria asked. "I care about my daughter."

"Maria, you are asking *me* for help, remember? So watch what you say about Vanessa."

"So will you help me and my daughter?" Maria asked again.

"I will help only when you stop talking badly about my girlfriend and her family, and I am going to ask Vanessa first. I am not going to do this if she doesn't want me to."

"You don't have to ask her," she said. "You just need to go to the hospital with me right now. Go sit with Emily, and see if your touch can work. No one has to know."

Goran thought about Vanessa, her family, his friends, and everyone that knew him. What would they do? What were they going to say?

"Come on," Maria begged.

"Oh hell," Goran said, and climbed into Maria's car.

"I am only doing this so Vanessa will not go to jail. If I do this, you will drop all the charges against Vanessa. And when Emily gets better, you two will leave Vanessa alone, understood?"

"Yeah, yeah," Maria said, "understood." She was only thinking of getting her daughter back.

This had better work, Goran thought. If Maria lied to him, then he will be the one charged with murder.

CHAPTER TWENTY-FOUR

EMILY WAS LAYING IN HER bed like she was the night before. Goran walked in the room for the first time since the fight. He could not even be sure that it was Emily. She was much worse than Vanessa. She had a breathing tube down her throat, and both her eyes were taped shut. He was truly shocked that Emily was still alive.

He sat down next to her, and Maria sat next to Goran. He put his hands on top of Emily's and prayed that she would move, or something. He could feel that holding Emily's hand would not do anything for her. Goran looked at Maria and shook his head.

"I am sorry," he said, "I did what you asked me to do."

"Please, Goran, stay here for while. Maybe she will wake up."

A nurse came in and checked on Emily. She checked her vitals, and then made some concerned noises.

"Is something wrong?" Maria asked.

"I am not sure, I have to go get a doctor," the nurse told her and walked out.

"What's going on?" Goran asked.

"I don't know, but I hope it is not bad for my poor Emily."

Maria looked at her daughter, and noticed that her finger was moving a little.

"Look Goran!" she yelled.

Goran jumped, and looked at Emily's hand. He could not believe it. Her fingers were moving!

Dr. Brown walked in then to check Emily, just like the nurse did.

"It looks like our little Emily is starting to wake up," he said. "The best thing to do now, is to leave her alone, so she can get as much rest as possible."

"Gladly," Goran said and walked out of the room.

Maria followed him out into the hallway, where they saw Jean and Alexander waiting outside of Vanessa's room. Great, Goran thought, now what will they think of me?

"Oh look, your family is here," Maria said.

"I am done here," Goran said. "I am leaving. I am glad your daughter is better."

"You cannot leave now," she said to him. "The doctors have to know that you saved my daughter's life. I saw it with my own eyes! I was there when you kissed Emily, and her finger moved." Maria raised her voice so that not only would Jean and Alexander be able to hear, but also Vanessa, laying in her room.

"Kissed?" Goran asked. "Are you out of your mind? I held her hand, lady, and that was all. For your information, I can leave any time I feel like. Not you, the doctors, or the police will stop me."

He saw Alexander and Jean shaking their heads at him. He walked towards them, knowing he had a lot explaining to do-if they were willing to listen.

"How is Vanessa?" he asked.

"Why do you care?" Alexander asked. "When was it that you cared most? When your lips were touching Emily's?"

"Alexander, that is enough," his mom said. "She is fine,

Goran. She is feeling better today, and she has talked a lot more than yesterday. Is it true what Maria said?"

"No ma'am," he answered. "I went to Emily's room, because her mother asked me to. She saw me walking this morning, and asked if I would hold Emily's hand to see if it might help her wake up. I made her promise me, if it worked that she would not press charges against Vanessa.

"Now Emily is coming out of the coma. She saw you guys outside of the room, that is why she said I kissed Emily, so that maybe you wouldn't want to talk to me."

"She is a weird woman," Jean said. "I am sorry that this happened to you. I don't believe a word she says. I know she will press charges, no matter what, or who, asks her not to. That is what kind of person she is."

"Really?" Goran asked, puzzled. "So she tricked me?"

"Yes, honey, she did, but, it is not your fault," Jean said. "She is a grown woman, and she should know, what goes around comes around."

"May I go and talk to Vanessa now?"

"Yes, go right ahead," Jean told him. Goran walked in, and Vanessa was sitting in bed watching television.

"How are you doing today?" he asked.

"I am fine," she said. "How is Emily?"

Her voice told Goranthat Vanessa had heard Maria. There was something else in her voice that told him to watch what he said next.

"You know her mom lied?" he asked.

"Goran, why would anyone lie? There is no reason to lie. Whether you kissed her, or not, you still went behind my back and saw her. You know how I feel about her, and you went anyway," Vanessa said.

She was trying to talk as slowly and quietly as possible. Her voice was not fully back yet, and the doctor said she should not talk much. She did not right now, though. Dammit, she was in love with this idiot, and he was going around the hospital kissing her enemies.

"I don't know who to believe," she said. "You, or her mom. I am sure Emily is not feeling as good as I am, but you are not her boyfriend, you are mine. Why were you there anyway?"

"Well, if you had asked me right away, you would not have had to use all of your voice," Goran answered. "I was walking to Darko's house, and Maria stopped me. She asked me to hold Emily's hand to see if she would come out of the coma."

"Why the hell would you say yes to her? She only wanted to trick you!" Vanessa yelled.

"Vanessa, calm down," he said. "I only did it so she would not press charges against you."

"Press charges?" Vanessa asked. "For what?"

Oops, Goran thought, no one told had her yet. Great, idiot. Not only did you mess up by helping Maria, you just got yourself in more trouble.

"Mom!" Vanessa yelled at the top of her lungs. Jean ran inside, and went to Vanessa's bed.

"What's the matter, honey?" she asked.

"Why am I getting charged? Who is charging me, and with what?" Vanessa asked.

"Nice going, idiot," Alexander said to Goran.

"Shut up," Goran told him.

"That's enough, both of you!" Jean said. "Why don't you both step outside, so I can talk to Vanessa alone?"

"Alexander, out!" Vanessa said. "And you," she looked at Goran, "don't go kissing the whole hospital while I am talking to my mom."

"Women," Goran said as he left the room, "you cannot be with them, or without them."

"You should be without one," Alexander said.

"You know you have a very big mouth," Goran told him. "I have my own problems, and I don't want to deal with you.

If you would please stay out of my way, that would be great. If not, I don't have to go far to put you in the hospital."

"Is that a threat?" Alexander asked. "Because, trust me, the mood I am in right now, that is the last thing you want to do!"

"I am not here to fight with you," Goran said.

"No, you are here to kiss half of the hospital, right?"

Goran took a step towards him. "I am asking you to leave me be."

"Or what?" Alexander asked. "You know, I bet my sister is in here because of you. If you think about it," Alexander went on, "she was at the party because of you. Of course Emily wants you, so they fought over you."

"Did you come up with that one all on your own?" Goran asked. Goran was about to say more, but he saw Darko, Marina, Ivan, and Amanda coming down the hall.

"You are not worth my trouble," Goran told Alexander, and left him standing alone in the hall.

Idiot, Alexander thought, maybe if he sees it my way then he might act smarter next time. Why was Maria yelling anyways, he wondered. Alexander was not going to stand around and wait for an answer. He went to Emily's room, hoping maybe he could overhear something. But before he got there, he was spotted by Goran and the rest of the group.

"Vanessa, come on," Jean said. "I know how important Goran is to you, and I know how much he likes you. Why are you being so difficult?"

"What do you mean, I am difficult?" she asked. "Mom, he was the one kissing Emily, not me."

"He did not kiss her, Vanessa."

"And you know this, how?" Vanessa asked.

"Because I know how conniving Maria and her daughter can be."

"Okay, so he did not kiss her, he still held her hand. Why?"

"Because," Jean began, "Maria thought that might help her daughter, and if Goran did it, then she wouldn't press charges against you."

"Why would she press charges against me?" Vanessa asked.

"Vanessa, honey, you almost killed Emily. What do you think happens to people that beat up on someone else, or kill them? Do you think they go free? No, Vanessa, they don't. There are laws, and Goran was trying to protect you. Not only did he try to help you out, but he also got himself in trouble with you. You really should listen to him," Jean said.

"Whose side are you on Mom?"

"Vanessa, I know you are the one in pain, but put yourself in his position. He is the one that was here last night, and today. You really think any other boy his age would stick around?"

"So you are saying I should just forget that he was touching that nasty thing, and then let him touch me?" Vanessa asked.

"That nasty thing has a name, and you almost killed her. Thank God you did not, or you would be in jail for the rest of your life."

Vanessa saw how much her mom was hurting. She knew her physical pain was nothing compared to the pain that her mom was feeling. She felt bad about what she did. She knew she was to blame for fighting, and she was to blame for almost killing Emily, but she deserved it.

"Mom, to tell you the truth I don't even know what we fought about. All I know is, I was hit first," Vanessa said.

"I know sweetie, I know, but every action has a consequence. And yours will be that you might be charged with attempted murder."

"Murder who? Vanessa asked. "She hit me so hard. Do you see that now I am going to be missing my teeth? What is she missing?"

"Vanessa, she was in a coma," Jean tried, calmly.

"I don't give a shit where she was, Mom. Sorry, I never talk to you like this, but who do they think they are? They are going to put me in jail, because *she* hit *me* first? Let them. I want to see the person who will come and take me to jail. Let them try."

"Vanessa, you need to calm down. You are not even supposed to talk. I can hear you all the way down the hall," a nurse said entering the room.

"Why does every one think they can tell me what to do?" Vanessa asked. "Vanessa calm down. Vanessa don't talk. Vanessa you will be going to jail."

"Where does it stop?" Vanessa asked her mom and the nurse. Vanessa dropped her head, and started to cry, not knowing when or if it would stop.

She knew Maria and Emily. When they wanted something, they did not stop until they got it. Right now they, wanted Vanessa in jail, and until she was there they but I know that no promise is good with them. They are very evil people, and I hate them, Vanessa thought.

"Vanessa, honey," Jean said. I know you are very upset right now, and that you don't want to talk, but we need to finish talking about Goran. You need to understand that you are mad at him for no reason. He did nothing but try to help you."

"That is just it, Mom. he tried to help me," Vanessa said through her tears. "He should have known that anything they say is a lie."

"How would he know that?" Jean asked. "They never lie to him."

"Mom, she just did!" Vanessa yelled. "She just lied to him

so he would go hold that stupid bitch's hand. Who do they think they are?"

"Vanessa, if you don't calm down, I will have to give you a shot. I know that is not what you want. You have other friends that would like to visit you, as well," the nurse cut in.

"I am sorry," Vanessa said. "I will settle down." I am not getting a shot, she thought, no way. I will calm down until I see that bitch again, then I will finish the job. Suddenly, she heard yelling from the hall.

"What is going on?" Vanessa asked.

"I don't know, but I will go find out," the nurse answered. "Are you sure you will be all right?"

"Yes ma'am," she said, "you can go and check."

The nurse left the room and headed down the hall. Vanessa and Jean were tried to hear what was going on, but they could not make out what was being said.

"Vanessa," Jean said, "I don't want you to get upset, but if Officer Johnson comes to talk to you, promise me you will stay calm."

"I promise, Mom," Vanessa said. "Mom, I am sorry I yelled. I am sorry I caused you pain, and I am sorry I got into a fight. If I do go to jail, that will be my fault, and I will have to stay there because I was the one fighting."

"Vanessa, I will do everything I can for you not to go, but if you have to, then I will get you out as soon as I can," Jean told her and took her daughter's hand. "You are my daughter, and if I have to, I will die for you. And for Alexander, too. You two are all that I have. If you had come home last night, there was something I was going to talk to you about, but I will wait until you get better."

"I am fine," Vanessa said. "What was it?"

"Well, we could go to America. If we get accepted, and if that is what you and Alexander want. I know it is a lot to think about," Jean said. "You have a boyfriend, and friends, and when we leave it will be just the three of us. Go to sleep, and we'll talk about it when you wake up."

"Stay the hell away from me!" Alexander suddenly yelled.

"Calm down," a nurse told him. "Don't you know that this is a hospital? If you two have a problem, then go outside and take care of it."

"Where were you going?" the nurse asked Alexander. "Why are you down this hall, when your sister is up the hall?"

"I wanted to go see Emily."

"Why?" Goran asked.

They were standing in the middle of the hall, between the girls' rooms. Maria heard all the yelling, and came outside to see what was going on.

"Oh look," Alexander said, "Goran cares why I was going to see that little bitch."

"Watch your language, young man," Officer Johnson said from behind him. "Answer the question, why did you want to see Emily?"

"Because it was something to do, and I wanted to," Alexander answered. "Why? Is that a crime? Are you going to charge me?" Alexander was looking straight at Maria.

"You children are nothing but trouble," Maria said. "Now Alexander, your sister is in the hospital."

"She is in the hospital, because your bitch daughter put her here," Alexander said.

"That's enough, Alexander," Jean said, coming up behind him. "I don't want to hear you talk like that. Apologize to Maria, right now."

"Why should I? Because of her daughter, my sister is laying in bed in pain."

"Yes, but so is Emily," Jean told him. "Now apologize, and come with me."

"I am sorry," he said through his teeth, then he walked over to his mom. "Why did you make me apologize, Mom?"

"Because, not only are you making it worse for your sister, you are making it worse for yourself, too. Maria enjoys seeing your sister here. She would like to see you here, too. With your words you will only end up hurting yourself."

"I am sorry, Mom," he said. "I just wanted to see what Emily looked like."

"Why? What difference would that make?" Jean asked.

"Have you not seen Vanessa?" Alexander asked. "I would like to know that Vanessa does not look worse than Emily."

"Alexander, did you forget that Emily was in a coma until today?"

"Yes, so? I just wanted to see. Why is it such a big deal?"

"Vanessa might go to jail, and if you don't stop making trouble, Maria will make sure you go, too. Now stop it, and let's go see your sister," Jean said to Alexander. "Why were you arguing with Goran?"

"Because I do not believe a word he said. I think he is trying to play my sister."

"And why would he want to do that?" Jean asked.

"Mom, you don't know nothing about teenagers these days, do you? You like Goran all you want," Alexander told her. "I will find out if he really likes my sister, my own way!"

CHAPTER TWENTY-FIVE

WITH EVERY DAY THAT WENT by, Emily got better, and it was almost time for her to get out of the hospital. She wanted revenge. She needed to see for herself that Vanessa was still with Goran. No matter what, she was going to separate them. It felt so good to hold his hand. It did not last more than five seconds, but to her that was all she needed. When she is out of this hole, she would make sure Vanessa got back in it.

She hated Vanessa. Not only did she have the guy Emily wanted, but she was out of the hospital before her, too. How much more did she have to take Emily wondered. There was talk that Vanessa's family might be leaving town, and going to America, but Emily didn't buy that for a minute. But maybe if they did go, then Goran would be all Emily's. He and Vanessa would have to break up, and Emily could have him to herself.

Even Officer Johnson did not come to see Emily anymore. The only person ever there was her mom, and she was getting on her nerves, too. Emily are you okay? Emily do you need anything? Emily this, and Emily that. She was getting sick of hearing her name all the time.

"Mom, I am fine," she would say, but did that stop her.

Her mom was still at the hospital every day, bringing her food, cookies, flowers and cards.

Jamie did not visit her at all. Emily even told her mom to personally go to Jamie's house, and ask her to visit and she still had not. She always gave some excuse, like Jamie was working, or at school, sick, or taking a bath.

Just wait until I get out, Emily thought, all hell will brake loose.

She could not wait to see Vanessa's face when she kissed Goran right in front of her. Emily had a great plan for when she got out. She was going to press charges against Vanessa, and then she would walk over her to house when Officer Johnson arrested her. Emily would pretend like she did not know anything. Then Goran would be all hers once again.

Emily was sleeping when Maria walked into her room. She had just got done talking to the doctors, and they told her that Emily was throwing up and she could not go home yet.

"My poor Emily" she said.

Emily opened her eyes, and saw her mom standing next to her, with eyes full of tears.

"Mom," Emily said, "I really don't feel good. It feels like someone is taking my insides out. I hurt so bad." She started to cry, and pressed the button for a nurse.

The nurse came in and gave her some medicine. Emily put them inside her mouth and pretended to swallow. When they were alone, Emily asked her mom if she would ask Goran to come and visit her.

"Oh Emily, honey, I am sure he is busy. I heard he is working so much these days."

"Please, Mom?" she asked. "it would make me feel so much better."

"Emily, I will try, but if I cannot get him to come, please don't be upset with me."

"Please try, Mom," Emily said again.

When her mom left the room, she took the medicine nurse gave her out of her mouth, and threw it in the trash.

"That is how it is done," she said aloud to herself. "Thank you, thank you. I know, I am the master."

She laid in her room watching television, when someone knocked on the door. That was fast, she thought. But instead of Goran, Jamie walked in.

"What took you so long to come and see me?" Emily asked her.

"I don't like hospitals," Jamie answered. "And you were very sick. I did not want to bother you."

"Bull crap," Emily said. "You were scared to see what I looked like."

"Well, yeah, you are right," Jamie admitted, "So how are you?"

"I am okay. My mom went to go get Goran for me, so I can get out of here with him by my side."

Jamie looked at her in surprise. "You are still hung up on him."

"You have no idea how it felt to hold his hand," Emily told her. "It felt magic, like something I have never experienced before. I don't want anyone else but him."

"And you really think he will come? Even though he is still with Vanessa, you think he will come to see you? Are you nuts?"

"Did you come here to insult me, or to keep me company?" Emily asked.

"Neither," Jamie answered. "I came to tell you that we got accepted to leave for America. I am saying my good byes early, because I was not sure if you would be out or not."

"Why the hell are you moving there?" Emily asked. "You don't have any family there. You don't speak English. What is it with all you people? Do you think life is better in America, or something?"

"It is way better than here," Jamie said. "My mom and dad

both lost their jobs, and we barely have any money. I am sure we will be all right, thanks for your support. Jamie got up to leave then turned around.

"Oh yeah, I almost forgot. Don't be stupid. Goran did not, does not, and will not ever want to be with you." Then Jamie walked out and left Emily staring after her.

When the hell did she get so bold, Emily wondered. She closed her eyes, and thought about Goran. How much better would her life be, if he was with her? She would never be home. All the people he hung out with would have to accept her, too. She heard a light knock on the door and opened her eyes. She almost got sick when she saw who it was.

"What the hell are you doing here?" Emily asked.

"Oh, I am sorry. Were you sleeping?" Alexander asked her.

"No, what do you need?"

"Do I have to need something, to come and visit you?"

"Yes. Your sister almost killed me, and you want me to believe you just came to see what I was doing?"

"No," Alexander said, "I came to see if you and your mother are still pressing charges against my sister."

"Of course we are. I cannot wait to get out of here, so I can make her pay for everything she did to me," Emily told him and pressed the nurse button. The nurse walked in before Alexander could say anything else.

"I am sorry, I am very tired," Emily said. "And he was bothering me. Will you please ask him to leave?"

"Sorry sir," the nurse said to Alexander, "but you have to leave."

"I am not done here," he said. "I need to stay and talk to her."

"No you don't," Emily said. "I am done talking to you, and your trash family."

The nurse pulled Alexander out by his arm.

"Bitch," Alexander said through his teeth. He was hoping

that Emily would have stopped thinking about the charges by now. His last hope was Goran. If he could get Goran to talk to Emily, maybe she would drop the charges. Where to find Goran today, he wondered.

Alexander walked home, and did not see Darko's car in his driveway, which meant Goran was not there. Just as he turned to go look somewhere else, Vanessa spotted him.

"Where are you going?" she asked.

"I was going for a walk, I did not know if anyone was home," Alexander lied. There was no way he would tell her he was looking for Goran. Alexander was on his way before she could ask any more questions.

Maria was looking for Goran, too. She just could not find him, but she had to. Emily was more sick now than she was three days ago. Driving back to the hospital, she spotted Goran and Darko at the store. She pulled over not knowing quite what to say.

"Hi Maria," Darko said. "How is Emily?"

"She is not good," she told him. "She asked me to look for Goran, and bring him back with me."

"Goran looked at her like had she just hit him.

"I am sorry, Maria," he said, "I have a date with Vanessa later, I cannot come."

"Please Goran?" she begged. "Emily is worse now, and I really need your help."

"I already helped you once," he said, "and you two are still planning on pressing charges against my girlfriend."

"This time, I promise it will be different," Maria said.

"And how will I know?" Goran asked. "I am not a toy you can play with."

"If you go, I promise I will never bother you again," Maria said. "And we'll drop all the charges against Vanessa."

"I don't know," Goran said.

"I will give you some time to think about it. I need some things from the store. By the time I am done, I hope you will find it in your heart to help my Emily." Maria turned around and entered the store.

"What do I do?" Goran asked Darko.

"I don't know man," Darko said. "If it was me, I would not go. Not only will this hurt Vanessa, you might even lose her over this. You have to ask yourself if it is worth it."

"I know I might lose Alexander walked into the store.

"Great," Goran said, "not only will I have to explain it to Vanessa, I have to tell her whole family, too."

"Hey guys," Alexander said.

"How come you are down here?" Darko asked.

"I was looking for you," Alexander pointed at Goran.

"Wow, I am a wanted man today," Goran said. "What can I do for you?"

"I was hoping you would talk to Emily, and see if she could be stopped from pressing charges against my sister." Darko and Goran looked at him in shock.

"Have you talked to Vanessa about this?" Goran asked.

"Are you crazy? If she knew I was even looking for you, she would kill me. If she knew you were going to do it, that would be even worse."

"Who said I was going to do it?" Goran asked.

"Come on, man," Alexander said. "You know that if we don't do anything, Vanessa will go to jail, and then what?"

"And if I go, Vanessa will hate me. I lose no matter what," Goran said.

"I will talk to her," Alexander said. They kept talking, not even noticing that Maria was listening.

"So you will do it?" Maria asked suddenly.

"Do what?" Alexander asked her.

"Emily sent me to find Goran, so she can talk to him. She is very sick again. I promised Goran I won't press charges if he goes," Maria told all of them.

"I did not say yes yet," Goran said.

"There is no time for thinking," Maria said. "My daughter

is sick, she wants to see you. There is nothing to think about. If you want to stay with your girlfriend, and you don't want her in jail, you will come with me."

"Fine. I will do it," Goran said. "Alexander, you are coming with me, because if anything happens, I want you there as a witness."

"I just came from there," Alexander said. "I went to ask Emily to drop the charges, and she said no. So I came looking for Goran, thinking maybe he could change her mind."

"You just made things worse," Maria told him. "She is very sick, and she needs her rest. Why would you go bother her?"

"She did not look sick to me," he answered. "Let's go and get this over with."

They headed to the hospital. Goran did not want to, but he knew he had to. He wanted to take care of Vanessa. He did not know how this would help, but it everyone else thought it was worth trying.

He had to see Emily, and he really disliked her. No matter how much her mom begged him to help her, he did not want to. He and Alexander walked in behind Maria. They were hoping Emily would be better, and just as they got to her door, they heard her laughing on the phone.

"Don't worry about it," Emily was saying. "My mom will do anything I ask her to. Just remember, you are the only one that knows that I am not really sick. I am doing this just so I can get Goran."

Maria looked at Goran, and his expression told her that Emily just blew any chance she ever had with him. They backed away from the door.

"I am sorry, Goran," Maria said. "I had no idea."

"As long as you drop the charges against Vanessa, I don't care.," Goran said. "I don't need your sorry, and I do not want to see her."

"Oh, come on," Alexander said. "Let's see how far she will go. It could be fun."

The moment they walked in, Emily put the phone down, and her smile disappeared.

"Oh, Mom, you found him for me! Thank you!"

"What do you want from me, Emily?" Goran asked.

"I just want you to hold my hand again, I am sure it would help me feel better so I can get out of here. Then you can take me home."

"That is why your mom had to look for me? Just so you can come home with me?" he asked.

Emily could see that Goran was mad, but why? She was sick, and he was mad at her? Maybe he cared, whatever his problem was she wouldn't let him leave without her.

"Who were you just talking to, Emily?" Maria asked her daughter.

"Jamie," Emily lied.

"Are you sure?" Maria asked.

"Mom, I know who was I talking to. I just don't know why you want to know."

"I will tell you why," Maria said. "I have been running around all day looking for Goran so you can feel better, and then I find out you were playing me for a fool. Did you really think that I was going to press charges against Vanessa?" Maria asked Emily.

"Well, that was the plan," Emily said.

"Well, I am not," Maria told her. "I heard you on the phone, telling whoever that was that you were playing sick."

"I am the one in the hospital," Emily said. "You cannot tell me what to do."

"Yes, I can. I am your mother, and you are underage, so no police will file the report without me."

"How does it feel when people find out you are a liar?" Alexander asked.

"Oh, shut up, Emily said, and looked at Goran. "You believe me, don't you? You know I am sick, and I *need* you."

"You don't need me. I am very sorry that I even thought of

helping you, or taking you home, or whatever you wanted me to do. I feel sorry for you," he said and walked out.

"Goran! Wait, don't go!" she cried. "I am sick! I need you! Please, come back!"

When the doors closed, it was Emily and Maria. Emily looked at her mother, her eyes full of hate.

"I hate you!" she yelled. "Look what you did! I cannot wait to get out of here, then I am moving to America with Jamie and her family."

Maria did not say anything, she knew her daughter would calm down. She would get home, and everything would be just like it was before.

"You will be fine, honey, I promise," she told her and left to look for a doctor. She found the doctor, and explained to him that Emily was playing sick ,just so she would get her way.

That afternoon, Emily was released to go home. Maria and Emily went home together, and lived in the same house, just like before.

CHAPTER TWENTY-SIX

VANESSA WAS OUT OF THE hospital, but she had lots of problems recovering. Her bruises disappeared, but her mouth did not heal. The doctors took out her six of her top teeth. It was embarrassing to smile, she did not want anyone to see her. When Goran came to see her, Jean told him that Vanessa was not feeling well, and did not want to be seen.

Vanessa was not the same girl anymore. She was ugly now. Emily not only took her boyfriend away, she took her looks, too. Vanessa knew Goran would not mind seeing her no matter how she looked, but to her it mattered.

"Come on, honey," Jean said, "this is the third time that Goran has been here today. Give him a chance."

"Chance for what mom?" Vanessa asked. "Chance for him, and everyone else, to make fun of me? To tell me that I am ugly? No, thank you. I would rather sit in this house all alone, than go out in public looking like this."

There was nothing Jean could do to change her mind. She walked out of the room, and went to see Goran, who was sitting in the kitchen.

"I am sorry," Jean said, "she won't come out."

"But why?" Goran asked. "I am here for her whenever she

needs me. I was in the hospital, I saw her when the ambulance came. Why can't I see her now?"

"Give her time," Jean told him.

"I am sorry, Jean," Goran said, "I don't know how much time I can give her. It seems like every time I come over, she doesn't want to see me. It makes me think she doesn't want to have anything to do with me. What if she won't change her mind?"

"She might," Jean answered.

"I am not going to come back anymore," he told her. "This is my last time. If she still wants to see me, she knows where I live."

"I will tell her," Jean said.

Jean tried to think of ways to change her daughter's mind. Jean knew it was going to be hard, but she had to try.

"Vanessa, Goran said he is not coming back anymore. If you want to see him, you will have to go to him. He said you know where to find him."

"Yeah, I do," Vanessa said with bitterness in her voice.

"It is not like he did not come here every day since you have been out, Vanessa. I don't know what more you want from him. No one else would wait for you as long as he has."

"Thank you, Mom. You are on his side, too. I wish Emily would have just killed me when she had the chance."

"Why are you so mean to the people that love you?" Jean asked.

"Maybe because none of you have to deal with this pain, and look like an ogre," Vanessa said.

"And that is our fault?" Jean asked her. When the words left her mouth, she wished she could take them right back.

"I am sorry," Jean said, "I did not mean it like that. But, Vanessa, honey, you are the one who was in the fight, and now you are taking it out on us. You are making all of us feel like we did something wrong, when you know that it is no one's fault but yours."

"Have I ever said it was your fault?" Vanessa asked her mom.

"No, you did not," Jean said. "You don't have to say it. We feel it when you won't come out and face us. Do you think Emily is hiding inside her house, not talking to anyone?"

"I don't care what she is doing," Vanessa answered. "I don't want to know that she even exists anymore."

"My point is," Jean said, "that I want you to get out today. I don't care if you want to, or not, you need to."

"Why are you so mean to me?" Vanessa asked and started to cry.

"Because I don't want to see my daughter lose a guy that really cares about her, and I don't want to see someone else take your place. I am not doing it to be mean to you, I am doing it because I love you."

"You have a very funny way of showing your love, Mom," Vanessa said. "Fine, I will get out today. But, I am not going to see Goran until I am ready."

"That is okay with me, as long as you are out of your room," Jean said and left the room.

"She will be out of her room today," Jean told Alexander. "Go find Goran, and drag him back here if you have to. He needs to be here today."

"Why me?" Alexander asked.

"You want your sister out of her room, don't you?" Jean asked him.

"No, not really," Alexander answered. "I know, Mom, I am going," he said when Jean gave him The Look.

Why do I have to get him, Alexander wondered. She wants Goran, she should go get him. But, he did it anyways. His mom always had ways of making him do things he did not want to do. He did not know where he was going to find Goran, so he started at Goran's house first, but he was not there.

"I think he went to Darko's," his dad, Milan told him. "How is you sister?"

"She is spoiled now, but she is good," Alexander told him.

"Tell her we are praying for her," Milan said and closed the door.

Great, Alexander thought, now I have to go to Darko's. He never liked Darko, or Goran for that matter, but his mom said to get him and he knows better than to not listen.

Seeing Darko's car in front of his house, Alexander knew they were home.

"Oh goody," Alexander said to himself. "All of them must be here." He walked in the house, and saw Darko's parents sitting at the kitchen table eating. Darko's mom, Yelena, noticed Alexander first.

"Hey Alexander," she said, "what brings you here?"

"I am looking for Goran. Have you seen him?" Alexander asked.

"Oh, they are all up in Darko's room. You know your way up," she said.

"Thank you," Alexander said.

"How is your sister?" Yelena asked. "I have not seen her around since she got out of the hospital."

"She is too shy to come out of her room," Alexander told her.

"I can understand that," Yelena said. "I would be, too but it was not her fault. She was provoked to do what she did."

"Is it okay for me to go up, and talk to Goran?" Alexander asked.

"Yes, go ahead. Tell your sister we are thinking of her," Yelena said.

"Yes ma'am, I will," he said and walked up the stairs to Darko's room.

He could hear them talking from the hallway. Must be all of them, he thought. Alexander knew it was bad to eavesdrop, but he could not help himself.

"I just don't know what else to do," he heard Goran say.

"I have done everything I can, every time I go there she won't talk to me."

"I don't know why you try," Marina said.

"Marina, of all people you should be the one to understand," Darko said. "You are her best friend."

"I *was* her best friend," she said. "I am not her friend anymore, I don't want to have anything to do with her. Don't ask me why, I have my reasons."

We all know your reasons," Darko told her. "You are mad that Ivan broke up with you, after he heard you were the one Emily was talking to when she was in the hospital. You were the one who was telling Emily to go after Goran, even though you knew what that would do to Vanessa."

This is better then me going inside, Alexander thought. This way I can find out everything I need to know, and I don't have to ask.

"So what?" Marina asked. "It is my right to talk to whoever I feel like, and no one can stop me."

"I don't want to stop you," Goran said. "I just don't want to lose her, that's all."

"You already have," Marina told him. "Can't you see that Vanessa doesn't want to be with you? You should move on, and find someone else better than she is. What do you see in her anyway?"

"Let me get this right," Goran said. "You want me to let Vanessa go, so I can be with you, don't you?"

"What do you mean?" Darko asked. "Why would you say that? You are my best friend, I thought you did not like my sister like that."

"I don't," Goran said, "but your sister has tried to kiss me many times when we are alone."

I knew it, Alexander thought, I knew she wanted him. I know I should go inside, but this is just too good to miss.

Amanda was just listening to them talk. She knew that Marina was talking to Emily, but did not say anything. Darko would have killed her. Amanda was the one who told her brother about Emily and Marina talking in the hospital, but he promised he would not tell anyone.

"I don't know why you are yelling at me," Marina said. "I can like whoever I want."

"Yes, you can," Darko said, "but not my best friend. You stole one already, and he broke up with you."

"How childish all of you are," Amanda said. "You are all yelling for no reason. I never wanted Vanessa around, because she is to quiet, and I knew Darko wanted her."

"If I wanted her, I would have had her," Darko said.

"What do you mean, you would have had her?" Goran asked.

"I am leaving," Marina said, "you all can fight over her all you want."

Before Marina could open the door, Alexander walked in.

"Wow," he said, "it was great to hear everything, but I had to crash this party."

"What the hell are you doing here? Where you spying on us?" Marina asked.

"Oh, don't act so innocent," he said. "I heard every word you said, and I would be ashamed if I was you."

"Ashamed of what?" Marina asked. "I am not the one spying on people."

"I was not spying," Alexander said, "I just did not want to be rude and interrupt."

"So you were standing there, listening what we were talking about?" Amanda asked.

Alexander said, "You were the only one I did not hear talk, you know what that means?"

"I have a feeling you are going to tell me."

"Well since you asked," he said, "I know you knew that Marina and Emily were talking on the phone. I know that you and Marina were working together to break up Goran and my sister. And, I know you told your brother that Marina was not good for him, and that is why he broke up with her.

"Didn't you people learn anything at Darko's party?" Alexander asked.

"Let me get this straight," Darko said, "Everyone keeps secrets, and I am always the last one to find out?"

"It seems that way," Goran said, "but this time it is not just you. I didn't know any of this, either."

"I am done talking," Amanda said and walked out of the room.

"So am I," Marina said and left right behind her.

"What are you doing here?" Darko asked Alexander.

"I came looking for Goran. My mom sent me. She said to bring you, even if you are kicking and screaming."

"Why?" Goran asked. "Is Vanessa okay?"

"If you ask me, she is just spoiled," Alexander said. "But, I guess my mom got her to come out, so she wants you there."

"Is it okay if I come with you?" Darko asked.

"Why would you want to?" Goran looked at him, surprised.

"Vanessa did not want to see anyone for weeks now. I think it will be best if I go by myself," Goran told Darko. "If she doesn't want to see me because you came along, we'll have problems."

Out on the road, they saw Amanda and Marina walking ahead of them. If they were all going to the same place, this would not be good.

Vanessa heard noises outside, so she got up to see what it was. She saw Marina and Amanda walking up her driveway, and behind them she saw Goran, Darko, and Alexander.

Wow, did my mom send Alexander to get the whole town, she wondered.

"I have a key," she heard Alexander say. "She must be in her room hiding, like she always does."

Vanessa heard the key in the lock, and ran back to her

room. She heard them all come inside, and then she heard a knock on her door.

"What?" she asked.

"Open the door," Alexander said. "People are here to see you."

"I did not ask for anyone," she said.

"Vanessa, will you let me in?" she heard Goran ask. "I am only asking for myself."

"God, why are you so stubborn and selfish?" Marina asked.

"I did not ask you to come over," Vanessa told her.

"If I don't," Marina asked, "are you going to beat me, like you did Emily?"

"Marina, stop it," Goran said. "Why are you girls even here?"

"We came over to see if she is going to let you see her."

"Why is that any of your business?" Goran asked. "This is between me and her."

Vanessa unlocked the door and stepped out. Darko and the girls had not seen her since the party, and they were surprised by how she looked. She still had a bruise eye, and her mouth was swollen. Vanessa turned to Goran.

"You want to come in my room, so we can talk?" she asked.

"We came to see you, too," Marina said. The girls had smirks on their faces.

"I don't care," Vanessa said. "I only wanted to see him, the rest of you can go away. I did not ask for you."

"Who do you think you are?" Marina asked.

"I am someone that doesn't need your sorry looks," Vanessa answered, and closed her door.

CHAPTER TWENTY-SEVEN

THERE WAS A LOT OF talk of people leaving for America. Maybe we could go too, Jean thought, I have to find out where I have to go. She was cleaning one of the bigger rooms in the post office when Officer Johnson came in.

"Hey Jean," he said, "I need to talk to you."

"What's wrong?" she asked.

"Nothing. I thought you would like to hear some good news. Maria came into the office today, and told us that she is not pressing charges against Vanessa. They are going to America in a couple of months."

"Oh, that is good news! I am glad they are not pressing charges. But, I was wondering myself where I would have to go to see if my family could go, too.

"Why would you want, too?" he asked. "You don't speak the language, and you don't know anyone there."

"Just because I don't speak the language, does not mean that I cannot learn. I am not stupid," Jean said.

"I am sorry, I did not mean anything by it. I am sure if you talk to Maria, she will tell you where to go. But just so you know, I like having you around."

"Thank you," Jean told him and went back to work.

Jean finished her shift and went to talk to Maria. It wasn't going to be easy talking to her. They had not talked since the girls' fight. Jean still felt hurt over the words Maria said about her and her kids. And look at me now, Jean thought, I have to go and ask for her help.

Jean knocked on the door and waited for someone to answer. After a minute, or two, no one came. She put her ear to the door and could hear voices, but she could not make out what was said. Jean knocked again. Emily peeked through the door, and saw Jean standing there.

"Yes?" she asked.

"Is your mom home?" Jean asked her.

"No, it is just me," Emily answered. She looked at Jean. Emily's eyes were trying to tell her something, but Jean could not make out what Emily was trying to say.

"May I come in?" Jean asked.

"Oh no, the place is a mess. And, Mom won't let me have people over when she is not home," Emily told her. Emily moved her mouth, but no sound came out. Jean tried to make out what Emily was saying.

It looked like, "Call police."

Emily was definitely in trouble, Jean knew because Emily was never this nice to her.

"Will you tell your mom to come by when she gets back?" Jean asked, then she nodded to Emily, letting her know that she knew there was trouble.

Emily closed the door, and Jean ran out to the street. Maria's house was not that far from the police station, and Jean ran in. She saw Officer Johnson sitting at his desk and when he saw her expression he jumped right up.

"What's wrong?" he asked.

"It is Emily. Someone is in her house, and she needs help!" Jean told him what happened, and what she knew.

"Are you sure she said to call us?" Officer Johnson asked her.

"Do I look sure?" Jean asked him. "I want you to go and

check it out." It took them about two minutes to get to Maria's house.

"You stay here," Johnson told Jean. "I am going to check it out."

Jean stayed in the car while he went to the door. Officer Johnson knocked just like Jean did, but no one was answering.

"Police!" he yelled. "Open the door!"

Still no one answered. Jean was getting scared, then she saw Maria's window. There was a young man coming out of it, on his left sleeve there was blood. Jean screamed very loudly, and Johnson looked at her.

Then he saw the man run towards the car, and Johnson took off after him. He jumped on him, and tackled him to the road. Cars stopped, and someone got out to help. Johnson put the man in cuffs, and sat him down in the car.

Jean hopped out, and went running towards the house. She saw blood and assumed the worst. Emily must be bleeding, or even worse. Officer Johnson caught up to her quickly.

"Slow down!" he told her. "Let me go in first."

He knocked the door down, and walked in very slowly. Jean was right behind him. The place was a mess. There was glass all over the floor. They walked in the kitchen, and saw Emily laying on the floor. She was bleeding, but alive.

Maria was on her almost home when she saw police car in front of her house. I wonder what Emily did now, she thought. She ran inside the house, and saw all the glass. Maria walked in the kitchen, and saw Officer Johnson and Jean leaning over Emily.

"What happened to my baby?" she cried.

"I think she was raped," Officer Johnson told her.

"Raped? By who?" Maria asked in shock.

"I have the guy in my car. I already called for back up, and the ambulance will be here in a minute."

"Why are you here?" Maria asked Jean.

"I came by to see you. When Emily opened the door, she signaled me to call the police. So I ran to the station and got Officer Johnson."

"So you saved my daughter," Maria said.

"I would not call it saved, yet," Johnson said. "She will have to be examined. I am going to talk to the boy in my car."

"I am going with you," Maria said.

"No. You wait here for ambulance. I will be right back."

"This is my only child! I am going to find out who did this to her, and you are not going to stop me."

There was a knock at the door. The ambulance had shown up. All of a sudden Maria's house became very small. There was no where for her to turn. She seen Jean, and a police officer, and then everything went black.

"Maria. Maria," she heard someone calling. Maria opened her eyes, and two paramedics were standing over her.

"Are you all right?" one of them asked.

"I am fine. What happened?" Maria asked.

"You fainted. And when you fell, you hit your head on the table. Are you sure you are all right?"

"I am good," she answered. Maria sat up very slowly, and everything came back to her.

"Where is my daughter?" she asked.

"She is on her way to the hospital. The police are outside waiting for you. I am Barry, I would be more than happy to take you to the hospital."

"Where are Jean, and Officer Johnson?"

"They are outside waiting, too" Barry told her.

Maria took a step forward, then had to sit back down.

"Will you please call them inside?" Maria asked Barry.

"I sure will," he said and walked out. It did not take him long to find Jean and Officer Johnson. Barry walked over to Johnson.

"What happened?" he asked Officer Johnson.

"I am not sure yet," Johnson told him.

"Don't give me that crap," Barry said.

"It is police business, I cannot tell you. Sorry," Johnson said and walked away.

"Asshole," Barry said. He looked around, and saw Jean outside talking to Johnson. Barry walked towards them, making sure they could not see him.

"So now what will happen?" he heard Jean ask.

"I am going back to the police station. I still have to go question the boy."

They caught him, Barry thought. Good, I won't have to go after him.

"I will stay with Maria," Jean said. "If you have to go, you can leave. I am sure Barry is still here, he can take her to hospital."

"Thank you Jean. You saved Emily's life," he told her and walked to his car.

Barry walked out of bushes where he was hiding, and almost scared Jean to death.

"What were you doing?" Jean asked.

"Nothing. I tried talking to Officer Johnson, and he would not tell me anything. I was hoping maybe you would tell me what happened."

"I am not sure I should be the one telling you," Jean said. "When Maria is ready to talk, I am sure she will. I think you should go inside and get her ready to go."

"Why won't anyone tell me what happened?" Barry asked.

"I would, but it is not my place," Jean told him.

Maria was inside trying to clean up the mess. "I wonder who he was?" she asked out loud.

"I have never seen him around," Jean answered from behind her.

"Damn woman!" Maria said. "You scared me to death!"

"I am sorry, but I think it is time for you to go to the

hospital. You need to check on Emily, and maybe get yourself checked, too."

"I will take you there," Barry said, walking into the room.

"Thank you," Maria said, then looked at Jean. "What were you doing here again?"

"I came to talk to you."

"About what?"

"That is not important right now," Jean told her. "You need to check on Emily. I can talk to you when you get back."

"Thank you, you saved my kid. I will be grateful to you for the rest of my life," Maria told her.

Maria and Barry headed to the ambulance, and Jean walked home. Jean was exhausted, not only did she work all day, but that was a lot to take in. Emily was Vanessa's age, what if something like that happened to her? No more just thinking about going somewhere.

Vanessa and Alexander were sitting on the couch when she walked in the house.

"Hi Mom," they said.

"Hi," Jean said. "We need to talk about something very serious. This will be hard for me to say, and even harder for us to do, but we'll have to try."

"Does this mean we might be going to America?" Vanessa asked, surprising Jean.

"How did you know?" Jean asked her.

"I heard people saying that Maria and Emily are leaving."

"Yes, it means we will try to go. I don't know where we are going just yet, but I want to try to get out of here."

"And why do we want to go?" Alexander asked.

"I know it will be hard," Jean said. "I don't want to leave all this behind, either, but I have to look for a better place than this. Did you hear what happened to Emily today?"

"No, what?" Alexander and Vanessa asked at the same time.

"Someone broke into her house today, and hurt her. I went there to talk to Maria, and when Emily opened the door, she told me to call the police."

"Cool! Mom is a hero," Alexander said.

"I would not say that," Jean told him. "Sadly, we were late. Emily was taken to the hospital."

"Does her mom know?" Vanessa asked.

"Yes, she got home right before the ambulance arrived. Barry took Maria to the hospital."

"Where is the guy?" Alexander asked. "Do they know who he is?"

"I don't know, the police took him," Jean said. "I did not recognize him."

"Poor Emily," Vanessa said. "She just came home from the hospital, and now she is right back in."

"Yes, but this time it is not her fault," Jean said. "This time something awful happened to her, and I don't want you two to tell anyone what I have just told you."

"Which part?" Alexander asked. "The part that we are leaving, or the one about Emily?"

"Don't tell anyone we are leaving yet, because we don't know for sure. I don't want anyone talking about Emily, either, because no one knows what really happened."

"I bet she called him, and when he tried something, she told him no. So he got mad," Alexander said.

"Alexander!" Jean yelled. "I don't want you talking like that. You don't know what happened, so don't go around spreading rumors."

"Fine, I won't say anything," he said. "I was saying that I think that is what happened."

"So what do we do now?" Vanessa asked.

"I am going to work in morning, and I will talk to people

to see where I go to sign us up to leave next month," Jean said.

"That soon?" Vanessa yelled. She stood up and started pacing the room. "Come on, Mom! I have to let everyone know I am leaving, which means I have to break up with Goran. How do I do all that in one month?"

"Don't tell him yet," Jean told her.

"Should I wait until the last minute? He will hate me!"

"You have to break up with him, because you will be going to a different country," Jean said. "I am sorry, Vanessa, but I am doing this for the family."

"Always for the family!" Vanessa cried. "Are you sure this is what we want?"

"I don't care. You are still my child," Jean said. "You will do what I tell you to."

"Then don't say you are doing this for the family," Vanessa said angrily, and walked off to her room.

"She will calm down, Mom," Alexander said. "I am sure she did not mean it, she is just upset because she has to leave Goran. She will get over it, eventually."

CHAPTER TWENTY-EIGHT

EMILY WOKE UP WITH A pounding headache. She looked around, and did not recognize where she was. She heard noises, but could not tell what they were.

"I think she is waking up," she heard a man's voice say.

"I am going to get a doctor. I will be right back," Emily thought it sounded like her mom.

"Mom," she tried to call to her, but nothing came out. What happened to me, Emily wondered. I don't remember anything, I cannot see very well, either.

"Mom?" she tried again, but this time only a moan came out.

"She will be right back," the voice said. "Can you see me?"

Emily tried to look, but could not see anything. She shook her head, and started to cry.

"It is okay," the man said. "I am Barry, I came with your mom. She went to get the doctors, they will be right back. Do you remember what happened to you?"

Emily shook her head again, and tried to turn so the man would not see her cry.

"Let me check her," the doctor said. "Can you step outside for a minute?" he asked Barry and Maria.

"I want to stay with her," Maria said.

"I will be waiting outside," Barry told them and walked out to the hallway.

"Emily, I am Doctor Baker," he said. "I am going to check your bruises while we wait for your head x-rays. Do you remember what happened today?"

She tried to talk, but the words still were not coming out.

"You don't need to talk," the doctor said. "If you know what happened, then nod your head yes. If you don't, shake no."

Emily shook her head no.

"You have a cut on your left eye, and your right eye is bruised. That is why it is so hard for you to see. You have some broken ribs, and your left arm is broken. I am going to give you some pain medicine, which will make you sleepy. When you wake up, you should feel a bit better."

The doctor left the room, and Emily felt the urge to cry. Her mom was right next to her, and made her feel safe. Deep inside she was scared. She didn't know what she was afraid of, but it was there. She felt someone touch her hand, and she jumped.

"Honey, it is just me," Maria said. "The doctor will give you medicine, then you can go to sleep. I will be right here when you wake up." That made Emily calm down, and she felt relaxed.

Emily fell asleep holding her mom's hand. Maria was remembering all the great moments she spent with her daughter. Not that Maria was a perfect parent. Maria had Emily when she was eighteen. She found a small apartment, and she found a job. She was worked all day while the church was babysitting Emily.

Maria worked at a factory planting flowers. One day, while she was working, her boss came in and asked her to come to the office. When she walked in, there was a young man standing next to her boss.

"Maria, I am glad you are here," her boss said. "This is Mark, and he needs your help. Will you please train him to do your job? Then I will train you how to do mine, so I can retire and know that I left my company in good hands."

"Yes sir," Maria said and looked at Mark. He had broad shoulders, and his skin was light. He had gorgeous blonde hair, and sky blue eyes.

Maria and Mark worked together side by side for over a year, before they went out on a date. They got married three years later.

But, Mark was nice and gentle with Emily, he gave her same love as if she were his own daughter. One night, after the war began, someone came to the house and took Mark. Maria never heard from him again. To this day she did not know if Mark was still alive.

Emily woke up, and was able to open her right eye. She saw her mother laying next to her, still holding her hand. Emily moved a little, trying not to wake her. Emily's memory was still foggy, and she could not remember why she was here. She could remember the doctor telling her what was all wrong with her, but nothing before that. Maria woke up when she felt Emily moving.

"How are you feeling?" she asked.

"I can talk now," Emily said. "Mom, what happened to me?"

"Let's not talk about it right now," Maria told her. "The most important thing is that you get better, and everything else will fall in to place. Are you in pain?"

"My right eye hurts, and my arm hurts."

There was a light knock at the door, and Officer Johnson walked in with Barry.

"Hi Emily," Officer Johnson said, "how are you feeling?"

"I can talk now," she said. "What happened?"

Officer Johnson looked at Maria, who signaled him not to tell Emily anything yet.

"Well, I was hoping you could tell me that," he said. "Can you?"

"That will have to wait," Maria said. "I want her to rest. Maybe she can talk to you some other time, if that is okay?"

"Of course we'll give her time to heal," Johnson said. "Could I have a word with you, Maria?"

"I will stay with Emily," Barry said.

"I will be right back, Sweetie," Maria said. "If you need anything, press this button, and a nurse will come in and help you." She lightly kissed Emily's cheek, and followed Officer Johnson to the hallway.

When they were outside, Maria looked at him and asked, "Do you think she knows something?"

"I was just going to ask her some questions?" he answered.

"My daughter has been through hell today."

"Maria calm down. I have a job to do."

"Your job is to find out what happened to my child, not drill her with questions."

"How am I going to find out what happened, if I don't ask questions?" Johnson asked.

"Didn't you catch the person who did this?"

"I have," Johnson answered, "but he is not talking yet. All I know, is that his name is Jovan, he is eighteen, and he is Emily's friend. He said she invited him to the house while you were out. Then Emily got all crazy, and started throwing stuff at him."

"You know that is a lie, right?" Maria asked.

"With Emily's past, I cannot sure what to believe until I hear her side."

"I cannot believe you just said that," Maria said and walked away. She walked into Emily's room, and asked Barry to leave. She needed to be alone with her daughter.

Barry stepped out into the hall, and found Johnson in a chair, writing in his notebook.

"What happened?" Barry asked him.

"Nothing," Johnson said. "Why are you still here?"

"I want to be here for Maria and Emily," he answered.

"Are you dating Maria?" Johnson asked.

"You are straight forward aren't you? I brought her here, and no I am not dating her."

"Just checking," Johnson said.

"Since when is it police business to ask about my private life?"

"Stay away from Maria," Johnson told him.

"Why?" Barry asked.

"None of your business," Johnson said and walked away from him.

Barry walked back to the room, and overheard Emily and Maria talking.

"What happened to you today, Emily, no one needs to know. If you don't want to talk about it, I will leave it alone," Maria said.

"Mom, I don't know what happened today. All I know is that I woke up here. I don't even remember what I was wearing this morning when you left the house."

Barry stepped in, and they stopped talking.

"Can I talk to you alone, Maria?" Barry asked.

They walked out to the hall, and he put his hand on Maria's shoulder, which made her very nervous. She shook his hand off, and sat down.

"Barry, I want to thank you for bringing me here, but can give me and Emily some privacy?"

"I wanted to stay here, and be with you, in case you need me," Barry told her.

"I won't need you," she said. "I am grateful to you for bringing me here, but I just want to be alone with my daughter." Barry sat down next to her.

"Maria, I will wait for you as long as it takes."

"I am sorry, Barry, if I gave you any ideas about me, but I am not looking for a man right now. As soon as Emily gets better, we are going to America."

Barry looked like someone had just slapped him in the face. Maybe Johnson was right, Barry thought, and left the hospital. He needed some fresh air, so he decided to walk home. When he got home, he opened a beer and sat down to think.

———————————————

Emily fell asleep once again. She dreamt that she was home waiting for her mom. They needed to go to the store, and her mom was late. There was a knock on the door, and she opened it. A man with brown hair and ugly glasses was standing there. He walked toward Emily, then pushed her down on the couch. She tried to fight him off, but he was a lot bigger and stronger than she was.

"You asked me to come over," he said to her.

"I don't even know who you are!" Emily cried.

"Sure you do. I am the same person you saw at the bar three nights ago. The one you gave your address to when you asked to take you home."

"I don't remember anything about you," she said.

The man got mad, and started to hit her. He hit her with his hands, then he threw her against the wall. It felt like all her bones were breaking. She tried to get up, and every time she would, he pushed her back down. Emily begged him to stop, but it did not seem to help. She heard someone at the door, and hoped that it was her mom.

Emily woke up crying, and looked around for her mom. Maria jumped up from her chair, and ran over to Emily.

"Baby, what happened? Why are you crying?"

"Was I raped, Mom?" Emily asked.

"Yes, honey. Do you know who did it?"

"All I know is that he was beating me up. I don't remember much, but I hope they catch him."

"They already have," Maria told her. "Jean was there, too. She called the police for you."

"I need to thank her when I get out of here," Emily said.

"Just rest now, honey. Everything else will come."

Emily closed her eyes and dreamed of some place far away. Some place where she was not afraid anymore. What ever happened she knew her mom would be always there for her.

When she woke up, Emily felt a lot better. The doctor told her that she had a broken arm, some broken ribs, and she was lucky she was still alive. If everything went well, she would go home next week, when she could walk on her own.

After a week in the hospital, Emily wanted to go home, but she was still to weak to walk on her own. Officer Johnson came to see her twice, and both times he asked her if she knew a tall man named Eric. She had heard of Eric before, but she did not remember him. The first thing she wanted to do when she get out of the hospital, was go to the police station and look at Eric, to see if she can remember anything. But first, she just had to get out of the hospital.

CHAPTER TWENTY-NINE

VANESSA DID NOT KNOW HOW to tell Goran that they were leaving. Why is life so unfair, she wondered. Everything about my life is unfair. Vanessa went looking for her mom. She had been avoiding her mom for two days now. Ever since Jean told them they were leaving, Vanessa did not want to talk to her. Alexander was sitting on the couch when she walked in the kitchen.

"Where is mom?" Vanessa asked.

"She is still at work," he told her. Alexander looked at her, and knew something was wrong. "Why do you need Mom?"

"I need to talk to her, and see if maybe she changed her mind about us leaving," Vanessa told him.

"I am sure she won't change her mind, Vanessa. She is doing something good for us. She is trying to find us a better life. Can't you at least try to be happy?" Alexander asked.

"How am I going to be happy? I have a boyfriend who is the best thing that has ever happened to me, and now I have to tell him that I am leaving. I will never see him again.

"I don't think it is fair to blame Mom," Alexander said, "but I can see why you are upset. Have you talked to Goran yet?"

"No, I have not. He is coming over tonight, and that is when I will tell him."

Jean walked in the house and looked at Vanessa. Vanessa tried to cover her face so her mom would not see that she was crying.

"What is the matter?" Jean asked her.

"Nothing," Vanessa answered. "Are we still leaving?"

"Yes we are," Jean said. "We will have to get our passports, our shots, and physicals. Then we will be all set to go. why?"

"I don't see why we have to go," Vanessa said. "I can see that no matter what I want, I will have to do what you tell me."

"Damn right, you will," Jean told her. "I am not going for myself, I am doing it for you and your brother. I am trying to do something good for our family."

"Whatever, Mom," Vanessa said and walked out of the house.

"Vanessa, come back here!" she heard her mom yell right before she slammed the door behind her.

I am not going back home anymore, she thought. I am going to find Goran, maybe we can find a place of our own. We can live here, and my mom can go where ever she wants to. As she walked away from her house, she saw Amanda walking towards her.

"Where are you going?" Amanda asked her.

"I am going to find Goran, and then we are going to find a place to live."

"Excuse me?" Amanda asked, stopping in her tracks.

"You heard right. I am going to find Goran, and we are looking for a place to live. I don't care about you, my mom, Darko, or anyone else. I am going to do this my way," she said and walked away.

"Okay," Amanda said, "I did not say anything! I was just wondering what you are going to do, because you are only sixteen. How will you live on your own, without your mom?

Have you thought about that? Do you think Goran's parents are going to let you and him live together? Have you even talked to him yet?"

"Amanda, why is this any of your business?" Vanessa asked.

"I just don't want you to make the biggest mistake of your life, Vanessa. Living with Goran, or any guy, will not be the same as living with your mom. If you think life is hard now, you have no idea what you are in for."

"How do you know what my life will be like if I live with him?"

"I don't know exactly, but I have bean living with Darko. I am back with my mom, now. I had to clean after him, cook for him, make sure he had clean clothes to wear, and I never even got a thank you for anything. But, if the things were not done the right way, I was the one he would blame."

"Darko and Goran are nothing alike. I am sure Goran would be different," Vanessa said. "I am still going to talk to him."

"You do what you want, but remember, nowhere is better than at home. I can vouch for that."

"No one will change my mind, I am going through with my plan."

Amanda left her alone, and walked to Darko's house. When she got there no one was outside, but his car and a new motorcycle. I wonder who is here, she thought. I hope this is not what Darko bought.

Amanda walked in and went upstairs to look for Darko. Maybe she would be able to talk to Goran before Vanessa did. She heard voices in Darko's room. That must be Goran, Amanda thought. She walked closer to the door and stopped dead in her tracks. She could not believe what she was hearing. How was that possible? How did Vanessa get here before her?

Inside the room, she heard another voice. Goran was there,

too. That must have been his bike outside. But how did they beat her there? She would just have to find out.

Right before she touched the door she heard Darko's voice say, "I will talk to my mom. I am sure she will have no problem with you staying here until you find yourself a place."

"Over my dead body," Amanda said to herself, and walked in the room.

"Oh, you are here, too," Darko said to her, like she was just some girl off the street, and not his girlfriend for over a year.

"I don't know what is going on here, and I don't care," Amanda said, "but she is not staying in your room, or your house. I will not allow it." She turned to Vanessa and looked her straight in the eyes.

"Listen, l I don't know what your plan is, but you better leave before I am the one putting you in the hospital."

"I would not say that," Goran said to Amanda. "You saw how long Emily was in the hospital because of Vanessa."

"I am not scared of her," Amanda said. "I am just curious who came to the decision that she will stay here, of all places? Why not at Goran's house?" She turned to Goran.

"She is your girlfriend, why is she staying in *my* boyfriend's house?"

"Amanda, I can see that you are upset with me," Vanessa began, but before she could finish her sentence, Amanda was on top of her. She felt pain in her chest, and covered her face with her hands. Vanessa was not going to fight Amanda. Goran and Darko pulled Amanda off of her, and Goran leaned over Vanessa.

"Are you okay?" he asked.

"I am fine." Vanessa got up and wiped her face. Amanda was still panting like a wild animal, waiting for her prey to recover so she could attack again. Vanessa got her things and left the room. Goran went after her.

When they made it outside, Vanessa started to cry. She did not know what she was crying about, but she had a heavy burden on her chest that she just had to get rid of. Goran hugged her tightly. He did not want to let her go, but it looked like he might have to.

"I don't think this is going to work," Vanessa said through her tears.

"We will work something out," Goran said.

"What is wrong with you?" Darko asked Amanda after Vanessa and Goran left.

"What is wrong with me?" Amanda yelled back. "Were you going to talk to me about her moving in here before you told her she could?"

Amanda was furious, and nothing Darko said would calm her down, but he did not care.

"I don't know why I would have to talk to you. You don't live here. You are just my girlfriend."

"Just your girlfriend?" she asked. "Maybe I should not be, so you can have *her* live with you."

"I know you are jealous of her, but she is with my best friend. I would not even dream of stealing her away from him," he told her calmly.

Hearing him say that was worse than him yelling at her.

"Darko what is wrong with you?" Amanda asked.

"Nothing. Just watching my girlfriend attack someone she calls her friend, because I am trying to help her. How would you feel if you had no where to go?"

"I don't think she should stay here," Amanda said in a calm voice.

"I don't think that is for you to decide," he said. "This is my parents' house. You need to apologize to Vanessa for jumping on her, and calling her names."

"I am not going to apologize to her for anything! She provoked me, and got what she deserved."

"Amanda, you have a hour to apologize to her. If you do not, we are over. I hope you will do the right thing," Darko said and walked out of his room. Closing the door behind him, he heard a plate hit the door. He opened the door, and after seeing the glass all over his room, just smiled and looked at Amanda.

"Very mature, honey," Darko said and closed the door again.

"God, I hate him now!" Amanda yelled. She cleaned up the all glass that she could. This was the perfect time to make it seem like she was in trouble, she thought. Amanda picked up a piece of glass, and moved it close to her arm. Just looking at it made her sick. She had no other choice. She wanted Darko back, but she was not going to apologize to Vanessa.

Darko was halfway down the stairs when he heard a loud scream from his room, he turned around and ran back up. Opening the door, he saw nothing but blood all over Amanda, and his room. He swore loudly, and picked her up. Coming down the stairs, he ran into his mom and dad, who also heard Amanda scream. She was unconscious and there was blood all over.

"Oh my god!" his mom cried. "What happened?"

"I don't know, I think she slit her wrists with glass," he said. "Call the ambulance, Mom! Don't just stand there!"

His mom called the ambulance, as Vanessa and Goran joined Darko.

"What happened?" Vanessa asked.

"We had a fight. I walked out, and she threw a plate. I guess she cut her wrists," he said.

"An ambulance is on the way," Darko's mom told them.

"I will stay with her. All of you an go back to whatever you were doing," Darko said.

"Do you want me to come with you?" Goran asked.

"No, I will be okay. Thanks though," Darko told him.

"What's wrong with him?" Darko's mom asked Goran.

317

"Nothing, I think he just needs some time alone. Last time we talked, he was not sure if he wanted to be with Amanda or not."

"I should go home," Vanessa said.

"I will walk you," Goran told her. They left Darko's mom standing alone.

Heading back to her house with Goran, Vanessa felt safe, but empty inside. She knew she had to talk to him, but she did not what to say. It seemed to her that he was feeling the same way she was. One of them had to start talking soon, though, because her house was not that far away.

Vanessa stopped and looked at Goran.

"I know I will probably never find someone as good as you are," she told him. "I know I will be very sorry for leaving you, and I will regret what I am about to do."

Goran looked at her confused. An hour ago, she was talking about how she wanted to live with him, but now she was saying that she would miss him?

"What are you talking about?" he asked.

"I am sorry. There is no easy way for me to say this. Goran, you are the best thing that has ever happened to me. You are an amazing boyfriend, and I would do anything to stay with you, but I think that will be impossible. I am not sure you are ready to be married, and we are too young, anyways. I am going to talk to my mom, and I will let you know when we are moving."

"Promise me something," he said.

"Anything," Vanessa told him.

Goran took her hands and kissed them. "No matter what happens, you will always stay in touch with me."

"Promise," she said, and kissed him. The kiss was salty from Vanessa's tears. She did not want to let go of Goran, though she knew she had to. One thing she knew for sure was that she would never forget Goran.

"Maybe we will see each other again," he said, surprising her.

"If we ever do, I will never let you go again," she told him. Vanessa looked into his eyes. Eyes that she would never forget, no matter if she was sixteen or sixty-one. Vanessa was in love.

"When are you guys leaving?" Goran asked her.

"I think next week sometime, but I am not sure." Vanessa looked at her watch and saw it was time for her to go inside.

"Just promise me you will not leave without saying good bye," he said. "I don't think I could live with out seeing you one last time."

"I promise I will tell you when we are leaving," Vanessa said. "I have to go inside now."

"I know, but I am not ready to let you go," Goran said holding her tightly. "I am very sorry that you have to leave, but maybe it is for the best. This was your second fight in, what, two months?" he asked, teasing her."

"I did not start either of those fights," she said. "I was there just for the beating."

"You beat up Emily pretty good."

"Oh I remember," she said, "but I have the scars to prove that I did not walk away from it, either."

"I am glad that is all over," he told her.

"Did you want to come inside?" Vanessa asked him.

"You don't think your mom will throw me out?" Goran asked surprised. Whenever he walked Vanessa home, she would never ask him to go inside.

"Right now, I don't care what my mother thinks," she answered. "If you want to come inside, you are more than welcome to."

Vanessa knew she was asking for trouble, but this was the last week she could spend with Goran. She opened the door, and Vanessa and Goran walked passed the kitchen and straight to her room. They sat down on her bed, still holding hands.

Vanessa turned to look at him, he seemed a lot different from just a moment ago. He was still holding her in his arms.

"Vanessa," he said, "I think it is time for us to do it."

"Do what?" she asked.

"Please, don't play games," he said. "You are only going to be here for one more week. I want to be the one and only you will sleep with."

"You must be out of your mind," she said. "What are you doing?" she asked him when Goran pressed his lips to the small of her back.

"Just relax, Vanessa. I have never done it, either, and I want you to be my first."

"No, Goran! The reason I have been with you this long, is because you have never asked me to sleep with you. I thought you cared about me, not what I can give you."

"I never wanted to be with anyone as much as I want to be with you," he told Vanessa.

"I don't care," she said. "I can see now that all you want is sex."

"What makes you think I want sex?" he asked with anger in his voice.

"Maybe, because you are getting angry about it!"

"I am not getting angry," Goran said calmly. "We have been dating for five months. I just thought it was time."

"I am sorry." Vanessa got off her bed, and turned on the light. "I want you out of my house."

"Fine, I am leaving," Goran said.

"Good. And don't think about coming to the airport when I leave."

"I don't know what your problem is," Goran said, "but your wish is my command." Goran slammed the door behind him.

"You don't have to wake up the whole house, idiot!" Vanessa yelled. She sat down on her bed and began crying. "Why would he do this to me now?" she asked herself.

Vanessa heard a knock on her door, and her mom walked in.

"Is everything okay?" Jean asked.

"Yes, sorry I woke you up," Vanessa told her. "I am okay now, you can go back to sleep."

"Who was that slamming doors?" her mom asked.

"I don't wan to talk about it, Mom," Vanessa said.

"Vanessa, you have been gone all day. Then you come home at midnight, after your curfew, and you tell me you don't want to talk after I am woken up by slamming doors?"

"I am sorry," Vanessa said. "That was Goran we had a fight. You won't have to worry about me staying here with him."

"I was not worried," Jean told her. "I knew you would make the right choice. Vanessa, you have always bean a smart girl. But, honey, can't you see that people are coming back to their houses? It is just a matter of time before someone comes knocking on our door."

"I am sorry, Mom," Vanessa said, and laid her head on her mom's lap. "Why are all guys the same?"

"I don't know, honey, but when you grow up, you will find that answer for yourself."

Vanessa fell asleep in her mother's lap feeling like the little girl that she still was.

CHAPTER THIRTY

EMILY HAD BEAN HOME FOR over a week, and no one had come to see her. No one except Barry. Emily wanted to ask him why he visited all the time, but she knew that it would upset her mom. He always came with something for her mom and her. If he brought Maria flowers, he made sure that Emily had some, too.

One night, when Maria was getting ready for a date night with Barry, Emily sat in her mom's room. Maria was wearing a long red dress cut low in the back. She looked beautiful.

"It is too much, isn't it?" Maria asked Emily.

"No, Mom, you look beautiful," Emily told her mom.

"I am just worried that he will get the wrong idea."

"Mom, you guys have been dating for a while now, I don't know why you think that he won't want something more from you."

"Emily, honey, you don't need to worry about that. I do like him, but I want to take it slow."

"Just don't take it too slow," Emily said and walked out of the room. She headed to the living room, where she heard a knock on the door.

"I got it!" she called, and opened the door. Never in a

million years, would Emily have dreamed of opening the door and finding who was standing there.

"Hi," Emily said.

"Hi," Goran answered.

Emily cleared her throat. "What are you doing here?" she asked, looking over his shoulder to see if Vanessa was with him.

"She is not here," Goran said.

"Who?" Emily asked. "I have not seen you for a while, why are you here? Where is Vanessa?"

"We are not together anymore," he answered.

"And you came here to make her jealous," Emily said. Deep down, she wanted him to tell her he was there just for her, but she knew that wasn't going to happen.

"No, I came here to apologize for all the things I have said and done to you."

"It is okay, I was not that good to you, either."

"But why did you wait until now, and not apologize before you guys broke up?" Emily asked.

"That would have upset Vanessa, and I did not want to do anything that would upset her."

"You are a very good boyfriend," Emily told him.

"Well, that was all I had, so I will leave you now." Goran turned and walked away.

"Who was that?" Maria asked as she walked down the stairs. "I thought I heard you talking to someone."

"It was Goran," Emily said. "He came to apologize."

"Really?" Maria asked. "Where is he now?"

"He just left," Emily said smiling. "He said, he and Vanessa are over. Maybe I still have a chance."

"Honey, I would not get my hopes up too high," Maria told her. "I don't want to see you get hurt."

"I will be fine, Mom, I promise," Emily said.

Maybe thinking about Goran was wrong, but she could not help herself. This was the best feeling in the world. She knew better then to dwell on it, though. She had been in the hospital because of it.

Emily was still thinking about Goran when Barry came over. He was dressed in a suit and tie. Emily had never seen him dressed like that before.

"Wow," she said, "you look awesome! Where are you guys going?"

"It is a surprise for your mom. Is she ready?" He suddenly stopped talking when he saw Maria on the stairs. He had never seen anyone more gorgeous than she was at that moment.

"You look stunning," he finally said.

"Thank you," Maria said smiling, "you look very good yourself."

"I hope you will love your surprise," Barry said.

"I am sure I will," Maria told him, and leaning in him for a kiss.

"You two kids have fun," Emily said as they walked out the door. "Barry," she yelled, "make sure my mother is home by eleven!"

"Yes ma'am!" he called back.

As Emily watched them leave, she saw Vanessa walking down the street. Vanessa and Emily had not talked for over six months, maybe it was time for them to stop fighting. Emily stepped out and stood on the porch. She waited for Vanessa to get closer so that she could tell her she was sorry for all the things she had done. Emily had heard Vanessa and her family were leaving, she did not know how many more chances she would get to apologize.

Why is Vanessa walking so slow, Emily asked herself. Was she talking to herself? Oh no, she was crying.

Vanessa had seen Emily standing on the porch. She was not on the mood to talk to her. Vanessa was crying because she was sorry that she told Goran to get out the night before. She did not want to leave knowing that the one guy she loved, hated her because she did not sleep with him. She did not want to deal with Emily, too. She walked closer, wiping her tears away.

"Vanessa."

"Emily."

"Are you all right?" Emily asked.

"I am fine," Vanessa answered, "thanks for asking."

"Why are you crying?" Emily asked.

"Just some things," Vanessa told her. "Nothing to worry about."

"Did you know Goran came to see me tonight?"

"Oh, he did?" Vanessa asked. That was hard to hear, but maybe she was lying.

"Don't look at me like that," Emily said.

"Like what?"

"Like I just killed your whole family. He was only here to tell me he was sorry for treating me like crap, that's all. He did not come over to ask me out, or anything like that."

"I was not thinking that," Vanessa said. "I know him a little better than that."

"What happened with you two?"

"What do you mean?" Vanessa asked.

"He said you broke up."

"I guess things just happened."

"Vanessa, I do not want to fight anymore. I am sorry for all the pain I have caused you. I promise, I am not going to be messing with you or with anyone else."

When Vanessa started to cry, Emily walked closer to her.

"I am sorry," Emily told her. "Did I say something to make you sad?"

"No," Vanessa said, "you have no idea how long I have wanted to hear you say that."

"I know I made a lot of bad decisions, but I don't think I want to be bad anymore."

"I never said you were bad," Vanessa told her.

"I know what I have done is bad, and I might not be able to, but I will try to fix it."

"I am glad to hear that," Vanessa said. "I would love to stay here, but I have to get to the store. My mom will have a cow, because I have been gone so long."

"Is there any way I can help you?" Emily asked.

That was a big surprise coming from Emily.

"Thank you," Vanessa said, "but there is nothing anyone can do but me." Vanessa walked away leaving Emily alone on the porch.

It was getting dark outside, Vanessa hated to be in the dark by herself. If she was lucky, maybe she would see Goran, and he would want to walk her home. But, that was wishful thinking. Vanessa heard a car behind her and she moved over so it could pass her. The car slowed down, and she prayed it would be someone she knew.

"Vanessa, why are you walking by yourself in the dark?" Darko asked.

"Oh thank God, it is you!" she said. "I saw someone walking towards me, and now I cannot see where they went."

"Get in the car," Darko told her."I will take you where you have to go."

Vanessa waited a minute, and then decided, "What the hell?" She got in the car, and they were on their way.

"So what is this, I hear you and Goran are not together anymore?"

"No, we are not," Vanessa said. "But, I am sure he did not tell you why."

"You want to bet? Goran tells me everything," Darko said.

"Okay, so if he tells you everything, why are we not together anymore?"

"Because you accused him of only wanting sex, and you did not want that. He just wanted to show you that he loves you, and that he will always be there for you."

"Really? Darko, do you think I am stupid? I know what guys want. I have been with Goran for months now. Not once did he ask me to sleep with him, until I am leaving. Then he was in my room looking at me like a hungry animal."

"Vanessa, calm down," Darko said. "I can assure you Goran did not want sex. He is a virgin, just like you are."

"How do you know I am?"

"Because you did not sleep with him yet."

"Darko, I don't want to fight with you. I don't care what he wanted, we are done. I am sure he will be better off without me."

"Whatever you say," Darko said. "I tried helping him, but he doesn't want my help. I try helping you, and you don't want it. I don't know how to help you guys anymore."

"Thank you for your concern," Vanessa told him. "I am glad I have friends like you. But we are here, and I am very glad you gave me a ride."

"Vanessa, don't make a big mistake, and let that guy go. A guy that loves you more than you can imagine."

"Thank you, Darko," she said, and got out of the car.

"You want me to wait for you?" he asked.

"No, thank you, I can walk home. I will be fine."

Vanessa walked in the store, and waited for Darko to drive away. I wonder if he is going to see Goran now, she thought. Thinking about Goran just made her sad, so she quickly got what she needed and headed home.

Vanessa got a bad feeling in her stomach as she was walking. It was darker now, and she became scared. What am I afraid of, she asked herself. There was no one around.

Suddenly she heard a car behind her, and Vanessa thought of Darko. It could be him, she hoped it was him. She made the mistake of turning around to look at the car. The minute she saw who it was, she wished she were not alone.

It was Dragan, a scare guy that was mean to everyone.

"Vanessa, get in the car!" Dragan yelled.

She could try running, but that would not help, so she got in.

"What are you doing?" Vanessa asked him.

"Oh nothing, just looking for someone to ride with me," Dragan answered.

"What do you want from me?" Vanessa asked.

"I will show you in a minute."

Vanessa hoped he would go to her house, but he did not. He passed righty by her house, and Vanessa got very scared. Horrible pictures started to run through her mind. She could see her mom waiting at the door. She could see Goran's face when they found her dead in a ditch somewhere.

Dragan stopped not far from her house, and got out of the car. Vanessa thought of locking the door, but Dragan was very strong, and she realized that maybe giving Dragan what he wanted was the only way she would get out in one piece.

Dragan came around to her side of the car, and opened the door. He practically dragged Vanessa out of her seat.

"Now take off your clothes," he demanded. "I enjoy watching girls undress. Emily was really good at it."

"I don't want to take my clothes off myself," Vanessa told him. "Why don't you take them off for me? I don't like Emily, I don't want to be anything like her. I am better."

Vanessa was not strong, but she was smart. She wanted him to get close so she could get him in his manhood. Then, he would never think about asking her to take off her clothes again.

"No," Dragan said, "I enjoy watching you do it."

"You have never seen me do it before," she said. "How do you know you will enjoy it?"

"News flash, Vanessa, maybe you should close your curtains the next time you are changing."

Vanessa gasped, but reminded herself to stay calm.

"Oh, come on," she said, "you know you will be a lot more satisfied if you come over and do it yourself."

"Fine," he said walking towards her. He walked slowly, and the closer he got, the more nervous Vanessa became.

Dragan finally reached her, and began to unbutton her shirt. Vanessa felt sick to her stomach, but knew she had to wait for perfect moment. The second Dragan put his mouth on her neck, she lifted her leg and kicked him. Vanessa had never heard a more painful sound in her life.

Dragan laid on the road and started to cry. He was having trouble breathing, and Vanessa saw the chance to get away. She ran all the way to her house without looking back. Thank goodness I am leaving, she thought, if he ever sees me again, I will be dead.

She ran inside the house, and locked the door behind her. She waited to hear a knock on the door, and to see Dragan standing there. But that did not happen, instead, she heard his car drive right passed her house.

"Thank God he is gone," Vanessa said aloud.

"Who?" Alexander asked from behind her. "What happened to you? Why is your shirt unbuttoned?"

Vanessa tried to answer his questions, but before she could, she fainted.

"Vanessa. Vanessa. Vanessa, open your eyes, honey. That's it. Look at me," she heard her mom say.

"What happened to you?" Jean asked. Alexander and Jean sat next to her, neither of them knowing what happened.

"Was anyone here?" Vanessa asked.

"No, honey," Jean answered. "Why? Who was it? What did they do?"

"I am going to kill someone," Alexander said.

"It is okay," Vanessa said, "I already took care of him."

"Him?" Alexander yelled. "Goran! Or Darko, maybe. Who ever it was, I will kill him."

"Alexander, calm down," Vanessa told him. "I will tell you who it was, if you promise you will not kill anyone."

"Fine," Alexander said, "I won't. Now, tell us."

"I was walking home, when I heard a car behind me. I thought it was Darko, or Goran, but it was Dragan."

"That maniac?" Alexander yelled. "Did he touch you? I will kill him!"

"No, Alexander. I took care of him," she said. "Stop interrupting me, I am trying to tell you what happened."

"Oh, alright already," he said. "Go on." Alexander was beyond mad. Vanessa had never seen her brother act like this. It made her feel safe, and she knew she could always count on him.

"Mom, did they found out who raped Emily," Vanessa asked.

Jean looked at her. "Yes, it was Dragan" she answered. "What did he do to you?"

"Nothing," she said, "he told me to take off my clothes. He told me he enjoyed watching Emily do it. I told him to come closer to me, and when he kissed my neck, I kicked him in the nuts."

"Ouch, go Vanessa!" Alexander said to her. "Did you hit him enough so he could not get up?"

"No, I just left him laying there," Vanessa said. "I feel so bad for Emily. He is ugly, and disgusting. His breath smells bad, and his car looks like trash."

"Are you going to report him to the police?" Alexander asked.

"No, I am going to wait and see if I can talk to Officer Johnson tomorrow," Vanessa said. "I hope he will be caught."

They heard a car pull into the driveway. Vanessa froze, thinking the worst. She was still sitting on the floor, unable to move, when she heard the doorbell.

"Jean, open up. It is me, Officer Johnson."

Jean stood up and opened the door. Not only was Officer Johnson there, Dragan was with him.

CHAPTER THIRTY-ONE

"What is *he* doing here?" Alexander asked.

"Dragan came to the station," Officer Johnson answered. "He said that Vanessa attacked him, so I came here to check it out."

"Vanessa is in the house," Jean said. "You can come in, but that garbage cannot."

"I would watch what I say," Dragan said. "My uncle is a lawyer, and he can make sure that your slut daughter goes to jail."

"Don't talk," Officer Johnson told him. "Jean, I just need to talk to Vanessa. I am sure she did not attack him, that it was the other way around, but I need her to tell me. So I can put him in jail for good, and not even his lawyer uncle will be able to save him."

"Whatever," Dragan said, and stepped back from the door and sat down on the steps.

"Vanessa, come here honey," Jean said. "Officer Johnson wants to talk to you."

"I will be there in a minute," Vanessa said. She was in her room changing her clothes, and she heard what they were talking about. Vanessa was glad she would be the one to put Dragan in jail.

Vanessa walked into the room, and when she saw Dragan, she stopped in her tracks and looked at Officer Johnson.

"Vanessa," Johnson said, "Dragan came to the station, and told us that you attacked him. Is that true?"

"Yes, I kicked him," she answered, "but did he tell you why?"

"No, he just said that you attacked him first, and he wants you arrested."

"I am sorry, but I think *he* should be the one to go to jail," Vanessa told Johnson. "He stopped his car, and pulled me in it. Then he threw me out of it, and told me to take my clothes off. He said that he enjoyed watching Emily do it. I told him that he should take my clothes off for me, and when he got close enough to me, I kicked him in the nuts. End of story.

"I would like to be excused," she said Vanessa stood and looked toward Dragan. "He is disgusting, and he should spend his life in jail."

"Tell your daughter, she is very lucky," Dragan said to Jean. "I could have killed her tonight if I wanted to."

"Is that a threat?" Officer Johnson asked. "If I were you, I would not open my mouth again. You are under arrest, and you will be spending lots of time in jail. I am sure there area few guys that would enjoy seeing you take your clothes off." Officer Johnson took Dragon to his car and walked back to the house.

"I am sorry," he told Jean. "Maybe it is for the best that you are leaving next week. I am wish you the best." Then he walked away. Jean closed the door and thanked her lucky stars that her daughter was fine, and that they were leaving soon.

The whole town was talking about Vanessa for the next few days. Darko came over to see her. He was alone, he did not come with Goran or his sister.

Darko and Vanessa were sitting in her room one day, when someone knocked on the door. Vanessa answered it, and she was shocked when she saw who was standing there. It was

Goran. Vanessa's heart skipped a beat. She wanted to be with him, but she was leaving soon.

"May I come in?" he asked after a long, awkward pause.

"Sure, I am sorry," she said. "It is not polite to stare."

Goran laughed at her, and walked passed her into the house. He smelled so good, Vanessa thought as he walked by her.

"Hey Darko," Goran said, "what brings you here?"

"I have been here for a while now," Darko said. "I should go."

"Well why run now? When I come over?" Goran asked, with anger in his voice.

"Stop your jealousy," Darko told him. "I am not here to take her away from you, I am here to talk to her. I like talking to her, she doesn't judge me or tells me what to do. She lets me make my own decisions."

"And that is why you are here?" Goran asked.

"Yes, that's why he is here," Vanessa answered for Darko. "Goran I have not stopped thinking about you since you walked out on me that night. I still love you, and I was wrong. Maybe you are not like other guys.

"I am glad you are here. I am leaving soon, we have all of our papers ready to go. I am sorry I called you a pig, and don't be mad at Darko he was not trying to put any moves on me. We are just friends, having friendly conversation."

Darko and Goran both laughed at her.

"I don't have any moves," Darko said. "All of them have been used up."

"Too bad," Vanessa said.

"I came to tell you that my mom and dad applied for us to leave, too," Goran told Vanessa.

"Maybe we'll be in the same city," Vanessa said.

"Don't get your hopes up," Goran said. "I think we are going to Texas."

"We are going to Michigan."

"And I am staying here," Darko said, looking at them.

"I am sorry you are staying here," Vanessa said to Darko.

"I am not," he said. "I am glad I am here. I can only handle one language at a time."

All three of them laughed. It is good to have them as friends, Vanessa thought. She knew she would never forget them, and she knew that Goran would stay in her heart forever. She wanted to spend every remaining moment with her two best friends. She and Goran were not dating anymore, they were just friends, and that was okay.

"I wish it could be like this all the time," Vanessa told Goran one night. They were outside laying on a blanket and talking.

"I wish so, too," Goran said. "Maybe then we would have our own house. I am sorry I was such a pig to you."

"Tell me the truth," Vanessa asked, "did you want sex with me that night?"

"Hell Vanessa, I want sex with you now, not only that night. But, I know we are not ready for that, so I just back off. I know I was wrong, and I beat myself up about it every day."

"Don't beat yourself up," Vanessa told him. Goran looked at her with his big brown eyes, and she felt the same electricity that she felt the night he first kissed her.

"Goran, don't look at me like that."

"Why not? Don't you still want me?"

"Yes, but I am leaving," Vanessa said.

"So am I. Will we ever be together again?" Goran asked.

"We might, but until then we will have to be best friends."

"I can be okay with that, I just don't want to lose you."

"And you won't," she said and put her head on his chest.

———

The day came when Vanessa and her family were leaving.

Everyone came out to say good bye, even old lady Anna. Vanessa was sad they were leaving, but she was happy to see so many people came to say good bye.

"This is not good bye," Goran told her. "This is see you later. No matter what, I will find you again. I will be with you."

"He hopes so," Darko said.

"I am sorry I was a bitch to you," Amanda said. "I wish you all the luck in the world, and don't forget to write." Vanessa suddenly remember Lidia's last words.

"I promise I won't," Vanessa said with tears in her eyes.

"Don't cry," Marina said, "you know we love you, even if we did not show it. We all have something to hide, don't we Goran."

"What do you mean?" Vanessa asked looking at Marina and then at Goran.

"I have nothing to hide," he said.

"Even now, when she is leaving, you won't tell her?" Marina asked him.

"Tell me what? Come on, guys, don't play games with me now," Vanessa said. "I only have three hours before I have to leave."

"I have nothing to say," Goran said.

"Yes, you do," Marina told him. "Vanessa, do you remember the night he said he wanted sex?"

"Yes," Vanessa answered, "but that was long ago. We don't care about it anymore."

"Did he tell you *why* he asked you for sex?" Marina asked.

"Marina, Vanessa is leaving today. She doesn't need to know," Darko said.

"I would like to hear it," Vanessa said.

"Fine," Marina said, "if you are not going to tell her, I will. It is bothering me."

"Someone better start talking," Amanda said. "I would love to hear this."

"Well, me and Goran were talking the night before he and Vanessa got into a fight," Marina said. "I told him, if he wanted to know what Vanessa would say about sex, he should just ask. So he did. When they stopped talking I felt really bad, but I promised him I would not say anything."

"Is that the truth?" Vanessa asked Goran.

"Yes, it is," he answered.

"So I was mad at you, because of something she told you to do."

"Yes," he said, "and it is over now."

"Yes it is. We will not talk about it anymore," Vanessa said. "I just hope that Marina will find someone to be with, so she won't have to be in other people's business."

Vanessa turned to Marina, "You are lucky I am leaving today, and I am not in the mood to fight."

"I know," Marina said. "I am glad that I told you the truth, though."

"Thank you," Vanessa said and hugged her.

"It is time to go," Jean called.

Darko was going to drive them to the airport, and Goran was going to ride along. Vanessa hugged Amanda, and they both started to cry.

"I never thought I would cry when you left," Amanda said.

"Me either," Vanessa said.

"I am sorry for everything I did to you," Amanda said hugging her.

"It is okay, we'll just have to forget about it," Vanessa told her.

Vanessa went to hug Emily next, and saw that her eyes were full of tears.

"Oh come on," Vanessa said. "Guys, we we'll still talk to each other."

"Yes, but you will be thousands of miles away from us."

"Will you ever come to visit?" Marina asked.

"Whenever I have a chance to," Vanessa said. As they were saying their good byes, they noticed a car stopping by the house. Two people got out, and started walking towards the house.

"Do you know them?" Amanda asked Vanessa.

"I've never seen them before in my life."

"Can I help you?" Jean asked the man and woman.

"Hi. My name is Bill, and this is my sister, Nancy. This house belonged to our parents. They were killed outside one night, and we were wondering who might live in it now."

"Well, we lived in it until today," Jean told them. "We were going to leave the keys with Anna just in case someone came back to the house."

"Thank you for taking care of the house for us," Nancy said. "Our parents would be very grateful."

"Where are you guys going, if I may ask?" Bill said.

"We are going to America. I am very happy you are here to take the keys to your parents' house," Jean told them.

Vanessa looked at her mom, and knew what she was thinking. They were very lucky that they were leaving.

Anna walked out from the backyard and saw Bill and Nancy.

"Oh my god!" she yelled. "You are alive!"

"Yes, we are Ms. Anna," Nancy said. "Have your kids come to visit you yet?"

"No, they don't come by," Anna told her.

"That is because you made them leave," Nancy said. "You stayed here and they left. I spoke to your daughter a couple times. You were a very bad mother to your kids. When the war began, you abandoned them. I would be ashamed to be called a mother if I were you." Then Nancy spit on her.

"That was not nice," Jean said. "I would love to stay, but we have to leave."

They climbed in the car, and Vanessa could not stop crying.

"Why are you crying?" Jean asked.

"Because this is the second time I am leaving all my friends, and telling them I will come back. I never once went to see Lidia and Tina. I wonder how they are doing."

"Honey, life is hard, and it is full of sacrifices."

"I know," Vanessa said, "maybe this time I won't have to leave, and disappoint more people."

"You are not disappointing anyone," Goran told her. "All you have to do is write to me." He was smiling at her, but deep inside he was crying, too.

They got to the airport, and boarded the plane. The plane was huge, and no one in their family had ever been on a plane. People were talking all around them. They sat all the way in the back. Vanessa looked outside, and she could see Goran and Darko standing and waving to them. Goran had written on a big card, in huge letters:

VANESSA, I WILL NEVER FORGET YOU! PROMISES
ARE FOREVER! I LOVED YOU THEN, I LOVE
YOU NOW, AND I WILL LOVE YOU FOREVER!

Those words stayed in Vanessa's head as the plane took off. She hoped life would be better now. They had fought for everything they had so far, and life had not been so good to them. As of this day, maybe things would change.